Hugo P. Thieme

Women of Modern France

Outlook

Hugo P. Thieme

Women of Modern France

1. Auflage | ISBN: 978-3-73262-889-6

Erscheinungsort: Frankfurt am Main, Deutschland

Erscheinungsjahr: 2018

Outlook Verlag GmbH, Frankfurt.

WOMAN

In all ages and in all countries

WOMEN OF MODERN FRANCE

by

HUGO P. THIEME, Ph.D.

Of the University of Michigan

THE RITTENHOUSE PRESS
PHILADELPHIA

PREFACE

Among the Latin races, the French race differs essentially in one characteristic which has been the key to the success of French women— namely, the social instinct. The whole French nation has always lived for the present time, in actuality, deriving from life more of what may be called social pleasure than any other nation. It has been a universal characteristic among French people since the sixteenth century to love to please, to make themselves agreeable, to bring joy and happiness to others, and to be loved and admired as well. With this instinctive trait French women have always been bountifully endowed. Highly emotional, they love to charm, and this has become an art with them; balancing this emotional nature is the mathematical quality. These two combined have made French women the great leaders in their own country and among women of all races. They have developed the art of studying themselves; and the art of coquetry, which has become a virtue, is a science with them. The singular power of discrimination, constructive ability, calculation, subtle intriguing, a clear and concise manner of expression, a power of conversation unequalled in women of any other country, clear thinking: all these qualities have been strikingly illustrated in the various great women of the different periods of the history of France, and according to these they may by right be judged; for their moral qualities have not always been in accordance with the standard of other races.

According as these two fundamental qualities, the emotional and mathematical, have been developed in individual women, we meet the different types which have made themselves prominent in history. The queens of France, in general, have been submissive and pious, dutiful and virtuous wives, while the mistresses have been bold and frivolous, licentious and self-assertive. The women outside of these spheres either looked on with indifference or regret at the all-powerfulness of this latter class, unable to change conditions, or themselves enjoyed the privilege of the mistress.

It must be remembered that in the great social circles in France, especially from the sixteenth to the end of the eighteenth centuries, marriage was a mere convention, offences against it being looked upon as matters concerning manners, not morals; therefore, much of the so-called gross immorality of French women may be condoned. It will be seen in this history that French women have acted banefully on politics, causing mischief, inciting jealousy and revenge, almost invariably an instrument in the hands of man, acting as a disturbing element. In art, literature, religion, and business, however, they have ever been a directing force, a guide, a critic and judge, an inspiration and companion to man.

The wholesome results of French women's activity are reflected especially in art and literature, and to a lesser degree in religion and morality, by the tone of elegance, politeness, *finesse*, clearness, precision, purity, and a general high standard which man followed if he was to succeed. In politics much severe blame and reproach have been heaped upon her—she is made responsible for breaking treaties, for activity in all intrigues, participating in and inciting to civil and foreign wars, encouraging and sanctioning assassinations and massacres, championing the Machiavelian policy and practising it at every opportunity.

It has been the aim of this history of French women to present the results rather than the actual happenings of their lives, and these have been gathered from the most authoritative and scholarly publications on the subject, to which the writer herewith wishes to give all credit.

HUGO PAUL THIEME.

University of Michigan.

Chapter I

Woman in politics

French women of the sixteenth, seventeenth, and eighteenth centuries, when studied according to the distinctive phases of their influence, are best divided into three classes: those queens who, as wives, represented virtue, education, and family life; the mistresses, who were instigators of political intrigue, immorality, and vice; and the authoresses and other educated women, who constituted themselves the patronesses of art and literature.

This division is not absolute by any means; for we see that in the sixteenth century the regent-mother (for example, Louise of Savoy and Catherine de' Medici), in extent of influence, fills the same position as does the mistress in the eighteenth century; though in the former period appears, in Diana of Poitiers, the first of a long line of ruling mistresses.

Queen-consorts, in the sixteenth as in the following centuries, exercised but little influence; they were, as a rule, gentle and obedient wives—even Catherine, domineering as she afterward showed herself to be, betraying no signs of that trait until she became regent.

The literary women and women of spirit and wit furthered all intellectual and social development; but it was the mistresses—those great women of political schemes and moral degeneracy—who were vested with the actual importance, and it must in justice to them be said that they not infrequently encouraged art, letters, and mental expansion.

Eight queens of France there were during the sixteenth century, and three of these may be accepted as types of purity, piety, and goodness: Claude, first wife of Francis I.; Elizabeth of France, wife of Charles IX.; and Louise de Vaudemont, wife of Henry III. These queens, held up to ridicule and scorn by the depraved followers of their husbands' mistresses, were reverenced by the people; we find striking contrasts to them in the two queens-regent, Louise of Savoy and Catherine de' Medici, who, in the period of their power, were as unscrupulous and brutal, intriguing and licentious, jealous and revengeful, as the most wanton mistresses who ever controlled a king. In this century, we find two other remarkable types: Marguerite d'Angoulême, the bright star of her time; and her whose name comes instantly to mind when we speak of the Lady of Angoulême—Marguerite de Navarre, representing both the good and the doubtful, the broadest sense of that untranslatable term *femme d'esprit*.

The first of the royal French women to whom modern woman owes a great and clearly defined debt was Anne of Brittany, wife of Louis XII. and the personification of all that is good and virtuous. To her belongs the honor of having taken the first step toward the social emancipation of French women; she was the first to give to woman an important place at court. This precedent she established by requesting her state officials and the foreign ambassadors to bring their wives and daughters when they paid their respects to her. To the ladies themselves, she sent a "royal command," bidding them leave their gloomy feudal abodes and repair to the court of their sovereign.

Anne may be said to belong to the transition period—that period in which the condition of slavery and obscurity which fettered the women of the Middle Ages gave place to almost untrammelled liberty. The queen held a separate court in great state, at Blois and Des Tournelles, and here elegance, even magnificence, of dress was required of her ladies. At first, this unprecedented demand caused discontent among men, who at that time far surpassed women in elaborateness of costume and had, consequently, been accustomed to the use of their surplus wealth for their own purposes. Under Anne's influence, court life underwent a complete transformation; her receptions, which were characterized by royal splendor, became the centre of attraction.

Anne of Brittany, the last queen of France of the Middle Ages and the first of the modern period, was a model of virtuous conduct, conjugal fidelity, and charity. Having complete control over her own immense wealth, she used it largely for beneficent purposes; to her encouragement much of the progress of art and literature in France was due. Hers was an example that many of the later queens endeavored to follow, but it cannot be said that they ever exerted a like influence or exhibited an equal power of initiation and self-assertion.

The first royal woman to become a power in politics in the period that we are considering was Louise of Savoy, mother of Francis I., a type of the voluptuous and licentious female of the sixteenth century. Her pernicious activity first manifested itself when, having conceived a violent passion for Charles of Bourbon, she set her heart upon marrying him, and commenced intrigues and plots which were all the more dangerous because of her almost absolute control over her son, the King.

At this time there were three distinct sets or social castes at the court of France: the pious and virtuous band about the good Queen Claude; the lettered and elegant belles in the coterie of Marguerite d'Angoulême, sister of Francis I.; and the wanton and libertine young maids who formed a galaxy of youth and beauty about Louise of Savoy, and were by her used to fascinate her son and thus distract him from affairs of state.

Louise used all means to bring before the king beautiful women through whom she planned to preserve her influence over him. One of these frail beauties, Françoise de Foix, completely won the heart of the monarch; her ascendency over him continued for a long period, in spite of the machinations of Louise, who, when Francis escaped her control, sought to bring disrepute and discredit upon the fair mistress.

The mother, however, remained the powerful factor in politics. With an abnormal desire to hoard money, an unbridled temper, and a violent and domineering disposition, she became the most powerful and dangerous, as well as the most feared, woman of all France. During her regency the state coffers were pillaged, and plundering was carried on on all sides. One of her acts at this time was to cause the recall of Charles of Bourbon, then Governor of Milan; this measure was taken as much for the purpose of obtaining revenge for his scornful rejection of her offer of marriage as for the hope of eventually bringing him to her side.

Upon the return of Charles, she immediately began plotting against him, including in her hatred Françoise de Foix, the king's mistress, at whom Bourbon frequently cast looks of pity which the furiously jealous Louise interpreted as glances of love. As a matter of fact, Bourbon, being strictly virtuous, was out of reach of temptation by the beauties of the court, and there were no grounds for jealousy.

This love of Louise for Charles of Bourbon is said to have owed most of its ardor to her hope of coming into possession of his immense estates. She schemed to have his title to them disputed, hoping that, by a decree of Parliament, they might be taken from him; the idea in this procedure was that Bourbon, deprived of his possessions, must come to her terms, and she would thus satisfy—at one and the same time—her passion and her cupidity.

Under her influence the character of the court changed entirely; retaining only a semblance of its former decency, it became utterly corrupt. It possessed external elegance and *distingué* manners, but below this veneer lay intrigue, debauchery, and gross immorality. In order to meet the vast expenditures of the king and the queen-mother, the taxes were enormously increased; the people, weighed down by the unjust assessment and by want, began to clamor and protest. Undismayed by famine, poverty, and epidemic, Louise continued her depredations on the public treasury, encouraging the king in his squanderings; and both mother and son, in order to procure money, begged, borrowed, plundered.

Louise was always surrounded by a bevy of young ladies, selected beauties of the court, whose natural charms were greatly enhanced by the lavishness of their attire. Always ready to further the plans of their mistress, they hesitated not to sacrifice reputation or honor to gratify her smallest whim. Her power was so generally recognized that foreign ambassadors, in the absence of the king, called her "that other king." When war against France broke out between Spain and England, Louise succeeded in gaining the office of constable for the Duc d'Alençon; by this means, she intended to displace Charles of Bourbon (whom she was still persecuting because he continued cold to her advances), and to humiliate him in the presence of his army; the latter design, however, was thwarted, as he did not complain.

To the caprice of Louise of Savoy were due the disasters and defeats of the French army during the period of her power; by frequently displacing someone whose actions did not coincide with her plans, and elevating some favorite who had avowed his willingness to serve her, she kept military affairs in a state of confusion.

Many wanton acts are attributed to her: she appropriated forty thousand crowns allowed to Governor Lautrec of Milan for the payment of his soldiers, and caused the execution of Samblancay, superintendent of finances, who had been so unfortunate as to incur her displeasure. It was Charles of Bourbon, who, with Marshal Lautrec, investigated the episode of the forty thousand crowns and exposed the treachery and perfidy of the mother of his king.

Finding that Bourbon intended to persist in his resistance to her advances, Louise decided upon drastic measures of retaliation. With the assistance of her chancellor (and tool), Duprat, she succeeded in having withheld the salaries which were due to Bourbon because of the offices held by him. As he took no notice of these deprivations, she next proceeded to divest him of his estates by laying claim to them for herself; she then proposed to Bourbon that, by accepting her hand in marriage, he might settle the matter happily. The object of her numerous schemes not only rejected this offer with contempt, but added insult to injury by remarking: "I will never marry a woman devoid of modesty." At this rebuff, Louise was incensed beyond measure, and when Queen Claude suggested Bourbon's marriage to her sister, Mme. Renée de France (a union to which Charles would have consented gladly), the queen- mother managed to induce Francis I. to refuse his consent.

After the death of Anne of Beaujeu, mother-in-law of Charles of Bourbon, her estates were seized by the king and transferred to Louise while the claim was under consideration by Parliament. When the judges, after an examination of the records of the Bourbon estate, remonstrated with Chancellor Duprat against the illegal transfer, he had them put into prison. This rigorous act, which was by order of Louise, weakened the courage of the court; when the time arrived for a final decision, the judges declared themselves incompetent to decide, and in order to rid themselves of responsibility referred the matter to the king's council. This great lawsuit, which was continued for a long time, eventually forced Charles of Bourbon to flee from France. Having sworn allegiance to Charles V. of Spain and Henry VIII. of England against Francis I., he was made lieutenant-general of the imperial armies.

When Francis, captured at the battle of Pavia, was taken to Spain, Louise, as regent, displayed unusual diplomatic skill by leaguing the Pope and the Italian states with Francis against the Spanish king. When, after nearly a year's captivity, her son returned, she welcomed him with a bevy of beauties; among them was a new mistress, designed to destroy the influence of the woman who had so often thwarted the plans of Louise—the beautiful Françoise de Foix whom the king had made Countess of Châteaubriant.

This new beauty was Anne de Pisseleu, one of the thirty children of Seigneur d'Heilly, a girl of eighteen, with an exceptional education. Most cunning was the trap which Louise had set for the king. Anne was surrounded by a circle of youthful courtiers, who hung upon her words, laughed at her caprices, courted her smiles; and when she rather confounded them with the extent of the learning which—with a sort of gay triumph—she was rather fond of showing, they pronounced her "the most charming of learned ladies and the most learned of the charming."

The plot worked; Francis was fascinated, falling an easy prey to the wiles of the wanton Anne. The former mistress, Françoise de Foix, was discarded, and Louise, purely out of revenge and spite, demanded the return of the costly jewels given by the king and appropriated them herself.

The duty assigned to the new mistress was that of keeping Francis busy with fêtes and other amusements. While he was thus kept under the spell of his enchantress, he lost all thought of his subjects and the welfare of his country and the affairs of the kingdom fell into the hands of Louise and her chancellor, Duprat. The girl-mistress, Anne, was married by Louise to the Duc d'Etampes whose consent was gained through the promise of the return of his family possessions which, upon his father's departure with Charles of Bourbon, had been confiscated.

The reign of Louise of Savoy was now about over; she had accomplished everything she had planned. She had caused Charles of Bourbon, one of the greatest men of the sixteenth century, to turn against his king; and that king owed to her—his mother—his defeat at Pavia, his captivity in Spain, and his moral fall. Spain, Italy, and France were victims of the infamous plotting and disastrous intrigues of this one woman whose death, in 1531, was a blessing to the country which she had dishonored.

At the time of the marriage of Francis I. to Eleanor of Portugal (one of the last acts of Louise), Europe was beginning to look upon France as ahead of all other nations in the "superlativeness of her politeness." The most rigid etiquette and the most punctilious politeness were always observed, fines being imposed for any discourtesy toward women.

After the death of Louise, the lot of managing the king and directing his policy fell to the share of his mistress, the Duchesse d'Etampes, who at once became all-powerful at court; her influence over him was like that of the drug which, to the weak person who begins its use, soon becomes an absolute necessity.

After the death of the dauphin, all the court flatteries were directed toward Henry, the eldest son of Francis. Though his mistress, Diana of Poitiers, ruled him, she exercised no influence politically; that she was not lacking in diplomacy, however, was proved by her attitude toward Henry's wife, Catherine, whom she treated with every indication of friendship and esteem, in marked contrast to the disdain exhibited by other ladies of the court. These two women became friends, working together against the mistress of the king —the Duchesse d'Etampes—and causing, by their intrigues, dissensions between father and son.

The duchess was not a bad woman; her dissuasion of Francis I. from undertaking war with Solyman II. against Charles V. is one instance of the use of her influence in the right direction. By some historians, she is accused of having played the traitress, in the interest of Emperor Charles V., during the war of Spain and England against France. It was she who urged the Treaty of Crépy with Charles V.; by it, through the marriage of the French king's second son, the Duke of Orleans, to the niece of Charles V., the duchess was sure of a safe retreat when her bitter enemy, Henry's mistress, should reign after the king's death. Her plans, however, did not materialize, as the duke died and the treaty was annulled.

The death of Francis I. occurred in 1547; with his reign ends the first period of woman's activity—a period influenced mainly by Louise of Savoy, whose relations to France were as disastrous as were those of any mistress. The influence exerted by her may in some respects be compared with that of Mme. de Pompadour; though, were the merits and demerits of both carefully tested, the results would hardly be in favor of Louise. Strong in diplomacy and intrigue, she was unscrupulous and wanton—morally corrupt; she did nothing to further the development of literature and art; if she favored men of genius it was merely from motives of self-interest.

With the accession of Henry II. his mistress entered into possession of full power. The absolute sway of Diana of Poitiers over this weakest of French kings was due to her strong mind, great ability, wide experience, fascination of manner, and to that exceptional beauty which she preserved to her old age. Immediately upon coming into power, she dispatched the Duchesse d'Etampes to one of her estates and at the same time forced her to restore the jewels which she had received from Francis I., a usual procedure with a mistress who knew herself to be first in authority.

After being thus displaced, the duchess spent her time in doing charitable work, and is said to have afforded protection to the Protestants. Eventually, hers was the fate of almost all the mistresses. Compelled to give up many of her possessions, miserable and forgotten by all, her last days were most unhappy.

Early in her career, Henry made Diana Duchesse de Valentinois. So powerful did she become that Sieur de Bayard, secretary of state, having referred in jest to her age (she was twenty years the king's senior), was deprived of his office, thrown into prison, and left to die. In her management of Queen Catherine, Diana was most politic; she never interfered, but constituted herself "the protectress of the legitimate wife, settling all questions concerning the newly born," for which she received a large salary. When, while the king was in Italy, the queen became ill, she owed her recovery to the watchful care of the mistress. The latter appointed to the vacant estates and positions members of her house—that of Guise. In time, this house gained such an ascendency that it conceived the project of setting aside all the princes of the blood royal.

Having (through one of her favorites) gained control of the royal treasury, Diana appropriated everything—lands, money, jewels. Her influence was so astonishing to the people that she was accused of wielding a magic power and bewitching the king who seemed, verily, to be leading an enchanted existence; he had but one thought, one aim—that of pleasing and obeying his aged mistress. To make amends for his adultery, he concluded to extirpate heretics. Such a combination of luxury and extravagance with licentiousness and brutality, such wholesale murder, persecution, and burning at the stake have never been equalled, except under Nero.

Michelet reveals the character of Diana in these words: "Affected by nothing, loving nothing, sympathizing with nothing; of the passions retaining only those which will give a little rapidity to the blood; of the pleasures preferring those that are mild and without violence—the love of gain and the pursuit of money; hence, there was absence of soul. Another phase was the cultivation of the body, the body and its beauty uniquely cared for by virile treatment and a rigid régime which is the guardian of life—not weakly adored as by women who kill themselves by excessive self-love." M. Saint-Amand continues, after quoting the above: "At all seasons of the year, Diana plunges into a cold bath on rising. As soon as day breaks, she mounts a horse, and, followed by swift hounds, rides through dewy verdure to her royal lover to whom—fascinated by her mythological pomp—she seems no more a woman but a goddess. Thus he styles her in verses of burning tenderness:

"'Hélas, mon Dieu! combien je regrette

Le temps que j'ai perdu en majeunesse!

Combien de fois je me suis souhaité

Avoir Diane pour ma seule maîtresse.

Mais je craignais qu'elle, qui est déesse,

Ne se voulût abaisser jusque là.'"

[Alas, my God! how much I regret the time lost in my youth! How often have I longed to have Diana for my only mistress! But I feared that she who is a goddess would not stoop so low as that.]

Catherine remained quietly in the palace, preferring her position, unpleasant as it was, to the persecution and possible incarceration in a convent which would result from any interference on her part between the king and his mistress. Without power or privileges, she was a mere figurehead—a good mother looking after her family. However, she was not idle; without taking part in the intrigues, she was studying them—planning her future tactics; in all relations she was diplomatic, her conversation ever displaying exquisite tact.

While France groaned under the burdens of seemingly interminable wars and exorbitant taxes, her king revelled in excessive luxury; the aim of his favorite mistress seemed to be to acquire wealth and spend it lavishly for her own pleasure. Voluptuousness, cruelty, and extravagance were the keynotes of the time. All means were used to procure revenues, the king easing any pangs of conscience by burning a few heretics whose estates were then quickly confiscated.

Diana, even at the age of sixty, still held Henry in her toils; an easy prey for the wiles of the flatterer, he was kept in ignorance of the hatred and anger heaping up against him. In the midst of riotous festivity, Henry II. died, a victim of the lance of Montgomery; and the twelve years' reign of debauchery, cruelty, and shameless extravagance came to an end.

Whatever else may be said of Diana, she proved to be a liberal patroness of art and letters; this was possible for her, since, in addition to inherited wealth and the gifts of lands and jewels from the king, she procured the possessions of many heretics whose confiscated wealth was assigned to her as a faithful servant and supporter of the church.

Her hotel at Anet was one of the most elaborate, tasteful, and elegant in all France; there the finest specimens of Italian sculpture, painting, and woodwork were to be seen. The king, upon making her a duchess, presented her with the beautiful château of Chenonceaux, which was so much coveted by Catherine. The latter attempted to make Diana pay for the château, thus interrupting her plans for building; upon discovering this, Henry sent his own artists and workmen to carry out Diana's desires. Such was the power of his mistress over the weak king that he respected her wishes far more than he did those of his queen. This was one of those instances in which Catherine saw fit to remain silent and plan revenge.

The death of Diana of Poitiers was that common to all women of her position. She died in 1566, forgotten by the world—her world. In her will she made "provision for religious houses, to be opened to women of evil lives, as if, in the depth of her conscience, she had recognized the likeness between their destiny and her own." Like the former mistresses, she had been required to give up the jewels received from Henry II.; but as this order was from Francis II. instead of from his mistress, the gems were returned to the crown after having passed successively through the hands of three mistresses.

Catherine's time had not yet come, for she dared not interfere when Mary Stuart (a beautiful, inexperienced, and impetuous girl of seventeen) gained ascendency over Francis II.—a mere boy. The house of Guise was then supreme and began its bloody campaign against its enemies; fortunately, however, its power was short-lived, for in 1560 the king died after reigning only seventeen months. At this point, Catherine enters upon the scene of action. Jealous of Mary Stuart and fearing that the young king, Charles IX., then but ten years old, might become infatuated with her and marry her, she promptly returned the fair young woman to Scotland.

The task before the regent was no light one; her kingdom was divided against itself, the country was overburdened with taxes, and discontent reigned universally. All who surrounded her were full of prejudice and actuated solely by personal aspirations—she realized that she could trust no one.

Her first act of a political nature was to rescue the house of Valois and solidify the royal authority. Some critics maintain that she began her reign with moderation, gentleness, impartiality, and reconciliation. This view finds support in the fact that during the first years she favored Protestantism; finding, however, that the latter was weakening royal power and that the country at large was opposed to it, she became its most bitter enemy. To the Protestants and their plottings she attributed all the disastrous effects of the civil war, all thefts, murders, incests, and adulteries, as well as the profanation of the sepulchres of the ancestors of the royal family, the burning of the bones of Louis XI. and of the heart of Francis II.

The Machiavellian policy was Catherine's guide; bitter experience had robbed her of all faith in humanity—she had learned to despise it and the judgment of her contemporaries. At first she was amiable and polite, seemingly intent upon pleasing those with whom she talked; in fact, it is said that she was then more often accused of excessive mildness and moderation than of the violence and cruelty which later characterized her. Experience having taught her how to deal with people, she never lost her self-control.

Subsequent history shows that any gentle and conciliatory policy of Catherine was merely a method of furthering her own interests, and was therefore not the outcome of any inborn feeling of sympathy or womanly tenderness. Whether her signing of the Edict of Saint-Germain, admitting the Protestants to all employments and granting them the privilege of Calvinistic worship in two cities of every province, and her refusal, upon the urgent solicitations of her son-in-law, Philip II., to persecute heretics were really snares laid for the Huguenots, is a matter which historians have not decided.

Inasmuch as the entire history of France plays about the personality of Catherine de' Medici, no attempt will be made to give a detailed chronological account of her career; the results, rather than the events themselves, will be given. M. Saint-Amand, in his work on *French Women of the Valois Court*, presents one of the strongest pictures drawn of Catherine. We shall follow him in the greater part of this sketch.

According to some historians, Catherine was a mere intriguer, without talent or ability, living but in the moment, often caught in her own snares; according to others, by her intelligence, ability, and strength of character she advanced a cause truly national—that of French unity; thus, she worked either the ruin or the salvation of France. Michelet calls her a nonentity, a stage queen with merely the externals—the attire—of royalty, remaining exactly on a level with the rulers of the smaller Italian principalities, contriving everything and fearing everything, with no more heart than she had sense or temperament. Being a female, she loved her young; she loved the arts, but cared to cultivate only their externalities. In this, however, Michelet goes to an extreme; for no woman ever lived who had so great a talent for intrigues and politics as she— a very type of the deceit and cunning which were inherent in her race. If she were not important, had not wielded so much influence and decided the fate of so many great men, women, and even states, she would not be the subject of so much writing, of such fierce denunciation and strong praise. To her family, France owes her finest palaces, her masterpieces of art—painting, bookmaking, printing, binding, sculpture.

M. Saint-Amand declares that "isolated from her contemporaries, Catherine de' Medici is a monster; brought back within the circle of their passions and their theories, she once more becomes a woman." But Catherine was the instigator, the embodiment of all that is vice, deceit, cunning, trickery, wickedness, and bold intrigue; she set the example, and her ladies followed her in all that she did; "the heroines bred in her school (and what woman was not in her school?) imitate, with docility, the examples she gives them." She was not only the type of her civilization,—brutal, gross, immoral, elegant, polished, and *mondain*,—but she was also its leader.

Greatness of soul, real moral force, strict virtue, are not attributes of the sixteenth-century woman—they are isolated and rare exceptions; these Catherine did not possess. Nor was she influenced deeply by her environments; the latter but encouraged and developed those qualities which were hers inherently,—will, intelligence, inflexible perseverance, tenacity of purpose, unscrupulousness, cruelty; hence, to say "She is the victim rather than the inspiration of the corruption of her time" is misleading, to say the least. If, upon her arrival at court, "she at once pleased every one by her grace and affability, modest air, and, above all, by her extreme gentleness," she could not have changed, say her defenders, into the perfidious, wicked, and cruel creature she is said to have become as soon as she stepped into power. "During the reign of Henry II., she wisely avoided all danger; faithful to her wifely duties, she gave no cause for scandal, and, realizing that she was not strong enough to overcome her all-powerful rival, she bided her time. She was loved and respected by everyone for her personal qualities and her benevolence." But why may it not be true that all this was but part of her politics, the politics in which she had been educated? Wise from experience, she foresaw the future and what was in store for her if she remained prudent and made the best of the surroundings until the time should come when she could strike suddenly and boldly.

Brought up from infancy amidst snares, intrigues, the clash of arms, the furious shouts of popular insurrections, tempests, and storms, she could not escape the influence of her early environment. Her talent for studying and penetrating the designs of her enemies, for facing or avoiding dangers with such sublime calmness and prudence, was partly inherited, partly acquired. That spirit she took with her to France, where her experience was widened and her opportunities for the study of human nature were increased.

It is not generally known that her mother was a French woman—a Madeleine de La Tour d'Auvergne, daughter of Jean, Count of Boulogne, and Catherine of Bourbon, daughter of the Count of Vendôme; thus, her gentler nature was a French product. Her mother and father both died when she was but twenty-two days old, and from that time until her marriage she was cast about from place to place. But from the very first she showed that talent of adapting herself to her surroundings, living amidst intrigues and discords and yet making friends. She has been called "the precocious heiress of the craftiness of her progenitors."

In her thirteenth year, after being sought by many powerful princes, Clement VII. (her greatuncle), in order to secure himself against the powerful Charles V., married her to Henry, Duke of Orleans, the second son of Francis I. Even at that early age she was fully aware of all the dreariness and danger attached to positions of power, and knew that the art of governing was not an easy one. She had studied Machiavelli's famous work, *The Prince*, which had been dedicated to her father, and it was from it, as well as from her ancestors, that she derived her wisdom and astuteness. Her childhood had prepared her for the work of the future, and she went at it with caution and reserve until she was sure of her ground.

She first proceeded to study the king, Francis I., watching his actions, extracting his secrets; a fine huntress and at his side constantly, she pleased him and gained his favor. Brantôme says she was subtle and diplomatic, quickly learning the craft of her profession; she sought friends among all classes and ranks, directing her overtures specially toward the ladies of the court, whom she soon won and gathered about her.

In 1536 the dauphin died, and Catherine's husband became heir to the throne of France. Though they had been married three years, no offspring had resulted, which unfortunate circumstance made her position a most uncertain one, especially as Diana of Poitiers was then at the height of her power, controlling Henry absolutely. A furious rivalry sprang up between the Duchesse d'Etampes, mistress of Francis I., and Diana and Catherine; the two mistresses formed two parties, and a war of slanders, calumnies, and unpleasant epigrams ensued. Queen Eleanor, the second wife of Francis I., took no active part, thus leaving all power in the hands of the mistress of her husband. (It was at this time that the Emperor Charles V. gained the Duchesse d'Etampes over to his cause.) Poets and artists, politicians and men of genius took sides, extolling the beauty of the one they championed. Catherine, although befriended and treated with apparent respect by Diana, remained a good friend to both women, thus evincing her tact. By keeping her own personality in the background, she won the esteem of both her husband and the king.

Brantôme leaves a picture of Catherine at this time: "She was a fine and ample figure; very majestic, yet agreeable and very gentle when necessary; beautiful and gracious in appearance, her face fair and her throat white and full, very white in body likewise.... Moreover, she dressed superbly, always having some pretty innovation. In brief, she had beauties fitted to inspire love. She laughed readily, her disposition was jovial, and she liked to jest." M. Saint-Amand continues: "The artistic elegance that surrounded her whole person, the tranquil and benevolent expression of her countenance, the good taste of her dress, the exquisite distinction of her manners, all contributed to her charm. And then she was so humble in the presence of her husband! She so carefully avoided whatever might have the semblance of reproach! She closed her eyes with such complaisance! Henry told himself that it would be difficult to find another woman so well-disposed, another wife so faithful to her duties, another princess so accomplished in point of instruction and intelligence. The *ménage à trois* (household of three) was continued, therefore, and if the dauphin loved his mistress, he certainly had a friendship for his wife. And, on her part, whenever she felt an inclination to complain of her lot, Catherine bethought herself that if she quitted her position she would probably find no refuge but the cloister, and that—taking it all around—the court of France (in spite of the humiliations and vexations one might experience there) was an abode more desirable than a convent;" this, then, is the secret of her submission. In spite of her beauty, mildness, and distinction of manner, she could not overcome the prestige of Diana.

After nine years, Catherine was still without children and began to fear the fate in store for her; but when she gave birth to a son in 1543, she felt assured that divorce no longer threatened her and she resolved that as soon as she came into power she would be revenged upon her enemies and Diana of Poitiers. When, in 1547, her husband succeeded his father as King of France, she did not feel that the time had yet arrived to interfere in any social or domestic arrangements or affairs of state; not until ten years later did she show the first sign of remarkable statesmanship or ability as a politician.

After the battle and capture of Saint-Quentin, France was in a most deplorable state; the enemy was believed to be beneath the walls of Paris; everybody was fleeing; the king had gone to Compiègne to muster a new army. Catherine was alone in Paris "and of her own free will went to the Parliament in full state, accompanied by the cardinals, princes, and princesses; and there, in the most impressive language, she set forth the urgent state of affairs at the moment.... With so much sentiment and eloquence that she touched the heart of everybody, the queen then explained to the Parliament that the king had need of three hundred thousand livres, twenty-five thousand to be paid every two months; and she added that she would retire from the place of session, so as not to interfere with the liberty of discussion; accordingly, she retired to another room. A resolution to comply with the wishes of her majesty was voted, and the queen, having resumed her place, received a promise to that effect. A hundred nobles of the city offered to give at once three thousand francs apiece. The queen thanked them in the sweetest form of words, and thus terminated this session of Parliament—with so much applause for her majesty and such lively marks of satisfaction at her behavior, that no idea can be given of them. Throughout the city, nothing was spoken of but the queen's prudence and the happy manner in which she proceeded in this enterprise" (Guizot). From this act dates Catherine's entrance into political consideration.

During the reign of Francis II., Catherine de' Medici exercised no influence at court, the king being completely under the dominion of his wife and the Duke of Guise, who was not favorable to the queen-mother's schemes and policies. Catherine, however, was plotting; caring little about religion so long as it did not further her plans, she connected herself with the Huguenots; her scheme was to bring the Guises to destruction and to form a council of regency which, while composed of the Huguenot leaders, was to be under her guidance. As this plan failed, bringing ruin to many princes, she deserted the Huguenots and allied herself with the Catholics.

She is next found attempting the assassination of the Duke of Condé, but she failed to accomplish that crime because her son, the king, refused his consent. Soon after, Francis II. died, it is said from the effect of poison dropped into his ear while he was sleeping; it is probable that this crime was committed at the instigation of the mother, since by his death and the accession of Charles IX. she became regent (1560). She was then all-powerful and in a position to exercise her long dormant talents.

Her first plan was to incapacitate all her children by plunging them "into such licentious pleasure and voluptuous dissipation that they were speedily unfitted for mental activity or exertion." Most unprejudiced historians credit her with the Massacre of Saint Bartholomew; she is said to have boasted about it to Catholic governments and excused it to Protestant powers. For a number of years, she had been planning the destruction of the Huguenot princes, and as early as 1565 she and Charles IX. had an interview with the Duke of Alva (representative of Philip II), to consult as to the means of delivering France from heretics. It was decided that "this great blessing could not have accomplishment save by the deaths of all the leaders of the Huguenots."

That fearful crime, the bloody Massacre of Saint Bartholomew, is familiar to everyone. The only excuse offered for this most heinous of Catherine's many offences is her intense sentiment of national unity; the actual reason for it is to be sought in the fact that as long as the Protestants retained their prestige and influence, Catherine and her Catholic party could not do as they pleased, could not gain absolute control over the government. History holds her more responsible than it does her weak son. The climax came on the occasion of the wedding of Marguerite of Valois with the Prince of Navarre, which meant the union of the branches—the Catholic and the Protestant. This resulted in the first breach between the king and Catherine; the latter at that time perpetrated one of her dastardly deeds by poisoning the mother of the Prince of Navarre —Jeanne d'Albret, her bitter enemy.

After the death of Charles IX., Henry III. was the sole survivor of the four sons of Catherine. Although her power was limited during his reign, she managed to continue her murderous plans and accomplished the death of Henry of Guise and his brother the cardinal, which crime united the majority of the Catholics of France against the king and was the cause of his assassination in 1589. This ended the power of Catherine de' Medici; when she died, no one rejoiced, no one lamented. Wherever she had turned her eyes, she had seen nothing but occasions for uneasiness and sadness; she had retired from court, feeling her helplessness and disgrace as well as the decline in power of that son in whom her hopes were centred. She decided to reënter the scene of action and save Henry. The stormy scenes of the Barricades and the League and the murder of the Duke of Guise hastened her death, which occurred in 1589.

Catherine de' Medici may rightfully be called the initiator and organizer of social and court etiquette and courtesy—of conventional and social laws. However great her political activity, she made herself deeply felt in the social and moral worlds also. She taught her husband the secret of being king; she introduced the *lever* audience; in the afternoon of every day, she held a reunion of all the ladies of the court, at which the king was to be found after dinner and every lord entertained the lady he most loved; two hours were spent in this pleasure which was continued after supper if there were no balls; bitter railleries and anything that passed the restrictions of good company were forbidden.

Her ladies of honor obeyed her as they would their God. Marguerite of Valois said of her: "I did not dare to speak to her, and when she looked at me I trembled for fear of having done something that displeased her." Ladies who had been delinquent were stripped and beaten with lashes; for correction— frequently for mere pastime—she would have them undressed and slapped vigorously with the back of the hand. Françoise of Rohan, cousin of Jeanne d'Albret, wrote the following poem:

"Plus j'ai de toi souvent esté battue,

Plus mon amour s'efforce et s'évertue

De regretter ceste main qui me bat;

Car ce mal-là m'estait plaisant esbat.

Or, adieu done la main dont la rigueur

Je préferais à tout bien et honneur."

[The more often I have been struck by you, the more my love struggles and strives to regret the hand that beats me; for that punishment was a pleasant pastime for me. Now farewell to the hand whose rigor I preferred to every fortune and honor.]

The following portrait and poetry, taken from M. Saint-Amand, does the subject full justice: "Catherine de' Medici represented with a sinister glance, deadly mien, mysterious and savage aspect—a spectre, not a woman—is not true to nature. Her self-possession, cool cunning, supreme elegance, imperturbable tranquillity, calmness, moderation, noble serenity, and dignified poise, gave her an individuality such as few women ever possessed. Gentle in crime and tragedy, polite like an executioner toward his victim—this Machiavellianism which is equal to every trial, which nothing alarms or surprises, and which with tranquil dexterity makes sport of every law of morality and humanity—this is the real character of Catherine de' Medici." The following burlesque poetry was composed for her:

"La reine qui ci-git fut un diable et un ange,

Toute pleine de blâme et pleine de louange,

Elle soutint l'Etat, et l'Etat mit à bas;

Elle fit maints accords et pas moins de débats;

Elle enfanta trois rois et trois guerres civiles,

Fit bâtir des châteaux et ruiner des villes,

Fit bien de bonnes lois et de mauvais édits.

Souhaite-lui, passant, enfer et paradis."

[The queen lying here was both devil and angel, blamed and praised; she both put down and upheld the state; she caused many an agreement and no end of disputes; she produced three kings and three civil wars; she built castles and ruined cities, made many good laws and many bad decrees. Wish her, passer-by, hell and paradise.]

With the reign of Henry IV.—the first king of the house of Bourbon, and the first king of the sixteenth century with a will of his own and the courage to assert it—begins a period of revelling, debauch, and the most depraved immorality. Three mistresses in turn controlled him—morally, not politically.

Henry was master of his own will, and, had he desired to do so, could have overcome his evil tendencies; instead, he openly countenanced and even encouraged dissoluteness and elegant debauchery, as long as he himself was not deprived of the lady upon whom his capricious fancy happened to fall. His advances were but seldom repulsed; but upon making his usual audacious proposals to the Marquise de Guercheville, he was informed that she was of too insignificant a house to be the king's wife and of too good a race to be his mistress; and when the king, in spite of this rebuff, made her lady of honor to his wife, Marie de' Medici, she continued to resist him and remained virtuous. Such types of purity, honor, and moral courage were very exceptional during this reign.

The three principal mistresses of this sovereign represent three phases of influence and three periods of his life. Corisande d'Andouins, Comtesse de Guiche and Duchesse de Gramont, fascinated him for eight years, while he was King of Navarre (1582-1590); to her he was deeply attached, and recompensed her for her devotion; this is called his *chevaleresque* period. The beautiful Gabrielle d'Estrées, Duchesse de Beaufort, was called his mate after victory; "she refined, sharpened, softened, and tamed his customs; she made him king of the court instead of the field." It was she who ventured to meddle in his politics, she whom Marguerite of Valois, his wife, so detested that she refused to consent to a divorce as long as Gabrielle (by whom he had several children) remained his mistress. The latter even went so far as to demand the baptism, as a child of France, of her son by the king. Sully, in a rage, declared there were no "children of France," and took the order to the king, who had it destroyed; he then asked his minister to go to his mistress and satisfy her, "in so far as you can." To his efforts she replied: "I am aware of all, and do not care to hear any more; I am not made as the king is, whom you persuade that black is white." Upon receiving this report, the king said: "Here, come with me; I will let you see that women have not the possession of me that certain malignant spirits say they have." Accompanied by Sully, he immediately went to the Duchesse de Beaufort, and, taking her by the hand, said: "Now, madame, let us go into your room, and let nobody else enter except Rosny. I want to speak to you both and teach you how to be good friends." Then, having closed the door, holding Gabrielle with one hand and Rosny with the other, he said: "Good God, madame! What is the meaning of this? So you would vex me from sheer wantonness of heart in order to try my patience? By God, I swear to you that, if you continue these fashions of going on, you will find yourself very much out in your expectations! I see quite well that you have been put up to all this pleasantry in order to make me dismiss a servant whom I cannot do without, and who has served me loyally for five-and- twenty years. By God, I will do nothing of the kind! And I declare to you that if I were reduced to such a necessity as to choose between losing one or the other, I could better do without ten mistresses like you than one servant like him." Shortly after this episode, Gabrielle died so suddenly that she was supposed to have been poisoned. Immediately after her death the divorce was granted, and Henry married Marie de' Medici.

The third mistress, Henriette de Balzac d'Entragues, Marquise de Verneuil, who led Henry IV. along a path of the worst debauchery, gained control over him by lewd, lascivious methods. While negotiations were being carried on for his divorce from Marguerite, only a few weeks after the death of Gabrielle, he signed a promise to marry Henriette; this, however, he failed to keep. She, more than any other of his mistresses, was the cause of national distress and of more than one ruinous war. When, after the marriage of the king to Marie de' Medici, Henriette began to nag, rail, intrigue, and conspire, she was disgraced by Henry, who at least had the courage to honor his own family above that of his mistresses. She is accused of having had, solely from motives of revenge, a hand in the death of the king.

Thus, around the queens-regent and the mistresses of the kings of France in the sixteenth century there is constant intriguing, murder, assassination, immorality, and debauchery, jealousy and revenge, marriage and divorce, honor and disgrace, despotism and final repentance and misery. The greatest and lowest of these women was Catherine de' Medici; Diana of Poitiers was famed as the most marvellously beautiful woman in France, and she was the most powerful and intelligent mistress until the time of Mme. de Pompadour. Amid all this bribery and corruption, elegant and refined immorality, there are some few types that represent education, family life, purity, and culture.

Chapter II

Woman in Family Life, Education, and Letters

The queens of France exerted little or no influence upon the cultural or political development of that country. Frequently of foreign extraction and reared in the strict religious discipline of Catholicism, they spent their time in attending masses, aiding the poor and, with the little money allowed them, erecting hospitals and other institutions for the weak and needy. Thus, they are, as a rule, types of gentleness, virtue, piety, and self-sacrifice.

The little information which history gives concerning them is confined mainly to their matrimonial alliances. To them, marriage represented nothing more than a contract—a union entered into for the purpose of settling some political negotiation; thus they were often cast upon strange and unfriendly soil where intrigues and jealousy immediately affected them.

Seldom did they venture to interfere with the intrigues of the mistress; in their uncertain position, any manifestation of resentment or opposition resulted in humiliation and disgrace; if wise, they contented themselves with quietly performing their functions as dutiful wives. Such women were Claude, daughter of Louis XII., and Eleanor of Spain—wives of Francis I.; lacking the power to act politically, both passed uneventful and virtuous lives in comparative obscurity. The wife of Charles IX.—Elizabeth of Austria, daughter of Maximilian II.—had absolutely no control over her husband; however, he condescended to flatter himself with having, as he said, "in an amiable wife, the wisest and most virtuous woman not only of France and Europe, but of the universe." Her nature is well portrayed in the answer she gave to the remark made to her, after the death of her husband: "Ah, Madame, what a misfortune that you have no son! Your lot would be less pitiful and you would be queen-mother and regent." "Alas, do not suggest such a disagreeable thing!" she replied. "As if France had not afflictions enough without my producing another to complete its ruin! For, if I had a son, there would be more divisions and troubles, more seditions to obtain the administration and guardianship during his infancy and minority; all would try to profit themselves by despoiling the poor child—as they wanted to do with the late king, my husband." Returning to Austria, she erected a convent, treated the nuns as friends and refused to marry again even to ascend the throne of Spain.

Louise de Vaudemont, wife of Henry III, was a French woman by birth and blood. After the death of the Princess of Condé, whom he passionately loved and desired to marry, Henry conceived an intense affection for Louise, daughter of Nicholas of Lorraine, Count of Vaudemont—a young lady of education and culture—"a character of exquisite sweetness lends distinction to her beauty and her piety; her thorough Christian modesty and humility are reflected in her countenance." Brantôme wrote: "This princess deserves great praise; in her married life she comported herself so wisely, chastely, and loyally toward the king that the nuptial tie which bound her to him always remained firm and indissoluble,—was never found loosened or undone,— even though the king liked and sometimes procured a change, according to the custom of the great who keep their full liberty." Soon after the marriage, however, Henry began to make life unpleasant for the queen, one of his petty acts being to deprive her of the moral ladies in waiting whom she had brought with her.

Louise de Vaudemont was a striking contrast to the perverted woman of the day; the latter, no longer charmed by the gentler emotions, sought the exaggerated and the eccentric, extraordinary incidents, dramatic situations, unexpected crises, finding all amusements insipid unless they involved fighting and romantic catastrophes. *"Billets doux* were written in blood and ferocity reigned even in pleasure."

In the midst of this turmoil, Louise busied herself with charity, appearing among the poor and distributing all the funds which her father gave her for pocket money; the evils of her surroundings threw her virtues, by contrast, into so much the brighter light. Though she held herself aloof from intrigues and rivalries, favoring no one and encouraging no slander, she was, strange to say, respected, admired and honored by Protestants and Catholics alike.

Calumny and all the agitations about her did not disturb Louise in her prayers. "The waves of the angry ocean broke at the foot of the altar as the queen knelt; but Huguenots and Catholics, leaguers and royalists, united to pay her homage. They were amazed to see such purity in an atmosphere so corrupt, such gentleness in a society so violent. Their eyes rested with satisfaction on a countenance whose holy tranquillity was undisturbed by pride and hatred. The famous women of the century, wretched in spite of all their amusements and their feverish pursuit of pleasure, made salutary reflections as they contemplated a woman still more highly honored for her virtues than for her crown." That she was not a mother was, with her, an enduring sorrow; even that, however, did not alter her calmness and benign resignation.

Louise de Vaudemont was indeed a bright star in a heaven of darkness—one of the best queens of whom French history can boast; she is an example of goodness and gentleness, of purity, charity, and fidelity in a world of corruption, cruelty, hatred, and debauch—where sympathy was rare and chastity was ridiculed. Although a highly educated woman, the faithful performance of her duties as queen and as a devout Catholic left her little time for literature and art; she remains the type of piety and purity—an ideal queen and woman.

A heroine in the fullest sense of that word was Jeanne d'Albret, the great champion of Protestantism; she was the mother of Henry IV. and the wife of the Duke of Bourbon, Count of Vendôme, a direct descendant of Saint Louis. This despotic, combative, and war-loving queen reigned as absolute monarch, and was as autocratic and severe as Calvin himself, confiscating church property, destroying pictures and altars—even going so far as to forbid the presence of her subjects at mass or in religious processions. "Her natural eloquence, the lightning flashes from her eyes, her reputation as a Spartan matron and an intractable Calvinist, all contributed to give her great influence with her party. The military leaders—Coligny, La Rochefoucauld, Rohan, La Noue—submitted their plans of campaign to her."

Though Jeanne was, perhaps, as fanatical, intolerant, and cruel as her adversaries, she was driven to this by the hostility shown her by the Catholic party—a party in which she felt she could place no confidence. Her retreat was amid rocks and inaccessible peaks, whence she defied both the pope and Philip II. She brought up her son—the future Henry IV.—among the children of the people, exercising toward him the severest discipline, and inuring him to the cold of the winter and the heat of the summer; she taught him to be judicious, sincere, and compassionate—qualities which she possessed to a remarkable degree. Chaste and pure herself, she considered the court of France a hotbed of voluptuousness and debauchery, and at every opportunity strengthened herself against its possible influence.

The political and religious troubles of Jeanne d'Albret began when Pope Paul IV. invested Philip II. of Spain with the sovereignty of Navarre—her territory; she resisted, and, following the impulses of her own nature, formally embraced Calvinism, while her weak husband acceded to the commands of the Church, and, applying to the pope for the annulment of his marriage, was prepared, as lieutenant-general of the kingdom, a position he accepted from the pontiff, to deprive his wife of her possessions. His death before the realization of his project made it possible for Jeanne to retain her sovereignty; alone, an absolute monarch, she declared Calvinism the established religion of Navarre. After the assassination of Condé she remained the champion of the Huguenots, defying her enemies and scorning the court of France.

So great were her power and influence over the soldiery that Catherine de' Medici, her bitter enemy, desiring to bring her into her power, or, at least, to conciliate her, planned a marriage between Jeanne's son and Marguerite of Valois—sister of Charles IX. When the suggestion that the marriage should take place came from the king of France, Jeanne d'Albret suspected an ambush; with the determination to supervise personally all arrangements for the nuptials, she set out for the French court. Venerated by the Protestants, and hated but admired by the Catholics, she had become celebrated throughout Europe for her beauty, intelligence, and strength of mind; thus, her arrival at Paris created a sensation.

She was so scandalized at the luxury and bold debauchery at court that she decided to give up the marriage; she had detected the intrigues and falsity of both the king and Catherine, and had a foreboding of evil. She wrote to her son Henry:

"Your betrothed is beautiful, very circumspect and graceful, but brought up in the worst company that ever existed (for I do not see a single one who is not infected by it) ... I would not for anything have you come here to live; this is why I desire you to marry and withdraw yourself and your wife from this corruption which (bad as I supposed it to be) I find still worse than I thought. Here, it is not the men who invite the women, but the women who invite the men. If you were here, you could not escape contamination without a great grace from God."

In the meantime, Catherine, undecided whether to strike immediately or to wait, was redoubling her kindness and courtesy and her affectionate overtures; her enemies were in her hands. Although Jeanne suspected that Catherine was capable of every perfidy, she at times believed that her suspicions were unjust or exaggerated. The situation between these two great women was indeed a dramatic one: both were tactful, powerful, experienced in war and diplomacy; both were mothers with children for whose future they sought to provide. Jeanne's hesitancy, however, was fatal; physically exhausted from suffering and sorrow, worry and excitement, she suddenly died, in the midst of her preparations for the marriage. While it is not absolutely certain that her death was due to poison, subsequent events lead strongly to the belief that Catherine was instrumental in causing it—that, probably, being but the first act toward the awful catastrophe she was planning.

"A few hours before her agony, Jeanne dictated the provisions of her will. She recommended her son to remain faithful to the religion in which she had reared him, never to permit himself to be lured by voluptuousness and corruption, and to banish atheists, flatterers, and libertines.... She begged him to take his sister, Catherine, under his protection and to be, after God, her father. 'I forbid my son ever to use severity towards his sister; I wish, to the contrary, that he treat her with gentleness and kindness; and that—above all— he have her brought up in Béarn, and that she shall never leave there until she is old enough to be married to a prince of her own rank and religion, whose morals shall be such that the spouses may live happily together in a good and holy marriage.'" D'Aubigné wrote of her: "A princess with nothing of a woman but sex—with a soul full of everything manly, a mind fit to cope with affairs of moment, and a heart invincible in adversity."

It was in deep mourning that her son, then King of Navarre, arrived at Paris; the eight hundred gentlemen who attended him were all likewise in mourning. "But," says Marguerite de Valois, "the nuptials took place in a few days, with triumph and magnificence that none others, of even my quality, had ever beheld. The King of Navarre and his troop changed their mourning for very rich and fine clothes, I being dressed royally, with crown and corsage of tufted ermine all blazing with crown jewels, and, the grand blue mantle with a train four ells long borne by three princesses. The people down below, in their eagerness to see us as we passed, choked one another." (Thus quickly was Jeanne d'Albret forgotten.) The ceremonies were gorgeous, lasting four days; but when Admiral Coligny, the Huguenot leader, was struck in the hand by a musket ball, the festive aspect of affairs suddenly changed. On the second day after the wounding of Coligny, and before the excitement caused by that act had subsided, Catherine accomplished the crowning work of her invidious nature, the tragedy of Saint Bartholomew.

Peace and quiet never appeared upon the countenance of Catherine de' Medici —that woman who so faithfully represents and pictures the period, the tendencies of which she shaped and fostered by her own pernicious methods; and Charles IX., her son, was no better than his mother. Saint-Amand, in his splendid picture of the period, gives a truthful picture of Catherine as well: "It is interesting to observe how curiously the later Valois represented their epoch. Francis I. had personified the Renaissance; Charles IX. sums up in himself all the crises of the religious wars—he is the true type of the morbid and disturbed society where all is violent; where the blood is scorched by the double fevers of pleasure and cruelty; where the human soul, without guide or compass, is tossed amid storms; where fanaticism is joined to debauchery, superstition to incredulity, cultured intelligence to depravity of heart. This wholly unbalanced character—which stretches evil to its utmost limits while preserving the knowledge of what is good, which mistrusts everybody and yet has at least the aspiration toward friendship and love, if not its experience—is it not the symbol and living image of its time?"

Marguerite de Valois, sister of Charles IX. and wife of Henry IV., by her own actions and intrigues exercised little influence politically; she was, above all else, a woman of culture and may be taken as an example of the type which was largely instrumental in developing social life in France. Famous for her beauty, talents, and profligacy, it seems that historians are prone to dwell too exclusively upon the last quality, overlooking her principal rôle—that of social leader.

She first came into prominence through her relations with the Duke of Guise who paid assiduous court to her for some time; for a while, no topic was more discussed than that of their marriage. When, however, Charles IX. heard that the duke had been carrying on a secret correspondence with his sister, he exclaimed, savagely: "If it be so, we will kill him!" Thereupon, the duke hurriedly contracted a marriage with Catherine of Clèves. That Marguerite, at this early date, had become the mistress of Henry of Guise is hardly likely and becomes even less probable when it is considered how closely she was watched by her mother, Catherine de' Medici.

Her marriage, previously mentioned, to Henry of Navarre was a mere political match, there being absolutely no love, no affection, no sympathy. This union was looked upon as the surest covenant of peace between Catholicism and Protestantism and put an end to the disastrous religious wars that had been carried on uninterruptedly for years; both the parties to this contract lived at court, leading an existence of pleasure and immorality. Remarkably intelligent, Marguerite was a scholar of no mean ability; she displayed much wit and talent, but no judgment or discretion; though conveying the impression of being rather haughty and proud, she lacked both self respect and true dignity. Her beauty was marvellous, but "calculated, to ruin and damn men rather than to save them."

Henry, the husband of Marguerite, was constantly sneered at and taunted by the Catholics; although Catholic in name he was Protestant at heart and keenly felt his false position. During Catherine's short term as queen-regent, he was held in captivity until the arrival of Henry III., when he escaped to his own Béarn people; for this, Marguerite was held responsible and kept under guard.

Although hating his religion, his wife went to live with him, tolerating his infidelities while he refused to tolerate her religion. The unhappiness of this marriage was not due to Marguerite alone; the first trouble arose when she discovered his love for his mistress, Gabrielle d'Estrées, and, thinking herself equally privileged, she began to indulge in the same excesses. The result of so many annoyances and debaucheries, so much vexation, was an illness; as soon as she became convalescent, she returned to her mother at court where she speedily gained the ill will of the king by her profligate habits, her quarrels with both Catholics and Protestants, her intimacy with the Duke of Guise, her plottings with her younger brother, her cutting satires on court favorites.

She was sent back to Henry, upon the way meeting with the mishap of being insulted by archers and, with her maids, led away prisoner. Her husband was with difficulty persuaded to receive her, and, finding him all attentive to his mistress, Marguerite fled to Agen, where she made war upon him as a heretic; unable to hold her position there on account of her licentious manner of living and the exorbitant taxes imposed upon the inhabitants, she fled again and continued moving from one place to another, causing mischief everywhere, "consuming the remainder of her youth in adventures more worthy of a woman who had abandoned her husband than of a daughter of France." At last, she was seized and imprisoned in the fortress of Usson; here she was supported mainly by Elizabeth of Austria, widow of Charles IX.

When her husband became King of France, he refused to liberate her until she should renounce her rank; to this condition she refused to accede until after the death of her rival, the mistress of Henry—Gabrielle d'Estrées, Duchess de Beaufort. After the annulment of the marriage, Marguerite said: "If our household has been little noble and less bourgeois, our divorce was royal." She was permitted to retain the title of queen, her debts were paid and other great concessions granted. Her subsequent relations with Henry IV. were very cordial and fraternal; she even revealed political plots to him.

When, after nearly twenty years of captivity, Marguerite returned to Paris (1605), she gained the favor of everybody—the king, dauphin, and court ladies. She was present at the coronation of Marie de' Medici, and, by being tactful enough to keep apart from all intrigues, quarrels, and jealousies, she managed to win the good will of the king's favorites. She became the social leader, the queen inviting her to all court ceremonies and consulting her on all disputed questions of etiquette—even going so far as to intrust her with the reception of the Duke of Pastrana, who had come to ask the hand of Elizabeth of France. It is reported that in her last years she led a worse life than in her earlier days—she had become a woman of the bad world, resorting to every possible means to hide her age and to gain any vantage ground. In order to be well supplied with blond wigs, she kept fair-haired footmen who were shorn from time to time to furnish the supply. In the latter part of her life, spent at Paris and its vicinity, she fell a victim to hypochondria, suffering the most bitter pangs of remorse and terrible fear at approaching death. To alleviate this, she founded a convent where she taught the children music. She died in 1615, in Paris, "in that blended piety and coquetry which formed the basis of a character unable to give up gallantries and love."

One of the very few historians who give due credit to her social importance and assign her the position she may rightfully command among French women of the sixteenth century is M. Du Bled. According to him, she was the leader of fashion, and in all its components she showed excellent taste and judgment. Forced to marry the king of Navarre, she said, after the ceremony: "I received from marriage all the evil I ever received, and I consider it the greatest plague of my life. They tell me that marriages are made in heaven; heaven did not commit such an injustice;" and this seems to be the secret of her "vicious life."

As soon as she discovered that the king's favorites were determined to make life hard and disagreeable for her, she sought consolation in love and the toilette, in balls and fêtes, in ballets and hunting, in promenades and gallant conversations, in tennis and carousals, and in an infinite variety of ingeniously planned pleasures. The spirit of chivalry, the habits of exalted devotion, were again in full sway about her. She worried little about virtue: "She had the gift of pleasing, was beautiful, and made full use of the liberality of the gods. Whatever may be said of her morals, it can truthfully be stated that she showed art in her love and practised it more in spirit than with the body." Music was a favorite art with her; she encouraged and rewarded singing, especially in the convent which she founded and where she spent almost all of her later days instructing the children.

Her court at Usson, where, as a prisoner, she lived for twenty years, was the most brilliant and least material of all France; there poets, artists, and scholars were held in high esteem, and were on familiar footing with Marguerite; the latter showed no despotism, but, with the most consummate skill, directed conversations and proposed subjects, encouraging discussion, and skilfully drawing from her friends the most brilliant repartees. She received people of distinction without ceremony.

She introduced the two elements which were combined in the eighteenth-century salon: a fine cuisine and freedom among her friends from the restraint usually imposed by distinction. She was, also, one of the first to have a circle —well organized according to modern etiquette—where the highest aristocracy, men of letters, magistrates, artists, and men of genius met on equal terms and in familiar and social intercourse; Montaigne, Brantôme, and other great writers dedicated their works to her. She also directed a select few, an academy, to instruct and distract herself. It is said that every coquette, every bourgeois woman, and almost every court lady endeavored to imitate her. When she died, at the age of sixty-two, poets and preachers sang and chanted her merits, and all the poor wept over their loss; she was called the queen of the indigent. Richelieu mentioned her devotion to the state, her style, her eloquence, the grace of her hospitality, her infinite charity. "She remains, *par excellence*, the one great sympathetic woman of the sixteenth century; her admirers, during life and after death, were legion. She shared in the lesser evils of the century, but it cannot be said that she participated in the brutalities, grossness, or glaring immoralities of her time; her weaknesses, compared with the great debauches of the age, seemed like virtues."

Such is this great woman of the sixteenth century, who has received almost universal condemnation at the hands of historians. It is to be taken into consideration that she was forced to marry a man whom she did not love, and to live in a country utterly uncongenial to her nature and opposed to the religion in which she was reared; furthermore, that her husband first defiled the marital union, thus driving her to follow the general tendencies of the time or to seek solace in religious activity, for which she had too much energy. After due consideration of the extenuating circumstances, her faults and vices, such as they were, may easily be condoned. Because she was the wife of a powerful Protestant king, she was condemned by Catholics and by them regarded with suspicion; and, in order to save herself, she was forced to commit unwise acts and even follies.

In fine, whatever may be said against Marguerite de Valois, whom despair drove to acts which are not generally pardoned, she stands foremost among the social leaders and cultured women of the sixteenth century, a century whose prominent women were notorious for their licentiousness and lack of conscience rather than famous for their virtue and womanly accomplishments. Undeniably powerful and brilliant, these unscrupulous women were never happy; usually proud, they finally suffered the most cruel humiliations; "voluptuous, they found anguish underlying pleasure." Their misfortunes are, possibly more interesting than those successes of which chagrin anxiety, and heavy hearts were the inseparable associates.

Religion, which in the sixteenth century was so badly understood, and practised even worse—obscured and falsified by fanaticism, disfigured and exaggerated by passion and hatred—was the secret cause of all downfalls crimes, horrors, intrigues, and brutality. Yet, it alone survives, and all the important figures of history return to it after a period of negligence and forgetfulness. In their religious aspect, the women of the sixteenth century differ as a rule, from those of the eighteenth, who, though equally powerful, witty, refined, sensual, frivolous, and scoffing, were far less devout; for "'tis religion which restores the great female sinners of the sixteenth century 'tis religion which saves a society ploughed up by so many elements of dissolution and so many causes of moral and material ruin, rescuing it from barbarism, vandalism, and from irretrievable decay;" but the women of the eighteenth century clung, to the end, to the scepticism and material philosophy which served them as their religion, their God.

Among the conspicuous women of the sixteenth century to whom, thus far, we have been able to attribute so little of the wholesome and pleasing, the womanly or love-inspiring, there is one striking exception in Marguerite d'Angoulême, a representative of letters, art, culture, and morality. With the study of this character we are taken back to the beginning of the century and carried among men of letters especially, for she formed the centre of the literary world. She, her mother, Louise of Savoy, and her brother, Francis I., were called a "trinity," to the existence of which Marguerite bore witness in the poem:

"Such boon is mine—to feel the amity

That God hath putten in our trinity

Wherein to make a third, I, all unfitted

To be that number's shadow, am admitted."

Marguerite inherited many of her qualities from her mother, "a most excellent and a most venerable dame," though anything but moral and conscientious; she, upon discovering that her daughter possessed rare intellectual gifts, provided her with teachers in every branch of the learning of the age. "At fifteen years of age, the spirit of God began to manifest itself in her eyes, in her face, in her walk, in her speech, and in all her actions generally." Brantôme says: "She had a heart mightily devoted to God and she loved mightily to compose spiritual songs. She devoted herself to letters, also, in her young days and continued them as long as she lived, in the time of her greatness, loving and conversing with the most learned folks of her brother's kingdom, who honored her so greatly that they called her their Mæcenas." Tenderness, particularly for her brother, seemed to develop in her as a passion.

Marguerite was a rare exception in a period described by M. Saint-Amand as one in which women were Christian in certain aspects of their character and pagan in others, taking an active part in every event, ruling by wit and beauty, wisdom and courage; an age of thoughtless gaiety and morbid fanaticism, and of laughter and tears, still rough and savage, yet with an undercurrent of subtle grace and exquisite politeness; an age in which the extremes of elegance and cruelty were blended, in which the most glaring scepticism and intense superstitions were everywhere evident; an age which was religious as well as debauched and whose women were both good and evil, innocent and intriguing. Everything was fluctuating; there was inconstancy even in the things most affected: pleasure, pomp, display. The natural outcome of this undefined restlessness was dissatisfaction; and when dissatisfaction brought in its train the inevitable reaction against falseness and immorality, Marguerite d'Angoulême stood at the head of the movement.

With her begins the cultural and moral development of France. It was she who encouraged that desire for a new phase of existence, which arose through contact with Italian culture. The men of learning—poets, artists, scholars—who soon gathered about the French court received immediate recognition from the king's sister, who had studied all languages, was gay, brilliant, and æsthetic. While her mother and brother were in harmony with the age, no better, no worse than their environment, Marguerite aspired to the most elevated morals and ideals; thus, she is a type of all that is refined, sensitive, loving, noble, and generous in humanity, a woman vastly superior to her time; in fact, the modern woman, with her highest attributes.

In Marguerite d'Angoulême contemporaries admired prudence, chastity, moderation, piety, an invincible strength of soul, and her habit of "hiding her knowledge instead of displaying it." "In an age wholly depraved, she approached the ideal woman of modern times; in spite of her virtue, she was brilliant and honored, the centre of a coterie that delighted in music, verse, ingenious dialogues and gossip, story telling, singing, rhyming. Deeply afflicted by the sad and odious spectacle of the vices, abuses, and crimes which unroll before her, she suffers through her imagination, mind and heart." Serious and sympathetic, she was interested in every movement, feeling with those who were persecuted on account of their religious opinions.

Various are the names by which she is known: daughter of Charles of Orléans, Count of Angoulême, Duchesse d'Alençon through her first marriage, and Queen of Navarre through her second, she was called Marguerite d'Angoulême, Marguerite of Navarre, of Valois, Marguerite de France, Marguerite des Princesses, the Fourth Grace, and the Tenth Muse. A most appreciative and just account of her life is given by M. Saint-Amand, which will be followed in the main outline of this sketch.

She was born in 1492, and, as already stated, received a thorough education under the direction of her mother, Louise of Savoy. At seventeen she was married to Charles III., Duke of Alençon; as he did not prove to be her ideal, she sought consolation in love for her brother, sharing the almost universal admiration for the young king, whose tendency to favor everything new and progressive was stimulated by her. She became his constant and best adviser in general affairs as well as in those of state. The foreign ambassadors sought her after having accomplished their mission, and were referred to her when the king was busy; they were enraptured, and carried back wonderful reports of Marguerite.

The world of art was opened to the French by a bevy of such painters and sculptors as Leonardo da Vinci, Rosso, Primaticcio, Benvenuto Cellini, and Bramante, and they were encouraged and fêted by Marguerite especially. In those days a new picture from Italy by Raphael was received with as much pomp and ceremony as, in olden times, were accorded the holiest relics from the East.

Men of letters gathered about the sister of the king, forming what might be termed a court of sentimental metaphysics; for the questions discussed were those of love. This refined gallantry, empty and vapid, formed the foundation of the seventeenth-century salon, where the language and fine points of sentiment were considered and cultivated until sentiment acquired poise, grandeur, and an air of dignity and reserve.

The period was one in which, during times of trial and misfortune, the presence of an underlying religious sentiment became unmistakable. In such an atmosphere, the propensity toward mysticism, which Marguerite had manifested as a child, grew more and more apparent. When Francis I. was captured at the battle of Pavia, his sister immediately sought consolation in devotion, the nature of which is well illustrated in a letter to the captive king:

"Monseigneur, the further they remove you from us, the greater becomes my firm hope of your deliverance and speedy return, for the hour when men's minds are most troubled is the hour when God achieves His masterstroke ... and if He now gives you, on one hand, a share in the pains which He has borne for you, and, on the other hand, the grace to bear them patiently, I entreat you, Monseigneur, to believe unfalteringly that it is only to try how much you love Him and to give you leisure to think how much He loves you. For He desires to have your heart entirely, as, for love, He has given you His own; He has permitted this trial, in order, after having united you to Him by tribulation, to deliver you for His own glory—so that, through you, His name may be known and sanctified, not in your kingdom alone, but in all Christendom and even to the conversion of the infidels. Oh, how blessed will be your brief captivity by which God will deliver so many souls from that infidelity and eternal damnation! Alas, Monseigneur! I know that you understand all this far better than I do; but seeing that in other things I think only of you, as being all that God has left me in this world,—father, brother, husband,—and not having the comfort of telling you so, I have not feared to weary you with a long letter, which to me is short, in order to console myself for my inability to talk with you."

After his incarceration in the gloomy prison in Spain where he was taken ill, Francis asked for the safe conduct of Marguerite; this was gladly granted. Ignorant of her future duty in Spain, she wrote: "Whatever it may be, even to the giving of my ashes to the winds to do you a service, nothing will seem strange, difficult or painful to me, but will be only consolation, repose, and honor." So impatient was she to arrive at her brother's side that she could not travel fast enough.

Her presence only increased his fever and a serious crisis soon came on, the king remaining for some time "without hearing or seeing or speaking." Marguerite, in this critical time, implored the assistance of God. She had an altar erected in her chamber, and all the French of the household, great lords and domestics alike, knelt beside the sick man's sister and received the communion from the hands of the Archbishop of Embrun, who, drawing near the bed, entreated the king to turn his eyes to the holy sacrament. Francis came out of his lethargy and asked to commune likewise, saying: "It is my God who will heal my soul and body; I entreat you that I may receive him." Then, the Host having been divided in two, the king received one half with the greatest devotion, and his sister the other half. The sick man felt himself sustained by a supernatural force; a celestial consolation descended into the soul that had been despairing. Marguerite's prayer had not been unavailing— Francis I. was saved.

She then proceeded to visit different cities and royalties, endeavoring to secure concessions for her brother. From the people in the streets as well as from the lords in their houses, she received the most unmistakable proofs of friendly feeling; in fact, her favor was so great that Charles V. informed "the Duke of Infantado that, if he wished to please the emperor, neither he nor his sons must speak to Madame d'Alençon." The latter, unable to secure her brother's release, planned a marriage between him and Eleanor of Portugal, sister of Charles V.; her successes at court and in the family of the emperor furthered this scheme. Brantôme says: "She spoke to the emperor so bravely and so courteously that he was quite astonished, and she spoke even more to those of his council with whom she had audience; there she produced an excellent impression, speaking and arguing with an easy grace in which she was proficient, and making herself rather agreeable than hateful or tiresome. Her reasons were found good and pertinent and she retained the high esteem of the emperor, his court and council."

Although she failed in her attempts to free the king, she succeeded, by arranging the marriage, in completely changing the rigorous captivity to which Charles had subjected him. Finally, by giving his two eldest sons as hostages, the king obtained his release, and in March, 1526, he again set foot, as sovereign, on French soil. Thus the king's life was saved and he was permitted to return to his country, Marguerite's devotion having accomplished that in which the most skilled diplomatist would have failed.

All historians agree that Marguerite d'Angoulême was a devout Catholic, but that she was too broad and liberal, intelligent and humane, to sanction the unbridled excesses of fanaticism. The acknowledged leader of moral reform, she protected and assisted those persecuted on account of their religious views and sympathized with the first stages of that movement which revolted against abuses, vice, scandals, immorality, and intrigue. With her, the question was not one of dogma, but concerned, instead, the religion which she considered most conducive to progress and reform. It grieved her to see her religion defile itself by cruel and inhuman persecutions and tortures, by intolerance and injustice. She felt for, but not with, the heretics in their errors. "She typifies her age in all that is good and noble, in artistic aspirations, in literary ideals, in pure politics—in short,—in humanity; in her is not found the chaotic vagueness which so often breaks out in license and licentiousness, cruelty, and barbarism."

During the absence in Spain of Francis I. and Marguerite, the mother-regent sought to gain the support and favor of Rome by ordering imprisonments, confiscations, and punishments of heretics; but upon the return of the king and his sister, the banished were recalled and tolerance again ruled. When (in 1526) Berquin was seized and tried for heresy, he found but one defender. Marguerite wrote to her brother, still at Madrid:

"My desire to obey your commands was sufficiently strong without having it redoubled by the charity you have been pleased to show poor Berquin according to your promise; I feel that He for whom I believe him to have suffered will approve of the mercy which, for His honor, you have had upon His servant and your own."

Marguerite had saved Berquin and had even taken him into her service. Her letter to the constable, Anne de Montmorency, shows her esteem of men of genius and especially of Berquin:

"I thank you for the pleasure you have afforded me in the matter of poor Berquin whom I esteem as much as if he were myself; and so you may say you have delivered me from prison, since I consider in that light the favor done me."

When on June 1, 1528, a statue of the Virgin was thrown down and mutilated by unknown hands, a reversion of feeling arose immediately, and even Marguerite was not able to save poor Berquin, and he was burned at the stake. Upon learning of his imminent peril, she wrote to Francis from Saint- Germain:

"I, for the last time, very humbly make you a request; it is that you will be pleased to have pity upon poor Berquin, whom I know to be suffering for nothing other than loving the word of God and obeying yours. You will be pleased, Monseigneur, so to act that it be not said that separation has made you forget your most humble and obedient sister and subject, Marguerite."

Encouraged by their success in that instance, the intolerant party began furious attacks upon her, one monk going so far as to say from the pulpit that she should be put into a sack and thrown into the Seine. Upon her publication of a religious poem, *Miroir de l'âme pécheresse*, in which she failed to mention purgatory or the saints, she was vigorously attacked by Beda, who had the verses condemned by the Sorbonne and caused the pupils of the College of Navarre to perform a morality in which Marguerite was represented under the character of a woman quitting her distaff for a French translation of the Gospels presented to her by a Fury. This was too much even for Francis, and he ordered the principal and his actors arrested; it was then that Marguerite showed her gentleness, mercy, and humanity by throwing herself at her brother's feet and asking for their pardon.

After but a short respite the persecution broke out anew, and with the full sanction of the king, who, upon finding at his door a placard against the mass, went even so far as to sign letters patent ordering the suppression of printing (1535). While away from the soothing influence of his sister, Francis I. was easily persuaded to sign, for the Catholic party, any permit of execution or cruelty. The life of Marguerite herself was constantly in danger, but in spite of persistent efforts to turn brother against sister, the king continued to protect and defend the latter; and though she gradually drew closer to Catholicism, she continued to protect the Protestants. She founded nunneries and showed a profound devotion toward the Virgin; although realizing the dangers and follies of the new doctrine, she had too much humanity to encourage cruelty.

The husband whom the king forced upon her was twelve years her junior, poor, and subsidized by Francis; by him she had a daughter, Jeanne d'Albret, who became the champion of Protestantism. Her married life at Pau, where she had erected beautiful buildings and magnificent terraces, was not happy; the subjects of love that formerly had amused her had lost their charm; and the incurable disease with which her brother was stricken caused her constant worry and mental suffering. When banquets, the chase, and other amusements no longer attracted Francis, he summoned Marguerite to comfort and console him; her devotion and goodness never failed. Unable to recover from the grief caused by his death in 1547, she expressed her sorrow in the most beautiful poems.

She gave the remainder of her life to religion and charity, abandoning her literary ambitions and plans. "The life after death gave her much trouble and many moments of perplexity and uneasiness. She survived her brother only two years, dying in 1549; the helper and protector of good literature, the defence, consolation, and shelter of the distressed, she was mourned by all France more than was any other queen." Sainte-Marthe says: "How many widows are there, how many orphans, how many afflicted, how many old persons, whom she pensioned every year, who now, like sheep whose shepherd is dead, wander hither and thither, seeking to whom to go, crying in the ears of the wealthy and deploring their miserable fate!" Poets, scholars, all learned and professional men, commemorated their protectress in poems and funeral orations. France was one large family in deep mourning.

Marguerite d'Angoulême must first be considered as the real power behind the supreme authority of her period, her brother the king; secondly, as a furtherer of the development and encouragement of good literature, good taste, high art, and pure morals; thirdly, as a critic of importance. She is entitled to the first consideration by the fact that as the confidential adviser of Francis I. she moulded his opinions and checked his evil tendencies: the affairs of the kingdom were therefore, to a large extent, in her hands. She collected and partly organized the chaotic mass of material thrown upon the sixteenth-century world, leaving its moulding into a classic French form to the next century; and by her spirit of tolerance she endeavored to further all moral development: thus is she entitled to the second consideration. Gifted with rare delicacy of taste, solidity of judgment, and the ability to select, discriminate, and adapt, she set the standards of style and tone: therefore, she is entitled to the third consideration.

The love of Marguerite for her brother, and her unselfish devotion to his interests, is a precedent unparalleled in French history until the time of Madame de Sévigné. In all her letters we find the same tenderness, gentleness, passion, inexhaustible emotion, sympathy, and compassion that distinguished her actions.

In her *Contes* (the *Heptameron*) *de la Reine de Navarre* we have an accurate representation of society, its manners and style of conversation; in it we find, also, remnants of the brutality and grossness of the Middle Ages, as well as reflections of the higher tendencies and aspirations of the later time. In having a thorough knowledge of the tricks, deceits, and follies of the professional lovers of the day, and of their object in courting women, Marguerite was able to warn her contemporaries and thus guard them against immorality and its dangers. In her works she upheld the purity of ideal love, exposing the questionable and selfish designs of the clever professional seducers. A specimen may be cited to show her style of writing and the trend of her thought:

"Emarsuite has just related the history of a gentleman and a young girl who, being unable to be united, had both embraced the religious life. When the story is ended, Hircan, instead of showing himself affected, cries: 'Then there are more fools and mad women than there ever were!' 'Do you call it folly,' says Oisille, 'to love honestly in youth and then to turn all love to God?' ...

'And yet I have the opinion,' says Parlemente, 'that no man will ever love God perfectly who has not perfectly loved some creature in this world.' 'What do you by loving perfectly?' asks Saffredant; 'do you call perfect lovers who are bashful and adore ladies from a distance, without daring to express their wishes?' 'I call those perfect lovers,' replies Parlemente, 'who seek some perfection in what they love—whether goodness, beauty or kindness—and whose hearts are so lofty and honest that they would rather die than perform those base deeds which honor and conscience forbid; for the soul which was created only to return to its Sovereign Good cannot, while it is in the body, do otherwise than desire to win thither; but because the senses, by which it can have tidings of that which it seeks, are dull and carnal on account of the sin of our first parents, they can show it only those visible things which most nearly approach perfection; and the soul runs after them, believing that in visible grace and moral virtues it may find the Sovereign Grace, Beauty and Virtue. But without finding whom it loves, it passes on like the child who, according to his littleness, loves apples, pears, dolls and other little things—the most beautiful that his eye can see—and thinks it riches to heap little stones together; but, on growing larger he loves living things, and, therefore, amasses the goods necessary for human life; but he knows, by the greatest experiences, that neither perfection nor felicity is attained by possessions only, and he desires true felicity and the Maker and Source thereof.'"

In her writings, much apparent indelicacy and grossness are encountered; but it must be remembered for whom she was writing, the condition of morality and the taste of the public at that time, and that she aimed faithfully to depict the society that lay before her eyes. It is argued by some critics that these indecencies could not have emanated from a pure, chaste woman; that Marguerite must have experienced the sins she depicted; but such reasoning is not sound. The expressions used by her were current in her time; there was greater freedom of manners, and coarseness and drastic language—examples of which are found so frequently in the writings of Luther—were very common.

Marguerite was less remarkable for what she did than for what she aspired to do. "She invoked, against the vices and prejudices of her epoch, those principles of morality and justice, of tolerance and humanity, which must be the very foundation of all stable society. She wished to make her brother the protector of the oppressed, the support of the learned, the crowned apostle of the Renaissance, the promoter of salutary reforms in the morals of the clergy; in politics, he was to follow a straight line and methodically advance the accomplishment of the legitimate ambitions of France."

She expressed the most modern ideas on the rights of woman, particularly on her relative rights in the married state:

"It is right that man should govern us as our head, but not that he should abandon us or treat us ill. God has so well ordered both man and woman, that I think marriage, if it is not abused, one of the most beautiful and secure estates that can be in this world, and I am sure that all who are here, no matter what pretense they make, think as much or more; and as much as man calls himself wiser than woman, so much the more grievously will he be punished if the fault be on his side. Those who are overcome by pleasure ought not to call themselves women any longer, but men, whose honor is but augmented by fury and concupiscence; for a man who revenges himself upon his enemy and slays him for a contradiction is esteemed a better companion for so doing; and the same is true if he love a dozen other women besides his wife; but the honor of woman has another foundation: it is gentleness, patience, chastity."

Désiré Nisard says that Marguerite d'Angoulême was the first to write prose that can be read without the aid of a vocabulary; in verse, she excels all poets of her time in sympathy and compassion; her poetry is "a voice which complains—a heart which suffers and which tells us so." "It is not so much her own deep sentiment that is reflected, but her emotion, which is both intellectual and sympathetic, volitional and spontaneous." Her letters were epoch-making; nothing before her time nor after her (until Madame de Sévigné) can equal them in precision, purity of language, sincerity and frankness of expression, passion and religious fervor.

In spite of what may be said to the contrary, her life was an ideal one, an example of perfect moral beauty and elevation; noble, generous, refined, pious, and sincere, she possessed qualities which were indeed rare in her time. She was attacked for her charity, and is to-day the victim of narrow sectarian and biased devotees. Her act of renouncing all gorgeous dress, even the robes of gold brocade so much worn by every princess, in order to give all her money to the poor; her protection of the needy and persecuted; her court of poets and scholars; her visits to the sick and stricken; even her untiring love for her brother and her acts of clemency—all have frequently been misinterpreted.

The greatest poets and men of letters of the sixteenth century were encouraged financially and morally or protected by Marguerite d'Angoulême —Rabelais, Marot, Pelletier, Bonaventure-Desperiers, Mellin de Saint-Gelais, Lefèvre d'Etaples, Amyot, Calvin, Berquin. Charles de Sainte-Marthe says: "In seeing them about this good lady, you would say it was a hen which carefully calls and gathers her chicks and shelters them with her wings."

Many critics believe that her literary work was imitative rather than original; even if this be true, it in no measure detracts from her importance, which is based upon the fact that she was the leading spirit of the time and typified her environment. Her followers, and they included all the intellectual spirits, looked up to her as the one incentive for writing and pleasing. Her disposition was characterized by restlessness, haste—too great eagerness to absorb and digest and appropriate all that was unfolded before her. She imitated the *Decameron* and drew up for herself a *Heptameron*; her poetry showed much skill and great ease, but little originality. Her extreme facility, her wonderfully active mind, her power of *causerie*, and her ability to discuss and write upon philosophical and religious abstractions, won the deep admiration and respect of her followers, who were not only content to be aided financially by her, but looked to her for guidance and counsel in their own work, though she never imposed her ideas and taste upon others. By her tact, she was able practically to control and guide the entire literary, artistic, and social development of the sixteenth century. Every form of intellectual movement of this period is impregnated with the spirit of Marguerite d'Angoulême.

With her affable and loving manners, her refined taste and superior knowledge, she was able to influence her brother and, through him, the government. Just as her mother controlled in politics, so did Marguerite in arts and manners. In her are found the main characteristics to which later French women owed their influence—a form of versatility which included exceptional tact and enabled the possessor to appreciate and sympathize with all forms of activity, to deal with all classes, to manage and be managed in turn.

The writings of Marguerite are quite numerous, consisting of six moralities or comedies, a farce, epistles, elegies, philosophical poems, and the *Heptameron*, her principal work—a collection of prose tales in which are reflected the customary conversation, the morals of polite society, and the ideal love of the time. They are a medley of crude equivocalities, of the grossness of the *fabliaux*, of Rabelais, and of the delicate preciosity of the seventeenth century. Love is the principal theme discussed—youth, nobility, wealth, power, beauty, glory, love for love, the delicate sensation of feeling one's self loved, elegant love, obsequious love; perfect love is found in those lovers who seek perfection in what they love, either of goodness, beauty, or grace—always tending to virtue.

Thoroughly to appreciate Marguerite d'Angoulême's position and influence and her contributions to literature, the conditions existing in her epoch must be carefully considered. It was in the sixteenth century that the charms of social life and of conversation as an art were first realized; all questions of the day were treated gracefully, if not deeply; woman began to play an important part, to appear at court, and, by her wit and beauty, to impress man. From the semi-barbaric spirit of the Middle Ages to the Italian and Roman culture of the Renaissance was a tremendous stride; in this cultural development, Marguerite was of vital importance. In intellectual attainments far in advance of the age, among its great women she stands out alone in her spirit of humanity, generosity, tolerance, broad sympathies, exemplary family life, and exalted devotion to her brother.

Of the other literary women of the sixteenth century, mention may be made of two who have left little or no work of importance, but who are interesting on account of the peculiar form of their activity.

Mlle. de Gournay, *fille d'alliance* of Montaigne, is a unique character. Having conceived a violent passion for the philosopher and essayist, she would have no other consort than her honor and good books. She called the ladies of the court "court dolls," accusing them of deforming the French language by affecting words that had apparently been greased with oil in order to facilitate their flow. She was one of the first woman suffragists and the most independent spirit of the age. In 1592, to see the country of her master, she undertook a long voyage, at a time when any trip was fraught with the gravest dangers for a woman.

She is a striking example of the effect of sixteenth-century sympathy, admiration, and enthusiasm; she was protected by some of the greatest literary men of the age—Balzac, Grotius, Heinsius; the French Academy is said to have met with her on several occasions, and she is said to have participated in its work of purifying and fixing the French language. Her adherence to the Montaigne cult has brought her name down to posterity.

M. du Bled relates a droll story in connection with her meeting Richelieu. Mlle. de Gournay was an old maid, who lived to the ripe age of eighty. Being a pronounced *féministe*, she—like her sisters of to-day—cultivated cats. The story runs as follows:

"Bois-Robert conducted her to the Cardinal, who paid her a compliment composed of old words taken from one of her books; she saw the point immediately. 'You laugh over the poor old girl, but laugh, great genius, laugh! everybody must contribute something to your diversion.' The Cardinal, surprised at her ready wit, asked her pardon, and said to Bois-Robert: 'We must do something for Mlle. de Gournay. I give her two hundred écus pension.' 'But she has servants,' suggested Bois-Robert. 'Who?' 'Mlle. Jamyn (bastard), illegitimate daughter of Amadis Jamyn, page of Ronsard.' 'I will give her fifty livres annually.' 'There is still dear little Piaillon, her cat.' 'I give her twenty livres pension, on condition that Piaillon shall have tripes.' 'But, Monseigneur, she has had kittens!' The Cardinal added a pistole for the little kittens."

A woman of large fortune, she spent it freely in study, in her household, and especially in alchemy. Her peculiar ideas about love kept her from falling prey to the wealth-seeking gallants of the time. She was one of the few women who made a profession of writing; she compiled moral dissertations, defences of woman, and treatises on language, all of which she published at her own expense; while they are of no real importance, they show a remarkable frankness and courage.

Mlle. de Gournay was, possibly, the first woman to demand the acceptance of woman on an equal status with man; for she wrote two treatises on woman's condition and rank, insisting upon a better education for her, though she herself was well educated. Following the events of the day with a careful scrutiny and interpreting them in her writings, she showed a remarkable gift of perspective and deduction and an intimate knowledge of politics. The fact that she was severely, even spitefully, attacked in both poetry and prose but proves that her writings on women were effective.

Some writers claim that the founding of the French Academy had its inception at her rooms, where many of the members met and where, later on, they discussed the work of the Academy. Her one desire for the language was to have it advance and develop, preserving every word, resorting to old ones, accepting new ones only when necessary. Thus, among French female educators, Mlle. de Gournay deserves a prominent place, because of her high ideals and earnest efforts in the study of the language, for the courage with which she advanced her convictions regarding woman, and for the high moral standard which she set by her own conduct.

In Louise Labé—*La Belle Cordière*—we meet a warrior, as well as a woman of letters. The great movement of the Renaissance, as it swept northward, invaded Lyons; there Louise Labé endeavored to do what Ronsard and the Pléiade were doing at Paris. A great part of her youth she passed in war, wearing man's apparel and assuming the name of "Captain Loys"; at an early age, she left home with a company of soldiers passing through Lyons on the way to lay siege to Perpignan, where she showed pluck, bravery, and skill. Upon her return, she married a merchant ropemaker, whence her sobriquet —*La Belle Cordière*.

She soon won a reputation by gathering about her a circle of men, who complimented her in the most elegant language and read poetry with her. Science and literature were discussed and the praises of love sung with passionate, inflamed eloquence. In this circle of congenial spirits, "she gave rise to doubts as to her virtue." As her husband was wealthy, she was able to collect an immense library and to entertain at her pleasure; she could converse in almost any language, and all travellers stopped at Lyons and called to see her at her salon. Her writings consisted of sonnets, elegies, and dialogues in prose; her influence, being too local, is not marked. Her greatest claim to attention is that she encouraged letters in a city which was beyond the reach of every literary movement. Such were the women of the sixteenth century; in no epoch in French history have women played a greater rôle; art, literature, morals, politics, all were governed by them. They were active in every phase of life, hunting with men, taking part in and causing duels, intriguing and initiating intrigues. "In the midst of battle, while cannon-balls and musket-shots rained about her, Catherine de' Medici was as brave and unconcerned as the most valiant of men. Diana of Poitiers was called the most wondrous woman, the woman of eternal youth, the beautiful huntress; it was she whom Jean Goujon sculptured, nude and triumphant, embracing with marble arms a mysterious stag, enamoured like Leda's swan."

In general, the women of that century "liked better to be feared than loved; they inspired mad passions, insensate devotions, ecstatic admirations. The epoch was one in which life counted for little, when balls alternated with massacres; when virtue was befitting only the lowly born and ugly(Brantôme recommends the beautiful to be inconstant because they should resemble the sun who diffuses his light so indiscriminately that everybody in the world feels it). It was the age of beauty—a beauty that fascinated and entranced, but the glow of which melted and killed; but this glow also reacted upon them that caused it and they became victims of their own passions—through either jealousy or their own weaknesses. No age was ever more luxurious, pompous, elegant, brilliant, and wanton, yet beneath all the glitter there were much misery and bitter repentance; amongst the violent wickedness there were noble and pure women such as Elizabeth of Austria and Louise de Vaudemont."

The whole century seemed to be afire and to tingle with that spirit of liberty, imitation, and experimentation, which, so often abused, led to much disaster. In spite of that unsettled and excited condition, the sixteenth century attained greater development, had more avenues of intellectual activity opened to it, imitated, thought and imagined more and produced as much as any other century; in every field, we find the names of its masters. As M. Faguet says, the sixteenth century was, in France, the century *créateur par excellence*; and in this, woman's part was, above all, political, her social, moral, and literary influence being less marked.

Chapter III

The Seventeenth Century: Woman at Her Best

In the seventeenth century, the influence exerted by the women of France, departing from the political aspect which had characterized it in the preceding century, became of a social, literary, religious, and moral nature, the last predominating. Inasmuch as the reins of government were in the hands of the king and his ministers, political affairs were but slightly affected by the feminine element. Woman, realizing the uselessness as well as danger of plotting against the inviolate person and power of the king, contented herself with scheming against those ministers whose attitudes she considered unfavorable to her plans.

Of all social and literary movements, however, woman was the acknowledged leader; in that institution of culture and development, the seventeenth century salon, her undisputed supremacy placed her in the position of patroness and protectress of men of letters. In the general religious movement her rôle was one of secondary importance; and as mistress, she ceased with the sixteenth century to be either active politically or disastrous morally and became merely a temporary recipient of capriciously bestowed wealth and favors. In order to fully comprehend woman's position and the exact nature of her influence in this century and the following one, the position and constitution of the nobility before, during and after the ministry of Richelieu, must be studied.

The great houses of Carolingian origin were those of Alençon, Bourgogne, Bourbon, Vendôme, Kings of Navarre, Counts of Valois, and Artois; the great gentlemen were the Dukes of Guise, Nemours, Longueville, Chevreuse, Nevers, Bouillon, Rohan, Montmorency, and, later, Luxembourg, Mortemart, Créqui, Noailles; names which are constantly met with in French history. Before the time of Louis XIV., men of such rank, when dissatisfied or discontented, might leave court at their will and were requested to return; but with Louis XIV., departure from court was considered a disgrace, and offending parties were permitted, not asked, to return.

Outside the army, there was open to the princes of the nobility no occupation in which they might expend their surplus energy; thus, being free from the burden of taxes, it was but natural that they should seek amusement in literature, society, and intrigue. The honor of their respective houses and the fear of being damned in the next world were their only sources of deep concern; other than these, they assumed no responsibilities, desiring absolute freedom from care.

Legal, judicial, and ecclesiastical offices were open to them but were little favored except as convenient means of obtaining revenues and positions otherwise not procurable. The first requisites toward advancement were bravery and skill, not learning; the majority of the members of the nobility much preferred buying a regiment to being president of a tribunal, and their primary ambition was to acquire a reputation for magnificence, heroism, and gallantry. They fought for glory, to show their skill and courage; the sentiment of patriotism was but weakly developed, and war was indulged in merely for the sake of fighting, passing the time, and being occupied. As in the preceding century, death was but little feared; in fact, the scorn of it was carried to the extreme. "The French went to death as though they were to be resuscitated on the morrow."

That man went to war was not sufficient proof of his bravery; in addition, he must, upon the smallest pretext, draw his sword, must fight constantly, and especially with adversaries better armed and larger in force; the love of woman was for such men only. Adventure was the fad: it is said of one seigneur that he took pleasure in going every night to a certain corner and, from pure malice, striking with his sword the first person who chanced that way; this unique pastime he continued until he himself was killed.

Marriage, until the eighteenth century, was not a union of affection, but merely an alliance between two families and in the interest of both; women, to preserve their identity after marriage, signed their family names. As maturity was reached at the age of twelve, marriage meant simply cohabitation. Until the Revolution, free marriages, or liaisons, were recognized as natural if not legitimate institutions, and the offspring of such unions, who were said to be more numerous than legitimate children, were legitimatized and became heirs simply through recognition by the father. (At first, princes were unwilling to accept, as wives, the natural daughters of kings; however, the Duke of Orleans and the Prince of Conti married the natural daughters of Louis XIV.) As a rule, titles could not be transmitted through females; when a woman married beneath her rank she lost her titles, but they were given to her children.

In the seventeenth century, woman's influence was of a nature vastly superior to that exerted by her in the sixteenth century, in that it rendered sacred both her and her honor; but, in spite of the refining restraint of the salon, brutality was still the main characteristic of man. To express beautiful sentiments in the midst of jealousies, rivalries, adventures, complaints, and despair, was the *savoir-vivre* of the Catherine de' Medici type of elegance brought from Italy in the sixteenth century. This caused the extremes of external fastidiousness and internal grossness to be embodied in the same individual; in the eighteenth century, man was, inwardly as well as outwardly, refined, mild, kind, a friend of pleasure; and therein lies the fundamental difference between the *honnête homme* of Louis XIV. and the *homme du monde* of Louis XV. The seventeenth century type of man is midway between that of the sixteenth and eighteenth—more polished and less gross than the former, yet lacking the knowledge and culture of the latter.

When in the seventeenth century the two all-powerful forces, brute force and money, of the preceding century were replaced by those of money and the pen, the decay of the impoverished and unintellectual nobility became but a question of time. The day when great gentlemen might scorn men of letters and learning was rapidly passing; with the French Academy arose a new spirit, a fresh impulse was given to intellectual attainments. Although treated as inferiors, the literary men of the seventeenth century spoke of the aristocracy in a spirit of raillery, but slightly veiled with respect; and the nobility while remaining, in its way, courageous and glorious, lost its prestige, force, and influence.

In the seventeenth century, money acquired a certain purchasing value which procured advantages and luxuries impossible in the preceding period when the brave man was worth infinitely more than the rich who, scorned and considered as a rapacious Jew, was isolated and in constant fear of being robbed or killed. As the number of government officials increased, individual fortunes grew; men became enormously wealthy through the various offices bought by them or given to them by the government. The financier was a king and many marriages of princes and dukes with daughters of men of wealth are recorded. Women of station, however, seldom married beneath their rank, because they lost their titles by so doing, and titles were still the only road to social success. As a rule, titles could not be transmitted through females; when a woman made a misalliance her titles were given to her children. Almost all rich men of the period, from the time of Louis XIII. to the Revolution, became nobles, as almost every brave man was made a knight up to the seventeenth century. It was possible for the wealthy to buy a marquisate or baronetage and give it to their children; a grand-marshal of France was no longer so powerful as a rich banker.

The complete change, under Louis XIV., of the customs of the time, caused numberless petty jealousies, scandals, and intrigues in the aristocracy, which could no longer maintain its old form and yet had to be considered by the government. The question of reform arose—how to restrict the number of nobles, which increased every year. Rank was bestowed for service and, sometimes, even for wealth; the old families, being poor, had no distinctive prestige except that given by their privileges at court; their titles no longer distinguished them from the newcomers, whom they gradually began to disdain, and the result was a general lowering of the standing, importance, and influence of nobility. Another party which gained prominence was that of the bench; the judges, as interpreters of the king's laws, became powerful, for law was absolute. A deadly rivalry sprang up between the parties of rank with no money or power and of power and money without rank.

The desire of every man of rank to be independent, to be a force in himself instead of a part of a unit which might be useful to the state as a whole, was one of the principal defects of the French aristocracy; poverty crushed it, idleness robbed it of its alertness, intriguing and gradual oppression reduced it to despair. Appointed to offices, its members failed in the performance of their duties; the latter fell to the under men who, while the aristocracy was busy at fêtes, in society, at the table, became experts in the affairs of the government—shrewd politicians and financiers. The new nobility, that of the robe, replaced that of the sword in all interests of the government except war; gradually, Parliament was made up of men who, having been elevated to the rank of nobility, retained their aversion to those who were noble by birth, recognizing only the king as their superior and refusing precedence to even the princes of the blood. Louis XIV., however, objecting to and fearing such a strong class as that of the robe, employed, wherever possible, people of lower rank. Thus it happened in the seventeenth century that the still powerful nobility of higher rank was scorned and kept down; but in the eighteenth century, when the gentlemen of the robe had become all-powerful and therefore constituted a dangerous party, it was they who became the objects of scorn and persecution, while the aristocrats of blood, the gentlemen of the court, recovered the royal favors through their political powerlessness.

French aristocracy really had no object, no *raison d'être*, after its disappearance from all governmental functions; it became an encumbrance to the state; having no particular part to play, it did nothing; this is one of the causes of its dissolution and of the Revolution as well. Thus France gradually passed from inequality of classes under the sanction of custom to equality of classes before the law: this change in the condition and constitution of the French nobility accounts for many intrigues and scandals and explains the social and moral actions of French women, as well as the difference in the nature of their activities in the seventeenth and eighteenth centuries.

The seventeenth was, *par excellence*, the century which can boast of that incomparable society the cult of which was the highest in all things—art, religion, philosophy, poetry, politics, war, and beauty. From the convent of the Carmelites to the Hôtel de Rambouillet, from the Place Royale to the various châteaux and salons, we must seek only that which is elevating and spiritual, beautiful and religious. In the famous society which kept pace with the political reputation and influence of France is found a coterie of women who combined remarkable beauty and intelligence with a high moral standard, and whose names are intimately connected with the history of France. Where again can we find such a galaxy of beauties as that formed by Charlotte de Montmorency, Mme. de Chevreuse, Mme. de Hautefort, Mme. de Montbazon, Mme. de Guémené, Mme. de Châtillon, Mme. de Longueville, Marie de Gonzague, Henriette de la Vallière, Mme. de Montespan, Mme. de Maintenon, without enumerating such great writers and leaders of salons as Mme. de Rambouillet, Mlle. de Scudéry, Mme. de Lambert, Mme. de Sévigné, and Mme. de la Fayette? The seventeenth century could tolerate no mediocrity; grandeur was in the very atmosphere; its political movements were great movements; it produced in art a Poussin, in letters a Corneille, in science and philosophy a Descartes.

The various movements of which woman was the head may be divided into two periods, and each period into two parts. The political women may well be grouped about Marie de' Medici,—whose career will not be given separate treatment, inasmuch as there was no drop of French blood in her veins,—and the social and literary women about Mme. de Rambouillet and her salon. In the latter half of the seventeenth century and at the beginning of the eighteenth, politics are represented by Mme. de Montespan—the mistress— and Mme. de Maintenon—the wife; social life and literature have their purest representative in Mme. de Lambert. The two queens of the seventeenth century, Anne of Austria and Maria Theresa, were without influence; the religious movement was represented by the galaxy of women of whom we write in a later chapter.

After the death of Henry IV., Marie de' Medici succeeded in having herself made queen-regent for Louis XIII., who was then but nine years old. A woman of no particular capacity, who had in no way adapted herself to French life and customs, she allowed herself to be governed by an adventurer, an Italian who understood and appreciated French ideals no more than did Marie; these two— the queen and Concini, her minister—immediately began to concoct plans to gain control of the state. The king was kept in virtual captivity until he reached the age of seventeen, when, having asserted his rights, Concini was killed, and Marie's dominant power and influence came to an abrupt end.

Louis XIII. reigned, with his minister, the Prince de Luynes, from 1617 to 1624, when he became reconciled to his mother and appointed her favorite, Richelieu, his minister. From 1610 to about 1640, Marie de' Medici exercised more or less influence, always of a nature disastrous to France.

After the king's death, Anne of Austria, as queen-regent, with Mazarin, directed the destinies of France. During the ministry of the two cardinals, Richelieu and Mazarin, occurred the political intrigues and astute diplomatic movements of Mme. de Chevreuse and the unwise and short-sighted aspirations of Mme. de Longueville. These intimate friends were women of the highest intelligence, most perfect beauty, and uncapitulating devotion, and were working for the same cause, though from different motives.

Mme. de Chevreuse was the daughter of M. de Rohan, Duke of Montbazon. She had married M. de Luynes, the minister of Louis XIII., who overthrew the power of Marie de' Medici, and who, by initiating his wife into his secrets, gave her the schooling and experience which she later used to such advantage. De Luynes presented her at court with instructions to ingratiate herself with the queen—Anne of Austria—and the king. In this design she succeeded so well that she was soon made superintendent of the household of the queen, and became as influential with Anne as was her husband with the king.

In 1621 M. de Luynes died; a year later his widow married Claude of Lorraine, Duke of Chevreuse; but as that was an unhappy union, she soon began her career as an intriguer. On the arrival of Lord Kensington, the English ambassador, she fell in love with him, that escapade being the first of a long series; the two proceeded to inveigle Queen Anne into a liaison with the Duke of Buckingham, which scheme, as history so well records, partly succeeded.

When Mme. de Chevreuse accompanied to England the new queen, Henriette-Marie, wife of Charles I., both Buckingham and Kensington outdid themselves in showing her attention, Richelieu, fearing her influence and intrigues at the court of England, hastened the recall of her husband, but she received through her friends, from the English monarch himself, an invitation to remain; during the time, she gave birth to a child.

Her next famous undertaking, which involved the lives of various persons of high rank, was the scheme to persuade Monsieur the Dauphin to refuse to marry Mlle. de Montpensier; Queen Anne was opposed to this union, and Mme. de Chevreuse gained to their cause a number of influential friends who were all madly in love with her. The ever vigilant Richelieu having discovered the plot, Monsieur confessed. In this conspiracy, M. de Chalais lost his head, other plotters lost their positions, and some were exiled. Mme. de Chevreuse was forced to retire to Lorraine; there she set in movement a vast plan against Richelieu and France, allying England and various princes, but, by the arrest of Montaigu, the plot was discovered, the alliance broken up, and peace restored.

In 1626, by request of England, Mme. de Chevreuse returned to France. For a time she was quiet and seemed to favor Richelieu, but she soon captivated one of his ministers, the Marquis of Châteauneuf. Richelieu discovered the latter's weakness, and, having captured his correspondence, sent him to prison, where he remained for ten years. The fair intriguer was exiled to Dampierre, the cardinal fearing to send her out of France on account of her influence with the Duke of Lorraine. She managed to steal into Paris at night and see the queen; when discovered, she was sent to Touraine where she began the dangerous task of carrying on the correspondence between the Dukes of Savoy and Lorraine and England, and between Spain and Queen Anne. Even when this correspondence was intercepted and the queen confessed all, Richelieu was afraid to banish Mme. de Chevreuse; though he believed her to be at the bottom of all the current intrigues, he knew that out of France she would stir up the rulers of England and Spain as well as the Duke of Lorraine and others hostile to the cardinal.

Violence being out of the question, because of her influence in England and of the prominence of her family, he decided to win her over by kindness; he even sent her money, but she was too shrewd to permit Richelieu to outwit her, always paying him back in his own coin. However, that kind of play was too dangerous for her and she escaped to Spain. As soon as her departure became known, Richelieu set to work every means in his power to bring her back, sending her an urgent invitation to return and promising to pardon her past. When his messages reached her, she was already in Madrid, where she was royally received as the friend of the king's sister, Anne; there, by means of her beauty and wonderful intelligence, she conquered every cavalier. When the war broke out between France and Spain, she left for England where she was welcomed like a visiting queen.

Richelieu, anxious for the support of the Duke of Lorraine in his war against Spain and Austria, needed the coöperation of Mme. de Chevreuse, and with that end in view sent ambassadors to London to arrange for her return; but an agreement was not an easy matter between two such astute politicians, and negotiations went on unsuccessfully for over a year. Her subtleness, apparent docility and invincible precautions were pitted against the artifices and dissimulation of the cardinal; both employed all the astute manœuvres of diplomacy and exhausted the resources of consummate skill in gaining the point desired by each. The cardinal failed to convince her of her safety.

Mme. de Chevreuse soon formed about her a circle of émigrés—Marie de' Medici, Duc La Vallette, Soubèse, La Vieuville, and many others. This coterie was in open correspondence with Spain, Austria, and the Duke of Lorraine. From every side, Richelieu felt the intriguing hand and influence of Mme. de

Chevreuse, and decided to put forth another effort to get her to return, this time sending her husband; but not sure of the latter's sincerity and in fear of him, the duchess concluded to leave England for Flanders, and, escorted by a squad of dukes and lords, departed like a queen.

At Brussels, she entered into open relations with Spain, drawing over the Duke of Lorraine. She was accused of being in the plot of Cinq-Mars and the Duke of Bouillon with Spain; when Richelieu exposed this to Queen Anne, the latter for the first time became her enemy. Just at this time of his triumph, Richelieu died, his death being followed soon after by that of Louis XIII., who left a special order for the exile forever of Mme. de Chevreuse, whom he called *Le Diable*. The queen-regent, however, recalled her, and set at liberty her friend, Châteauneuf, who had been imprisoned for ten years.

When Mme. de Chevreuse returned to Paris after an absence of ten years, her beauty was still unimpaired, she possessed an experience such as no man of the day could boast, was personally acquainted with nearly every great statesman and aware of the weak points in every court of Europe. While she could now count on the support of the majority of the princes, plots were being formed about the queen-regent, the object of which was to persuade the latter to give up the friends who had served her faithfully for so many years. La Rochefoucauld was sent to meet Mme. de Chevreuse and to inform her of the change of attitude of the queen-regent; as her devoted friend, he advised her to abandon, for the present, all hopes of governing the queen and to devote herself entirely to regaining her favor and to preparing for the possible fall of Mazarin.

After securing the release of her friend Châteauneuf, Mme. de Chevreuse set to work to restore him to his former office of Guard of the Seals, but did not succeed. She then turned her attention to undermining the power of Mazarin, agitating all émigrés returning to France and starting the most outspoken denunciation of the policy of the cardinal, his injustice and tyranny against the nobility. The cries of disapproval became so general that Mazarin was kept busy warding off the blows aimed at him by his enemy; the latter succeeded in placing Châteauneuf as *Chancelier des ordres du roi* and in having his estates restored to him, while Alexandre de Campion she placed in the household of the queen. Mazarin, living in constant dread of her, managed to thwart two of her cherished schemes—the restoration to the Duke of Vendôme of the government of Brittany and the placing of Châteauneuf in the ministry—upon the success of which depended her own influence and power.

Finding that ruse, flattery, insinuation, and ordinary court intrigues were of no avail, she turned to other methods. The Importants, a party made up of adventurers and a large number of the nobility, were making themselves felt more and more; they were opposed to Richelieu and Mazarin, and Mme. de Chevreuse became their chief and instigator. Failing to succeed with the cardinal's own methods, she decided to assassinate him, but the plot was discovered, the Duke of Beaufort was arrested and all the princes of the party of the Importants were ordered to leave Paris. Mme. de Chevreuse was compelled to depart from court and retire to Dampierre, and then to Touraine, where she did everything in her power to assist the friends who had compromised themselves for her. During her first exile she had had the consolation of the friendship of the queen; but now she was banished by the very friend whom she had served so well and who had up to this time been able and willing to afford her comfort and protection. Through Lord Goring, Count Craft, and the Commander de Jars, she opened up correspondence and negotiations with England, but was again surprised by the vigilant Mazarin and sent to Angoulême; determining to escape, after many hardships, she successfully reached Liège; from there, as head of all foreign intrigues against France, she continued to thwart Mazarin's foreign policy.

As soon as the first signs of the Fronde broke out, Mme. de Chevreuse became active and succeeded in attracting to her the young Marquis de Laigues with whom, later on, she contracted a *mariage de conscience*. As ambassador of the Fronde, she prevailed upon Spain to promise troops and subsidies to her party. After the peace of 1649, she went to Paris where she found almost all her friends ready to follow her and to pay her homage. It was she who conceived the idea of an aristocratic league which, under the auspices of the two great princes of the blood, the Duke of Orléans and the Prince of Condé, would unite the best part of the nobility.

Her plan was to marry her daughter to the Prince de Conti and the young Duc d'Enghien to one of the daughters of the Duke of Orléans. The contracts were signed and all was in readiness when Mazarin was exiled, and the following Frondists came into power: the Duke of Orléans at court, Condé and Turenne at the head of the army, Châteauneuf in the Cabinet, Molé in Parliament, while Mme. de Chevreuse and Mme. de Longueville managed to keep harmony among all. Queen Anne in a short time annulled the marriage contracts; and on the return of Mazarin, Mme. de Chevreuse took up her work with him, the cardinal being wise enough to appreciate the fact that she was a greater force with than against him.

Strange as it may seem, Mme. de Chevreuse in time became the great acting and controlling force of royalty, winning over the Duke of Lorraine and becoming a staunch friend to both the regent and the cardinal; after the death of the latter, she became all-powerful, and it may be said that she made Colbert what he was. In the fulness of her power, she gradually retired, having seen, in turn, the passing away or the fall of Richelieu, Mazarin, Louis XIII., Anne of Austria, the Queen of England, Châteauneuf, the Duke of Lorraine, her daughter, and the Marquis de Laigues. She ceased plotting, renounced politics and intrigues, and retired to the country, where she died in 1679.

Mme. de Chevreuse was undoubtedly one of the most important political characters of the seventeenth century, just as she was also one of its greatest beauties—possibly the most seductive and charming woman of her epoch. A consummate diplomat and an untiring worker, she was at the head of more intrigues and plots, had more thrilling adventures, controlled and ruined more men, than any other woman of her century, if not of all French history. Thinking little of religion, she was yet in the very midst of the Catholic party; unswerving in her friendships, she scorned danger, opinion, fortune, for those whom she loved or whose cause she espoused; an implacable foe, she was the most dreaded enemy of both Richelieu and Mazarin.

With a remarkable ability for grasping the details of an antagonist's position she combined all the other qualities of an astute politician; thus, upon the desired consummation of her plots she brought to bear a sagacity, finesse, and energy that baffled all her adversaries. With her, politics became a passion and a necessity; even while in exile, her zeal was unflagging and she intrigued over all Europe. Scorning peril as well as all petty restraints, and characterized by courage, loyalty, and devotion, she was without an equal among the members of her sex.

Mme. de Hautefort, while less powerful than Mme. de Chevreuse and of quite a different type, is associated with her in the history of the time. Pure, beautiful, and virtuous, she everywhere inspired love and respect; without political aspirations and seeking neither power nor favors, she refused to deliver her soul or betray her friends for Richelieu or Mazarin; she was their enemy, but not their rival.

Because of her desire to serve the queen, of whom she was an intimate friend, and to further her interests, she was connected with the first intrigues of Mme. de Chevreuse, but as an innocent and disinterested party. Louis XIII. conceived an ardent attachment for her, and Richelieu endeavored to win her over to his policies, but she remained faithful to her queen and refused to sacrifice her honor to the king.

The cardinal did not rest until he had prevailed upon the king to exile her, ostensibly for only fifteen days; and as her unselfishness and generosity had made an impression upon the whole court, her departure was much regretted, though no demonstration was made. When, after the king's death, Mme. de Hautefort returned to Paris, she soon reëstablished herself in the affection, admiration, and respect of her associates.

As Mazarin gained ascendency over Queen Anne, that regent changed her policy and abandoned her former friends. Mme. de Hautefort was opposed to the queen on account of her liaison with her minister and her lack of fidelity to those who, in time of trouble, had served her so well. As *dame d'atours*, she was forced either to close her eyes to all scenes between the cardinal and Anne or to combat the regent and resign. She was not to be tempted by the honors and favors with which the two sought to purchase her criminal connivance or her silence; preferring poverty and exile to a guilty conscience, she soon retired to the convent of the Daughters of Sainte-Marie, where she was followed by her admirers, who were willing to place themselves and their fortunes at her disposal. At the age of thirty she accepted the hand of the Duke of Schomberg, and, away from the court and its intrigues, lived in peace.

Indifferent to the powerful, but kind and compassionate to the poor and oppressed, Mme. de Hautefort is a type of those great women of the seventeenth century who stood for honor, courage, generosity, sympathy, and virtue; fervently, even austerely, religious, she was yet far removed from anything resembling bigotry. Among the ladies of the Hôtel de Rambouillet, she was one of the most popular; her vivacity, modesty, and reserve, combined with a tall figure, imposing bearing, and large, expressive blue eyes, won the hearts of many cavaliers, among whom the most prominent were the Dukes of Lorraine and La Rochefoucauld.

A close second to Mme. de Chevreuse in influence and power, was Mme. de Longueville, a woman of exquisite and aristocratic beauty, of brilliant mind, and an adept in the art of conversation. Tender and kind, but ambitious, she, like many others of her time and sex, had two distinct periods—one of conquest and one of penitence and pious devotion.

Born in a prison at Vincennes during the captivity of her father, the great Henry of Bourbon, Prince of Condé, she in time developed remarkable personal charms. Her early days were spent at the convent of the Carmelites and at the Hôtel de Rambouillet, her mind—in these opposite worlds of religion and society—being divided between pious meditations and romantic dreams. At the time of the execution at Toulouse of her uncle, M. de Montmorency, she seriously considered entering the Carmelite convent.

Upon making her social début, she immediately became one of the leaders about whom all the gallants gathered. She formed a fast friendship with Mme. de Sablé, Mme. de Rambouillet, Mme. de Bouteville, and Mlle. du Vigean. Her beauty, which was quite phenomenal, soon became the subject of poetry. Voltaire wrote:

"De perles, d'astres et de fleurs,

Bourbon, le ciel fit tes couleurs,

Et mit dedans tout ce mélange

  L'esprit d'un ange!

L'on jugerait par la blancheur

De Bourbon, et par sa fraicheur,

Qu'elle a prit naissance des lis."

[The heaven made thy colors, Bourbon, of pearls, of stars, of flowers, and to all this mixture added the spirit of an angel. One would judge by the whiteness and freshness of Bourbon that she was born of the lilies.]

In 1642, at the age of twenty-three, she was married, against her will, to M. de Longueville who was, after the princes of the blood, the greatest seigneur of France; he was old and indifferent, and enamored of another woman, while she was young and full of hopes, ambitions, and love. His conduct, being anything but correct, immediately set the young wife, with her instincts of refinement and principles and habits of the *précieuses*, against her husband. The advent of a rival in the person of Mme. de Montbazon, one of the most noted beauties of the day, made the state of affairs even more unpleasant, the humiliation being so much keener because it was on account of her charms that Montbazon was preferred to the wife. The latter's fate was a cruel one; she could not respect her husband, and, for her, respect was the only road to love. She continued to live at the Hôtel de Longueville and to attend all court functions, where, through her beauty, she early became the object of much attention from the young lords, among whom Coligny seemed to impress her more than any other.

About this time occurred the deaths of Richelieu and Louis XIII., and the Importants, flocking to Paris to regain their rights and to share in the spoils of the new regency, began to make themselves felt. The leaders expected great favors from Anne of Austria who had been forced into obedience by the cardinal, but she was a great disappointment to them. A born lady of leisure, she was only too glad to be relieved of the arduous duties of government, and this her minister, Mazarin, quickly proceeded to do; his first object was to crush the influence of the Importants, who were very powerful in the salons, society, and politics.

The house of Condé declared in favor of Mazarin, but at first this did not affect Mme. de Longueville, whose kindness of heart and indifference to politics and intrigues were generally known. Probably, she never would have taken a part in the Fronde had it not been for the rival who had been seeking, by every possible means, to injure her reputation—a design which Mme. de

Montbazon well-nigh accomplished by declaring that two letters which, at a reception, had fallen from the pocket of Coligny had been written by Mme. de Longueville. In reality, they had been written by Mme. de Fouquerolles to the Marquis of Maulevrier. Mme. la Princesse, mother of Mme. de Longueville demanded full reparation, threatening that unless it was at once granted the house of Condé would withdraw from court, and Mazarin managed to induce the queen to compel Mme. de Montbazon to apologize publicly. It may be of interest to give, in full, the apology, to show the nature of court etiquette, hypocrisy, and intrigue of that day. Mme. de Montbazon called at the hôtel of the princess and spoke the following words, which were written on a paper attached to her fan: "Madame, I come here to attest that I am innocent of the spitefulness of which they accuse me, there being no person of honor capable of uttering such a calumny; and if I had committed such a crime, I would have submitted to the punishments that the queen would have imposed upon me, would never have shown myself before the world again, and would have asked your pardon. I beg you to believe that I shall never be lacking in the respect that I owe you because of the opinion which I have of the merit and virtue of Mme. de Longueville." To which the princess replied: "I very willingly receive the assurance you give me of having had no part in the spitefulness that was published, deferring all to the order the queen has given me."

After this episode, the princess refused to be in the same place with Mme. de Montbazon. On one occasion, Mme. de Chevreuse had invited the queen to a collation at a place where the queen enjoyed walking; she requested the princess to join her, giving her word of honor that Mme. de Montbazon would not be there; she was present, however, and the princess was about to leave when the queen ordered Mme. de Montbazon to feign illness and retire; this she refused to do and remained, whereupon the queen and the princess left, and shortly afterward Mme. de Montbazon received orders to leave Paris.

This excited the Importants to fever heat and a plot was formed, with Mme. de Chevreuse as the leader, to assassinate the cardinal. Shortly after this, Coligny, as champion of the cause of Mme. de Longueville, challenged the Duc de Guise to a duel. The whole court was made up of two parties: the Importants with Mme. de Montbazon and Mme. de Chevreuse; and Condé and Mme. de Longueville with their friends; the result was the death of Coligny. Mme. de Longueville was a true *précieuse* and hardly loved Coligny, but allowed him and any other to serve and adore her in a respectable way—a principle followed by the better women of the age, such as Mme. de Rambouillet and Mme. de Sablé.

Some time after these occurrences, Mme. de Longueville was stricken with smallpox which, fortunately, did not impair her beauty; it was said, on the contrary, that in taking away its first flower it left all the brilliancy which, joined to her culture and charming languor, made her one of the most attractive persons in France. La Rochefoucauld has left the following picture of her: "This princess had all the advantages of *esprit* and beauty to as great a degree as if nature had taken pleasure in completing, in her person, a perfect work; but these qualities shone less brilliantly on account of one characteristic which led her to imbibe so thoroughly the sentiments of those who adored her that she no longer recognized her own."

After her twenty-fifth year, Mme. de Longueville became more and more imbued with the general spirit of the seventeenth century: coquetry and *bel esprit* became her chief occupation. The glory of her brother, the Duc d'Enghien, who was rapidly becoming a power, and the probability of the house of Condé becoming dangerous, made Mazarin realize that Mme. de Longueville was to be reckoned with, inasmuch as she had full control over D'Enghien and was constantly instilling new ideas into his mind and requesting from him the distribution of all sorts of favors. Mazarin, in 1646, succeeded in causing her withdrawal to Münster for one year; there she ruled as queen of the Congress. On the death of her father, the Prince of Condé, and at the request of her mother to come home for her lying-in, the husband of Mme. de Longueville consented to her return to Paris.

In the meantime, everything was being done by the Importants to win over the house of Condé and cause a breach between it and Mazarin. The court at this time was in full glory; to amuse the queen-regent, Mazarin was lavishing money on artists from Italy, and the nobility outdid itself in its attempts to rival royalty in elegance and luxury. Upon her return, everyone paid homage to Mme. de Longueville; it was at this period that La Rochefoucauld, who was anxious about his position at court, as he was accused of being in league with the Importants and was therefore refused the favors he desired, met Mme. de Longueville who was in the height of her glory and in full control of the most prominent house of the time—that of the Duc d'Enghien and the Prince de Conti, her brothers.

In order to conquer for himself what the cardinal would not grant him, La Rochefoucauld put forth every effort to win Mme. de Longueville; captivated by his fine appearance, his chivalry and, above all, by his powerful intellect, she gave herself up entirely, willing to share his destiny, to sacrifice all her interests, even those of her family, and the deepest sentiment of her life—the tenderness for her brother.

France at this time, 1648, was in a position to gain for herself a peace with the world at her own terms, and her future seemed to be without a cloud. It was the Fronde that checked her growth and glory, and the cause of this was the estrangement of the house of Condé through the action of Mme. de Longueville in passing with her husband over to the party of the Importants, she being the first of her family to forsake the government. Under the leadership of La Rochefoucauld, she cast her lot with the opposing party, allowing herself to be identified with the interests of those who had endeavored to tarnish her early reputation. Becoming a leader with Mme. de Chevreuse and Mme. de Montbazon (her rival), she easily won over her young brother, the Prince de Conti. After the imprisonment of her husband and her two brothers, she began her real career as a woman of tactics, politics, and generalship.

With the connivance of Mme. de Chevreuse and the Princess Palatine, a general plan had been formed to create a new government by the union of the aristocracy. The marriage, already spoken of, between the Duke of Enghien and one of the daughters of the Duke of Orléans and that arranged between the Prince of Conti and the daughter of Mme. de Chevreuse were to have united the Fronde with the house of Condé. The alliances, however, were declared off, and Mme. de Chevreuse went over to the cardinal and the queen; Condé's fall and Mazarin's success followed, being the result, mainly, of the determination of Mme. de Chevreuse to avenge herself upon Condé for having consented to the breaking of the marriage contracts.

Mme. de Longueville did all in her power to continue the conflict that Condé had undertaken, but, exhausted by continual excitement and ill success, she was compelled to retire. After this, her life, spent in Normandy, at the Carmelites' convent and at Port Royal, became a long penance, which increased in austerity until she died in 1679. Thus, her career was at first one of unblemished brilliancy, then a period of elegant and intellectual debauch, and finally one of expiation.

"Her politics," says Sainte-Beuve, "considered in the *ensemble*, are nothing more than a desire to please, to shine—a capricious love. Her character lacked consistency and self-will, her mind was keen, ready, subtle, ingenious, but not reasonable."

In her convent life, her crowning virtue was humility. Her enemies did not cease to attack her, but she received all their affronts with the noblest resignation. The following testimonies are taken from a Jansenist manuscript of 1685:

"She never said anything to her own advantage. She made use of as many occasions as she could find for humiliating herself without any affectation. What she said, she said so well that it could not be better said. She listened much, never interrupted, and never showed any eagerness to speak. She spoke sensibly, modestly, charitably, and without passion. To court her was to speak with equity and without passion of everyone and to esteem the good in all. Her whole exterior, her voice, her face, her gestures, were a perfect music; and her mind and body served her so well in expressing what she wished to make heard, that she appeared the most perfect actress in the world."

Her love for La Rochefoucauld was the secret of her failure in life. When she experienced the disappointments of her married life and discovered that her dream of being loved by her husband could not be realized, she looked to other sources for diversion. She was not an intriguing woman like Mme. de Chevreuse, but one of ambitions which were incited by her love for and interest in the objects of her affection. Although she carried on flirtations with Coligny and the Duke of Nemours, she really loved no one but La Rochefoucauld, to whom she sacrificed her reputation and tranquillity, her duties and interests. For him she took up the cause of the Fronde; for him she was a mere slave, her entire existence being given up to his love, his whims, his service; when he failed her, she was lost, exhausted, and retired to a convent at the age of thirty-five and in the full bloom of her beauty. Her professed lover simply used her as a means to an end, seeking only his own interests in the Fronde, while she sought his; and this is the explanation of her seeming inconsistency of conduct. In her religious life she was happy and contented; surrounded by her friends, she lived peacefully for over twenty years.

Thus, Marie de' Medici, a foreigner, Mme. de Chevreuse, and Mme. de Longueville represent the political women of the first half of the seventeenth century; Anne of Austria, who was of foreign extraction, was a mere tool in the hands of Mazarin, and exerted little influence in general.

One of the principal differences between the conspicuous political women of the sixteenth and those of the seventeenth centuries lies in the possession by the latter of less personal force than that wielded by the former, who allowed nothing to thwart their plans. The women of both periods were beautiful, but those of the earlier one were of a magnetic and sensual type, "inspiring insensate passions and exciting a feverish unrest," thus ruling man through his lower instincts. The lack of refinement, sympathy, and charity reflected in their actions is in glaring contrast to the dignity, repose, reserve, and womanly modesty and grace displayed by their less masterful successors of the seventeenth century.

Chapter IV

Woman in Society and Literature

At the beginning of the seventeenth century, after the death of Henry IV., there were three classes in France,—the nobility, clergy, and third estate,— each with a distinct field of action: the nobility dominated customs, morality, and the government; the clergy supervised instruction and education; the third estate furnished the funds, that is, its work made possible the operations of the other classes.

At court, various dialects and diverse pronunciations were in use by the representatives of the different provinces; the written language, though understood generally, was not used. Warriors were largely in evidence among the members of the nobility and court; entirely indifferent to decency of expression, purity of morals, and refinement of manners, and even boasting of their scorn of all restrictions, they took their boisterous rudeness into the drawing room where their influence was unlimited. The king, being of the same class, knew no better, or, if he did, had not the moral courage to compel a change; thus, the institution of a reformatory movement fell to the lot of woman.

Then, however, woman was but little better than man; to gain his esteem, she would first have to make radical changes in her own behavior and become self-respecting. The customs of the time placed many disadvantages in the way of her social and moral reform. As a rule, the young girl was confined to a convent until she reached marriageable age; when that came and with it an undesired husband, she was ready for almost any prank that would relieve the monotony of her uncongenial marital relations. The convents themselves were so corrupt or so easily corruptible, that, very frequently, young girls did not leave them with unstained purity. To certain of these institutions, women and men of standing often bought the privilege of access at any time, to drink, dine, sleep, or attend sacred exercises with other persons; thus, libertinage was not uncommon within the walls of those so-called religious establishments.

Mme. de Rambouillet felt most keenly the degradation of woman and resolved to act against it by combating everything that could offend taste or delicacy. As in the beginning of every great age, all things tended to greatness. A period of discipline and coördination set in, and elegance, grace, and refinement became the most pronounced characteristics of the time; rough, crude, robust, vigorous, and energetic characteristics, combined with coarseness and brutality, were eliminated during the seventeenth century. The women who caused this general purification of morals and language were given the name of *précieuses* and the movement that of *préciosité*.

The extent to which the *précieuses* went in inventing locutions by which they were to be recognized as elegant, is generally exaggerated; Livet says that out of six hundred women hardly thirty could be accused of such fatuity. The wiser and more conservative women did adopt a large number of expressions which were necessary for refinement of language and these classicisms were exaggerated by some of the provincial classes who received their expressions from books and the theatre; such authors as Corneille, etc., were studied and their poetic licenses introduced into spoken language. These follies, pictured by Molière, naturally afforded much amusement in cultured circles where every event of the day was discussed, from the vital affairs of the government to the æsthetic interests of art and literature.

The tremendous vogue of the seventeenth century salons or drawing rooms naturally gave a stimulus to literature; but, as they were so numerous and as each one claimed its large coterie of literary men, they proved to be disastrous to some while helpful to others. Two distinct classes of writers arose: the one, serious, elevated, thoughtful, classical, and independent of the salon, is well represented by Molière, Pascal, Boileau; the other, light, affected, gallant, superficial, was composed of the innumerable unimportant writers of the day.

The salon movement must not be confounded with two other social movements or forces—those of court and society; while at the former all was formality, the latter was still gross and brutish. The Marquis de Caze, at a supper seized a leg of mutton and struck his neighbor in the face with it, sprinkling her with gravy, whereupon she laughed heartily; the Count of Brégis, slapped by the lady with whom he was dancing, tore off her headdress before the whole company; Louis XIII., noticing in the crowd admitted to see him dine a lady dressed too *décolleté*, filled his mouth with wine and squirted the liquid into the bosom of the unfortunate girl; the Prince of Condé, indulging in customary brutishness, ate dung and had the ladies follow his example; these are fair illustrations of social *elegances*.

As will be seen, nothing of this nature occurred in the salon of Mme. de Rambouillet, whose object was to charm her leisure hours, distract and amuse the husband whom she adored, and be agreeable to her friends. Her amusements were most original—concerts, mythological representations, suppers, fireworks, comedies, readings, always something new, often in the form of a surprise or a joke. Of the latter, the best known is the one played on the Count of Guise whose fondness for mushrooms had become proverbial; on one occasion when he had consumed an immense number of them at table, his valet, who had been bribed, took in all his doublets; on trying to put them on again, he found them too narrow by fully four inches. "What in the world is the matter—am I all swollen—could it be due to having eaten too many mushrooms?" "That is quite possible," said Chaudebonne; "yesterday you ate enough of them to split." All the accomplices joined in ridiculing him, and he began to squirm and show a somewhat livid color. Mass was rung, and he was compelled to attend in his chamber robe. Laughing, he said: "That would be a fine end—to die at the age of twenty-one from having eaten too many mushrooms." In the meantime, Chaudebonne advised the use of an antidote which he wrote and handed to the count, who read: "Take a good pair of scissors and cut your doublet." Only then did the victim comprehend the joke.

One day, Voiture, having met a bear trainer, took him with his animals to the room of the Marquise de Rambouillet; she, turning at the noise, saw four large paws resting upon her screen. She readily forgave the author of the surprise. Du Bled relates many more of these innocent jokes.

Among the congenial people of the salons, the relations were always of the most cordial, friendly, free, and intimate nature; they were like the members of a large family. By them, love was not considered a weakness but a mark of the elevation of the soul, and every man had to be sensitive to beauty. When the Duchesse d'Aiguillon presented to society her nephew, who later became the Duke of Richelieu, she advised and encouraged him to complete his education and make of himself an *honnête homme* by association with the elder Mlle. du Vigean and other women; the object of this procedure was to polish his manners, elevate his instincts, and develop ease in deportment toward the ladies. There was no hint of the vulgar or licentious pleasures which became the characteristics of love in the eighteenth century.

The woman who inaugurated the movement toward purity of morals, decency of language, polish of manners, and courtesy to woman, was Mme. de Rambouillet. Cathérine de Vivonne, Marquise de Rambouillet, whose mother was a great Roman lady and whose father had been ambassador to Rome, inherited that pride of race and independence of spirit for which she was so well known. In 1600, she was married, at the age of twelve, to the Marquis de Rambouillet who was her senior by eleven years, but who treated her with deference and respect rare at that time. Husband and wife were perfectly congenial, and their happy and peaceful life was a great contrast to that led by the majority of the married couples of the day. Absolutely irreproachable in conduct, she set a worthy example for all women who knew her.

Her high ideals, independence of character, family duties, and the general debauchery, which was incompatible with her rigid chastity and "precocious wisdom," caused her to withdraw from the court in 1608; two years later, she decided to open her salon to such aristocratic and cultured persons as appreciated womanly grace, wit, and taste. Her familiarity with Italian and

Spanish history and art placed her at the head of intellectual as well as moral movements. She surrounded herself with the distinguished men and women of the day, and her salon, which in every detail was decorated and arranged for pleasure, immediately became, through the exquisite charm with which she presided, the one goal of the cultured; her blue room was the sanctuary of polite society and she was its high priestess.

The highest ambition of the *habitué* of the salon was to sing, dance, and converse artistically and with refinement. A reaction against the general social state immediately set in, even the brusque warriors acquiring a refinement of speech and manners; and as conversation developed and became a power, the great lords began to respect men of letters and to cultivate their society. Anyone who possessed good manners, vivacity, and wit was admitted to the salon, where a new and more elevating sociability was the aspiration.

Mme. de Rambouillet was very particular in the choice of friends, and they were always sincere and devoted, knowing her to be undesirous of political favors and incapable of stooping to intrigue. Even Richelieu could not, as compensation to him for a favor to her husband, induce her to act as spy on some of the frequenters of her salon.

While not a woman of remarkable beauty, she was the personification of reason and virtue; her unassuming frankness, exquisite tact, and exceptional reserve discouraged all advances on the part of those gallants who frequented every mansion and were always prepared to lay siege to the heart of any fair woman. Her wide culture, versatility, modesty, goodness, fidelity, and disinterestedness caused her to be universally sought. Mlle. de Scudéry, in her novel *Cyrus*, leaves a fine portrait of her:

"The spirit and soul of this marvellous person surpass by far her beauty: the first has no limits in its extent and the other has no equal in its generosity, goodness, justice, and purity. The intellect of Cléomire (Mme. de Rambouillet) is not like that of those whose minds have no brilliancy except that which nature has given them, for she has cultivated it carefully, and I think I can say that there are no *belles connaissances* that she has not acquired. She knows various languages, and is ignorant of hardly anything that is worth knowing; but she knows it all without making a display of knowing it; and one would say, in hearing her talk, 'she is so modest that she speaks admirably of things, through simple common sense only'; on the contrary, she is versed in all things; the most advanced sciences are not beyond her, and she is perfectly acquainted with the most difficult arts. Never has any person possessed such a delicate knowledge as hers of fine works of prose and poetry; she judges them, however, with wonderful moderation, never abandoning *la bienséance* (the seemliness) of her sex, though she is far above it. In the whole court, there is not a person with any spirit and virtue that does not go to her house. Nothing is considered beautiful if it does not have her approval; no stranger ever comes who does not desire to see Cléomire and do her homage, and there are no excellent artisans who do not wish to have the glory of her approbation of their works. All people who write in Phénicie have sung her praises; and she possesses the esteem of everyone to such a marvellous degree that there is no one who has ever seen her who has not said thousands of favorable things about her—who has not been charmed likewise by her beauty, *esprit*, sweetness, and generosity."

Mlle. de Scudéry describes the salon of Mme. de Rambouillet in the following:

"Cléomire (Mme. de Rambouillet) had built, according to her own design, a place which is one of the finest in the world; she has found the art of constructing a palace of vast extent in a situation of mediocre grandeur. Order, harmony, and elegance are in all the apartments, and in the furniture also; everything is magnificent, even unique; the lamps are different from those of other palaces, her cabinets are full of objects which show the judgment of her who chose them. In her palace, the air is always scented; many baskets full of magnificent flowers make a continual spring in her room, and the place which she frequents ordinarily is so agreeable and so imaginative as to make one feel as if she were in some enchanted place."

The very names of the frequenters of the salon of Mme. de Rambouillet testify to the prominence of her position in the world of culture: Mlle. de Scudéry, Mlle. du Vigean; Mmes. de Longueville, de la Vergne, de La Fayette, de Sablé, de Hautefort, de Sévigné, de la Suze, Marie de Gonzague, Duchesse d'Aiguillon, Mmes. des Houlières, Cornuel, Aubry, and their respective husbands; the great literary men: Rotrou, Scarron, Saint-Evremond, Malherbe, Racan, Chapelain, Voiture, Conrart, Benserade, Pellisson, Segrais, Vaugelas, Ménage, Tallemant des Réaux, Balzac, Mairet, Corneille, Bossuet, etc. In the entire period of the French salon, no other such brilliant gathering of men and women of social standing, princely blood, genuine intelligence, and literary ability ever assembled from motives other than those of politics or intrigue; here was a gathering purely social and for purposes of mutual refinement. The nobility went through a process of polishing, and the men of letters sharpened their intelligence and modified their manners and customs.

Julie, Duchess of Montausier, and Angélique, daughters of Mme. de Rambouillet, were popular, but the former lost much of her charm after she sacrificed her independence of thought and action by becoming governess of the children of the queen. Julie was the centre of attraction for all perfumed rhymesters, all sighers in prose and verse, who thronged about her. The stern and unbending Duke of Montausier was so under her influence that in 1641 he arranged and laid before her shrine the famous *guirlande* which was illustrated by Robert and to which nineteen authors contributed. After her marriage to the duke, the Hôtel de Rambouillet may be said to have ceased to exist, as madame, who was seventy years of age, had for a number of years kept herself in the background, and Julie had become the acknowledged leader.

With the outbreak of the Fronde, friends were separated by their individual interests and the reunions at the salon were interrupted from about 1650 to 1652. After the death of her husband, Mme. de Rambouillet retired, to reside with her daughter, Mme. de Montausier; after that, she seldom appeared in public. She hardly lived to see the spirit of the salon changed to the real *préciosité*—the direction and aim she gave to it being gradually abandoned.

In her salon, for nearly fifty years, no pedantry, no loose manners, no questionable characters, no social or political intrigues, no discourtesies of any kind, were recorded; hers was a reign of dignity and grace, of purity of language, manners, and morals. She died in 1665, at the advanced age of seventy-seven, esteemed and mourned by the entire social and intellectual world of France. Her influence was incalculable; it was the first time in the history of France that refined taste, intellectuality, and virtue had won importance, influence, and power.

It must be remembered that in the first period of the salon there were no blue-stockings, no pedants: these were later developments. It was, primarily, a gathering which found pleasure in parties, excursions, concerts, balls, fireworks, dramatic performances, living tableaux; the last form of amusement very strongly influenced the development of the art, for in the galleries there appeared a surprisingly large number of portraits of the women of the day in character—sometimes as a nymph, sometimes as a goddess.

The salon, in its first phase, showed and developed tolerance in religion as well as in art and literature. It also encouraged progress and displayed acute discrimination, keeping pace with the time in all that was new and meritorious. It developed individual liberty, public interest, criticism, good taste, and the elegant, clear, and precise conversational language in which France has excelled up to the present day.

When about to build the Hôtel Pisani, Mme. de Rambouillet, having no love for architects, planned its construction without their assistance. She revolutionized the architecture of the time by introducing large and high doors and windows and putting the stairway to one side in order to secure a large suite of rooms. She was also the first to decorate a room in other colors than red or tan. The construction of her hôtel completely changed domestic architecture; and it may be noted that when the Luxembourg was to be built, the designers were instructed to examine, for ideas, the Hôtel de Rambouillet.

Legouvé gives as the object and mission of Mme. de Rambouillet: "to combat the sensualism of Rabelais, Villon, and Marot, to reform society through love by reforming love through chastity; to place women at the head of civilization, by beginning a crusade against vice in the disguise of sentiment. The word 'fame' must, in the seventeenth century, apply to both man and woman, meaning honor for the one and purity for the other. Her ideal falls with the accession of Louis XIV.; the dazzling luxury of royalty hardly conceals, under its exterior elegance, the profound and deep-seated grossness of Versailles and Marly."

To Mme. de Rambouillet, then, belongs the distinction of having been the first to bring together men of letters and great lords on a footing of social equality and for mutual benefit. Her salon and friends continued in the seventeenth century what Marguerite d'Angoulême had begun in the first part of the sixteenth—an intellectual, social, and moral reform.

Many salons which were all more or less patterned after that of Rambouillet sprang into existence. Among these the Academy of the Vicomtesse d'Auchy, with Malherbe as president and tyrant, was of little influence as far as women were concerned. The members were all of second-rate importance, and Malherbe tolerated only the discussion of his verses, while Mme. d'Auchy was better known for her splendid neck than for any intellectuality. Every salon had a master of ceremonies, who performed the rite of presentation; these men were frequently abbés, and some of them, such as Du Buisson and Testu, became famous.

Among the most noted of these salons was that of the celebrated beauty, Ninon de Lenclos, she who called the *précieuses* the "Jansenists of love," an expression which became very popular. Her salon was situated on the Rue des Tournelles. Ninon de Lenclos was a woman of the most brilliant mind and exquisite taste, and it was at her hôtel that Molière first read his *Tartuffe* before Condé, La Fontaine, Boileau, Lulli, Racine, and Chapelle, and it was there that he received the principal ideas for his drama.

Ninon became famous for making staunch friends of her former lovers, in which connection some interesting tales are told. She was the mother of two children; upon the arrival of the first, a heated discussion arose between Count d'Estrées and Abbé d'Effiat, both claiming the honor of paternity. When the mother was consulted, she made no attempt to conceal her amusement; finally, the rivals threw dice for "father or not father."

The other child, whose father was the Marquis de Gersay, was the victim of an unnatural passion for his mother with whom, when a young man, he fell desperately in love, being ignorant of their relation. While pleading his cause, he learned from her lips the secret, and, in despair, blew out his brains, a tragedy which apparently had no effect upon the mother. At one time, at the request of the clergy Ninon was sent, for impiety, to the convent of the Benedictines at Lagny.

Among her friends she counted the greatest men and women of the day and her salon was the foyer of *savoir-vivre*, of letters and art. At the age of sixty she met the Great Condé, who dismounted to greet her, something that he very seldom did, as he was not in the habit of paying compliments to women. The saying: *Elle eut l'estime de Lenclos* [she had the esteem of Lenclos] became a popular manner of expressing the fact that a certain woman was especially esteemed. Even to the last (she died at the age of eighty-five), Ninon preserved her grace, beauty, and intelligence. Colombey calls her *La mère spirituelle de Voltaire* [the spiritual mother of Voltaire].

The generality of women had their lovers; even the famous Mlle. de Scudéry, in spite of her homeliness—she was a dark, large-boned, and lean sort of old maid—had admirers galore; among the latter was Pellisson who was said to be so ugly "that he really abused the privilege—which man enjoys—of being homely."

The hôtel of the famous poet Scarron—Hôtel de l'Impécuniosité—received almost all the frequenters of Ninon's salon. At the former place there were no restrictions as to the manner of enjoyment; after elevating and edifying conversation at the salon of Ninon, the members would repair to that of Scarron for a feast of *broutilles rabelaisiennes* [Rabelaisian tidbits].

The salon of Mme. de Montbazon had its frequenters who, however, were attracted mainly by her beauty; she was, to use the words of one of her friends, "One of those beauties that delight the eye and provoke a vigorous appetite." Her salon was one of suitors rather than of intellectuality or harmless sociability.

The most famous of the men's salons was the Temple, constructed in 1667 by Jacques de Souvré and conducted from 1681 to 1720 by Phillipe de Vendôme and his intendant, Abbé de Chaulieu. These reunions, especially under the latter, were veritable midnight *convivia*; he himself boasted of never having gone to bed one night in thirty years without having been carried there dead drunk, a custom to which he remained "faithful unto death." His boon companion was La Duchesse de Bouillon. Most of his frequenters were jolly good persons, utterly destitute of the sense of sufficiency in matters of carousing; the better people declined his invitations.

After that of Mme. de Rambouillet, there were, in the seventeenth century, but two great salons that exerted a lasting influence and that were not saturated with the decadent *préciosité*. Of these the salon of Mlle. de Scudéry has been called the salon of the *bourgeoisie*, because the majority of its frequenters belonged to the third estate, which was rapidly acquiring power and influence.

Mlle. de Scudéry, who was born in 1608 and lived through the whole century, saw society develop, and therefore knew it better than did any of her contemporaries. Having lost her parents early in life, her uncle reared her and she received advantages such as fell to the lot of few women of her condition; she was given an excellent education in literature, art, and the languages.

Until the marriage of her brother, she was his constant and devoted companion, exiling herself to Marseilles when he was appointed governor of Notre Dame de La Garde, and returning to Paris with him in 1647. She first collaborated with him in a literary production of about eighty volumes. In their works, the brother furnished the rough draft, the dramatic episodes, adventures, and the Romanesque part, while she added the literary finish through charming character sketches, conversation, sentimental analyses, and letters. With a strong inclination toward society, and constantly fulfilling its obligations, she would from day to day write up her conversations of the evening before.

An interesting anecdote is told in connection with the travels and coöperation of Mlle. de Scudéry and her brother; once, on the way to Paris, while stopping over night at Lyons, they were discussing the fate of one of their heroes, one proposing death and the other rescue, one poison and the other a more cruel death; a gentleman from Auvergne happened to overhear them and immediately notified the people of the inn, thinking it was a question of assassinating the king; the brother and sister were thrown into prison and only with great difficulty were they able to explain matters the next morning. From this incident Scribe drew the material for his drama, *L'Auberge ou les Brigands sans le Savoir.*

At the Hôtel de Rambouillet where Mlle. de Scudéry was received early, she won everyone by her modesty, simplicity, *esprit*, and lovable disposition, and, in spite of her homeliness and poor figure, she attracted many platonic lovers. She was one of the few brilliant and famous women of the seventeenth century whose popularity was due solely to admirable qualities of mind and soul. With her, friendship became a cult, and it was in time of trouble that her friends received the strongest proof of her affection. She preferred to incur disgrace and the disfavor of Mazarin rather than forsake Condé and Madame de Longueville; to them she dedicated the ten volumes, successively, of her novel, *Cyrus*; the last volume was published after Mme. de Longueville's retirement and partial disgrace.

After the brilliant society of the Hôtel de Rambouillet had been broken up by the marriage of Julie and the operations of the Fronde, and after her brother's marriage in 1654, Mlle. de Scudéry became independent and established the custom of receiving her friends on Saturday; these receptions became famous under the name of *Samedi*, and besides the regular rather bourgeois gathering, the most brilliant talent and highest nobility flocked to them, regardless of rank or station, wealth or influence. Pellisson, the great master, the prince, the Apollo of her Saturdays, was a man of wonderfully inventive genius, and possessed in a higher degree than any of his contemporaries the art of inventing surprises for the society that lived on novelty. When, on account of his devotion to Fouquet, he was imprisoned in the Bastille, Mlle. de Scudéry managed to persuade Colbert to brighten his confinement by permitting him to see friends and relatives. Part of every day she spent in his prison, conversing and reading; and this is but one instance of her fidelity and friendship.

Mlle. de Scudéry, considering all men as aspirants for authority who, when husbands, degenerate into tyrants, preferred to retain her independence. Her ideas on love were very peculiar and were innovations at the time: she wished to be loved, but her love must be friendship—a pure, platonic love, in which her lover must be her all, her confidant, the participator in her sorrows and her conversation; and his happiness must be in her alone; he must, without feeling passion, love her for herself, and she must have the same feeling toward him. These sentiments are expressed in her novels, from which the following extracts are taken:

"When friendship becomes love in the heart of a lover or when this love is mingled with friendship without destroying it, there is nothing so sweet as this kind of love; for as violent as it is, it is always held somewhat more in check than is ordinary love; it is more durable, more tender, more respectful, and even more ardent, although it is not subject to so many tumultuous caprices as is that love which arises without friendship. It can be said that love and friendship flow together like two streams, the more celebrated of which obscures the name of the other." ... "They agreed on even the conditions of their love; for Phaon solemnly promised Sapho (Mlle. de Scudéry)—who desired it thus— not to ask of her anything more than the possession of her heart, and she, also, promised him to receive only him in hers. They told each other all their thoughts, they understood them even without confessing them. Peace, however, was not so completely established that their affection could not become languishing or cool; for, although they loved each other as much as one can love, they at times complained of not being loved enough, and they had sufficient little difficulties to always leave something new to wish for; but they never had any troubles that were serious enough to essentially disturb their repose."

Mlle. de Scudéry was mistress of the art of conversation, speaking without affectation and equally well on all affairs, serious, light, or gallant; she objected, however, to being called a *savante*, and she was far from resembling the false *précieuses* to whom she was likened by her enemies. The occupations of her salon were somewhat different from those of the salon of Mme. de Rambouillet. M. du Bled describes them as follows:

"What they did in the salon of Mlle. de Scudéry you can guess readily: they amused themselves as at Mme. de Rambouillet's, they joked quite cheerfully, smiled and laughed, wrote farces in prose and poetry. There were readings, *loteries d'esprit*, sonnet-enigmas, *bouts-rimés* (rhymes given to be formed into verse), *vers-échos*, fine literary joustings, discussions between the casuists. This salon had its talkers and speakers, those who tyrannized over the audience and those who charmed it, those who shot off fireworks and those who prepared them, those who had made a symphony of conversation and those who made of it a monologue and had no flashes of silence. They did not follow fashion there—they rather made it; in art and literature as in toilets, smallness follows the fashion, pretension exaggerates it, taste makes a compact with it."

A specimen of the *énigme-sonnets* may be of interest, to show in what intellectual playfulness and trivialities these wits indulged:

"Souvent, quoique léger, je lasse qui me porte.

Un mot de ma façon vaut un ample discours.

J'ai sous Louis le Grand commencé d'avoir cours,

Mince, long, plat, étroit, d'une étoffe peu forte.

"Les doigts les moins savants me taillent de la sorte;

Sous mille noms divers je parais tous les jours;

Aux valets étourdis je suis d'un grand secours.

Le Louvre ne voit point ma figure à sa porte.

"Une grossière main vient la plupart du temps

Me prendre de la main des plus honnêtes gens.

Civil, officieux, je suis né pour la ville.

"Dans le plus rude hiver j'ai le dos toujours nu:

Et, quoique fort commode, à peine m'a-t-on vu,

Qu'ausitôt négligé, je deviens inutile."

[Often, although light, I weary the person who carries me. A word in my manner is worth a whole discourse. I began under Louis the Great to be in vogue,—slight, long, flat, narrow, of a very slight material.

The most unskilled fingers cut me in their way; under a thousand different forms I appear every day; I am a great aid to the astonished valets. The Louvre does not see my face at its door.

A coarse hand most of the time receives me from the hand of the nicest people. Civil, officious, I am born for the city.

In the coldest weather, my back is always bare; and, although quite convenient, scarcely have they seen me, when I am neglected and useless.— Visiting card.]

A more interesting one and one that caused no little amusement is the following:

"Je suis niais et fin, honnête et malhonnête,

Moins sincère à la cour qu'en un simple taudis.

Je fais d'un air plaisant trembler les plus hardis,

Le fort me laisse aller, le sage m'arrête.

"A personne sans moi l'on ne fait jamais fête:

J'embellis quelquefois, quelquefois, j'enlaidis.

Je dédaigne tantôt, tantôt j'applaudis;

Pour m'avoir en partage, il faut n'être pas bête.

"Plus mon trône est petit, plus il a de beauté.

Je l'agrandis pourtant d'un et d'autre côté,

Faisant voir bien souvent des défauts dont on jase.

"Je quitte mon éclat quand je suis sans témoins,

Et je me puis vanter enfin d'être la chose

Qui contente le plus et qui coûte le moins."

[I am both stupid and bright, honest and dishonest; less sincere at court than in a simple hovel; with a pleasant air, I make the boldest tremble, the strong let me pass, the wise stop me.

There is no joy to anyone without me; I embellish at times, at times I distort; I disdain and I applaud; to share me, one must not be stupid.

The smaller my throne, the greater my beauty; I enlarge it, however, on both sides, often showing defects which are made sport of.

I leave my brilliancy when I am without witness, and I can boast of being the thing which contents the most and costs the least.—A smile.]

Critics often reproach Mlle. de Scudéry for having portrayed herself—as Sapho—in a flattering light in her novel *Cyrus*; but it must be remembered that at that time this was a common custom, women of the highest quality indulging in such pastimes, there even being a prominent salon where verbal portraiture was the sole occupation. No one has written more or better on the condition of woman, for she, above all, had the experience upon which to base her writings. The idea of woman's education and aim, which was generally entertained by the intelligent and modest women of the seventeenth century, is well expressed by Mlle. de Scudéry in the following:

"The difficulty of knowing something with seemliness does not come to a woman so much from what she knows as from what others do not know; and it is, without doubt, singularity that makes it difficult to be as others are not, without being exposed to blame. Seriously, is not the ordinary idea of the education of women a peculiar one? They are not to be coquettes nor gallants, and yet they are carefully taught all that is peculiar to gallantry without being permitted to know anything that can strengthen their virtue or occupy their minds. Don't imagine, however, that I do not wish woman to be elegant, to dance or to sing; but I should like to see as much care devoted to her mind as to her body, and between being ignorant and *savante* I should like to see a road taken which would prevent annoyance from an impertinent sufficiency or from a tiresome stupidity. I should like very much to be able to say of anyone of my sex that she knows a hundred things of which she does not boast, that she has a well-balanced mind, that she speaks well, writes correctly, and knows the world; but I do not wish it to be said of her that she is a *femme savante*. The best women of the world when they are together in a large number rarely say anything that is worth anything and are more ennuyé than if they were alone; on the contrary, there is something that I cannot express, which makes it possible for men to enliven and divert a company of ladies more than the most amiable woman on earth could do."

Mlle. de Scudéry considered marriage a long slavery and preferred virtuous celibacy enlivened by platonic gallantry. When youth and adorers had passed away, she found consolation in interchanges of wit, congenial conversation, and the cultivation of the mind by study. Making of love a doctrine, a manual of morals or *savoir-vivre*, has had a refining effect upon civilization; but the process has rendered the emotion itself too subtle, select, narrow, enervating, and exhausting; it has resulted in the production of splendid books with heroes and heroines of the higher type, and has purified the atmosphere of social life; this phase of its influence, however, is felt by only a set of the élite, and its adherents are scattered through every age and every country. Mlle. de Scudéry was a perfect representative of that type, but healthy and normal rather than morbidly æsthetic.

An opposition party soon arose, formed by those, especially, who entertained different ideas of the sphere and duties of woman. Just as the type of the salon of Mme. de Rambouillet degenerated among the aristocracy into those of the Hôtel de Condé, Mme. de Sablé, and Mlle. de Luxembourg, so the type of the salon of Mlle. de Scudéry gave rise to a number of literary salons among the *bourgeoisie*. The aim of the latter institutions was to imitate her example in endeavoring to spread the taste for courtesy, elegant manners and the higher forms of learning; all these aspirations, however, drifted into mere affectation, while the requisites of welcome at the original salon were simplicity, freedom from affectation, delicacy, amiability, and dignity.

As a writer, Mlle. de Scudéry occupies no mean position in the history of French literature of the seventeenth century. Her descriptions and anecdotes possess a wonderful charm and display unusual power of analysis; in them, Victor Cousin recognizes a truly virile spirit. In the history of the French novel, she forms a transition period, her productions having both a psychological interest and a historical value of a very high degree. Through her finesse and marvellous feminine penetration, her truthful, delicate and fine portraitures, which were widely imitated later, she has exerted an extensive influence.

With Mlle. de Scudéry "we have substance, real character painting, true psychological penetration, and realism in observation," while previously the novel, under such men as Gomberville and La Calprenède, was imaginative and full of fancy. Her talent, then, in that field, lay in the analysis and development of sentiments, in delineation of character, in the creation and reproduction of refined and ingenious conversations, and in her reflections on subjects pertaining to morality and literature—in all of which she displayed justness and entire liberty and independence of thought. Her poetry, delicate compliment or innocent gallantries, was a mere bagatelle of the salon.

Charming as well as accomplished, Mlle. de Scudéry was as intelligent, witty, and intellectual a woman as could be found in the seventeenth century; and in the history of that period she retains an undisputed position as one of its great leaders of thought and progress. Her salon, inasmuch as the salon of Mme. de Lambert was not opened until 1710, and therefore the discussion of it belongs properly to the beginning of the eighteenth century, really closes the literary progress of the seventeenth century.

The influence of the seventeenth century salon was of a threefold nature—

literary, moral, and social. According to the salon conception, artistic, literary, or musical pleasure being derived from form and mode of expression, it possessed a special and unique interest in proportion to the efforts made and the difficulties surmounted in attaining that form and expression: thus, woman introduced a new standard of excellence.

Préciosité treated language not as a work of art, but as a medium for the display of individual linguistic dexterity; giving no thing its proper name, it delighted in paraphrase, allusion, word play, unexpected comparisons and abundance of metaphors, and revelled in the elusive, delicate, subtle, and complex. Hence conversation turned constantly to love and gallantry; thus woman developed to a wonderful degree, unattainable to but few, the art of conversation, politeness and courtesy of manners, and social relations, at the same time purifying language and enriching it.

French women of the seventeenth century are condemned for having treated serious things too lightly; and it is said that "in confining the French mind to the observation of society and its attractions, she has restricted and retarded a more realistic and larger activity." In answer to this it may be asserted that the French mind was not prepared for a broader field until it had passed through the process of expurgating, refining, drilling, and disciplining. If *préciosité* influenced politics, it was by developing diplomacy, for, from the time that this spirit began to spread, French diplomacy became world-renowned.

The social influence of the movement may be better appreciated by considering the condition of woman in earlier periods. Having practically no position except that of housewife or mother, she was merely a source of pleasure for man, for whom she had little or no respect. The *précieuses*, on the contrary, exacted respect, honor, and a place beside man, as rights that belonged to them.

As the outcome of their desire to think, feel, and act with greater delicacy, women introduced propriety in expression, finesse in analysis, keenness of *esprit*, psychological subtleness: qualities that surely tended to higher standards of morality, purer social relations, finer and more subtle diplomacy, more elegance and precision in literature. Therefore, *préciosité* in France had a wholesome influence, which was possible because woman had won for herself her rightful position, and her aspirations were toward social and moral elevation.

In general, the women of France have always been conscious of their duty, their importance, and their limitations, appreciating their power and cultivating the characteristics that attract man and retain his respect and attention: sociability, morality, *esprit*, artistic appreciation, sensitiveness, tact. These qualities became manifest to a remarkable degree in French women of the seventeenth century, and created in every writer, great or unimportant, the desire to win their favor. Thus, Corneille strove to write dramas with which he might establish the reign of decency on a stage the liberties of which had previously made the theatre inaccessible to woman; hence, his characters of humanity (Cid) and politeness (Menteur).

The purpose of the French Academy itself was not different from that of the *précieuses*. Richelieu, realizing that every great talent accepted the discipline of these women, sought to use this power for his own ends by interesting the world of letters in the accomplishment of his plans for a general political unity. Thus, when the first period of *préciosité* had reached its highest point and was beginning to decline, and other smaller and envious social groups were forming about Paris and causing a conflict of ideas, Richelieu conceived the scheme of joining all in a union, with strong ideals and with a language as dignified as the Latin and the Greek. The result was the formation of the French Academy. From this time begins the decline of the authority of woman; for while she still exerted a powerful influence, it was no longer absolute. After the decline of the Hôtel de Rambouillet, feminine influence became more general, expending itself in petty rivalries, gossip, intrigues, and partaking of the nature of that court life which was filled by the young king with parties, feasts, collations, walks, carousals, boating, concerts, ballets, and masquerades—a mode of living that gave rise to a new standard of politeness, which was freer and looser than that of *préciosité*.

As the power of the young king became stronger, his favor became the goal of all men of letters. Although woman still to some extent controlled the destinies of those who were struggling for recognition and reputation, her influence was of a secondary nature, that of the king being supreme. Woman seemed to be overcoming the influence of woman—Mme. de Montespan replaced Mlle. de La Vallière, and she was in turn replaced by Mme. de Maintenon.

The degeneration of the king was accompanied by that of literature, society, and morals. The characteristic inclination of the day was eagerly to seek and grasp that which was new, and the noble, forceful, and dignified style of language of the previous period was replaced by one of much lighter description; many female writers directed their efforts entirely toward amusing, pleasing, and gaining applause.

In the beginning of the eighteenth century, with Mme. de Lambert as its leader, there was a renascence of the *préciosité* of the Hôtel de Rambouillet, women protesting against the prevalent grossness and indecency of manners. The salon of Mme. de Lambert was the great antechamber to the Academy, election to which was generally gained through her. A new aristocracy was forming, a new society arose; from about 1720 to 1750, libertinism and atheism, licentiousness and intrigue, crept into the salons.

The new aristocracy was of doubtful and impure source, cynical in manner, unbridled in habits, over-fastidious in taste, and politically powerful. In this society woman began to be felt as a political force. M. Brunetière said: "Mme. de Lambert made Academicians; the Marquise de Prie made a queen of France; Mme. de Tencin made cardinals and ambassadors." Montesquieu wrote: "There is not a person who has any employment at the court in Paris or in the provinces, who has not the influence (and sometimes the injustices which she can cause) of a woman through whom all favors pass;" and M. Brunetière added: "This woman is not his wife." The popular spirit in literature was one of subtleness, irony, superficial observations on manners and customs. From the beginning of the eighteenth century up to the eve of the Revolution, woman's influence continued to increase, but that influence was mainly in the direction of politics. Thus, in every period in French history, a group of women effectively moulds French thought and language, and directs intellectual activity in general.

After the death of Louis XIV., society passed under the rule of the regent, the Duke of Orléans—the personification of gallantry and affability, of depravity which was a mania, and of licentiousness which was a disease. From this atmosphere the salon of Mme. de Lambert became a refuge to those who still cherished the ideals of the good old times of Mme. de Rambouillet; it was distinguished by its refined sentiment and polished manners, which were like those of the seventeenth century at its best.

Mme. de Lambert believed that the demands of the time were just the opposite of those of the seventeenth century: "What a multitude of tastes nowadays— the table, play, theatre! When money and luxury are supreme, true honor loses its power. Persons seek only those houses where shameful luxury reigns." In her own salon, none might enter who were not of the small number of the elect.

Very little is known of the life of Mme. de Lambert. She was born in 1647, and, in spite of the unfavorable surroundings of her youth and of a dissolute, extravagant, and unrefined mother, the observance of decorum and honor became the actuating principle of her life. Until her marriage (in 1666) to Henri de Lambert, Marquis de Bris en Auxerrois, she was in the midst of the grossest licentiousness and freedom of manners; when married, she entered a family the very opposite of her own.

She was a woman who believed in the power of ambitious energy. To her son she once said: "Nothing is less becoming to a young man than a certain modesty that makes him believe that he is not capable of great things. This modesty is a languor of the soul, which prevents it from soaring and rapidly carrying itself to glory."

At first she lived in the Hôtel de Lambert (in the Ile Saint-Louis), renowned for its splendidly sculptured decorations, painted ceilings, panels, and staircases. Her famous Salon des Muses and Cabinet d'Amours were filled with the finest works of art and the most exquisite paintings. There the élite of all classes were entertained until the death of her husband (1686), when the hôtel was closed; it was not reopened until 1710.

Though left with immense wealth, her affairs were in a very complicated state. While actively employed in untangling her difficulties, she at the same time superintended the education of her son and daughter. After long and trying lawsuits, she managed to put her fortune in order and established herself at Paris, where the Duc de Nevers ceded to her, for life, a large portion of the magnificently furnished Palais Mazarin, now the National Library. On the completion of her work in remodelling this palace and furnishing it with the most costly and beautiful panel paintings by Watteau and other artists, she inaugurated her Tuesday and Wednesday dinner parties.

One remarkable characteristic of her company was the age of her intimate associates—the Marquis de Saint-Aulaire, Fontenelle, Mme. Dacier, and her husband, Louis de Sacy, all of whom, as well as Mme. de Lambert herself, had passed threescore and more; but they still kept alive the cherished memories of the brilliant society of their youth. Mme. de Lambert did not personally know Mme. de Rambouillet, but she visited the latter's daughter, Julie d'Angennes, from whom she learned the customs and etiquette in vogue at the Hôtel de Rambouillet.

The Wednesday dinners of Mme. de Lambert were to her intimate friends, while every Tuesday afternoon she received a general circle which indulged in general conversation and read and discussed books which were about to be published; gambling, which seemed to be the principal means of entertaining in those days, had no place there. Fontenelle says: "It was, with very few exceptions, the only house which had been preserved from the epidemic of gambling—the only house where persons congregated simply for the sake of talking sensibly and with *esprit*. Those who had their reasons for considering it bad taste that conversation was still carried on in any place, cast mean reflections, whenever they could, against the house of Mme. de Lambert." In the evening, she received only a few select friends with whom she talked seriously. Her salon soon became the envy of those who were not admitted (and they were numerous), and was the object of many calumnies and attacks.

During this time she found leisure to write two treatises of practical morality, *Avis d'une mère à son fils*, and *Avis d'une mère à sa fille*, which appeared without her permission. The manuscripts, lent to friends, fell into the hands of a publisher; and although the authoress endeavored to prevent the distribution of the works by buying up the entire editions, they were published outside of France. The two works written to her children form an important contribution to the educational literature of the time; in them the religion of the eighteenth century is first defined.

"Above all these duties—civil and human (says the mother to her son)—is the duty you owe to the Supreme Being. Religion is a commerce established between God and man through the grace of God to man and through the duty of man to God. Elevated souls have for their God sentiments and a cult apart, which do not resemble at all those of the people; everything issues from the heart and goes to God."

In these works, she attacked also the fad of free-thinking in vogue among the young men of the time. She was one of the few women of that age who could not separate themselves from reason and thought, even in religion; the latter was a matter for the reason and the intellect to decide, and was thus an elevated product of the mind rather than an instinct coming from the heart, or a positive revelation as it was in the seventeenth century. In this view, Madame de Lambert indicated the beginning of the later eighteenth-century spirit.

Mme. de Lambert taught her children to be satisfied with nothing but the highest attainable object. She advised her son to choose his friends from among men above him, in order to accustom himself to respectful and polite demeanor; "with his equals he might cultivate negligence and his mind might become dull." She desired her children to think differently from the people —"Those who think lowly and commonly, and the court is filled with such." To their servants they were to be good and kind, for humanity and Christianity make all equal. She was the first to use those words, "humanity" and "equality," which later became the bywords of everyone, and the first to teach that conscience is the best guide. "Conscience is defined as that interior sentiment of a delicate honor which assures you that you have nothing with which to reproach yourself."

Possibly the most important and lasting effect of Mme. de Lambert's influence resulted from the expression of her ideas on the education of young women who "are destined to please, and are given lessons only in methods of delighting and pleasing." She was convinced that in order to resist temptation and be normal, women must be educated, must learn to think. Her counsels to her daughter are remarkable for an unusual insight into the temperament of her sex and for an extreme fear that makes her call to her aid all precautions and resources. She thus advises her daughter:

"Try to find resources within yourself—this is a revenue of certain pleasures. Do not believe that your only virtue is modesty; there are many women who know no other virtue, and who imagine that it relieves them of all duties toward society; they believe they are right in lacking all others and think themselves privileged to be proud and slanderous with impunity. You must have a gentle modesty; a good woman may have the advantages of a man's friendship without abandoning honesty and faithfulness to her duties. Nothing is so difficult as to please without the use of what seems like coquettishness. It is more often by their defects than by their good qualities that women please men; men seek to profit by the weaknesses of good and kind women, for whose virtues they care nothing, and they prefer to be amused by persons not very estimable than to be forced merely to admire virtuous persons."

This is a most faithful description of the society of her time, and it was because her treatises struck home that they were severely criticised; but, nothing daunted, she carried out her plans in her own way, resorting neither to intrigue nor artifice. Many of her sayings became household maxims, such as —"It is not always faults that undo us; it is the manner of conducting ourselves after having committed them."

Her reflections on women might be called the great plea, at the end of the seventeenth century, for woman's right to use her reason. After the severe and cruel satire of Molière, attacking women for their innocent amusements, they gave themselves up entirely to pleasure. "Mme. de Lambert now wrote to avenge her sex and demand for it the honest and strong use of the mind; and this was done in the midst of the wild orgies of the Regency."

Mme. de Lambert was not a rare beauty, but she possessed recompensing charms. M. Colombey asserts that she became convinced of two things, about which she became highly enthusiastic: first, that woman was more reasonable than man; secondly, that M. Fontenelle, who presided over or filled the functions of president of her salon, was always in the right. He was indeed in harmony with the tone of the salon, being considered the most polished, brilliant, and distinguished member of the intellectual society of Paris, as well as one of the most talented drawing room philosophers. He made the salon of Mme. de Lambert the most sought for and celebrated, the most intellectual and moral of the period.

Mme. de Lambert has, possibly, exercised more influence upon men—and especially upon the Forty Immortals of her time—than did any woman before or after her. The Marquis d'Argenson states that "a person was seldom received at the Academy unless first presented at her salon. It is certain that she made at least half of our actual Academicians."

Her salon was called a *bureau d'esprit*, which was due to the fact that it was about the only social gathering point where culture and morality were the primary requisites. As she advanced in years, she became even more influential. After her death in 1733, her salon ceased to exist, but others, patterned after hers, soon sprang up; to those, her friends attached themselves —Fontenelle frequented several, Hénault became the leader of that of Mme. du Deffand.

The finest résumé that can be given of Mme. de Lambert, is found in the letters of the Marquis d'Argenson: "Her works contain a complete course in the most perfect morals for the use of the world and the present time. Some affectation of the *préciosité* is found; but, what beautiful thoughts, what delicate sentiments! How well she speaks of the duties of women, of friendship, of old age, of the difference between actual character and reputation!"

The salon of Mme. de Lambert forms a period of transition from the seventeenth century type in which elegance, politeness, courtesy, and morality were the first requisites, to the eighteenth century salon in which *esprit* and wit were the essentials demanded. It retained the dignity, discipline, refinement, and sentiments of morality of the Hôtel de Rambouillet; it showed, also, the first signs of pure intellectuality. The salons to follow, will exhibit decidedly different characteristics.

Chapter V

Mistresses and Wives of Louis XIV

The story of the wives and mistresses of Louis XIV., embraces that which is most dramatic morally (or immorally dramatic) in the history of French women. The record of the eighteenth century heroines is essentially a tragic one, while that of those of the previous century is essentially dramatic in its sadness, remorse, and repentance.

The mistress, as a rule, was unhappy; there were few months during the period of her glory, in which she was entirely free from anxiety or in which her conscience was at rest. Mme. de Montespan "was for so many years the sick nurse of a soul worn out with pride, passion, and glory." Mme. de Maintenon wrote to one of her friends: "Why cannot I give you my experience? Why cannot I make you comprehend the ennui which devours the great, and the troubles that fill their days? Do you not see that I am dying of sadness, in a fortune the vastness of which could not be easily imagined? I have been young and pretty; I have enjoyed pleasures; I have spent years in intellectual intercourse; I have attained favor; and I protest to you, my dear child, that all such conditions leave a frightful void." She said, also, to her brother, Count d'Aubigné: "I can hold out no longer; I would like to be dead." It was she too, who, after her successes, made her confession thus: "One atones heavily for the pleasures and intoxications of youth. I find, in looking back at my life, that since the age of twenty-two—which was the beginning of my fortune—I have not had a moment free from sufferings which have constantly increased."

M. Saint-Amand gives a description of the women of Louis XV. which well applies to those of his predecessor: "These pretended mistresses, who, in reality, are only slaves, seem to present themselves, one after the other, like humble penitents who come to make their apologies to history, and, like the primitive Christians, to reveal publicly the miseries, vexations, and remorses of their souls. They tell us to what their doleful successes amounted: even while their triumphal chariot made its way through a crowd of flatterers, their consciences hissed cruel accusations into their ears; like actresses before a whimsical and variable public, they were always afraid that the applause might change into an uproar, and it was with terror underlying their apparent coolness that they continued to play their sorry part…. If among these mistresses of the king there were a single one who had enjoyed her shameful triumphs in peace, who had called herself happy in the midst of her dearly bought luxury and splendor, one might have concluded that, from a merely human point of view, it is possible to find happiness in vice. But, no—there is not even one!" Massillon, the great preacher of truth and morality, said: "The worm of conscience is not dead; it is only benumbed. The alienated reason presently returns, bringing with it bitter troubles, gloomy thoughts, and cruel anxieties"—a true picture of every mistress.

The remarkable power and influence of these women, the love and adoration accorded them, ceased with their death; the memory of them did not survive overnight. When, during a terrible storm, the remains of the glorious Mme. de Pompadour were being taken to Paris, the king, seeing the funeral cortége from his window, remarked: "The Marquise will not have fine weather for her journey."

Each one of these powerful mistresses represents a complete epoch of society, morals, and customs. Mme. de Montespan—that woman whose very look meant fortune or disfavor—with all her wit and wealth, her magnificence and pomp and superb beauty—she, in all her splendor, is a type of the triumphant France, haughty, dictatorial, scornful and proud, licentious and decayed at the core. Voluptuousness and haughtiness were replaced by religiosity and repentance in Mme. de Maintenon, with her temperate character, consistency, and propriety.

The Regency was a period of scandal and wantonness, personified in the Duchess of Berry. The licentious and extravagant, yet brilliant and exquisite, frivolous but charming, intriguing and diplomatic, was represented by the talented and politically influential Mme. de Pompadour. Complete degeneracy, vice with all manner of disguise thrown off, adultery of the lowest order, were personified in the common Mme. du Barry, who might be classed with Louise of Savoy of the sixteenth century, while Mme. de Pompadour might be compared with Diana of Poitiers.

In this period the queens of France were of little importance, being too timid and modest to assert their rights—a disposition which was due sometimes to their restricted youth, spent in Catholic countries, sometimes to a naturally unassuming and sensitive nature. To this rule Maria Theresa, the wife of Louis XIV., was no exception. She inherited her sweetness of disposition and her Christian character from her mother, Isabella of France, the daughter of Henry IV. and Marie de' Medici. She was pure and candid; a type of irreproachable piety and goodness, of conjugal tenderness and maternal love; and recompensed outraged morality for all the false pride, selfish ambition, depravity, and scandals of court. She is conspicuous as a model wife, one that loved her husband, her family, and her children.

Around Maria Theresa may be grouped the noble and virtuous women of the court of Louis XIV., for she was to that age what Claude of France was under Francis I., Elizabeth of Austria under Charles V., Louise de Vaudemont under

Henry III. However, in extolling these women, it must be remembered that they had not, as queens, the opportunity to participate in debauchery, licentiousness, and intrigue, as had the mistresses of their husbands; they had no power, were not consulted on state or social affairs, and had granted to them only those favors to the conferring of which the mistresses did not object.

Maria Theresa was a perfect example of the self-sacrificing mother and devoted wife. Her feelings toward the king are best expressed by the Princesse Palatine: "She had such an affection for the king that she tried to read in his eyes whatever would give him pleasure; providing he looked kindly at her, she was happy all day." Mme. de Caylus wrote: "That poor princess had such a dread of the king and such great natural timidity that she dared neither to speak to him nor to run the risk of a tête-à-tête with him. One day, I heard Mme. de Maintenon say that the king having sent for the queen, the latter requested her to go with her so that she might not appear alone in his presence: but that she (Mme. de Maintenon) conducted her only to the door of the room and there took the liberty of pushing her so as to make her enter, and that she observed such a great trembling in her whole person that her very hands shook with fright."

From about 1680, especially after the death of Mlle. de Fontanges, his last mistress, Louis XIV. began to look with disfavor upon the women of doubtful morality and to advance those who were noted for their conjugal fidelity. He became more attentive to the queen—a change of attitude which was due partly to the influence of Mme. de Maintenon and partly to the fact that he was satiated with the excesses of his debauches, by which his physical system had been almost wrecked. He would not have dared to legitimatize his bastard children, had he not been so thoroughly idolized by his greatest heroes and most powerful ministers. As an illustration, it may be remarked that the Great Condé proposed the marriage of his son to the king's daughter by Mlle. de La Vallière.

The queen became so religious that she derived more enjoyment from praying at the convents or visiting hospitals than from remaining at her magnificent apartments. She waited upon the sick with her own hands and carried food to them; she never meddled in political affairs or took much interest in social functions.

Timidity, an instinctive shrinking from the slanders, calumnies, and intrigues of the court, appeared to be the most pronounced characteristic of queens who seemed to believe themselves too inferior to their husbands to dare to offer any political counsel. While none of them were superior intellectually, they possessed dignity, good sense, and tact, "a reverential feeling for the sanctity of religion and the majesty of the throne," an admirable resignation, a painful docility and submission—qualities which might have been turned to the advantage of their owners and the state, had the former been more self-assertive.

The infidelities of their husbands caused the queen-consorts constant torture; they were forced to behold the kings' favorites becoming part of their own households and were compelled to endure the presence, as ladies in waiting, of those who, as their rivals, caused them to suffer all possible torments of jealousy and outraged conjugal love.

First among the mistresses of Louis XIV. was Mlle. de La Vallière, whom Sainte-Beuve mentions as the personification of the ideal of a lover, combining disinterestedness, fidelity, unique and delicate tenderness with a touching and sincere kindness. When, at the age of seventeen, she was presented at court, the king immediately selected her as one of his victims. Her beauty was so striking, of such an exquisitely tender type, that no woman actually rivalled her as queen of beauty. Distinguished by blond hair, dark blue eyes, a most sympathetic voice, and a complexion of rare whiteness mingled with red, she was guileless, animated, gentle, modest, graceful, unaffected, and ingenuous; although slightly lame, she was, by everyone, considered charming.

Mlle. de La Vallière was the mother of several children of whom Louis XIV. was the father. On realizing that she had rivals in the favor of the sovereign, she fled several times from the Tuileries to the convent; on her second return, the king, about to go to battle, recognized his daughter by her, whom he made a duchess. Remorse overcame the mistress so deeply that she, for the third and final time, left court. Especially on the rise to power of Mme. de Montespan was she painfully humiliated, suffering the most intense pangs of conscience. The evening before her final departure to the convent, she dined with Mme. de Montespan, to drink "the cup to the dregs and to enjoy the rejection of the world even to the last remains of its bitterness."

Guizot describes this period most vividly: "When Mme. de Montespan began to supplant her in the king's favor, the grief of Mlle. de La Vallière was so great that she thought she would die of it. Then she turned to God, penitent and in despair; twice she sought refuge in a convent at Chaillot. On leaving, she sent word to the king: 'After having lost the honor of your good graces I would have left the court sooner, if I could have prevailed upon myself never to see you again; but that weakness was so strong in me that hardly now am I capable of sacrificing it to God. After having given you all my youth, the remainder of my life is not too much for the care of my salvation.'" The king still clung to her. "He sent M. Colbert to beg her earnestly to come to

Versailles that he might speak with her. M. Colbert escorted her thither and the king conversed for an hour with her and wept bitterly. Mme. de Montespan was there to meet her, with open arms and tears in her eyes." "It is all incomprehensible," adds Mme. de Sévigné; "some say that she will remain at Versailles and at court, others that she will return to Chaillot; we shall see."

Mlle. de La Vallière remained three years at court, "half penitent," she said, humbly, detained by the king's express wish, in consequence of the tempers and jealousies of Mme. de Montespan who felt herself judged and condemned by her rival's repentance. Attempts were made to turn Mlle. de La Vallière from her inclination for the Carmelites': "Madame," said Mme. Scarron to her, one day, "here are you one blaze of gold; have you really considered that, before long, at the Carmelites' you will have to wear serge?" She, however, was not to be dissuaded from her determination and was already practising, in secret, the austerities of the convent. "God has laid in this heart the foundation of great things," said Bossuet, who supported her in her conflict; "the world puts great hindrances in her way, and God great mercies; I have hopes that God will prevail; the uprightness of her heart will carry everything before it."

"When I am in trouble at the Carmelites'," said Mlle. de La Vallière, as for the last time she quitted the court, "I shall think of what those people have made me suffer." "The world itself makes us sick of the world," said Bossuet in the sermon which he preached on the day she took the veil; "its attractions have enough of illusion, its favors enough of inconstancy, its rebuffs enough of bitterness. There is enough of bitterness, enough of injustice and perfidy in the dealings of men, enough of inconsistency and capriciousness in their intractable and contradictory humors—there is enough of it all, to disgust us."

When, in 1675, she took the final vows, she cut off her beautiful hair and devoted herself to the church and to charity, receiving the veil from the queen, whose forgiveness she sought before entering the convent. The king showed himself to be such a jealous lover, that when Mlle. de La Vallière entirely abandoned him for God, he forgot her absolutely, never going to the convent to see her.

She was by far the most interesting and pathetic of the three mistresses of Louis XIV.; her heart was superior to that of either of her successors, though her mind was inferior; she belonged to a different atmosphere—such kindness, charity, penitence, resignation, and absolute abandonment to God were rare among the conspicuous French women. Sainte-Beuve says: "She loved for love, without haughtiness, coquetry, arrogance, ambitious designs, self-interest, or vanity; she suffered and sacrificed everything, humiliated herself to expiate her wrong-doing, and finally surrendered herself to God, seeking in prayer the treasures of energy and tenderness; through her heart, her mental powers attained their complete development."

The fate of Mlle. de La Vallière was the same as that of nearly all royal mistresses; abandoned and absolutely forgotten by her lover, she sought refuge and consolation in religion and God's mercy. "She was dead to me the day she entered the Carmelites'," said the king, thirty-five years later, when the modest and fervent nun at last expired, in 1710, without having ever relaxed the severities of her penance.

Of an entirely different type from Mlle. de La Vallière was that haughtiest and most supercilious of all French mistresses, Mme. de Montespan. The picture drawn by M. Saint-Amand does her full justice: "A haughty and opulent beauty, a forest of hair, flashing blue eyes, a complexion of splendid carnation and dazzling whiteness, one of those alluring and radiant countenances which shed brightness around them wherever they appear, an incisive, caustic wit, an unquenchable thirst for riches and pleasure, luxury and power, the manners of a goddess audaciously usurping the place of Juno on Olympus, passion without love, pride without true dignity, splendor without harmony—that was Mme. de Montespan." And these qualities were the secret of her success as well as of her fall.

From this description it can easily be divined of what nature was her influence and how she gained and held her power over the king. She won Louis XIV. entirely by her sensual charms, provoked him by her imperious exactions, her ungovernable fits of temper, and her daring sarcasm; always extravagant and unreasonable, she talked constantly of balls and fêtes, the glories of court and its scandals. Most exacting, yet never satisfied, she had no regard for the interests or honor of the weak king, to whose lower nature only she appealed.

Mme. de Montespan was of noble birth, being the youngest daughter of Rochechouart, first Duke of Mortemart. She was born in 1641, at the grand old château of Tonnay-Charente, and was educated at the convent of Sainte-Marie. Brought up religiously, she at first evinced a much greater tendency toward religion than toward worldly ambition and vanity. Mme. de Caylus, in her *Souvenirs*, wrote that "far from being born depraved, the future favorite had a nature inherently disinclined to gallantry and tending to virtue. She was flattered at being mistress, not solely for her own pleasure, but on account of the passion of the king; she believed that she could always make him desire what she had resolved never to grant him. She was in despair at her first pregnancy, consoled herself for the second one, and in all the others carried impudence as far as it could go."

She was known first as Mlle. Tonnay-Charente, and was maid of honor to the Duchess of Orléans. When, at the age of twenty-two, she married the Marquis de Montespan and became lady in waiting to the queen, her beauty, wit, and brilliant conversational powers at once made her the centre of attraction; for several years, however, the king scarcely noticed her. Upon secretly becoming his mistress in 1668 and openly being declared as such two years later, her husband attempted to interfere, and was unceremoniously banished to his estates; in 1676 he was legally separated from her. She persuaded the king to legitimatize their children, who were confided to Mme. Scarron,—afterward Mme. de Maintenon,—who later influenced the king to abandon his mistress.

Mme. de Montespan's power, lasting fourteen years, was almost unlimited, and was the epoch of courtiers intoxicated with passion and consumed by vice, infatuated with the king and his mistress, whose title as *maîtresse-en- titre* was considered an official one, conferring the same privileges and demanding the same ceremonies and etiquette as did a high court position. The only opposition incurred was from the clergy, who eventually, by uniting their forces with the influence of Mme. de Maintenon, brought about the disgrace of the mistress.

When, in 1675, she desired to perform her Easter duties publicly at Versailles, the priest refused to grant absolution until she should discontinue her wanton, adulterous life. She appealed to the king, and he referred the decision of the matter to Bossuet, who decided that it was an imperative duty to deny absolution to public sinners of notorious lives who refused to abandon them. This was immediately before her legal separation from her husband.

Influenced by the preaching of men like Bourdaloue and Bossuet, the king resolved to abandon his powerful mistress; in 1686 she was finally separated from Louis XIV., but did not leave Versailles until 1691, when, becoming reconciled to her fate, she decided to retire to a convent. Bossuet became her spiritual adviser, and described her habits in the following letter to the king:

"I find Mme. de Montespan sufficiently tranquil. She occupies herself greatly in good works. I see her much affected by the verities I propose to her, which are the same I uttered to your majesty. To her—as to you—I have offered the words by which God commands us to yield our whole hearts to him; they have caused her to shed many tears. May God establish these verities in the depths of the hearts of both of you, in order that so many tears, so much suffering, so many efforts as you have made to subdue yourselves, may not be in vain."

The king did not wholly abandon his mistress; from a material point of view, she was more powerful than ever, for Louis XIV. gave orders to his minister, Colbert, to do for Mme. de Montespan whatever she wished, and her wishes caused a heavy drain upon the treasury. The king continued to pay court to other favorites, such as the Princesse de Soubèse and Mlle. de Fontanges; the latter was his third mistress, but her career was of short duration, as one of the last acts of Mme. de Montespan was, it is said, the poisoning of Mlle. de Fontanges; this, however, is not generally accepted as true, although the Princesse Palatine wrote the following which throws suspicion upon the former favorite: "Mme. de Montespan was a fiend incarnate, but the Fontanges was good and simple. The latter is dead—because, they say, the former put poison in her milk. I do not know whether or not this is true, but what I do know well is that two of the Fontanges's people died, saying publicly that they had been poisoned." With the increasing influence of Mme. de Maintenon, the king completely forgot his former mistress.

Mme. de Montespan was possibly the most arrogant and despotic of all French mistresses and she was, also, the most humiliated. She had inspired no confidence, friendship, love, or respect in Louis XIV., who eventually looked with shame and remorse upon his relations with her. It took her sixteen years to overcome her terrible passion and to give up the court forever. Not until 1691 did she become reconciled to departure from Versailles; thenceforth, penitence conquered immoral desires. M. Saint-Amand says she not only "arrived at remorse, but at macerations, fasts, and haircloths. She limited herself to the coarsest underlinen and wore a belt and garters studded with iron points. She came at last to give all she had to the poor;" she also founded a hospital in which she nursed the sick.

While at the convent, she tried, in vain, to effect a reconciliation with her husband; not until every avenue to a social life was cut off from her, did she entirely surrender herself to charity and the service of God. In her latest years, she was so tormented by the horrors of death that she employed several women whose only occupation was to watch with her at night. She died in 1707, forgotten by the king and all her former associates; Louis XIV. formally prohibited her children, the Duke of Maine, the Comte de Toulouse, the Comte de Vexin, and Mlles. de Nantes, de Blois, and de Tours, from wearing mourning for her.

A striking contrast to Mme. de Montespan in character, disposition, morality, and birth was Mme. de Maintenon, one of the greatest and most important women in French history. What is known of her is so enveloped in calumny and falsehood and made so uncertain by dispute, that to disentangle the actual facts is almost an impossibility, despite the glowing tribute paid to her in the immense work published recently by the Comte d'Haussonville and M. Gabriel Hanotaux.

It would seem that the more the history of Mme. de Maintenon is studied, the more one is led away from a first impression—which usually proves to be an erroneous one. Thus, M. Lavallée, in his first work, *Histoire des Français*, wrote that she "was of the most complete aridity of heart, narrow in the scope of her affections, and meanly intriguing. She suggested fatal enterprises and inappropriate appointments; she forced mediocre and servile persons upon the king; she had, in fine, the major share in the errors and disasters of the reign of Louis XIV." A few years later he wrote, in his *Histoire de la maison royale de Saint-Cyr*: "Mme. de Maintenon gave Louis XIV. none but salutary and disinterested counsels which were useful to the state and instrumental in making less heavy the burdens of the people."

Opinion in general, especially French opinion, has been very bitter toward her. History has even reproached her with having been a usurper, a tyrant, and a selfish master. The great preacher, Fénelon, wrote to her:

"They say you take too little part in affairs. Your mind is more capable than you think. You are, perhaps, a little too distrustful of yourself, or, rather, you are too much afraid to enter into discussions contrary to the inclination you have for a tranquil and meditative life."

Is this picture, left by Emile Chasles and accepted by M. Saint-Amand, truthful? "This intelligent woman, far from being too much heeded, was not enough so. There was in her a veritable love for the public welfare, a true sorrow in the midst of our misfortunes. To-day, it is necessary to retrench much from the grandeur of her worldly power and add a great deal to that of her soul." M. Saint-Amand believes her sincere when she wrote to Mme. des Ursins:

"In whatever way matters turn, I conjure you, madame, to regard me as a person incapable of directing affairs, who heard them talked too late to be skilful in them, and who hates them more than she ignores them.... My interference in them is not desired and I do not desire to interfere. They are not concealed from me, but I know nothing consecutively and am often badly informed."

The opinions of her contemporaries are not always flattering, but such are possibly due to envy and jealousy or to some purely personal prejudice. Thus, when the Duchess of Orléans, the Princesse Palatine, calls her "that nasty old thing, that wicked devil, that shrivelled-up, filthy old Maintenon, that concubine of the king," and casts upon her other gross aspersions that are unfit to be repeated, one must remember that the calumniator was a German, the daughter of the Elector Palatine Charles-Louis, a woman honest in her morals, but shameless in her speech, who loved the beauties of nature more than those of the palaces; more shocked at hypocrites than at religion or irreligion, she took Mme. de Maintenon to be a type of the impostors whom she detested. It was her son who became regent, and it was her son who married one of the illegitimate daughters of Louis XIV.—an alliance of which his mother had a horror.

The memoirs of Saint-Simon are interesting, but the odious picture he has drawn of Mme. de Maintenon is hardly in accord with later appreciations. M. Saint-Amand sums up the two classes of critics thus:

"The revolutionary school which likes to drag the memory of the great king through the mire, naturally detests the eminent woman who was that king's companion, his friend and consoler. Writers of this school would like to make of her a type not only odious and fatal, but ungraceful and unsympathetic, without radiance, charm or any sort of fascination. She is too frequently called to mind under the aspect of a worn old woman, stiff and severe, with tearless eyes and a face without a smile. We forget that in her youth she was one of the prettiest women of her time, that her beauty was wonderfully preserved, and that in her old age she retained that superiority of style and language, that distinction of manner and exquisite tact, that gentle firmness of character, that charm and elevation of mind, which, at every period of her life, gained her so much praise and so many friends."

Mme. de Maintenon was born in prison. Her maiden name was Françoise d'Aubigné. She was the granddaughter of Agrippa d'Aubigné, the historian. Her father had planned to settle in the Carolinas, and his correspondence with the English government, to that effect, was treated as treason; he was thrown into prison, where his wife voluntarily shared his fate and where the future Mme. de Maintenon was born. After the death of her father, she was confided to her aunt, Mme. de Villette, a Calvinist, who trained her in the principles of Protestantism. Because of the refusal of her daughter to attend mass, her mother put her in charge of the Countess of Neuillant who, with great difficulty, converted Françoise back to Catholicism.

At the home of the Countess of Neuillant, she often met Scarron, the comic poet—a paralytic and cripple—who offered her money with which to pay for admission to a convent, a proposition which she refused; subsequently, however, the countess sent her to the Ursulines to be educated. When, after two years, she lost her mother and was thus left without home, fortune, or future prospects, she consented, at the age of seventeen, to marry the poet. Thus, born in a prison, without even a dowry, harshly reared by a mother who was under few obligations to life, more harshly treated in the convent, introduced as a poor relation into the society of her aunt and to the friends of her godmother, the Countess of Neuillant, she early learned to distrust life and suspect man, and to restrain her ambitions.

Exceedingly beautiful, graceful, and witty, she soon won her way to the brilliant and fashionable society of the crippled wit, buffoon, and poet, who was coarse, profane, ungodly, and physically an unsightly wreck. In this society, which the burlesque poet amused by his inexhaustible wit and fancy, and his frank, Gallic gayety, she showed an infinite amount of tact and soon made his salon the most prominent social centre of Paris. There, Scarron, never tolerated a stupid person, no matter of what blood or rank.

When asked what settlement he proposed to make upon his wife, he replied: "Immortality." At another time, he remarked: "I shall not make her commit any follies, but I shall teach her a great many." On his deathbed he said: "My only regret is that I cannot leave anything to my wife with whom I have every imaginable reason to be content." In this free-and-easy salon, a young noble said, soon after the marriage of Scarron: "If it were a question of taking liberties with the queen or Mme. Scarron, I would not deliberate; I would sooner take them with the queen."

The reputation made by the young Mme. Scarron gained her many influential friends, especially among court people. At the death of her husband, in 1660, to avoid trouble with his family, she renounced the marriage dowry of twenty-four thousand livres. Her friends procured her a pension of two thousand livres from the queen. Thus freed from care, she lived according to her inclination, which tended toward pleasing and doing good; taking good cheer and her services voluntarily and unaffectedly to all families, she gradually made herself a necessity among them—thus she laid the foundation of her future greatness. She was received by the best families, grew in favor everywhere, and even won over all her enemies. Modest, complaisant, promptly and readily rendering a favor, prudent, practical and virtuous, her one desire was to make friends, not so much for the purpose of using them, but because she realized that a person in humble circumstances cannot have too many friends.

Her portrait as a widow is admirably drawn by M. Saint-Amand: "Mme. Scarron seeks esteem, not love. To please while remaining virtuous, to endure, if need be, privations and even poverty, but to win the reputation of a strong character, to deserve the sympathy and approbation of honest persons —such is the direction of all her efforts. Well dressed, though very simply; discreet and modest, intelligent and *distingué*, with that patrician elegance which luxury cannot create, but which is inborn and comes by nature only; pious, with a sincere and gentle piety; less occupied with herself than with others; talking well and—what is much rarer—knowing how to listen; taking an interest in the joys and sorrows of her friends, and skilful in amusing and consoling them—she is justly regarded as one of the most amiable as well as one of the superior women in Paris. Economical and simple in her tastes, she makes her accounts balance perfectly, thanks to an annual pension of two thousand livres granted her by Queen Anne of Austria."

When Mme. Scarron was about to leave Paris because of lack of funds and the loss of her pension, after the death of Queen Anne, her friend Mme. de Montespan, the king's mistress, interfered in her behalf and had the pension renewed, thus inadvertently paving the way for her own downfall. Three years later Mme. Scarron was established in an isolated house near Paris, where she received the natural children of Louis XIV. and Mme. de Montespan, as they arrived, in quick succession, in 1669, 1670, 1672, 1673, and 1674. There, acting as governess, she hid them from the world. This is the only blemish upon the fair record of her life. It is maintained by her detractors that a virtuous woman would not have undertaken the education of the doubly adulterous children of Louis XIV. (thus, in a way, encouraging adultery), and that she would have given up her charge upon the first proposals of love.

However deep this stain may be considered, one must remember that the standard of honor at the court of Louis XIV. did not encourage delicacy in matters of love, and Mme. Scarron knew only the standard of society; her morality was no more extraordinary than was her intelligence, and it was to her credit that she preserved intact her honor and her virtue. At first the king looked with much dissatisfaction upon her appointment, not admiring the extreme gravity and reserve of the young widow; however, the unusual order of her talents and wisdom soon attracted his attention, and her entrance at court was speedily followed by quarrels between the mistress and Louis XIV. In 1674 the king, wishing to acknowledge his recognition of her merits, purchased the estate of Maintenon for her and made her Marquise de Maintenon.

Her primary object became the gaining of the favor of Mme. de Montespan; for this purpose she taught herself humility, while toward the king she directed the forces of her dignity, reserve, and intellectual attainments. Being the very opposite of the mistress who won and retained him by sensuous charms (in which the king was fast losing pleasure and satisfaction), she soon effected a change by entertaining her master with the solid attainments of her mind— religion, art, literature.

Mme. de Maintenon was always amiable and sympathetic, kind and thoughtful, never irritating, crossing, or censuring the king; wonderfully judicious, modest, self-possessed, and calm, she was irreproachable in conduct and morals, tolerating no improper advances. Although the characteristics and general deportment of Mme. de Montespan were entirely different from those of Mme. de Maintenon, the latter entertained true friendship for her benefactress, displaying astonishing tact, shrewdness, and self-control.

If Mme. de Maintenon were not, at first, loved by the king, it was because she appeared to him too ideal, sublime, spirituelle, too severely sensible. Then came the turning point; at forty years of age she was "a beautiful and stately woman with brilliant dark eyes, clear complexion, beautiful white teeth, and graceful manners;" sedate, self-possessed, and astonished at nothing, she had learned the art of waiting, and studied the king—showing him those qualities he desired to see.

Her aim became to take the king from his mistress and lead him back to the queen. After gaining his confidence by her sincerity and trustworthiness, and making herself indispensable to him, she succeeded in bringing about the desired separation, through the medium of the dauphiness, whom she won over to her cause. Thus, without perfidy, hypocrisy, intrigue, or manœuvring, by simply being herself, she replaced the haughty and beautiful Mme. de Montespan.

When, after the queen's death, and after having lived about the king for fifteen years, "she had succeeded in making the devotee take precedence of the lover, when piety had overcome passion, when religion had effected its change, then Louis the Great offered his hand in marriage to her who had only veneration, gratitude, and devotion for him, but no passion or love." Reasons of state demanded the secrecy of the marriage; for had he raised her to the throne, political complications would have arisen and disturbed his subsequent career; Mme. de Maintenon fully appreciated the intricacies of the situation, and was therefore content to remain what she was.

She came to the king when he was beginning to feel the effects of his former mode of life; he needed fidelity and friendship, and he saw these in her. His feelings for her are well described in the following extract by M. Saint-Amand:

"To sum up: the king's sentiment for her was of the most complex nature. There was in it a mingling of religion and of physical love, a calculation of reason and an impulse of the heart, an aspiration after the mild joys of family life and a romantic inclination—a sort of compact between French good sense, subjugated by the wit, tact, and wisdom of an eminent woman, and Spanish imagination allured by the fancy of having extricated this elect woman from poverty in order to make her almost a queen. Finally, it must be noted that Louis XIV., always religiously inclined, was convinced that Mme. de Maintenon had been sent to him by Heaven for his salvation, and that the pious counsels of this saintly woman, who knew how to render devotion so agreeable and attractive, seemed to him to be so many inspirations from on High."

It must not be inferred, however, that the feeling for Mme. de Maintenon was purely ideal. "He was unwilling to remarry," says the Abbé de Choisy, "because of tenderness for his people. He had, already, three grandsons, and wisely judged that the princes of a second marriage might, in course of time, cause civil wars. On the other hand, he could not dispense with a wife and Mme. de Maintenon pleased him greatly. Her gentle and scintillating wit promised him an agreeable intercourse which would refresh him after the cares of royalty. Her person was still engaging and her age prevented her from having children."

As his wife, Mme. de Maintenon took more interest in the king and his family than she did in the affairs of the kingdom. To be the wife of the hearth and home, to educate the princes, to rear the young Duchess of Bourgogne, granddaughter of Louis XIV., to calm and ease the old age of the king and to distract and amuse him, became her sole objects in life. Her power, thus directed, became almost unbounded; she was the dispenser of favors and the real ruler, sitting in the cabinet of the king; and her counsels were so wise that they soon became invaluable.

At court, she opposed all foolish extravagance, such as the endless fêtes and amusements of all kinds which had become so popular under Mme. de Montespan—a procedure which caused her the greatest difficulties and provoked revolts and quarrels in the royal family. By her prudence, tact, wisdom, and the loyalty of her friendship, she won and retained the respect and favor—if not the love—of everyone. Her reputation was never tarnished by scandal. "When one reflects that Louis XIV. was only forty-seven years old and in the prime of life and Mme. de Montespan in the full blaze of her marvellous beauty, that this woman of humble birth, in her youth a Protestant, poor, a governess, the widow of a low, comic poet, should win so proud a man as Louis XIV., seems incredible."

When one considers that throughout life her one aspiration was an irreproachable conduct, that her manner of action was always defensive, never offensive, that her chief aim was to restore the king to the queen (who died in her arms) and not to replace his mistress, one cannot withhold admiration and esteem from this truly great woman who accomplished all those honorable designs.

The obstacles to be conquered before reaching her goal were indeed numerous, but she managed them all. There were so many persons hostile to her,—mistresses and intriguers, bishops and priests, courtesans and valets, princes and members of the royal family,—to overcome whom she had to be on her guard, make use of every opportunity, show a rare knowledge of society and court, a profound skill and address, resolution and will; and she was equal to all occasions.

Her greatest defect was the narrowness of her religious views. Entirely in the hands of her spiritual advisers, obeying them faithfully and blindly, she was not inclined to theological investigation, but was sincerely devout. More interested in the various persons than in doctrines, she showed a passion for making bishops, abbots, and priests, as well as for negotiating compromises, reconciling *amours propres* and doing away with all religious hatred. Lacking, above all else, clearness of conception, promptness and firmness of decision, she was finally persuaded to encourage the bigotry of Louis XIV. and his intolerance toward those who differed from him. Hence, in 1685, she permitted that fearfully destructive persecution of the Protestants, which caused over three hundred thousand of France's most solid people to leave the country; and by her fanaticism and false zeal, she caused the king to be a party to that awful catastrophe.

"This one act of hers counterbalances nearly all her virtues, and we remember her more as the murderess of thousands of innocents than as the calm and virtuous governess. But we must remember the nature of her advisers and the eternal policy of the Catholic Church, which are ever identical with absolutism. To uphold the institutions and opinions already established, was the one sentiment of the age; innovation, progress, were destructive—Mme. de Maintenon became the watchful guardian of royalty and the Church." Such is the verdict of English opinion. M. Saint-Amand judges the affair differently:

"A woman as pious and reasonable as she was, animated always by the noblest intentions, loving her country and always showing sympathy for the poor people—not merely in words but in deeds as well—detesting war and loving justice and peace, always moderate and irreproachable in her conduct —such a woman cannot be the mischievous, crafty, malicious, and vindictive bigot imagined by many writers; she did not encourage such an act, nor would her nature permit to do so.... The prayer she uttered every morning, best portrays the woman and her rôle: 'Lord, grant me to gladden the king, to console him, to sadden him when it must be for Thy glory. Cause me to hide from him nothing which he ought to know through me, and which no one else would have courage to tell him.' ... To Madame de Glapion she said: 'I would like to die before the king; I would go to God; I would cast myself at the foot of His throne; I would offer Him the desires of a soul that He would have purified; I would pray Him to grant the king greater enlightenment, more love for his people, more knowledge of the state of the provinces, more aversion for the perfidy of the countries, more horror of the ways in which his authority is abused: and God would hear my prayers.'"

This pious woman was weary of life before her marriage, and but changed the nature of her misery upon reaching the highest goal open to a woman. Marly, Versailles, Fontainebleau were only different names for the same servitude.

When she had attained her desire, she thought her repose assured; instead, her ennui, her disgust of life and the world, only increased; realizing this, she began to direct her thoughts entirely toward God and her aspirations toward things not of this earth—hence the almost complete absence of her influence in politics.

She was never happy, and that her life was a disappointment to her may be gathered from the following words from her pen: "Flee from men as from your mortal enemies; never be alone with them. Take no pleasure in hearing that you are pretty, amiable, that you have a fine voice. The world is a malicious deceiver which never means what it says; and the majority of men who say such things to young girls, do it hoping to find some means of ruining them."

Her most intense desire seemed to be to please, and be esteemed—to receive the *honneur du monde*, which appeared to be her sole motive for living. When in power, she did not use her influence as the intriguing women of the epoch would have done, because she did not possess their qualities—taste, breadth of vision, and selfish ambitions. Her objects in life were the reform of a wicked court, the extirpation of heresy, the elevation of men of genius, and the improvement of the society and religion of France. After the death of the king (in 1715), she retired to Saint-Cyr, and spent the remainder of her life in acts of charity and devotional exercises.

After the king's death she dismissed all her servants and disposed of her carriages as well, "unable to reconcile herself to feeding horses while so many young girls were in need," as she said. For almost four years she peacefully and happily lived in a very modest apartment. She seldom went out and then only to the village to visit the sick and the poor. On June 10, 1717, when she was eighty-one years old, Peter the Great went to Saint-Cyr for the purpose of seeing and talking to the greatest woman of France. He found her confined to her bed; the chamber being but dimly lighted, he thrust aside the curtain in order to examine the features of the woman who had ruled the destinies of France for so many years. The Czar talked to her for some time, and when he asked Madame de Maintenon from what she was suffering, she replied: "From great old age." She died on August 15, 1719, and was buried in the choir of the church of Saint-Cyr, where a modest slab of marble indicated the spot where her body reposed until, in 1794, when the church was being transformed into hospital wards, "the workmen opened the vault, and took out the body and dragged it into the court with dreadful yells and threw it, stripped and mutilated, into a hole in the cemetery."

The greatest work of Mme. de Maintenon was the founding of the Seminary of Saint-Cyr, which the king granted to her about the time of their marriage and of his illness; it was probably intended as the penance of a sick man who wished to make reparation for the wrongs inflicted upon some of the young girls of the nobility, and as a wedding gift to Mme. de Maintenon. There, aided by nuns, she cared for and educated two hundred and fifty pupils, dowerless daughters of impoverished nobles. It was "the veritable offspring of her who was never a daughter, a wife, nor a mother." There she was happy and content; there she recalled her own youth when she was poor and forsaken; there she found respite from the turmoils and agitations of Versailles; there she was supreme; there she governed absolutely and was truly loved.

For thirty years she was queen at Saint-Cyr, visiting it every other day and teaching the young girls for whom it was a protection against the world. Since childhood, she had been so accustomed to serve herself, to wait upon others and to care for the smallest details of the management of the household, that she introduced this spirit into society and at Saint-Cyr, where she managed every detail, from the linen to the provisions; this showed a reasonable and well-balanced mind, but not any high order of intelligence.

Of the young girls in her charge, she desired to make model women, characterized by simplicity and piety; they were to be free from morbid curiosity of mind, were to practise absolute self-denial and to devote their lives to a practical labor. Her advice was: "Be reasonable or you will be unhappy; if you are haughty, you will be reminded of your misery, but if you are humble, people will recall your birth.... Commence by making yourself loved, without which you will never succeed. Is it not true that, had you not loved me or had you had an aversion for me, you would not have accepted, with such good grace, the counsels that I have given you? This is absolutely certain—the most beautiful things when taught by persons who displease us, do not impress but rather harden us."

A counsel that strikes home forcibly to-day, one which strongly attacks the modern fad of neglecting home for church, is expressed well in one of her letters: "Your piety will not be right if, when married, you abandon your husband, your children and your servants, to go to the churches at times when you are not obliged to go there. When a young girl says that a woman would do better properly to raise her children and instruct her servants, than to spend her morning in church, one can accommodate one's self to such religion, which she will cause to be loved and respected."

At the hour of leisure, she gave the girls those familiar talks which were anticipated by them with so much pleasure, and extracts from which are still cherished by the young women of France. She believed that the aim of instruction for young girls should be to educate them to be Christian women with well-balanced and logical minds. With her varied experience of the ups and downs of life, she gradually came to the conclusion that, after all, there is nothing in the world so good as sound common sense, but one that is not enamored of itself, which obeys established laws and knows its own limits. Her sex is intended to obey, thus her reason was a Christian reason.

"You can be truly reasonable only in proportion as you are subservient to God.... Never tell children fantastic stories, nor permit them to believe them; give them things for what they are worth. Never tell them stories of which, when they grow to independent reasoning, you must disillusion them. You must talk to a girl of seven as seriously and with as much reason as to a young lady of twenty. You must take part in the pleasures of children, but never accommodate them with a childish language or with foolish or puerile ways.

You can never be too reasonable or too sane. Religion, reason, and truth are always good."

To appreciate the importance of Mme. de Maintenon's position and the revolutionary effect which her attitude produced upon the customs of the time, one must remember with what she had to contend. Hers was a period of passion and adventure—a period which was followed by sorrow and disaster. The novels of Mlle. de Scudéry, which were at the height of their popularity, had over-refined the sentiments; the *chevaleresque* heroes and picturesque heroines turned the heads of young girls, who dreamed of an ideal and perfect love; their one longing was for the romantic—for the enchantments and delights of life. In this stilted and amorous atmosphere, Mme. de Maintenon preserved her poise and fought vigorously against the fads of the day. The young girls under her care were taught to love just as they were taught to do other things—with reason. Also, she guarded against the weaknesses of nature and the flesh. "Than Mme. de Maintenon, no one ever better knew the evils of the world without having fallen prey to them," says Sainte-Beuve; "and no one ever satisfied and disgusted the world more, while charming it at the same time."

Mme. de Maintenon's ideal methods of education were not immediately effective; there were many periods of hardship, apprehension, and doubt. Thus, when Racine's *Esther* (written at the request of Mme. de Maintenon, to be presented by the pupils at Saint-Cyr) was performed, there sprang up a taste for poetry, writing, and literature of all kinds. The acting turned the girls' thoughts into other channels and threatened to counteract the teachings of simplicity and reason; no one ever showed more genuine good sense, wholesomeness of mind, and breadth of view, than were displayed by Mme. de Maintenon in dealing with these disheartening drawbacks.

In endeavoring to impress upon those young minds the correct use of language and the proper style of writing, she wrote for them models of letters which showed simplicity, precision, truth, facility, and wonderful clearness; and these were imitated by them in their replies to her.

She wished, above all, to make them realize that her experience with that social and court life, for which they longed, was one of disappointment: that was a world apart, in which amusing and being amused was the one occupation. She had passed wearily through that period of life, and sought repose, truth, tranquillity, and religious resignation; to make those young spirits feel the fallacy of such a mode of existence was her earnest desire, and her efforts in that direction were characterized by a zeal, energy, and persistence which were productive of wonderful results. That was one phase of her greatness and influence.

But Mme. de Maintenon was somewhat too severe, too narrow, too strict,—one might say, too ascetic,—in her teaching. There was too little of that which, in this world, cheers, invigorates, and enlivens. Her instruction was all reason, without relieving features; it lacked what Sainte-Beuve calls the *don des larmes* (gift of tears). Hers was a noble, just, courageous, and delicate judgment; but it was without the softening qualities of the truly feminine, which calls for tears and affection, tenderness and sympathy.

She remains in educational affairs the greatest woman of the seventeenth century, if not of all her countrywomen. M. Faguet says: "This widow of Scarron, who was nearly Queen of France, was born minister of public instruction." She powerfully upheld the cause of morality, was a liberal patroness of education and learning, and all aspiring geniuses were encouraged and financially aided by her. It was she who impressed upon Louis XIV. the truth of the existence of a God to whom he was accountable for his acts—a teaching which contributed no little to the general purification of morals at court.

The writings of Mme. de Maintenon occupy a very high place in the history of French literature; in fact, her letters have often been compared with those of Mme. de Sévigné, although, unlike the latter, she never wrote merely to please, but to instruct, to convert, and to console. In her works there was no pretension to literary style; they were sermons on morals, characterized by discretion and simplicity, dignity and persuasiveness, seriousness and earnestness; Napoleon placed her letters above those of Mme. de Sévigné. M. Saint-Amand says of her writings: "More reflection than vivacity, more wisdom than passion, more gravity than charm, more authority than grace, more solidity than brilliancy—such are the characteristics of a correspondence which might justify the expression, the style is the woman."

He gives, also, the following discriminating comparison between the two writers: "Enjoyment, Gallic animation, good-tempered gayety, fall to the lot of Mme. de Sévigné; what marks Mme. de Maintenon is experience, reason, profundity. The one laughs from ear to ear—the other barely smiles. The one has pleasant illusions about everything, admiration which borders on *naïveté*, ecstasies when in the presence of the royal sun: the other never permits herself to be fascinated by either the king or the court, by men, women, or things. She has seen human grandeur too close at hand not to understand its nothingness, and her conclusions bear the imprint of a profound sadness. At times Mme. de Sévigné, also, has attacks of melancholy, but the cloud passes quickly and she is again in the sunshine. Gayety—frank, communicative, radiant gayety—is the basis of the character of this woman who is more witty, seductive, and amusing than is any other. Mme. de Sévigné shines by imagination—Mme. de Maintenon by judgment. The one permits herself to be dazzled, intoxicated—the other always preserves her indifference. The one exaggerates the splendors of the court—the other sees them as they are. The one is more of a woman—the other more of a saint."

Mme. de Maintenon may be called "a woman of fate," She was never daughter, mother, or wife; as a child, she was not loved by her mother, and her father was worthless; married to two men, both aged beyond their years, she was, indeed, but an instrument of fate. Truthful, candid, and discreet she was entirely free from all morbid tendencies, and was modest and chaste from inclination as well as from principle. Though outwardly cold, proud, and reserved, yet in her deportment toward those who were fortunate enough to possess her esteem, she was kind—even loving. While not intelligent to a remarkable degree, she was prudent, circumspect, and shrewd, never losing her self-control. When once interested, and convinced as to the proper course, she displayed marvellous strength of will, sagacity, and personal force. Beautiful and witty, she easily adapted herself to any position in which she might be placed; though intolerant and narrow in her religious views, she was otherwise gentle, charitable, and unselfish. Therefore, it is evident that she possessed, to a greater degree than did any other woman of her time, unusual as well as desirable qualities—qualities that made her powerful and incomparable.

Chapter VI

Mme. de Sévigné, Mme. de La Fayette, Mme. Dacier, Mme. de Caylus

The seventeenth century was, in French history, the greatest century from the standpoint of literary perfection, the sixteenth century the richest in naissant ideas, and the eighteenth the greatest in the way of developing and formulating those ideas; and each century produced great women who were in perfect harmony with and expressed the ideals of each period of civilization.

It is not within the limits of reason to expect women to rival, in literature, the great writers such as Corneille, Racine, Molière, Bossuet, La Fontaine, Descartes, Pascal—most of whom were but little influenced by femininity; there were those, however, among the sex, who were conspicuous for elevation of thought, dignity in manner and bearing, and brilliancy in conversation— attributes which they have left to posterity in numberless exquisite and charming letters, in interesting and invaluable memoirs, or in consummate psychological and social portraitures incorporated into the form of novels. Among female writers of letters, Mme. de Sévigné wears the laurel wreath; Mme. de La Fayette, with Mlle. de Scudéry, is the representative of the novel; Mme. Dacier was the great advocate of the more liberal education of women; and the *Souvenirs* of Mme. de Caylus made that authoress immortal.

The association of La Rochefoucauld, the Cardinal de Retz, the Chevalier de Meré, Mme. de La Fayette, and Mme. de Sévigné, was responsible for almost everything elevating and of interest produced in the seventeenth century. Of that highly intellectual circle, Mme. de Sévigné was the leading spirit by force of her extraordinary faculty for making friends, her wonderful talent as a writer, her originality and her charming disposition. She gave the tone to letters; M. Faguet says that her epistles were all masterpieces of amiable badinage, lively narration, maternal passion, true eloquence. More than that, they are important sources of historical knowledge, inasmuch as they contain much information concerning the politics of the day, and furnish an excellent guide to the etiquette, fashions, tastes, and literature of the writer's period.

Mme. de Sévigné was the most important figure of the time, being to that third prodigiously intellectual epoch of France what Marguerite de Navarre was to the sixteenth century, and the Hôtel de Rambouillet to the beginning of the seventeenth century. She represented the style, *esprit*, elegance, and *goût* of this greatest of French cultural periods. Her life may be considered as having had two distinct phases—one connected with an unhappy marriage and the other the period of a restless widowhood.

Marie de Rabutin-Chantal, Marchioness of Sévigné, was born at Paris, in 1626; at the age of eighteen months she lost her father; at seven years of age, her mother; at eight, her grandmother; at ten, her grandfather on her mother's side; she was thus left with her paternal grandmother, Mme. de Chantal, who had her carefully educated under the best masters, such as Ménage and Chapelain (court favorites), from whom she early imbibed a genuine taste for solid reading; from these instructors she learned Spanish, Italian, and Latin.

In 1644, she was married to the Marquis Henri de Sévigné, who was killed six years later in a duel, but who had, in the meantime, succeeded in making a considerable gap in her immense fortune, in spite of the precautions of her uncle, the Abbé of Coulanges. Henceforward, her interests in life were centred in the education of her two children; to them she wrote letters which have brought her name down to posterity as, possibly, the greatest epistolary writer that the history of literature has ever recorded.

Mme. de Sévigné was but nineteen years old when, after the marriage of Julie d'Angennes, the frequenters of the Hôtel de Rambouillet began to disperse, and she was in much demand by the successors of Mme. de Rambouillet. While the women of the reign of Louis XIII.—Mmes. de Hautefort, de Sablé, de Longueville, de Chevreuse, etc.—were exceedingly talented talkers, they were poor writers: but in Mme. de Sévigné, Mme. de La Fayette, and Mlle. de Scudéry both arts were developed to the highest degree.

Mme. de Sévigné was on the best terms with every great writer of her time— Pascal, Racine, La Fontaine, Bossuet, Bourdaloue, La Rochefoucauld. She was a woman of such broad affections that numerous friends and admirers were a necessary part of her existence. Of all the eminent women of the seventeenth century, she had the greatest number of lovers—suitors who frequently became her tormentors. Ménage, her teacher, who threatened to leave her never to see her again, was brought back to her by kind words, such as: "Farewell, friend— of all my friends the best." The Abbé Marigny, that "delicate epicurean, that improviser of fine triolets, ballads, vaudevilles, that enemy of all sadness and sticklers for morality," charmed her, at times, with sentimental ballads, such as the following:

"Si l'amour est un doux servage,

Si l'on ne peut trop estimer

Les plaisirs ou l'amour engage,

Qu'on est sot de ne pas aimer!

"Mais si l'on se sent enflammer

D'un feu dont l'ardeur est extrême,
Et qu'on n'ose pas l'exprimer,
Qu'on est sot alors que l'on aime!
"Si dans la fleur de son bel âge,
Une qui pourrait tout charmer,
Vous donne son cœur en partage,
Qu'on est sot de ne point aimer!
"Mais s'il faut toujours s'alarmer,
Craindre, rougir, devenir blême,
Aussitôt qu'on s'entend nommer,
Qu'on est sot alors que l'on aime!
"Pour complaire au plus beau visage
Qu'amour puisse jamais former,
S'il ne faut rien qu'un doux langage,
Qu'on est sot de ne pas aimer!
"Mais quand on se voit consumer.
Si la belle est toujours de même,
Sans que rien la puisse animer,
Qu'on est sot alors que l'on aime!

"L'ENVOI.

"En amour si rien n'est amer,
Qu'on est sot de ne pas aimer!
Si tout l'est au degré suprême,
Qu'on est sot alors que l'on aime!
[If love is a sweet bondage,
If we cannot esteem too much
The pleasures in which love engages,
How foolish one is not to love!
But if we feel ourselves inflamed

With a passion whose ardor is extreme,

And which we dare not express,

How foolish we are, then, to love!

If in the flower of her youth

There is one who could charm all.

And offers you her heart to share,

How very foolish not to love!

But if we must always be full of alarm—

Fear, blush and become pallid,

As soon as our name is spoken,

How foolish to love!

If to please the most beautiful countenance

That love can ever form,

Only a mellow language is necessary,

How foolish not to love!

But if we see ourselves wasting away,

If the belle is always the same

And cannot be animated,

How very foolish to love!

ENVOY.

If in love, nothing is bitter,

How dreadfully foolish not to love!

If everything is so to the highest degree,

How awfully foolish to love!]

Tréville went so far as to say that the figure of Mme. de Sévigné was beautiful enough to set the world afire. M. du Bled divides her lovers into three classes: the first was composed of her literary friends; the second, of those enamored, impassioned suitors, loving her from good motives or from the opposite, who strove to compensate her for the unfaithfulness of her husband while alive and for the ennui of her widowhood; the third class was composed of her Parisian friends, of whom she had hosts, court habitués who were leaders of society.

Representatives of the second class were the Prince de Conti, the great Turenne, various counts and marquises, and Bussy-Rabutin, who was a type of the sensual lover and the more dangerous on account of the privileges he enjoyed because of his close relationship to Mme. de Sévigné. His portrait of her is interesting: "I must tell you, madame, that I do not think there is a person in the world so generally esteemed as you are. You are the delight of humankind; antiquity would have erected altars to you, and you would certainly have been a goddess of something. In our century, when we are not so lavish with incense, and especially for living merit, we are contented to say that there is not a woman of your age more virtuous and more amiable than are you. I know princes of the blood, foreign princes, great lords with princely manners, great captains, gentlemen, ministers of state, who would be off and away for you, if you would permit them. Can you ask any more?"

Such eulogies came not only from men like the perfidious and cruel cousin, but from her friends everywhere. The finest of these is the one by her friend Mme. de La Fayette, contained in one of the epistolary portraits so much in vogue at that time, and which were turned out, *par excellence*, in the salon of Mlle. de Luxembourg: "Know, madame,—if by chance you do not already know it,—that your mind adorns and embellishes your person so well that there is not another one on earth so charming as you when you are animated in a conversation in which all constraint is banished. Your soul is great, noble, ready to dispense with treasures, and incapable of lowering itself to the care of amassing them. You are sensible to glory and ambition, and to pleasures you are less so; yet you appear to be born for the latter, and they made for you; your person augments pleasures, and pleasures increase your beauty when they surround you. Joy is the veritable state of your soul, and chagrin is more unlike to you than to anyone. You are the most civil and obliging person that ever lived, and by a free and calm air—which is in all your actions—the simplest compliments of seemliness appear, in your mouth, as protestations of friendship."

The originality which gained Mme. de Sévigné so many friends lay principally in her force, wealth of resource, intensity, sincerity, and frankness.
M. Scherer said she possessed "surprises for us, infinite energy, inexhaustible variety—everything that eternally revives interest."

The interest of the modern world in this remarkable woman is centred mainly in her letters. Guizot says: "Mme. de Sévigné is a friend whom we read over and over again, whose emotions we share, to whom we go for an hour's distraction and delightful chat; we have no desire to chat with Mme. de Grignan (her daughter)—we gladly leave her to her mother's exclusive affection, feeling infinitely obliged to her for having existed, inasmuch as her mother wrote letters to her. Mme. de Sévigné's letters to her daughter are superior to all her other epistles, charming as they all are; when she writes to M. Pomponne, to M. de Coulanges, to M. de Bussy, the style is less familiar, the heart less open, the soul less stirred; she writes to her daughter as she would speak to her—it is not a letter, it is an animated and charming conversation, touching upon everything, embellishing everything with an inimitable grace."

She had married her daughter to the Comte de Grignan, a man of forty, twice married, and with children, homely, but wealthy and aristocratic; writing to her cousin, Bussy-Rabutin, concerning this marriage, she said: "All these women (the count's former wives) died expressly to make room for your cousin." By marrying her daughter to such a man she encouraged all the questionable proprieties of the time. Mme. de Sévigné's affection for that daughter amounted almost to idolatry; it was to her that most of the mother's letters were written, telling her of her health, what was being done at Vichy, and about her business and for that child the authoress gave up her life at Paris in order to economize and thereby to help Mme. de Grignan in her extravagance, her son-in-law being an expert in spending money.

The intensity of her nature is well reflected in her letter upon the separation from her daughter: "In vain I seek my darling daughter; I can no longer find her, and every step she takes removes her farther from me. I went to St. Mary's, still weeping and dying of grief; it seemed as if my heart and my soul were being wrenched from me and, in truth, what a cruel separation! I asked leave to be alone; I was taken into Mme. du Housset's room, and they made me up a fire. Agnes sat looking at me, without speaking—that was our bargain. I stayed there till five o'clock, without ceasing to sob; all my thoughts were mortal wounds to me. I wrote to M. de Grignan (you can imagine in what key). Then I went to Mme. de La Fayette's, and she redoubled my griefs by the interest she took in them; she was alone, ill, and distressed at the death of one of the nuns; she was just as I should have desired, I returned hither at eight; but oh, when I came in! can you conceive what I felt as I mounted these stairs? That room into which I always used to go, alas! I found the doors of it open, but I saw everything upturned, disarranged, and your little daughter, who reminded me of mine.... The wakenings of the night were dreadful. I think of you continuously—it is what devotees call habitual thought, such as one should have of God, if one did one's duty. Nothing gives me diversion; I see that carriage which is forever going on and will never come near me. I am forever on the highways; it seems as if I were sometimes afraid that the carriage will upset with me; the rains there for the last three days, drove me to despair. The Rhone causes me strange alarm. I have a map before my eyes—I know all the places where you sleep. This evening you are at Nevers; on Sunday you will be at Lyons where you will receive this letter. I have received only two of yours—perhaps the third will come; that is the only comfort I desire; as for others, I seek none."

The letters of Mme. de Sévigné contain a great number of sayings applicable to habits and conduct, and these have had their part in shaping the customs and in depicting the time. To be modest and moderate, friendly, and conciliatory, to be content with one's lot and to bow to circumstances, to be sincere, to cultivate good sense and good grace—these counsels have been and still are, according to French opinion, the basis of French character: and Mme. de Sévigné's own popularity and success attest their wisdom.

She had not the gift of seeing things vividly and reproducing them in living form; her talent was a rarer one—it induced the reader to form a mental picture of the scene described, so vivid as to be under the illusion of being present in reality; and this is done with so much grace, charm, happy ease and naturalness, that to read her letters means to love the writer. What mother or friend would not fall a willing victim to the charm of a woman who could write the following letter?

"You ask me, my dear child, whether I continue to be really fond of life; I confess to you that I find poignant sorrows in it, but I am even more disgusted with death; I feel so wretched at having to end all thereby, that, if I could turn back again, I would ask for nothing better, I find myself under an obligation which perplexes me; I embark upon life without my consent, and so must I go out of it; that overwhelms me. And how shall I go? Which way? By what door? When will it be? In what condition? Shall I suffer a thousand, thousand pains which will make me die desperate? Shall I have brain fever? Shall I die of an accident? How shall I be with God? What shall I have to show Him? Shall fear, shall necessity bring me back to Him? Shall I have sentiment except that of dread? What can I hope? Am I worthy of heaven? Am I worthy of hell? Nothing is such madness as to leave one's salvation in uncertainty, but nothing is so natural. The stupid life I lead is the easiest thing in the world to understand; I bury myself in these thoughts and I find death so terrible that I hate life more because it leads me thereto, than because of the thorns with which it is planted. You will say that I want to live forever, then; not at all; but, if my opinion had been asked, I would have preferred to die in my nurse's arms; that would have removed me from the vexations of spirit and would have given me heaven full surely and easily."

Mme. de Sévigné never bored her readers with her own reflections. She differed from her contemporaries, who seemed to be dead to nature's beauty, in her striking descriptions of nature. A close observer, she knew how to describe a landscape; animating and enlivening it, and making it talk, she inspired the reader with love of it.

"I am going to be alone and I am very glad. Provided they do not take away from me the charming country, the shore of the Allier, the woods, streams, and meadows, the sheep and goats, the peasant girls who dance the *bourrée* in the fields, I consent to say adieu; the country alone will cure me.... I have come here to end the beautiful days and to say adieu to the foliage—it is still on the trees, it has only changed color; instead of being green, it is golden, and of so many golden tints that it makes a brocade of rich and magnificent gold, which we are likely to find more beautiful than the green, if only it were not for the changing part."

If the style of her letters did not make her the greatest prose writer of her time, it certainly entitled her to rank as one of the most original. The prose of the seventeenth century lacked "easy suppleness in lively movement, and imagination in the expression"—two qualities which Mme. de Sévigné possessed in a high degree. The slow and grave development, the just and harmonious equilibrium, the amplitude, are in her supplanted by a quick, alert, and free *saillie*; the detail and marvellous exactness are enriched by color, abundance of imagery, and metaphors. M. Faguet says she is to prose what La Fontaine is to poetry.

The literary style of Mme. de Sévigné is not learned, studied, nor labored. In an epoch in which the language was already formed, she did what Montaigne did a century before, when, we may almost assert, he had to create the French language. Her most striking expressions are her own—newly coined, not taken from the vocabulary in usage. Her style cannot be duplicated, and for this reason she has few imitators. Her letters show that they were improvised —her pen doing, alone, the work over which she seemed to have no control when communicating with her daughter; to the latter she said: "I write prose with a facility that will kill you."

Mme. de Sévigné was possibly not a beautiful woman, but she was a charming one; broad in the scope of her affections, she found the making of friends no difficult task. M. Vallery-Radot leaves the following picture of her: "A blonde, with exuberant health, a transparent complexion, blue eyes, so frank, so limpid, a nose somewhat square, a mouth ready to smile, shoulders that seem to lend splendor to her pearl necklace. Her gayety and goodness are so in evidence that there is about her a kind of atmosphere of good humor."

M. du Bled most admirably sums up her character and writings in the following: "She is the person who most resembles her writings—that is, those that are found; for alas! many (the most confidential, the most interesting, I think) are lost forever: in them she is reflected as she reflects French society in them. Endowed—morally and physically—with a robust health, she is expansive, loyal, confiding, impressionable, loving gayety in full abundance as much as she does the smile of the refined, as eager for the prattle of the court as for solid reading, smitten with nobiliary pride, a captive of the prejudices, superstitions and tastes of her caste (or of even her coterie), with her pen hardly tender for her neighbor—her daughter and intimates excepted. A manager and a woman of imagination, a Frondist at the bottom of her soul, and somewhat of a Jansenist—not enough, however, not to cry out that Louis

XIV. will obscure the glory of his predecessors because he had just danced with her—faithful to her friends (Retz, Fouquet, Pomponne) in disgrace and detesting their persecutors, seeking the favor of court for her children. In the salons, she is celebrated for her *esprit*—and this at an age when one seldom thinks about reputation, when one is like the princess who replied to a question on the state of her soul, 'At twenty one has no soul;' and she possesses the qualities that are so essential to style—natural *éclat*, originality of expression, grace, color, amplitude without pomposity and abundance without prolixity; moreover, she invents nothing, but, knowing how to observe and to express in perfection everything she had seen and felt, she is a witness and painter of her century: also, she loves nature—a sentiment very rare in the seventeenth century."

Mme. de Sévigné was endowed with the best qualities of the French race—good will and friendliness, which influence one to judge others favorably and to desire their esteem; of a very impressionable nature, she was gifted with a natural eloquence which enabled her to express her various emotions in a light or gay vein which often bordered on irony. Affectionate and appreciative and tender and kind to everyone in general, toward those whom she loved she was generous to a fault and unswerving in her fidelity.

Her last years were spent in the midst of her family. She died in 1696, of small-pox, thanking God that she was the first to go, after having trembled for the life of her daughter, whom she had nursed back to health after a long and dangerous illness. Her son-in-law, M. de Grignan, wrote to her uncle, M. de Coulanges:

"What calls far more for our admiration than for our regret, is the spectacle of a brave woman facing death—of which she had no doubt from the first days of her illness—with astounding firmness and submission. This person, so tender and so weak towards all whom she loved, showed nothing but courage and piety when she believed that her hour had come; and, impressed by the use she managed to make of that good store in the last moments of her life, we could not but remark of what utility and of what importance it is to have the mind stocked with the good matter and holy reading for which Mme. de Sévigné had a liking—not to say a wonderful hunger."

In order to give an idea of the place that Mme. de Sévigné holds in the opinion of the average Frenchman, we quote the final words of M. Vallery-Radot:

"To take a place among the greatest writers, without ever having written a book or even having thought of writing one—this is what seems impossible, and yet this is what happened to Mme. de Sévigné. Her contemporaries knew her as a woman distinguished for her *esprit*, frank, playful and sprightly humor, irreproachable conduct, loyalty to her friends, and as an idolizer of her daughter; no one suspected that she would partake of the glory of our classical authors—and she, less than any one. She had immortalized herself, without wishing or knowing it, by an intimate correspondence which is, to-day, universally regarded as one of the most precious treasures and one of the most original monuments to French literature. To deceive the *ennui* of absence, she wrote to her daughter all that she had in her heart and that came to her mind—what she did, wished to do, saw and learned, news of court, city, Brittany, army, everything—sadly or gayly, according to the subject, always with the most keen, ardent, delicate, and touching sentiments of tenderness and sympathy. She amuses, instructs, interests, moves to tears or laughter. All that passes within or before her, passes within and before us. If she depicts an object, we see it; if she relates an event, we are present at its occurrence; if she makes a character talk, we hear his words, see his gestures, and distinguish his accent. All is true, real, living: this is more than talent—it is enchantment. Generations pass away in turn; a single one, or, rather, a group escapes the general oblivion—the group of friends of Mme. de Sévigné."

A woman with characteristics the very opposite of those of Mme. de Sévigné, but who in some respects resembled her, was Mme. de La Fayette. Of her life, very little is to be said, except in regard to her lasting friendship and attachment for La Rochefoucauld. She was born in 1634, and, with Mme. de Sévigné, was probably the best educated among the great women of the seventeenth century. She was faithful to her husband, the Count of La Fayette, who, in 1665, took her to Paris, where she formed her lifelong attachment for the great La Rochefoucauld, and where she won immediate recognition for her exquisite politeness and as a woman with a large fund of common sense.

After her marriage, she seemed to have but one interest—La Rochefoucauld, just as that of Mme. de Maintenon was Louis XIV. and that of Mme. de Sévigné—her daughter. These three prominent women illustrate remarkably well that predominant trait of French women—faithfulness to a chosen cause; each one of the three was vitally concerned in an enduring, a legitimate, and sincere attachment, which state of affairs gives a certain distinction to the society of the time of Louis XIV.

Mme. de La Fayette, like Mme. de Sévigné, possessed an exceptional talent for making and retaining friends. She kept aloof from intrigues, in fact, knew nothing about them, and consequently never schemed to use her favor at court for purposes of self-interest. Two qualities belonged to her more than to any of her contemporaries—an instinct which was superior to her reason, and a love of truth in all things.

Compared with those of Mme. de Rambouillet, it is said that her attainments were of a more solid nature; and while Mlle. de Scudéry had greater brilliancy, Mme. de La Fayette had better judgment. These qualities combined with an exquisite delicacy, fine sentiment, calmness, and depth of reason, the very basis of her nature, are reflected in her works. Sainte-Beuve says that "her reason and experience cool her passion and temper the ideal with the results of observation." She was one of the very few women playing any rôle in French history who were endowed with all things necessary to happiness— fortune, reputation, talent, intimate and ideal friendship. Extremely sensitive to surroundings, she readily received impressions—a gift which was the source of a somewhat doubtful happiness.

In her later days, notwithstanding terrible suffering, she became more devout and exhibited an admirable resignation. A letter to Ménage will show the mental and physical state reached by her in her last days: "Although you forbid me to write to you, I wish, nevertheless, to tell you how truly affectedI am by your friendship. I appreciate it as much as when I used to see it; it is dear to me for its own worth, it is dear to me because it is at present the only one I have. Time and old age have taken all my friends away from me.... I must tell you the state I am in. I am, first of all, a mortal divinity, and to an excess inconceivable; I have obstructions in my entrails—sad, inexpressible feelings; I have no spirit, no force—I cannot read or apply myself. The slightest things affect me—a fly appears an elephant to me; that is my ordinary state.... I cannot believe that I can live long in this condition, and my life is too disagreeable to permit me to fear the end. I surrender myself to the will of God; He is the All-Powerful, and, from all sides, we must go to Him at last. They assure me that you are thinking seriously of your salvation, and I am very happy over it."

There probably never existed a more ideal friendship between two French women, one more lasting, sincere, perfect in every way, than that of Mme. de Sévigné and Mme. de La Fayette. The major part of the information we possess regarding events in the life of Mme. de La Fayette is obtained from their letters. Said Mme. de Sévigné: "Never did we have the smallest cloud upon our friendship. Long habit had not made her merit stale to me—the flavor of it was always fresh and new. I paid her many attentions, from the mere promptings of my affection, not because of the propriety by which, in friendships, we are bound. I was assured, too, that I was her dearest consolation—which, for forty years past, had been the case."

Shortly before her death, she wrote to Mme. de Sévigné: "Here is what I have done since I wrote you last. I have had two attacks of fever; for six months I had not been purged; I am purged once, I am purged twice; the day after the second time, I sit down at the table; oh, dear! I feel a pain in my heart—I do not want any soup. Have a little meat, then? No, I do not wish any. Well, you will have some fruit? I think I will. Very well, then, have some. I don't know—I think I will have some by and by. Let me have some soup and some chicken this evening…. Here is the evening, and there are the soup and the chicken; I don't desire them. I am nauseated, I will go to bed—I prefer sleeping to eating. I go to bed, I turn round, I turn back, I have no pain, but I have no sleep either. I call—I take a book—I close it. Day comes—I get up— I go to the window. It strikes four, five, six—I go to bed again, I doze until seven, I get up at eight, I sit down to table at twelve—to no purpose, as yesterday…. I lay myself down in my bed, in the evening, to no purpose, as the night before. Are you ill? Nay, I am in this state for three days and three nights. At present, I am getting some sleep again, but I still eat mechanically, horsewise—rubbing my mouth with vinegar. Otherwise, I am very well, and I haven't so much as a pain in my head."

Her depressing melancholy kept her indoors a great deal; in fact, after 1683, after the death of the queen, who was one of her best friends, she was seldom seen at court. Mme. de Sévigné gives good reason for this in her letter:

"She had a mortal melancholy. Again, what absurdity! is she not the most fortunate woman in the world? That is what people said; it needed that she should die to prove that she had good reason for not going out and for being melancholy. Her reins and her heart were all gone—was not that enough to cause those fits of despondency of which she complained? And so, during her life she showed reason, and after death she showed reason, and never was she without that divine reason which was her principal gift."

Her liaison with La Rochefoucauld is the one delicate and tender point in her life, a relation that afforded her much happiness and finally completed the ruin of her health. M. d'Haussonville said: "It is true that he took possession of her soul and intellect, little by little, so that the two beings, in the eyes of their contemporaries, were but one; for after his death (1680) she lived but an incomplete and mutilated existence."

Some critics have ventured to pronounce this liaison one of material love solely, others are convinced of its morality and pure friendship. In favor of the latter view, M. d'Haussonville suggests the fact that Mme. de La Fayette was over thirty years of age when she became interested in La Rochefoucauld, and that at that age women rarely ally themselves with men from emotions of physical love merely. At that age it is reason that mutually attracts two beings; and this feeling was probably the predominant one in that case, because her entire career was one of the most extreme reserve, conservatism, good sense, and propriety. However, other proofs are brought forward to show that there was between the two a sort of moral marriage, so many examples of which are found in the seventeenth century between people of prominence, both of whom happened to have unhappy conjugal experiences.

French society, one must remember, was different from any in the world; it seems to have been a large family gathering, the members of which were as intimate, took as much interest in each other's affairs, showed as much sympathy for one another and participated in each other's sorrows and pleasures, as though they were children of the same parents.

In his early days, La Rochefoucauld found it convenient, for selfish purposes, to simulate an ardent passion for Mme. de Longueville, of which mention has been made in the chapter relating to Mme. de Longueville. In his later period, he had settled down to a normal mode of life and sought the friendship of a more reasonable and less passionate woman. He himself said:

"When women have well-informed minds, I like their conversation better than that of men; you find, with them, a certain gentleness which is not met with among us; and it seems to me, besides, that they express themselves with greater clearness and that they give a more pleasant turn to the things they say."

Mme. de La Fayette exercised a great influence upon La Rochefoucauld—an influence that was wholesome in every way. It was through her influential friends at court that he was helped into possession of his property, and it was she who maintained it for him. As to his literary work (his *Maxims*), her influence over him was supposed to have somewhat modified his ideas on women and to have softened his tone in general. She wrote: "He gave me wit, but I reformed his heart." M. d'Haussonville has proved, without doubt, that her restraint modified many of his maxims that were tinged with the spirit of the commonplace and trivial. While Mme. de Sablé—essentially a moralist and a deeply religious woman—was more of a companion to him, and though his maxims were, for the greater part, composed in her salon, Mme. de La Fayette, by her tenderness and judgment, tempered the tone of them before they reached the public.

Mme. de La Fayette will always be known, however, as the great novelist of the seventeenth century. Two novels, two stories, two historical works, and her memoirs, make up her literary budget. M. d'Haussonville claims that her memoirs of the court of France are not reliable, because she was so often absent from court; also, in them she shows a tendency to avenge herself, in a way, upon Mme. de Maintenon, whose friend she was until the trouble between this lady and Mme. de Montespan occurred. The latter was the intimate friend of Mme. de La Fayette. As for her literary work proper, her desire to write was possibly encouraged, if not created, by her indulgence in the general fad of writing portraitures, in which she was especially successful in portraying Mme. de Sévigné. Her literary effort was, besides, a revolt of her own taste and sense against the pompous and inflated language of the novels of the day and against the great length of the development of the events and adventures in them. Thus, Mme. de La Fayette inaugurated a new style of novel; to show her influence, it will be well to consider the state of the Romanesque novel at the period of her writing.

In the beginning of the century, D'Urfé's novels were in vogue; these works were characterized by interminable developments, relieved by an infinite number of historical episodes. All characters, shepherds as well as noblemen, expressed the same sentiments and in the same language. There was no pretension to truth in the portraying of manners and customs.—A reaction was natural and took the form of either a kind of parody or gross realism. These novels, of which *Francion* and *Berger Extravagant* were the best known, depicted shepherds of the Merovingian times, heroes of Persia and Rome, or procurers, scamps, and scoundrels; but no descriptions of the manners of decent people (*honnêtes gens*) were to be found.

The novels of Mlle. de Scudéry, while interesting as portraitures, are not thoroughly reliable in their representation of the sentiments and environment of the times; on the other hand, those of Mme. de La Fayette are impersonal —no one of the characters is recognizable; yet their atmosphere is that of the court of Louis XIV., and the language, never so correct as to be unnatural, is that used at the time. Her novels reflect perfectly the society of the court and the manner of life there. "Thus," says M. d'Haussonville, "she was the first to produce a novel of observation and sentiment, the first to paint elegant manners as they really were."

Her first production was *La Princesse de Montpensier* (1662); in 1670, appeared *Zayde*, it was ostensibly the work of Segrais, her teacher and a writer much in vogue at the time; in 1678, *La Princesse de Clèves*, her masterpiece, stirred up one of the first real quarrels of literary criticism. For a long time after the appearance of that book, society was divided into two classes—the pros and the cons. It was the most popular work of the period.

M. d'Haussonville says it is the first French novel which is an illustration of woman's ability to analyze the most subtile of human emotions. Mme. de La

Fayette was, also, the first to elevate, in literature, the character of the husband who, until then, was a nonentity or a booby; she makes of him a hero —sympathetic, noble, and dignified.

In no fictitious tale before hers was love depicted with such rare delicacy and pathos. In her novel, *La Princesse de Clèves*, "a novel of a married woman, we feel the woman who has loved and who knows what she is saying, for she, also, has struggled and suffered." The writer confesses her weakness and leaves us witness of her virtue. All the soul struggles and interior combats represented in her work the authoress herself has experienced. As an example of this we cite the description of the sentiments of Mme. de Clèves when she realizes that her feeling toward one of the members of the court may develop into an emotion unworthy of her as a wife. She falls upon her knees and says:

"I am here to make to you a confession such as has never been made to man; but the innocence of my conduct and my intentions give me the necessary courage. It is true that I have reasons for desiring to withdraw from court, and that I wish to avoid the perils which persons of my age experience. I have never shown a sign of weakness, and I would not fear of ever showing any, if you permitted me to withdraw from court, or if I still had, in my efforts to do right, the support of Mme. de Chartres. However dangerous may be the action I take, I take it with pleasure, that I may be worthy of your actions, I ask a thousand pardons; if I have sentiments displeasing to you, I shall at least never displease you by my actions. Remember, to do what I am doing, one must have for a husband more friendship and esteem than was ever before had. Have pity on me and lead me away——and love me still, if you can."

La Princesse de Clèves is a novel of human virtue purely, and teaches that true virtue can find its reward in itself and in the austere enjoyment of duty accomplished. "It is a work that will endure, and be a comfort as well as a guide to those who aspire to a high morality which necessitates a difficult sacrifice."

M. d'Haussonville regards the novels of Mmes. de Charrière, de Souza, de Duras, de Boigne, as mere imitations or as having been inspired by that masterpiece of Mme. de La Fayette. He says: "In fact, novels in general, that depict the struggle between passion and duty, with the victory on the side of virtue, emanate more or less from it."

Taine wrote: "She described the events in the careers of society women, introducing no special terms of language into her descriptions. She painted for the sake of painting and did not think of attempting to surpass her predecessors. She reflects a society whose scrupulous care was to avoid even the slightest appearance of anything that might displease or shock. She shows the exquisite tact of a woman—and a woman of high rank."

Mme. de La Fayette is one of the very rare French writers that have succeeded in analyzing love, passion, and moral duty, without becoming monotonous, vulgar, brutal, or excessively realistic. Her creations contain the most minute analyses of heart and soul emotions, but these never become purely physiologic and nauseating, as in most novels. This achievement on her part has been too little imitated, but it, alone, will preserve the name of Mme. de La Fayette.

Mme. de Motteville is deserving of mention among the important literary women of the seventeenth century. She is regarded as one of the best women writers in French literature, and her memoirs are considered authority on the history of the Fronde and of Anne of Austria. The poetry of Mme. des Houlières was for a long time much in vogue; to-day, however, it is not read. The memoirs of Mlle. de Montpensier are more occupied with herself than with events of the time or the numerous princes who tarried about her as longing lovers. Guizot says: "She was so impassioned and haughty, with her head so full of her own greatness, that she did not marry in her youth, thinking no one worthy of her except the king and the emperor, and they had no fancy for her." The following portrait of her was sketched by herself:

"I am tall, neither fat nor thin, of a very fine and easy figure. I have a good mien, arms and hands not beautiful, but a beautiful skin—and throat, too. I have a straight leg and a well-shaped foot; my hair is light and of a beautiful auburn; my face is long, its contour is handsome, nose large and aquiline; mouth neither large nor small, but chiselled and with a very pleasing expression; lips vermilion, not fine, but not frightful, either; my eyes are blue, neither large nor small, but sparkling, soft, and proud like my mien. I talk a great deal, without saying silly things or using bad words. I am a very vicious enemy, being very choleric and passionate, and that, added to my birth, may well make my enemies tremble; but I have, also, a noble and kindly soul. I am incapable of any base and black deed; and so I am more disposed to mercy than to justice. I am melancholic, and fond of reading good and solid books; trifles bore me—except verses, and them I like, of whatever sort they may be; and undoubtedly I am as good a judge of such things as if I were a scholar."

Possibly the greatest female scholar that France ever produced was Mme. Dacier, a truly learned woman and one of whom French women are proud; during her last years she enjoyed the reputation of being one of the foremost scholars of all Europe. It was Mme. de Lambert who wrote of her:

"I esteem Mme. Dacier infinitely. Our sex owes her much; she has protested against the common error which condemns us to ignorance. Men, as much from disdain as from a fancied superiority, have denied us all learning; Mme. Dacier is an example proving that we are capable of learning. She has associated erudition and good manners; for, at present, modesty has been displaced; shame is no longer for vices, and women blush over their learning only. She has freed the mind, held captive under this prejudice, and she alone supports us in our rights."

Tanneguy-Lefèvre, the father of Mme. Dacier, was a savant and a type of the scholars of the sixteenth century. He brought up his sons to be like him—instructing them in Greek, Latin, and antiquities. The young daughter, present at all the lessons given to her brothers, acquired, unaided, a solid education; her father, amazed at her marvellous faculty for comprehending and remembering, soon devoted most of his energy to her. He was, at that time, professor at the College of Saumur; and he was conspicuous not only for the liberty he exhibited in his pedagogical duties, but for his general catholicity.

After the death of her father, the young daughter went to Paris where her family friends, Chapelain and Huet, encouraged her in her studies, the latter, who was assistant preceptor to the dauphin, even going so far as to request her to assist him in preparing the Greek text for the use of the dauphin. She soon eclipsed all scholars of the time by her illuminating studies of Greek authors and of the quality of the new editions which she prepared of their works, but she was continually pestered on account of her erudition and her religion, the Protestant faith, to which she clung while realizing that it had been the cause of the failure of her father's advancement.

From that time appeared her famous series of translations of Terence and Plautus, which were the delight of the women of the period and which gave her the reputation of being the most intellectual woman of the seventeenth century. In 1635, when nearly thirty years of age, she married M. Dacier, the favorite pupil of her father, librarian to the king and translator of Plutarch—a man of no means, but one who thoroughly appreciated the worth of Mlle. Lefèvre. This union was spoken of by her contemporaries as "the marriage of Greek and Latin."

Two years after their marriage, after long and serious deliberation, both abjured Protestantism, adopted the Catholic religion, and succeeded in converting the whole town of Castres—an act which gained them royal favor, and Louis XIV. granted them a pension of two thousand livres. Sainte-Beuve states that their conversion was perfectly sincere and conscientious. In all their subsequent works were seen traces of Mme. Dacier's powerful intellect, which was much superior to that of her husband. Boileau said: "In their production of *esprit*, it is Mme. Dacier who is the father."

Besides her translations of the plays of Plautus, all of Terence, the *Clouds* and *Plutus* of Aristophanes, she published her translation of the *Iliad* and *Odyssey* (1711-1716), which gave her a prominent place in the history of French literature, especially as it appeared at the time of the "quarrels of the ancients and moderns," which concerned the comparative merits of ancient and modern literature.

Mme. Dacier thoroughly appreciated the grandeur of Homer and knew the almost insurmountable difficulties of a translation; therefore, when in 1714 the *Iliad* appeared in verse (in twelve songs by La Motte-Houdart), preceded by a discourse on Homer, in which the author announced that his aim was to purify and embellish Homer by ridding him "of his barbarian crudeness, his uncivil familiarities, and his great length," the ire of Mme. Dacier was aroused, and in defence of her god she wrote her famous *Des Causes de la Corruption du Goût* (Causes of the Corruption of Taste), a long defence of Homer, to which La Motte replied in his *Réflexions de la Critique* This rekindled the whole controversy, and sides were immediately formed.

Mme. Dacier was not politic; although she sustained her ideas well and displayed much erudition and depth of reason, she is said to have injured her cause by the violence of her polemic. Her immoderate tone and bitter assaults upon the elegant and discerning favorite only detracted from his opponent's favor and grace. Voltaire said: "You could say that the work of M. de La Motte was that of a woman of *esprit*, while that of Mme. Dacier was of a *homme savant*. He translated the *Iliad* very poorly, but attacked very well." Mme. Dacier's translation remained a standard for two centuries. She and her adversary became reconciled at a dinner given by M. de Valincour for the friends of both parties; upon that festive occasion, "they drank to the health of Homer, and all was well."

Mme. Dacier died in 1720. "She was a *savante* only in her study or when with savants; otherwise, she was unaffected and agreeable in conversation, from the character of which one would never have suspected her of knowing more than the average woman." She was an incessant worker and had little time for social life; in the evening, after having worked all morning, she received visits from the literary men of France; and, to her credit may it be added, amid all her literary work, she never neglected her domestic and maternal duties.

A woman of an entirely different type from that of Mme. Dacier, one who fitly closes the long series of great and brilliant women of the age of Louis XIV., who only partly resembles them and yet does not quite take on the faded and decadent coloring of the next age, was Mme. de Caylus, the niece of Mme. de Maintenon. It was she who, partly through compulsion, partly of her own free will, undertook the rearing of the young and beautiful Marthe- Marguerite de Villette. Mme. de Maintenon was then at the height of her power, and naturally her beautiful, clever, and witty niece was soon overwhelmed by proposals of marriage from the greatest nobles of France. To one of these, M. de Boufflers, Mme. de Maintenon replied: "My niece is not a sufficiently good match for you. However, I am not insensible to the honor you pay me; I shall not give her to you, but in the future I shall consider you my nephew."

She then married the innocent young girl to the Marquis de Caylus, a debauched, worthless reprobate—a union whose only merit lay in the fact that her niece could thus remain near her at court. At the latter place, her beauty, gayety, and caustic wit, her adaptable and somewhat superficial character and her freedom of manners and speech, did not fail to attract many admirers. Her frankness in expressing her opinions was the source of her disgrace; Louis XIV. took her at her word when she exclaimed, in speaking of the court: "This place is so dull that it is like being in exile to live here," and forbade her to appear again in the place she found so tiresome. Those rash words cost her an exile of thirteen years, and only through good behavior, submission, and piety was she permitted to return.

She appeared at a supper given by the king, and, by the brilliancy of her beauty and *esprit*, she attracted everyone present and soon regained her former favor and friends. From that time she was the constant companion of Mme. de Maintenon, until the king's death, when she returned to Paris; at that place her salon became an intellectual centre, and there the traditions of the seventeenth century were perpetuated.

Sainte-Beuve said that Mme. de Caylus perfectly exemplified what was called urbanity—"politeness in speech and accent as well as in *esprit*." In her youth she was famous for her extraordinary acting in the performance, at Saint-Cyr, of Racine's *Esther*. Mme. de Sévigné wrote: "It is Mme. de Caylus who makes Esther." Her brief and witty *Souvenirs* (Memoirs), showing marvellous finesse in the art of portraiture, made her name immortal. M. Saint-Amand describes her work thus:

"Her friends, enchanted by her lively wit, had long entreated her to write— not for the public, but for them—the anecdotes which she related so well. Finally, she acquiesced, and committed to paper certain incidents, certain portraits. What a treasure are these *Souvenirs*—so fluently written, so unpretentious, with neither dates nor chronological order, but upon which, for more than a century, all historians have drawn! How much is contained in this little book which teaches more in a few lines than interminable works do in many volumes! How feminine it is, and how French! One readily understands Voltaire's liking for these charming *Souvenirs*. Who, than Mme. de Caylus, ever better applied the famous precept: 'Go lightly, mortals; don't bear too hard.'"

She belonged to that class of spontaneous writers who produce artistic works without knowing it, just as M. Jourdain wrote prose, and who do not even suspect that they possess that chief attribute of literary style—naturalness. What pure, what ready wit! What good humor, what unconstraint, what delightful ease! What a series of charming portraits, each more lifelike, more animated, still better than all the others! "These little miniatures—due to the brush of a woman of the world—are better worth studying than is many a picture or fresco."

Chapter VII

Woman in Religion

The entire religious agitation of the seventeenth century was due to women. Port-Royal was the centre from which issued all contention—the centre where all subjects were discussed, where the most important books were written or inspired, where the genius of that great century centred; and it was to Port-Royal that the greatest women of France went, either to find repose for their souls or to visit the noble members of their sex who had consecrated their lives to God—Mère Angélique, Jacqueline Pascal. Never in the history of the world had a religious sect or party gathered within its fold such an array of great minds, such a number of fearless and determined heroines and *esprits d'élite*. A short account of this famous convent must precede any story of its members.

The original convent, Port-Royal des Champs, near Versailles, was founded as early as 1204, by Mathieu of Montmorency and his wife, for the Cistercian nuns who had the privileges of electing their abbess and of receiving into their community ladies who, tired of the social world, wished to retire to a religious asylum, without, however, being bound by any religious vows. Later on, the sisters were permitted to receive, also, young ladies of the nobility.

These privileges were used to such advantage that the institution acquired great wealth; and through its boarders, some of whom belonged to the most important families of France, it became influential to an almost incalculable degree. For four centuries this convent had been developing liberal tendencies and gradually falling away from its primitive austerity, when, in 1605, Sister Angélique Arnauld became abbess and undertook a thorough reform. So great was her success in this direction that, after having effected similar changes at the Convent of Maubuisson and then returned to Port-Royal des Champs, the latter became so crowded that new and more commodious quarters had to be obtained.

The immense and beautiful Hôtel de Cluny, at Paris, was procured, and a portion of the community moved thither, establishing an institution which became the best known and most popular of those French convents which were patronized by women of distinction. The old abbey buildings near Versailles were later occupied by a community of learned and pious men who were, for the most part, pupils of the celebrated Abbé of Saint-Cyran, who, with Jansenius, was living at Paris at the time that Mère Angélique was perfecting her reforms; she, attracted by the ascetic life led by the abbé, fell under his influence, and the whole Arnauld family, numbering about thirty, followed her example.

Soon "the nuns at Paris, with their numerous and powerful connections, and the recluses at Port-Royal des Champs, together with their pupils and the noble or wealthy families to which the latter belonged, were imbued with the new doctrines of which they became apostles." The primary aim was to live up to a common ideal of Christian perfection, and to react against the general corruption by establishing thoroughly moral schools and publishing works denouncing, in strong terms, the glaring errors of the time, the source of which was considered, by both the Abbé of Saint-Cyran and Jansenius, to lie in the Jesuit Colleges and their theology. Thus was evolved a system of education in every way antagonistic to that of the Jesuits.

At this time the convent at Paris became so crowded that Mère Angélique withdrew to the abbey near Versailles, the occupants of which retired to a neighboring farm, Les Granges; there was opened a seminary for females, which soon attracted the daughters of the nobility. An astounding literary and agricultural activity resulted, both at the abode of the recluses and at the seminary: by the recluses were written the famous Greek and Latin grammars, and by the nuns, the famous *Memoirs of the History of Port-Royal* and the *Image of the Perfect and Imperfect Sister*; a model farm was cultivated, and here the peasants were taught improved methods of tillage. During the time of the civil wars the convent became a resort where charity and hospitality were extended to the poor peasants.

"The mode of life at Port-Royal was distinguished for austerity. The inmates rose at three o'clock in the morning, and, after the common prayer, kissed the ground as a sign of their self-humiliation before God. Then, kneeling, they read a chapter from the Gospels and one from the Epistles, concluding with another prayer. Two hours in the morning and a like number in the afternoon were devoted to manual labor in the gardens adjoining the convent; they observed, with great strictness, the season of Lent." Their theories and practices, and especially their sympathy with Jansenius, whose work *Mars Gallicus* attacked the French government and people, aroused the suspicions of Richelieu. When in 1640 the Port-Royalists openly and enthusiastically received the famous work, *Augustinus*, of Jansenius, the government became the declared opponent of the convent. Saint-Cyran had been imprisoned in 1638, and not until after the death of Richelieu, in 1642, was he liberated. After the appearance, in 1643, of Arnauld's *De la Fréquente Communion*, in which he attacked the Jesuits for admitting the people to the Lord's Supper without due preparation, two parties formed—the Jesuits, supported by the Sorbonne and the government, and the Port-Royalists, supported by Parliament and illustrious persons, such as Mme. de Longueville.

In 1644, the nuns were dispersed by order of Louis XIV., against whose despotic caprices two Jansenist bishops had fought in support of the rights of the pope. The Paris convent remained closed until 1669, when it and the one at Chevreuse, near Versailles were made independent of each other, a proceeding which resulted in the two institutions becoming opponents. In 1708 the Convent of Port-Royal des Champs was suppressed, and, a year later, the beautiful and once prosperous community was destroyed, the buildings being levelled to the ground. In 1780 the Paris convent was abolished; five years later the structure was converted into a hospital, and in 1814 it became the lying-in asylum of *La Maternité*.

In those two convents, which were practically one, was fomented and developed the entire religious movement of the seventeenth century, to which period belong the general study and development of theology, metaphysics, and morality. Such great, good, and brilliant women as the Countess of Maure, Mlle. de Vandy, Anne de Rohan, Mme. de Brégy, Mme. de Hautefort, Mme. de Longueville, Mme. de Sévigné, Mme. de La Fayette, and Mme. de Sablé were inmates of Port-Royal, or its friends and constant visitors.

Port-Royal may have been the cause of the civil war waged by the Frondists against the government. It did bring on the struggle between the Jesuits, who were all-powerful in the Church, and the Jansenists. The latter denied the doctrine of free will, and taught the absolutism of religion, the "terrible God," the powerlessness of kings and princes before God—a doctrine which brought down upon them the wrath of Louis XIV., for whom their notion of virtue was too severe, their use of the Gospel too excessive, and their Christianity impossible.

In its purest form, Port-Royalism was a return to the sanctity of the primitive church—an attempt at the use, in French, of the whole body of Scriptures and the writings of the Church Fathers; it aimed to maintain a vigorous religious reaction in the shape of a reform, and that reform was vigorously opposed by the Catholic Church.

One family that is associated with Port-Royal gave to its cause no less than six sisters; the latter all belonged to the Convent of Port-Royal and were attached to the Jansenist party; of them, the Archbishop of Paris said that they were "as pure as angels, but as proud as devils." They were related to the one great Arnauld family, of which Antoine and his three sons—Robert, Henri, and the younger Antoine, called "the great Antoine"—were illustrious champions of Port-Royal.

Marie Jacqueline Angélique, the oldest among the three abbesses, was born in 1591, and, at the early age of fourteen, was made abbess of Port-Royal des Champs; it was she who, after having instituted successful reforms at Port-Royal, was sent to reform the system of the Abbey of Maubuisson, thus initiating the important movement which later involved almost all France. She became convinced that she had not been lawfully elected abbess and resigned, securing, however, a provision which made the election of abbesses a triennial event. To her belongs the honor of having made Port-Royal anew. She was a woman capable of every sacrifice,—a wonderful type in which were blended candor, pride, and submission,—and she exhibited indomitable strength of will and earnest zeal for her cause.

Her sister, Agnes, but three years younger than Marie, also entered the convent, and, at the age of fifteen, was made mistress of the novices; during the absence of her sister, at Maubuisson, she was at the head of the convent; from that time, she governed Port-Royal alternately with her sister, for twenty-seven years. Her work, *The Secret Chapter of the Sacrament*, was suppressed at Rome, but without bringing formal censure upon her.

The last of those great abbesses was Mère Angélique, who lived through the most troublous and critical times of Port-Royal (1624 to 1684). At the age of twenty she became a nun, having been reared in the convent by her aunt, Marie, who was the most perfect disciple of Saint-Cyran. Mère Angélique was especially conspicuous for her obstinacy, and when the nuns were forced to accept the formulary of Pope Alexander VI., she, alone, was excepted, because of that well known characteristic. Upon the reopening of Port-Royal (in 1689), her powerful protectress, Mme. de Longueville, died and the persecutions were renewed; Mère Angélique endeavored to avert the storm, but all in vain; amidst her efforts, she collapsed. She was also a writer, her *Memoirs of the History of Port Royal* being the most valuable history of that institution.

Thus, about those three women is formed the religious movement which involved both the development of religious liberty, free will, and morality, and of the philosophical literature of the century—a century which boasts such writers and theologians as Nicole, Pascal, Racine, etc.

The mission of Port-Royal seems to have been preparation of souls for the struggles of life, teaching how to resist oppression or to bear it with courage, and how, for a righteous cause, to brave everything, not only the persecutions of power—violence, prison, exile,—but the ruses of hypocrisy and the calumny of opposing opinion. The Port-Royalist nun combated and taught how to combat; she lacked humility, but possessed an abundance of courage which often bordered upon passion.

One of the most pathetic and striking illustrations of the fervent devotion which was a characteristic product of Port-Royal, is supplied by Jacqueline Pascal, sister of the great Blaise Pascal. Young, *spirituelle*, very much sought after and the idol of brilliant companions, at the age of twenty-six she abandoned the world to devote herself to God. At thirty-six years of age she died of sorrow and remorse for having signed an equivocal formulary of Pope Alexander VI., "through pure deference to the authority of her superiors." The papal decision concerning Jansenius's book, already mentioned, was drawn up in a formula "turned with some skill, and in such a way that subscription did not bind the conscience; however, the nuns of Port-Royal refused to sign." Jacqueline Pascal wrote:

"That which hinders us, what hinders all the ecclesiastics who recognize the truth from replying when the formulary is presented to them to subscribe is: I know the respect I owe the bishops, but my conscience does not permit me to subscribe that a thing is in a book in which I have not seen it—and after that, wait for what will happen. What have we to fear? Banishment and dispersion for the nuns, seizure of temporalities, imprisonment, and death if you will; but is not that our glory and should it not be our joy? Let us either renounce the Gospel or faithfully follow the maxims of that Gospel and deem ourselves happy to suffer somewhat for righteousness' sake. I know that it is not for daughters to defend the truth, though, unfortunately, one might say that since the bishops have the courage of daughters, the daughters must have the courage of bishops; but, if it is not for us to defend the truth, it is for us to die for the truth and to suffer everything rather than abandon it."

She subscribed, "divided between her instinctive repugnance and her desire to show herself an humble daughter of the Catholic Church." She said: "It is all we can concede; for the rest, come what may,—poverty, dispersion, imprisonment, death,—all those seem to me nothing in comparison with the anguish in which I should pass the remainder of my life, if I had been wretch enough to make a covenant with death on the occasion of so excellent an opportunity for proving to God the sincerity of the vows of fidelity which our lips have pronounced." According to Mme. Périer, the health of the writer of the above epistle was so undermined by the shock which all that commotion had caused her, that she became dangerously ill, dying soon after. Thus was sacrificed the first victim of the formulary.

Cousin says that few women of the seventeenth century were as brilliantly endowed as Jacqueline Pascal; possessing the finesse, energy, and sobriety of her brother, she was capable of the most serious work, and yet knew perfectly how to lead in a social circle. Also, she was most happily gifted with a talent for poetry, in relation to which her reputation was everywhere recognized; at the convent, she consulted her superiors as to the advisability of continuing her verse making; and upon being told that such occupation was not a means of winning the grace of Jesus Christ, she abandoned it.

Cousin maintained that the avowed principle of the Port-Royalists was the withdrawal from all worldly pleasure and attachment. "'Marriage is a homicide; absolute renunciation is the true régime of a Christian.' Jacqueline Pascal is an exaggeration of Port-Royal, and Port-Royal is an exaggeration of the religious spirit of the seventeenth century. Man is too little considered; all movement of the physical world comes from God; all our acts and thoughts, except those of crime and error, come from and belong to Him. Nothing is our own; there is no free will; will and reason have no power. The theory of grace is the source of all truth, virtue, and merit—and for this doctrine Jacqueline Pascal gives up her life."

Among the great spirits of Port-Royal, the women especially were strong in their convictions and high in their ideals. They naturally followed the ideas of man and naturally fell into religious errors; but their firmness, constancy, and heroism were striking indeed. Their aspiration was the imitation of Christ, and they approached their model as near as ever was done by man. In an age of courtesans, when convictions were subservient to the pleasure of power, they set a worthy example of strength of mind, firmness of will, purity, and womanliness. M. du Bled says:

"Port-Royal was the enterprise of the middle-class aristocracy of France; you can see here an anticipated attempt of a sort of superior third estate to govern for itself in the Church and to establish a religion not Roman, not aristocratic and of the court, not devout in the manner of the simple people, but freer from vain images and ceremonies, and freer, also, as to the temporal in the face of worldly authority—a sober, austere, independent religion which would have truly founded a Gallican reform. The illusion was in thinking that they could continue to exist in Rome—that Richelieu and Louis XIV. would tolerate the boldness of this attempt."

A celebrated woman of the seventeenth century, one who really belongs to the circle of Mme. de Longueville and Mme. de La Fayette, but who early in life, like Mme. de Longueville, devoted herself to religion and retired to live at Port-Royal, and is therefore more intimately associated with the religious movement, was Mme. de Sablé, a type of the social-religious woman.

Mme. de Sablé is a heroine of Cousin, whom we closely follow in this account of her career. According to that writer, she is a type of the purely social woman, a woman who did less for herself than for others, in aiding whom she took delight, a woman who was the inspiration of many writers and many works.

Mlle. de Souvré married the wealthy Marquis of Sablé, of the house of Montmorency, of whom little is known. He soon abandoned her; and she, most unhappy over unworthy rivals, fell very ill, retired from society for a time, and then reappeared; her career as a society woman then began. At an early age, by force of her decided taste for the high form of Spanish gallantry, then so much in vogue, and her inclination to all things intellectual, she became one of the leaders of the Hôtel de Rambouillet. She, Mmes. de Sévigné, de Longueville, and de La Fayette formed that circle of women who idealized friendship.

Within a few years she lost her father, husband, two of her brothers, and her second son; and after putting her financial affairs into order, she and her friend, the Countess of Maure, took up their quarters at the famous Place Royale; there they decided to devote their lives to letters, and there assembled their friends, men and women, regardless of rank or party, personal merit being the only means of access. Mmes. de Sablé and de Rambouillet were called the arbiters of elegance and good taste.

To her friends, Mme. de Sablé was always accommodating and showed no partiality; well informed, she was constantly approached for counsel and favors; discreet and trustworthy, the most important secrets were intrusted to her—a confidence which she never betrayed. During the Fronde she remained faithful to the queen and Mazarin, but did not become estranged from her friends, so many of whom were Frondists, and who chose her as their counsellor, arbitrator, and pacifier.

About 1655 she began to realize her unsettled position in the world and to long for a place where she might, modestly and becomingly, spend her declining years. She was then fifty-five years of age. The ideas of Jansenism had so impressed the great people of the day, that she decided to retire to Port- Royal, to end her days with sympathizers of the spiritual life around her and her former friends whenever she desired them. There she gathered about her the most exclusive and aristocratic people of the day: La Rochefoucauld, the Prince and Princess of Conti, Condé, Monsieur,—brother of Louis XIV.,— Mme. de La Fayette, Mme. de Hautefort, and others.

At her apartments, not only were religious and literary affairs discussed, but the most delicate and delicious dishes were prepared and elixirs and remedies for disease compounded. Famous people were led to seek her, through her reputation and influence, and through friendship, for she seldom left her house. Mme. de Sablé possessed all the qualities that attract and hold, nothing extraordinary or rare, but abundant politeness and elegance.

It was not long before she began to withdraw from even her friends, still continuing, however, her fine cuisine, the remarkable care of her health, and her medical experiments. Her dinners became celebrated, and invitations to them were much in demand; about them there were no signs of opulence, but her gatherings were distinguished for refinement and taste. Her friends were constantly asking her for her recipes, of the preparation of which no one but herself knew the secret.

At the salon of Mme. de Sablé originated many famous literary works, such as the *Conférences sur le Calvinisme*, works on Cartesian philosophy, the *Logique de Port-Royal*, *Questions sur l'Amour*, *Les Maximes*, etc. She will be remembered as the initiator of many maxims, in the composition of which she excelled. A number of her sayings concerning friendship have been preserved. Two treatises, in the form of maxims, on the education of children and on friendship, respectively, are supposed to have come from her pen; from them La Rochefoucauld conceived the ideas he utilized in his famous *Maxims*.

La Rochefoucauld's maxims were composed according to the chance of conversation, which gave rise to various subjects and led to his serious reflection upon them. Cousin even goes so far as to say that the *Pensées* of Pascal would never have been published in that form had not the *Maxims* enjoyed such favor. Pascal often visited Port-Royal and naturally followed the general reflective tendency of its society. His *Discours sur les Passions de l'Amour* possibly originated at the salon of Mme. de Sablé, because the subject of which that work treated was one much discussed there. La Rochefoucauld was in the habit of sending his maxims to Mme. de Sablé with the message: "As you do nothing for nothing, I ask of you a carrot soup or mutton stew."

When La Rochefoucauld entered the society of Mme. de Sablé, he had seen much of life, was familiar with most of the adventures and intrigues of the Fronde and the society of the time; he himself had acted his part in all, and at the age of fifty was ready to put his experience into a permanent form of reflection. His *Maxims* created a stir, through the clearness and elegance of their character, their fine analyses of man as he was in the seventeenth century, and through their truthfulness and general applicability to men of every country. From all the illustrious women of the day, either he or Mme. de Sablé received letters of criticism or suggestion—eulogies and condemnations of which he took notice in his next edition. This shows the intense interest felt in the appearance of any new literary production.

Cousin says that the whole literature of maxims and reflections issued directly from the salon of a kind and good woman who had retired to a convent with no other desire than to live over her life, to recall her past and what she had seen and felt therein; and upon her society, that woman impressed her own tastes, elegance, and seriousness. Her great act of benevolence was her protection of Port-Royal. When, after the death in 1661 of Mother Angélique Arnauld, that institution became the object of persecution and its tenants were either imprisoned or compelled to seek refuge in the various families of Paris, Mme. de Sablé remained faithful to its principles; she lived with her friends,

Mme. de Longueville and Mme. de Montausier, until 1669, when, with the coöperation of Mme. de Longueville, who exerted all her influence for Port-Royal, she finally succeeded in bringing about its reopening. At least, Cousin ascribes this result to Mme. de Sablé, but he may have somewhat exaggerated her influence in this respect. From her retreat at Port-Royal, she kept up a constant correspondence with her friends all over France; she lived there until 1678, with but one intimate friend, Mme. de Longueville.

Mme. de Sablé had remarkable gifts; her mission in politics, religion, and literature seems to have been to excite to action, to stimulate and to bring out to its fullest value, the talents and genius of others. In her modest salon, she inspired the great and illustrious work which will keep her memory alive as long as the *Maxims* and *Pensées* are read. Her name will be connected with that of Mme. de Longueville, because of their ideal friendship, and with that of Port-Royal because of her ardent and self-sacrificing support of it in the time of its direst persecution, when any exhibition of sympathy was dangerous in the extreme; and finally, her name will always be connected with that small circle of French society of the seventeenth century, which was noble, moral, and elevating to an unusual degree.

Somewhat later in the century a different movement was started by a woman, which involved many of the highest in rank at court. This took the form of a kind of mystical enthusiasm, running into a theory of pure love, and was instigated by Mme. Guyon, a widow, still young, and gifted with a lofty and subtile mind. After losing her husband, whom she had converted to her religious views, she went, in 1680, to Paris to educate her children. Becoming interested in religion, she went to Geneva, where she became very intimate with a priest who was her spiritual director, and whom she soon wholly subjected to her influence. On account of their views on sanctification, they were ordered to leave.

After travelling over Europe for a number of years, and writing several works, including *Spiritual Torrents* and *Short and Easy Method of Making Orison with the Heart*, the widow returned to Paris, with the intention of living in retirement; but so many persons of all ranks sought her out, that she organized, for ladies of rank, meetings for purposes of prayer and religious conversation. The Duchess of Beauvilliers, the Duchess of Béthune, the Countess of Guiche, the Countess of Chevreuse, and many others, with their husbands, became her devoted adherents.

According to Mme. Guyon, prayer should lose the character of supplication, and become simply the silence of a soul absorbed in God. "Why are not simple folks so taught? Shepherds, keeping their flocks, would have the spirit of the old anchorites; and laborers, whilst driving the plow, would talk happily with God. In a little while, vice would be banished and the kingdom of God would be realized on earth." Thus, her doctrine was directly opposite to the theories of the Jansenists.

At that time, 1687 to 1688, all religious movements, however quiet, were condemned at Rome; and the teachings of Mme. Guyon were found to differ very little from those of the Spanish priest Molinas. The first arrest, that of her friend Lacombe, was soon followed by that of Mme. Guyon herself, by royal order; she was released through the intercession of Mme. de Maintenon, who was fascinated by her to the extent of permitting her to teach her doctrines at Saint-Cyr, Upon the appearance of her *Method of Prayer*, an examination was instituted by Bossuet and Fénelon, who marked out a few passages as erroneous—a procedure to which she submitted. However, Bossuet himself wrote a treatise against her *Method of Prayer*, in which he cast reflections upon her character and conduct; to that work Fénelon refused to subscribe, which antagonistic proceeding brought on the great quarrel between those two absolute ecclesiasts. In fact, Fénelon became imbued with the doctrines of Mme. Guyon.

She was imprisoned at various times; and when a letter was received from Lacombe, who had been imprisoned at Vincennes for a long time, exhorting her to repent of their criminal intimacy, Mme. Guyon's cause was hopeless. She was sent to the Bastille, her son was dismissed from the army, and many of her friends were banished. In 1702 she was released from prison and banished to Diziers; she passed the remainder of her life in complete retirement at Blois.

Fénelon had written a treatise, *Maxims of the Saints*, which was said to favor Mme. Guyon's doctrines, and which was sent to Rome for examination. He defined her doctrine of divine love in the following maxim, which was condemned at Rome:

"There is an habitual state of love of God, which is pure charity without any taint of the motive of self-interest. Neither fear of punishment nor desire of reward has, any longer, part in this love; God is loved, not for the merit, but for the happiness to be found in loving Him."

Such a doctrine made repentance unnecessary, destroyed all effort to withstand evil, and did not acknowledge the need of a Redeemer. This the great Bossuet foresaw; consequently, he, as the supreme religious potentate of his inferior in rank, Fénelon, demanded the condemnation by the latter of the works of Mme. Guyon. The refusal cost Fénelon exile for life. To Mme. de Maintenon he wrote a letter which shows the sincerity of his devotion to a friend in disgrace, even though his own reputation was thereby endangered:

"So it is to secure my own reputation that I am wanted to subscribe that a lady —my friend—would plainly deserve to be burned, with all her writings, for an execrable form of spirituality which is the only bond of our friendship. I tell you, madame, I would burn my friend with my own hands, and I would burn myself joyfully, rather than let the Church be imperilled; but here is a poor, captive woman, overwhelmed with sorrows; there is none to defend her, none to excuse her; all are afraid to do so. I maintain that this stroke of the pen, given from a cowardly policy and against my conscience, would render me forever infamous and unworthy of my ministry and my position."

Thus, in the seventeenth century, religious agitations and religious reform were the work preëminently of women; but that reform and those agitations were productive of good results to a far greater degree than was any similar movement in any other century, with the possible exception of the nineteenth. The seventeenth century was, as mentioned before, a century of stability, one that toned down and crushed all violations and abuses of the standard established by authority. Woman, in her constant striving for the complete emancipation and gradual purification of her sex, rebelled against the power of established authority; she did not consciously or intentionally violate law and order, but in her intense desire to act for good as she saw it, and in her noble efforts to ameliorate all undesirable conditions, she created commotion and confusion. The seventeenth-century woman is conspicuous as a champion of religion, moral purity, and social reform; therefore, her influence was mainly social, religious, moral, and literary, while that of the woman of the sixteenth century was mainly political. This difference was the result of the greater advantages of education and training enjoyed by the females of the later period.

In the beginning of the seventeenth century, young girls were granted greater privileges and received more attention from men and society than did their predecessors; they thus had more opportunities for mental development, more occasion to become aware of the temptations and injustices of life, without falling prey to them. Such young girls as Julie d'Angennes, Mlle. d'Arquenay, and Mlle. de Pisani, took part in the balls, fêtes, garden parties, and all amusements in which society indulged. They met young men of their own age and became intimately acquainted with them, morals were purer, marriages of affection were much more frequent, and the state of married life was much more congenial, than in any other century. Young men paid court to the older ladies, to refine their manners and sharpen their intellects, but not for any immoral purpose. To a certain extent women were more world-wise when they reached the marriageable age, and inspired respect and admiration rather than passion and desire as in the next century.

Young girls of the seventeenth century were early placed in a convent, and when they left it they were ready for marriage; in the meantime, they frequently visited home and associated with their parents and brothers; at the convents intellectual intercourse with people of high rank and men of letters was encouraged. Yet the discipline at those institutions was very rigid, the boarders being more carefully watched then than later on; two nuns always accompanied them on their walks, and when not busy with their studies, to prevent the mind from wandering, they were kept busy with their hands; "the transports of the soul of the young girl, as every reflection of the intelligence, are watched and held in check, every one of her inclinations opposed, all originality suppressed."

At first the convents were reproached for stifling all culture and development and applying only correction and mortification of the flesh. Mme. de Maintenon opposed such a state of affairs, but her methods discouraged true independence. The happiness of her charges was her one aim, but they had no voice in the matter. When of marriageable age, they were given a trousseau and a husband; however, they were taught to be reasonable.

In that century, the young girl, mixing more generally in society, received greater consideration—hence, she became more active and conspicuous. It will be seen that the rôle played by the eighteenth century woman was not so much played by the young woman as it was by the woman of mature years, of the mother, the counsellor—the indispensable element of society. There were three classes of women—young women, mature women who sought consideration, and old women who received respect and deference, and who, as arbiters of culture, upheld the principles already established.

A young man making his début had to find favor with one of those classes which decided his future reputation and the extent of his favor at court, and assigned him his place and grade, upon which depended his marriage. All education was directed to the one end—social success. The duty of the tutor charged with the instruction of a young son was to give a well-rounded, general education; by the mother, he was taught politeness, grace, amiability —a part of his training to which more importance was attached than to the intellectual portion. Whenever a young man was guilty of misconduct toward a woman, his mother was notified of the occurrence, on the same evening, and he promptly received his reprimand. This spirit naturally fostered that rare politeness, exquisite taste and tact in conversation, in which the eighteenth century excels.

But where did the young girls receive the education which gave them such prestige—that consummate art of conversation exemplified in Mme. de Boufflers, Mme. de Luxembourg, Mme. de Sabran, the Duchess of Choiseul, the Princess of Beauvau, the Countess of Ségur? The sons were educated in the usages of the *bonne compagnie* by the mothers, but the daughters did not enjoy that attention, for, at the age of five or six years, they were sent to the convent; there the mother's influence could not have reached them, and they never left the convent except to marry. The middle class imitated the higher class, and family life became practically impossible. All men of any importance had a charge at court or a grade in the army, and lived away from their families. A large number of women were attached to the queen, spending the greater part of their time at Versailles; the little time passed at their homes was entirely occupied in preparation for the evening *causeries* at the salons, in reading new books, acquiring information upon current events, and in superintending the making of the many necessary and always elaborate gowns; as M. Perey so well says, "as the toilettes and hairdressing took up the greater part of the morning, they devoted the time used by the *coiffeur*, in constructing complicated edifices that crushed down the heads of women, to the reading of new books."

Nearly every large establishment kept open house, dining from twenty to thirty persons every day. They dined at one, separated at three, were at the theatre at five, and returned with as many friends as possible—the more, the greater the reputation for hospitality and popularity. Under such circumstances, the mother had no time for the daughters, nor were the conversations at those dinners food for young, innocent girls—and innocence was the first requirement of a marriageable young woman.

The great convents were the Abbaye-aux-Bois and Penthemont, where the daughters of the wealthiest and highest families were educated. In those convents or seminaries, strange to say, the young girls were taught the most practical domestic duties, as well as dancing, music, painting, etc. Such teachers as Molé and Larrive gave instruction in declamation and reading, and Noverre and Dauberval in dancing; the teaching nuns were all from the best families. The most complete costumes, scenic decorations, and other equipments of a complete theatre were supplied, special hours being set aside for the play. However, much intriguing went on there, and many friendships and lifelong enmities were formed, which later led to serious troubles.

Often, from the midst of a group of young girls of from ten to fifteen years of age, one would be notified of her coming marriage with a man she had never seen, and whom, in all probability, she could not love, having given her heart to another. If it turned out to be an uncongenial marriage, a separate life would be the result, and, while still absolutely ignorant of the world, those young married women would fall prey to the charms of young gallants or men of quality, and a liaison would follow.

The difference between a liaison of the seventeenth century and one of the eighteenth led to one essential difference in the standards of social and moral etiquette; in the former period, a liaison meant nothing more censurable than an intimate friendship, a purely platonic love; the lover simply paid homage to the lady of his choice; it was an attraction of common intellectual interests and usually lasted for life; in the eighteenth century, a liaison was essentially immoral, rarely a union of interests, but rather one of passions and physical propensities. Such relations developed and fostered deceit, intrigues, infidelity, and rivalry, one woman endeavoring to allure the lover of another; affairs of that nature were the chief topic of conversation in social circles, and were soon reflected in every phase of the intelligent world. This will be seen in the study of the eighteenth century.

Chapter VIII

Salon Leaders
Mme. de Tencin, Mme. Geoffrin, Mme. du Deffand, Mlle. de Lespinasse, Mme. du Châtelet

In studying the vast numbers of salons of the eighteenth century, three types are discernible, each of which was prominent and in full sway throughout the century up to the Revolution. To the first class belong the great literary and philosophical salons which, though not political in nature, finally changed politics; such were the circles of Mme. de Tencin, Mme. Geoffrin, Mme. du Deffand, Mlle. de Lespinasse, Mme. Necker, Mme. d'Epinay, Mme. de Genlis; with these every literary student is familiar. The second class includes the smaller and less important literary, philosophical, and social salons—those of Mme. de Marchais, Mme. de Persan, Mme. de Villars, Mme. de Vaines, and of D'Alembert, D'Holbach, Helvétius. The third class is of a social nature exclusively, good breeding and good tone being the essentials; its conspicuous features were the dinners and suppers of Suard, Saurin, the Abbés Raynal and Morellet, of the Palais-Royal of Mme. de Blot, of the Temple of the Prince of Conti, those of Mme. de Beauvau, Mme. de Gramont, M. de La Popeliniére, and others.

The distinctions thus made will not hold throughout, but they facilitate the presentation of a subject that is exceedingly complicated. It may almost be said that each generation of the eighteenth century had a salon with a different physiognomy; those of 1710, 1730, 1760, and 1780 were all inspired by different motives, causes, and events, and were all led by women of different histories and aspirations, whose common idol was man, but whose ideas of what constituted a hero were as widely different as was the constitution of society in the respective periods. Not until the middle of the reign of Louis XIV. did social life become detached from Versailles, and, spreading out and circulating in a thousand hôtels, showed itself in all its force, splendor, and elegance. The celebrated women of the regency—Mme. de Prie, Mme. de Parabère, Mme. de Sabran—had no salon, while those of the Marquis d'Alluys and the Hôtels de Sully, de Duras, de Villars, and the suppers of Mme. de Chauvelin were of a distinctly different type from those of the earlier and the later periods.

In a certain sense, the salons changed the complexion of the age. The eighteenth century itself was friendly and generous; it was, also, impatient and inexperienced, seeing things not as they were but as it wished them to be, compelling science and art to serve its purpose. It was frank, often brutally frank, a characteristic due partly to the conversational license of the salons. With its Fontenelle, Voltaire, Piron, etc., it was indeed a happy century. A *bon mot* was the event of the day and travelled over all the civilized world.

Feeling keenly the need of a guiding principle, the need of a more substantial foundation in education, the women of the century thought and wrote much on that subject; such was, for the most part, the work of the great salons, but in them the philosophical tenets of the age were also discussed. The spirit of criticism thus created and cultivated, which finally spread through all classes of society, gradually conquered the new power in the state—public opinion which, at the end of the century, ruled supreme in all its strength and vehemence, defying every effort of the government to stifle it. The highest form of agreeable and intellectual society which the world has ever seen attained to its most complete development in these salons.

Every century has had its specialty: the twelfth had its crusades, the sixteenth its religious struggles, the seventeenth its grand *goût*, the eighteenth its conversation and love of reason, the nineteenth its political struggles; and each one displayed the French passion for *esprit*; the eighteenth, however, was, *par excellence*, the century of *esprit*, and it was most remarkably developed in woman.

"Such astonishingly loquacious people as lived in Paris in the eighteenth century! ineffective, sardonic, verbose, sociable, intellectual, elegant, immoral —grand gentlemen and ladies, with tears for mimic woes and none for actual ones, praise for wit, rewards for cleverness, and absolute ignorance of the destinies they were preparing for themselves;" such is the story of women and society of the eighteenth century. Among these women the salon leaders will be found the most attractive, and the most influential in literature, theory of government, and social and moral development; to the mistresses belongs the title of "politicians."

La Ménagerie de Mme. de Tencin was one of the earliest of the eighteenth-century salons, although, in the strict sense of the word, Mme. de Tencin's salon was of a political rather than a literary nature. Successively nun, mistress, mother, she was one of the shrewdest women of the century. Born in 1681, she early became a nun; but such was the character of her life at the convent that it was not long before she became a mother. In 1714 she abandoned her conventual life and went to Paris, where she rose to influence as the mistress of Cardinal Dubois and of the regent, the Duke of Orléans. At Paris her real activity began; she arrived at that gay capital with no other collateral than a pretty face and an extraordinary cunning, which soon brought her a fortune. Fertile in resources of all kinds, she succeeded immediately, and gained for her nephew the cardinal's hat. In 1717 was born to her the afterward famous d'Alembert, whom she left upon the steps of the church Saint-Jean-le-Rond; afterward, when he had become eminent and her power was waning, she unsuccessfully used every means at her command to gain his favor and recognition; the father of that child was the Chevalier Destouches.

About 1726, when lovers were numerous and friends plentiful, the death of Lafresnaye occurred at her salon. In his testament he stated that his death was caused by Mme. de Tencin; however, she was too shrewd, cunning, and careful to be guilty of permitting any weak points to appear in her plots, and it was not difficult for her to clear herself of that charge by the verdict of the judges, who considered the accusation a posthumous vengeance.

The great literary men whom Mme. de Tencin gathered about her, Fontenelle, Montesquieu, Mairan, Marivaux, Helvétius, Marmontel, were called her menagerie, or her *bêtes*. Among them, Marivaux received a pension of one thousand écus from her, besides drawing at will upon the exchequer of an old maid by the name of Saint-Jean. Marmontel, desirous of writing tragedies, took lessons from the famous Mlle. Clairon—at his friend's expense. To give a correct idea of the character of woman's influence upon the literary style of that century, the words of Marmontel may be quoted: "He who wishes to write with precision, energy, and vigor, may live with man only; but he who in his style wishes to have subtleness, amenity, charm, flexibility, will do well, I think, to live with woman."

Mme. de Tencin exerted an immense influence upon the men of her circle, especially socially; for example, she married the wealthy M. de La Popelinière to Mlle. Dancourt. She was one of the few really consummate diplomats; later on, she became less associated with intrigues, and gave lessons in current diplomacy, with which she was perfectly familiar. Her counsel to her pupils was to gain friends among women rather than among men. "For," she would say, "we do whatever we wish with men; they are so dissipated, or so preoccupied with their personal interests, that to give attention to them would be to neglect your own interests."

Every New Year's Day the *bêtes* of her menagerie received two yards of velvet, to make knickerbockers to be worn at her receptions; this custom was observed up to the last year of the existence of her salon. Her receptions were among the first of the kind in France. Like the majority of salon leaders, she was an authoress of no mean ability. Her novels were widely read at the time —*Le Siège de Calais* and *Les Malheurs de l'Amour*. Her memoirs, throwing light upon the intrigues and plots, social animosities, and general state of the society of the time, are historically valuable. She died in Paris, in 1749.

Among all the great salons, that of Mme. de Tencin was the only one in which gambling was indulged in on a wholesale scale; fortunes changed hands every evening, a large part of the gains always falling to the lot of the hostess, as a sort of "rake off." She herself was a professional at the business, and by receiving private information from headquarters, through her famous friend Law, the *contrôleur-général*, and her lover Dubois, she was able to acquire an immense fortune which she distributed freely among her friends and favorites. Her place among the literary salon leaders depends mainly upon her endeavors to advance the interests of the aspiring young authors who were willing to place themselves under her protection.

After the death of Mme. de Tencin and that of Mme. de Châtelet, who had received many of the celebrities of the time, there remained but two distinguished, purely literary and philosophical salons open in Paris. By right of precedence, the *bêtes* should have gone over to the salon of Mme. du Deffand, as she had been established some years when Mme. Geoffrin began to receive at her residence, which gained its first renown through the exquisite dinners served there. But the *bêtes* all flocked to the *salon bourgeois*, and consequently a more brilliant gathering never assembled in a salon; here sat, enjoying the liberal hospitalities, Fontenelle, Montesquieu, Mairan, Marmontel, Helvétius, Diderot, D'Alembert, Thomas, D'Holbach, Hume, Morellet, Mlle. de Lespinasse, the Marquis de Duras, Comtesses d'Egmont and de Brionne. Here, conversation—which, in the eighteenth century, was not only a discussion or a dissertation, but an art—reached its highest development; the members did not need to be eloquent, to expatiate upon some theory or science; the conversation moved about the members, and they had to be a part of it.

Mme. Geoffrin was born in Paris in 1699, and was the daughter of M. Rodet, *valet de chambre* of the dauphiness, Duchesse de Bourgogne, mother of Louis XV. When barely fifteen she was married to the wealthy M. Geoffrin, the so-called founder of the celebrated *Manufacture des Glaces de Gobelins*. Through his wealth and his associations with people of nobility who bought his ware, she was soon encouraged in her desire to entertain the nobility; and her *esprit*, tact, intelligence, and admirable taste in dress were all effective in bringing about the desired results.

Her career was one of continual successes. When she opened her salon, in 1741, she instituted the custom of receiving her friends at table, not only men of letters, but artists, architects, builders, painters, sculptors, all men of genius and prominence. Monday was the day reserved for artists exclusively; Marmontel, who lived with Mme. Geoffrin for ten years "as her tenant," and the indispensable Abbé Morellet were the exceptions who might be present upon that day. From the very beginning she formed the habit of permitting conversation to go just so far, then cutting it off with her famous: *Voil qui est bien!*

Her husband was the *maître d'hôtel*, of whom many interesting anecdotes are told; the best and one that illustrates well the appreciation of individuals in those days is the following, which is so admirably told by Lady Jackson that we quote from her: "For some years, there sat at the bottom of Mme. Geoffrin's dinner and supper table a dignified-looking, white-haired old gentleman, bland in manner, but very modest and retiring, speaking only when spoken to, but looking very happy when the guests seemed to enjoy the good cheer set before them. When, at last, his customary place became vacant, and some brilliant butterfly of madame's circle of *visiteurs flottants*, who, perhaps, had smiled patronizingly upon the silent old gentleman, becoming aware of his absence, would, perchance, carelessly inquire what had become of her constant dinner guest, madame would reply: *Mais, c'était mon mari. Hélas! il est mort, le bon homme.* [Why, that was my husband! alas, he is dead, poor man!] Just so little was the consideration shown this worthy creature in his own house! Yet it both pleased and amused him to sit there silently and gaze at the throng of rank, fashion, and learning, assembled in his wife's salon, and to witness her social success."

After the death of Mme. Geoffrin's husband, the immense fortune passed under her own management, whereupon began her real career as a social arbitress, during which she is said to have tempered both opinions and characters. Thomas said of her that "she was, in morals, like that divinity of the ancients which maintained or reëstablished limits." She was a great patroness of arts and her rooms were decorated with pictures by Vanloo, Greuze, Vernet, Robert, etc. She and her salon became, in time, the acknowledged judge and dictator of matters literary and artistic. Whenever a financier wished to purchase a certain work of art, it was taken to her Monday dinner, where the artists determined its artistic value and fixed the price. Her house was a real museum; there the precious Mariette collection was on permanent exhibition.

Besides her Monday dinners to artists and her Wednesday dinners to the literary world, she gave private luncheons to a select few who were especially congenial. At those functions, such celebrities as the Comtesses d'Egmont and de Brionne, the Marquise de Duras, and the Prince de Rohan were frequent guests.

Mme. Geoffrin was shrewd and tactful enough to avoid politics and not to permit discussions of a political nature at her salon—precautions which she observed to keep the government from interfering with her fortune and mode of living. Her salon and dinners became so famous that every foreigner going to Paris had the ambition to be received at Mme. Geoffrin's; when any aspirant was successful in this, she would say to her friends: *Soyons aimables* [Let us be kind]. She spent freely of her immense fortune constantly seeking and aiding the poor. Persons who refused to accept her charity found little favor with her; Rousseau was one of these. It was her habit to go frequently to see friends, merely to ascertain their wants and to satisfy them. The Abbé Morellet, Thomas, D'Alembert, and Mlle. de Lespinasse (the only lady admitted to her Wednesdays) were given liberal pensions. Upon each New Year's Day, in commemoration of Mme. de Tencin, she sent each Wednesday guest a velvet cap. Her motto was: *Donner et pardonner* [Give and forgive].

Stanislas, King of Poland, her *protégé*, whom she had rescued from the debtor's prison in Paris, and to whom she had shown many favors, upon being elected King of Poland in 1764, said to her: *Maman, votre fils est roi* [Mamma, your son is king]. Two years later, when she paid him a visit, the leading members of the Polish nobility met her on the road, and the king had a special residence prepared for her. As she passed through Vienna, Joseph II. received her, and the Empress Maria entertained her at dinner. Upon her return to Paris, after this triumphal tour through Europe, the members of the world of literature and art, and even the ministers and the nobility, flocked to see her; this demonstration was the more remarkable from the fact that she wielded no political influence, her only desire and pleasure seeming to lie in aiding her friends.

Mme. Geoffrin was too practical and had too much good common sense to be vain. The majority of men were influenced by and favored her, and, which seemed strange, she had few enemies among her own sex. Mme. Necker said: "The old age of Mme. Geoffrin is like that of old trees, whose age we know by the space they cover and the quantity of roots they spread. She has seen all the illustrious men of the century; she has discovered, with sagacity, their peculiarities and their defects. She judges them by their conduct, never by their talents."

In her best years, she was intimately associated with the Encyclopædists, to whom she paid over one hundred thousand francs for the publication of their work. Of all the great women of that century, she was the closest friend of the philosophers and free-thinkers, being called *La Fontenelle des Femmes*. She was always ready with an answer; one day a friend pointed out to her the house of the farmer-general Bouvet, and asked her: "Have you ever seen anything as magnificent and in better taste?" She replied: "I would have nothing to say if Bouvet were the *frotteur* [floor polisher] of it."

Mme. Geoffrin, more than any other woman of the salons, possessed the three essential qualifications of a salon leader,—good sense, tact, and intelligence. She had also *esprit*, perfect simplicity, precision, and faultless taste; though a sceptic, she was a diplomat who perfectly understood the art of manœuvring. In short, Mme. Geoffrin was an intellectual authority, a sort of minister to society, and her salon was the great centre and rendezvous, a veritable institution of the eighteenth century. This seems the more remarkable when we consider that she belonged to the bourgeoisie, and that by dint of her exquisite tact, her almost infallible judgment, her admirable taste in dress, and her keen intelligence, she created for herself a position which was the envy of all Europe. Such women are rare. During the last eighteen months of her life, though suffering from paralysis and rheumatism, which she contracted at a religious fête at Notre-Dame, she was unremitting in her attention to her friends and the poor; and up to her death, in 1777, her friends were faithful to her.

That spirit, or malady, which penetrated and ruled almost every creature in the eighteenth century found its most notable victim in Marie de Vichy-Chamrond—Mme. du Deffand. She, so to speak, yawned out her life in a blasé society without faith or ideal. That horrible affliction, with all its painful symptoms, ennui, whose origin was seen to lie in an excess and abuse of *esprit* in a society that based all its pleasures and happiness upon the mind without any higher interest than the self, infected a whole century with an "irremediable disenchantment of others and one's self." This self-cult, or life in and for the mind, developed sagacity, justness of views, and an incomparable penetration, but it neglected all the elements necessary to contentment and those other pleasures, of which the first is love for one's fellow beings. Mme. du Deffand exemplified this stage of mental unbalance; and when she wrote of her former friend and companion: "Mlle. de Lespinasse died to-day at two o'clock; formerly, that would have been an event for me; to-day, it is nothing at all," she gave an idea of the indifference which was characteristic of the society of the time—an indifference which developed into an incurable malady and an all-consuming egoism, stifling the heart-beat of that world which was weary of everything and yet was unwilling to close its eyes.

Marie de Vichy-Chamrond was born in 1697, of a noble family. She began the same manner of life as that followed by most French women, being reared in the Convent of Madeleine de Frénel, where, when quite young, she evinced a strong spirit of impiety, giving expression to the most sceptical opinions upon religious subjects, to the great dismay of her superiors and parents. At the age of twenty she was married to the Marquis du Deffand, who had but his brevet of colonel of a regiment of dragoons, and whose intelligence and fortune were of a *nullité rare*. However, her marriage was a sort of emancipation which enabled her to enter society; and it is asserted that she soon became the mistress of Philippe of Orléans, the regent, from whom she received six thousand francs life income.

As the result of a disagreement, she separated from her husband, and then began a life of pleasure among the gayest of the most fashionable world, where, through the power of her brilliancy, wit, charm, and fascinating beauty, she immediately became a leader. After passing through all the phases of social life and its varied experiences—from the society of Mme. de Prie, the type of the dissolute woman of the Regency, from the famous suppers of the regent, whose ingenious inventions of lewd and wanton pleasures made him notorious, from an association with the intriguing Duchesse de Maine, to all the great and influential social centres of Paris—in short, after pursuing a career of fashionable dissipation, she became reconciled to her husband, and lived with him in peace and happiness for a short time; but six months of regular life affected her behavior toward the poor marquis to such a degree that he thought it best to leave her. After that episode, she returned to her lover; and, rejected by him and her friends, and becoming the subject of the gossip of the entire city, she sought consolation from one acquaintance after another, and was miserable all the time.

At the age of about thirty-four, Mme. du Deffand returned to a kind of regular life, and, in time, won a reputation for *esprit*, regained her honorable friends and established for herself a kind of accepted authority. Thus, when she opened a salon in 1742, she was able to attract a brilliant company, which became famous after 1749, when she took apartments in the Convent Saint- Joseph. Here wit and polished manners, taste, vivacity, and good sense were the requisites; literature, politics, and philosophy were not tolerated, but "sparkling *bons mots*, glancing epigrams, witty verses, were the avenues to social success."

Until her dotage this woman, who, from a natural selfishness and lack of sympathy, was incapable of loving with the characteristic ardor of the women of her time, by knowing how to inspire love in others, controlled and held near her the famous men and women of her age. When she began to realize the calamity of her failing sight, which was probably due to her general state of restlessness and the resultant physical decay, she received, as companion, a relative, Mlle. de Lespinasse, who undertook the most difficult, disagreeable, and ungrateful task of waiting on the marquise. As Mme. du Deffand arose in time to receive at six, mademoiselle soon announced to the friends that herself would be visible at an earlier hour. Thus, it happened that Marmontel, Turgot, Condorcet, and d'Alembert regularly assembled in mademoiselle's room—a proceeding which soon led to a rupture between the two women and a breach between Mme. du Deffand and d'Alembert. The marquise was therefore left alone, blind, but too proud to tolerate pity, yet by her conversation retaining her power of fascination. It was about this time that Horace Walpole became connected with her life. Upon the death of Mme. Geoffrin, she, hearing of the imposing ceremonies and funeral orations, exclaimed: *Voilà bien du bruit pour une omelette au lard.* [A great ado about a lard omelet!] Her latter years were dragged out most miserably, being marked by a singular feverishness and unavailing efforts toward the acceptance of some faith. Her death, in 1780, finally brought her relief.

The career of Mme. du Deffand actually began as early as 1730, when she opened her establishment on the Rue de Beaune, at the time that she became attached to the president Hénault, who presided over her salon for more than thirty years. The famous salon Du Deffand at the Convent Saint-Joseph was not opened until 1749; there she was very particular as to those whom she received, and access to her salon was a matter of difficulty. Grimm was never received, and Diderot was present but once. The conversation was always intellectual, and whenever she tired of French vivacity, she would spend an evening with Mme. Necker.

A letter of Walpole to Montagu leaves, on the whole, a splendid picture of her: "I have heard her dispute with all sorts of people, upon all sorts of subjects, and never knew her to be in the wrong. She humbles the learned, sets right their disciples, and finds conversation for everybody. As affectionate as Mme. de Sévigné, she has none of her prejudices, but a more universal taste; and with the most delicate frame, her spirits hurry her through a life of fatigue that would kill me were I to remain here."

The simple furnishings of her apartments, which were very spacious and had been occupied by the famous Mme. de Montespan, stood out in striking contrast to the elegance of her visitors. Here she gathered about her her two lovers, *le Président* Hénault and Pont de Veyle, besides D'Alembert, Turgot, Voltaire, Montesquieu, Necker, Walpole, the Abbés Barthélemy and Pernetty, the Chevalier de Lisle, de Formant, *le Docteur* Gatti, Hume, Gibbon, Baron de Gleichen, and many other celebrities, including the Princesses de Beauvau, de Poix, de Talmont, the Duchesses de Choiseul, d'Aiguillon, de Gramont, the Maréchale de Luxembourg, the Marquises de Boufflers and du Châtelet, the Comtesses de Rochefort, de Broglie, de Forcalquier, Mme. Necker, Lady Pembroke, De Lauzun, and many others, all of whom were society leaders. Whenever Mme. du Deffand had a special supper, it was said that Paris was at Mme. du Deffand's.

Her salon, above all others, was the centre of cosmopolitanism, where all great men, foreigners and natives, found means of social intercourse, and where, more than in any other salon, were assembled the great beauties of the day, represented especially by the Countesses de Forcalquier and Choiseul-

Beaupré, Duchesse de La Vallière. Gallantry and beauty were found in the Maréchale de Luxembourg and the Comtesse de Boufflers. The philosophical movement of the Encyclopædists and Economists was not encouraged at all. Thus, in Mme. du Deffand's salon, we find neither pure philosophy nor religion, nor the air of pedants and *déclamateurs*; it was a royalist salon without illusion, hence indifferent to all questions. It represented the perfect type of the French model of *esprit de finesse*,—that is, precision,—and its leader possessed a keen insight into human character.

This wonderful woman, who, during a period of over forty years, had held at her feet the élite of the French world, at the age of about threescore and ten, fell desperately in love with a man of fifty—Horace Walpole. She who had never loved with her heart, but only with her mind, then declared it better to be dead than not to love someone. Although her actions and letters were pitiful in the extreme, her epistles are invaluable for their incomparable portraitures and keen reflections upon persons and events of the time. She attracted Walpole by the possibilities that were opened up to him by her position in society, and by her brilliant conversation, in which she scoffed at the clergy and the philosophers, showing a profound insight into human nature and the society of the time as well as into politics. Their correspondence shows one of the most pitiful, pathetic, and lamentable love tales in the history of society. He looked upon her friendship as a most valuable acquisition by which he was kept in touch with all the scandals and stories of society, of which he was so fond, and she mistook that friendship for love. He felt himself flattered in being the one preferred by such a distinguished old lady of high society.

All critics are at a loss for the explanation of such a love in a woman of seventy. Was it the result of the lifetime of disappointment of a woman who had constantly sought love but had never found it? Was it, thus, the hallucination of the childish old age of the woman who was physically consumed by incessant social functions and all-night reading? Mme. du Deffand sees in Walpole her ideal, and she gives expression to her feelings, regardless of propriety; for she is childish and irresponsible. To a certain extent, the same was true of Mme. de Staël, but she was still physically healthy and young enough to enjoy life and the realization of that which she had so long desired— an ideal affection. In the case of Mme. du Deffand, the soul was willing, but the body failed. Her emotion can scarcely be termed love, but is rather to be designated as a mental hallucination, an exaggerated intellectual affection bordering upon sentimentality—the outgrowth of that morbid imagination developed from her long suffering from ennui.

She was a woman destined to pass by the side of happiness without ever reaching it. She hardly had enjoyed what may be called friendship; she was always either suspicious of it and of her friends' sentiments, or she herself broke off relations for some trivial reason. This woman, however, always longed to believe her friends sincere, but never succeeded. "Her friends either leave her, they die, or they are far away; or, if present, faithful and attached to her, she cannot believe in their affection; her cursed scepticism deceived her heart."

Mme. du Deffand was one of the few women of the eighteenth century who saw reality and nothing but reality, and admitted what she saw; she was gifted with such quick penetration and such mental facility that she stands out prominently as one of the brightest and most intellectual of the spiritual women of her time. This quickness of perception and tendency to follow a mere impression made it difficult for her to examine closely, to be patient of details; too sure of herself, too emotional, too passionate, she displayed injustice, vehemence, over-enthusiasm; easily bored and disgusted, she was, at the same time, susceptible to infatuation. Scherer said: "She is a superior man in a body of a nervous and weak woman."

She was a woman dominated by her reason—a characteristic which led to an incurable ennui, thus causing her terrible suffering, but equipping her with a penetration which saw through the world and knew man, whom she divided into three classes: *les trompeurs, les trompés, les trompettes*. According to her judgment, man is either fatiguing or, if brilliantly endowed, usually false or jealous; but she realized, also, her own shortcomings, the incompleteness of her faculties. "The force of her thought does not reach talent; her intelligence is active and responsive, but fails to respond. She often shows a sovereign disdain for herself, everybody, and everything. She arrives at a point in life when she no longer has passion, desire, or even curiosity; she detests life, and dreads death because she does not know that there is another world. She is not happy enough to do without those whom she scorns, and must therefore seek diversion in the conversation of stupid people, preferring anything to solitude; this refers to the time when her best friends are no more and when she herself is out of her former *milieu*); she was too old, or lived too long; she belongs to another age."

By her friends she was called the feminine Voltaire, and the celebrated philosopher and she were drawn together by a very similar habit of mind, although, to her intimates, she scorched Voltaire; but in writing to him she would overwhelm him with compliments, calling him the only orthodox representative of good taste. In general, she detested philosophers, because their hearts were cold and their minds preoccupied with themselves.

Mme. du Deffand had an inherent passion for simplicity, frankness, justice, and a hatred for deceit and affectation; but, strange as it may seem, her nature required variety in her pleasure—new people, new pursuits, new amusements, new agitations for her hungry mind; she was too critical to be contented and to put implicit trust in her friends. An agnostic, always endeavoring to probe into the nature of things, the possession of a personal, living faith was yet the strongest desire of her heart; all her life she longed for the peace that religion affords, but this was denied her, although she had the spiritual assistance of the most famous of the clergy, attended church, had her oratory, her confessor, and faithfully studied the Bible; all was vain—belief would not come to her. The marriage tie was not sacred to her, which was the case with many of the French women of the day, but she went further in lacking all reverence for religious ceremony, though she respected the beliefs of others.

She was all wit and intellectuality. In order to keep her friends from falling under the spell of ennui, she devoted herself to the culinary art, and her suppers became famous for their rare dishes. "She is an example of the type that was predominant in the time—one that had lived too much and was dying from excess of knowledge and pleasure; but she sought that which did not exist in that age,—serenity, peace, faith. She was passionate, sensitive, and sympathetic, in a cold, heartless, and unfeeling world. She needed variety; being bored with society, solitude, husband, lovers, herself, nothing remained for her but to await deliverance by death." This came to her in 1780.

In matters literary, Mme. du Deffand preserved an absolute liberty and independence of opinion. She refused to accept the verdicts of the most competent judges; with instinctive attractions and repulsions, she found but few writers that pleased her. Boileau, Lesage, Chamfort, were her favorites. She said that Buffon was of an unendurable monotony. "He knows well what he knows, but he is occupied with beasts only; one must be something of a beast one's self in order to devote one's self to such an occupation."

As a writer, she showed remarkable good sense, admirable sincerity, rare judgment, justness, and precision; depth and charm were present in a less degree than were other desirable qualities, but she exhibited excellent *esprit*. She was probably the most subtile, and at the same time the most fastidious person of the century. The best portraits of her were written by her own pen; two of them we give, one written at the beginning of her career in 1728, the other at its end in 1774.

"Mme. la Marquise du Deffand is an enemy of all falseness and affectation. Her talk and countenance are always the faithful interpreters of the sentiment of her soul. Her form is not fine nor bad. She has *esprit*, is reasonable and has a correct taste. If vivacity at times leads her off, truth soon brings her back. After she falls into an ennui which extinguishes all the light of her mind, she finds that state insupportable and the cause of such unhappiness, that she blindly embraces all that presents itself, without deliberation."

(1774.) "They believe Mme. du Deffand to possess more *esprit* than she really has; they praise and fear her, but she merits neither the one nor the other. As far as her *esprit* is concerned, she is what she is; in regard to her form, to her birth and fortune—nothing extraordinary, nothing distinguished. Born without great talent, incapable of great application, she is very susceptible to ennui, and, not finding any resource within herself, she resorts to those that surround her and this search is often without success."

Mme. du Deffand arouses our curiosity because she was such an exceptional character, led such a strange life, made and retained friends in ways so different from those of the noted heroines of the salons. In her youth, she was beautiful and fascinating, with numerous lovers and numberless suitors, but she grew even more famous as her age increased; when infirm and blind, and living in a convent, she ruled by virtue of her acknowledged authority and was still able to cope with the greatest philosophers, the chief and dean of whom, Voltaire, wrote the following four lines:

"Qui vous voit et qui vous entend

Perd bientôt sa philosophie;

Et tout sage avec Du Deffand

Voudrait en fou passer sa vie."

[He who sees and hears you,

Soon loses his philosophy.

Wise he who with Du Deffand

Insane would pass his life.]

Living long enough to witness the reigns of three kings and one regent, she was brilliant enough to reign over the intellectual and social world for over fifty years, by virtue of her intellectuality, keenness, and wit; yet, among all the great women of France, she is truly the one who deserves genuine pity and sympathy.

The salon of Mlle. de Lespinasse, her rival, was of a different type, being exclusively intellectual, but permitting absolute liberty of expression of opinions. Born in 1732, at the house of a surgeon of Lyons, she was the illegitimate daughter of the Comtesse d'Albon and was baptized as the child of a man supposed to be named Claude Lespinasse. From 1753 she was the constant attendant to Mme. du Deffand, her mother's sister-in-law, for a period of ten years, until she became completely worn out physically, morally, and mentally by incessant care and endless all-night readings. An attempt to end her existence with sixty grains of opium failed. Owing to the jealousy of

Mme. du Deffand, a separation ensued in 1764, when she retired some distance from the Convent Saint-Joseph to very modest apartments, where, by means of her friends, she was able to receive in a dignified way. The Maréchale de Luxembourg completely fitted up her apartment, the Duc de Choiseul succeeded in getting her an annual pension from the king, and Mme. Geoffrin allowed her three thousand francs.

The majority of the members of her salon were from that of Mme. du Deffand, having followed Mlle. de Lespinasse after the rupture of the two women; besides these, there were Condorcet, Helvétius, Grimm, Marmontel, Condillac, Bernardin de Saint-Pierre, and many others. As her hours for receiving were after five o'clock, her friends were made to understand that her means were not such as to warrant suppers or dinners, four o'clock being the dinner hour in those days.

Her salon immediately became known as the official encyclopædia resort, Mme. du Deffand dubbing it *La Muse de l'Encyclopédie*. D'Alembert was the high priest, and it was not long before he was comfortably lodged in the third story of her house, Mlle. de Lespinasse having nursed him through a malignant fever which the poor man had contracted in the wretched place where he lodged. A strange gathering, those salons! Mlle. de Lespinasse, one of the leaders in the social world, with a prominent salon, was the illegitimate daughter of a Comtesse d'Albon, and her presiding genius was the illegitimate son of Mme. de Tencin; here we find the wealthiest and most elegant of the aristocracy coming from their palaces to meet, in friendly social and intellectual intercourse, men who lived on a mere pittance, dressed on almost nothing, lodged in the most wretched of dens, boarding wherever a salon or palace was opened to them. Surely, intellect was highly valued in those days, and moral etiquette was at a low ebb!

Mlle. de Lespinasse possessed two characteristics which were prominent in a remarkable degree—love and friendship. She appeared to interest herself in everybody in such a way as to make him believe that he was the preferred of her heart; loving everybody sincerely and affectionately, she "lacked altogether the sentimental equilibrium." Especially pathetic was her love for two men—the Count de Mora, a Spanish nobleman, and a Colonel Guibert, who was celebrated for his relations with Frederick the Great; although this wore terribly on her, consuming her physical force, she always received her friends with the same good grace, but often, after their departure, she would fall into a frightful nervous fit from which she could find relief only by the use of opium.

Her love for Guibert was known to her friends, but was a secret from her platonic lover, D'Alembert. When, after a number of years of untold sufferings which even opium could not relieve, she died in 1776, having been cared for to the last by D'Alembert, the Duke de La Rochefoucauld, and her cousin, the Marquis d'Enlezy, it was with these words on her dying lips, addressed to Guibert: "Adieu, my friend! If ever I return to life, I should like to use it in loving you; but there is no longer any time." When D'Alembert read in her correspondence that she had been the mistress of Guibert for sixteen years, he was disconsolate, and retired to the Louvre, which was his privilege as Secretary of the Academy. He left there only to go walking in the evening with Marmontel, who tried to console him by recalling the changeableness of humor of Mlle. de Lespinasse. "Yes," he would reply, "she has changed, but not I; she no longer lived for me, but I always lived for her. Since she is no longer, I don't know why I am living. Ah, that I must still suffer these moments of bitterness which she knew so well how to soothe and make me forget! Do you remember the happy evenings we used to pass? What is there now? Instead of her, when coming home, I find only her shadow! This Louvre lodging is itself a tomb, which I enter only with fright."

Mlle. de Lespinasse died of grief for a lover's death, but she left a group of lovers to lament her loss. In many respects she was not unlike Mlle. de Scudéry; exceptionally plain, her face was much marked with smallpox, a disfigurement not uncommon in those days; her exceedingly piercing and fine eyes, beautiful hair, tall and elegant figure, excellent taste in dress, pleasing voice and a most brilliant talent for conversation, combined to make her one of the most attractive and popular women of her time. As previously stated, she was the only female admitted to the dinners given by Mme. Geoffrin to her men of letters.

Mme. du Deffand's friend, *le Président* Hénault, left the following portrait of Mlle. de Lespinasse: "You are cosmopolitan—you are suitable to all occasions. You like company—you like solitude. Pleasures amuse, but do not seduce you. You have very strong passions, and of the best kind, for they do not return often. Nature, in endowing you with an ordinary state, gave you something with which to rise above it. You are distinguished, and, without being beautiful, you attract attention. There is something piquant in you; one might obstinately endeavor to turn your head, but it would be at one's own expense. Your will must be awaited, because you cannot be made to come. Your cheerfulness embellishes you, and relaxes your nerves, which are too highly strung. You have your own opinion, and you leave others their own. You are extremely polite. You have divined *le monde*. In vain one would transplant you—you would take root anywhere. In short, you are not an ordinary person."

The salon of Mlle. de Lespinasse was unique. Everyone was at perfect liberty to express and sustain his own opinions upon any subject, without danger of offending the hostess, which, as has been seen, was not the case in the salon of Mme. Geoffrin. Her high and sane intellectual culture permitted her to listen to all discussions and to take part in all. She had no strong prejudices, having read—for Mme. du Deffand—nearly everything that was read at that time; also, she had the talent of preserving harmony among her members by drawing from each one his best qualities.

A woman who played a prominent part in society during the Regency, but who had no salon in the proper sense of that word, was Mme. du Châtelet, commonly called Voltaire's Emilie. She was especially interested in sciences, mathematics, geometry, and astronomy, and did more than any other woman of that time to encourage nature study. It was at her Château de Cirey that Voltaire found protection when threatened with a second visit to the Bastille; and there, from time to time for sixteen years, he did some of the best work of his life. It was Mme. du Châtelet who encouraged him, sympathized with him, and appreciated his mobile humor as well as his talent. During these years, while he was under the influence of madame, appeared *Mérope*, *Alzire*, the *Siècle de Louis XIV*, etc.

Mme. du Châtelet was the one great *femme savante* of that century. In the preface to her *Traduction des Principes Mathématiques de Newton*, Voltaire wrote: "Never was a woman so *savante* as she, and never did a woman merit less the saying, *she is a femme savante*. She did not select her friends from those circles where there was a war of *esprit*, where a sort of tribunal was established, where they judged their century, by which, in recompense, they were severely judged. She lived for a long time in societies which were ignorant of what she was, and she took no notice of this ignorance. The words precision, justness, and force are those which correctly describe her elegance. She would have written as Pascal and Nicole did rather than like Mme. de Sévigné; but this severe firmness and this tendency of her *esprit* did not make her inaccessible to the beauties of sentiment."

Maupertuis, the astronomer, wrote: "What a marvel, moreover, to have been able to combine the fine qualities of her sex with the sublime knowledge which we believe uniquely made for us! This enterprising phenomenon will make her memory eternally respected."

Chapter IX

Salon Leaders—(Continued)
Mme. Necker, Mme. d'Epinay, Mme. de Genlis:
Minor Salons

It seems strange indeed that in a century in which the universal impulse was toward pleasure, and sameness of personality was visible everywhere, the types of great women showed such an absolute dissimilarity. The contrast between the natural inclinations of Mme. Necker, the wife of the great minister of finance, and the atmosphere in which she lived, makes the study of her a most interesting one. Born in Switzerland, the daughter of Curchod, a poor Protestant minister, "with patriarchal morals, solid education, and strong good sense," this moral and stern woman was thrown into the midst of depraved elegance, refined licentiousness, and physical debauchery. Sincere, chaste, enthusiastic, and essentially religious, she remained so amidst all the corruption and physical and mental degeneracy of the age.

Critics have made much ado over her marriage, a union of pure love and mutual inclinations, amidst the marriages of mere convenience and the gallant liaisons, such as those of Mme. du Deffand and *le Président* Hénault, and Mme. d'Epinay and Grimm. The matrimonial selection of Susanne Curchod was natural in a girl of her serious make-up, her moral education and her pure ancestry of the strict Protestant type. As a girl of sixteen, she had given evidence of remarkable mental ability and had acquired a wide knowledge—physics, Latin, philosophy, metaphysics—when she was sent to Lausanne, possibly with the idea of meeting a future husband with whom she could become thoroughly acquainted before giving up her independence. There she became the centre of a group or academy of young people, who, under her leadership, discussed subjects of every nature. At first she showed a tendency toward *préciosité* and the spirit of the blue-stocking rather than toward the seriousness and dignity which marked her later career.

It was at Lausanne that she met and fell in love with Gibbon, the English historian; this love affair met with opposition from Gibbon's father, and, after the death of the father of his fiancée, a calamity which left her poor and necessitated her teaching for a living, the Englishman, by his actions and manner toward her, compelled the breaking of their engagement. When, later in life, he went to her salon, they became intimate friends, enjoying "the intellectual union which had been impossible for them in their earlier days."

Thus, at the age of twenty-four, Mlle. Curchod, beautiful, virtuous, and accomplished, and at the height of her reputation in a small town in

Switzerland, was left an orphan. She was taken to Paris by Mme. de Vermenoux, a wealthy widow, who was sought in marriage by M. Necker, banker and capitalist; but, as she was unable to make up her mind to a definite answer, his attention was attracted to her young companion. The result was that, after a few months' sojourn in Paris, Mlle. Curchod became the wife of M. Necker, an event which caused rejoicing from Lausanne to Geneva. Their characters are well portrayed in two letters, written by them to their friends after their marriage. M. Necker wrote, in reply to a letter of congratulation:

"Yes, sir; your friend (Mlle. Curchod) was indeed willing to have me, and I believe myself as happy as one can be. I cannot understand how it can be you whom they congratulate, unless it is as my friend. Will money always be the measure of opinion? That is pitiable! He who wins a virtuous, kind, and sensible woman—has he not made a good transaction, whether or not she be seated on sacks of money? Humanity, what a poor judge you are!"

Shortly after her marriage, Mme. Necker wrote to one of her friends: "My dear, I have married a man who, according to my ideas, is the kindest of mortals, and I am not the only one to judge thus. I had had a liking for him ever since I learned to know him. At present, I see, in all nature, only my husband. I take notice of other men only in so far as they come more or less up to the standard of my husband, and I compare them only for the pleasure of seeing the difference." The marital relations of this loving pair lasted throughout life; and among great women of the eighteenth century, Mme. Necker is one of the few examples of ideal marriage relations.

Soon after their marriage, the Neckers took up their quarters at the Rue Michel-le-Comte, where they began to receive friends. As at that time every day in the week was reserved by other salons,—Monday and Wednesday at Mme. Geoffrin's, Tuesday at Helvétius's, Thursday and Sunday at the Baron d'Holbach's,—Mme. Necker was compelled to appoint Friday as her reception day. She soon succeeded in attracting to her hôtel the best *esprit* of Paris: Diderot, Suard, Grimm, Comte de Schomberg, Marmontel, D'Alembert, Thomas, Saint-Lambert, Helvétius, Ducis, Bernardin de Saint- Pierre, the Abbés Raynal, Armand, and Morellet, Mme. Geoffrin, Mme. du Deffand, Mme. de Marchais, Mme. Suard, the Maréchale de Luxembourg, the Duchesse de Lauzun, the Marquise de La Ferté-Imbault, Mme. de Boufflers.

Among these visitors, most of whom were atheists, Mme. Necker preserved her own religious opinions and piety, although her friends at Geneva never ceased to be concerned about her. Her admirers were many, but they were kept within the bounds of propriety and never attempted any gallant liberties with the hostess—except her ardent admirer Thomas, the intensity of whose eulogies upon her she was forced to check occasionally. It was not long before she became very influential in filling the vacant seats of the Academy. In this and many other respects, her salon may be compared with that of Mme. de Lambert.

Mme. Necker's idea of conducting a salon and its conversation was much the same as the management of a state; she believed that the hostess must never join in the conversation as long as it goes on by itself, but, ever watchful, must never permit disturbances, disagreements, improprieties, or obstacles; she must animate it if it languish; she must see that conversation never takes a dangerous, disagreeable, or tiresome turn, and that it never brings into undue prominence one man especially, as this makes others jealous and displeases the entire society; it must always interest and include all members. The discussions at Mme. Necker's were literary and philosophical; and to prevent even the possibility of tedium, frequent readings were given in their place.

It was at the salon of Mme. Necker that Bernardin de Saint-Pierre first read his *Paul et Virginie*, which received such a cold and indifferent welcome that the author, utterly discouraged, was on the point of burning his manuscript, when he was prevailed upon by his friend Vernet, the great artist, to preserve all his works. Mme. Necker was always quite frank and outspoken, often showing a cutting harshness and a rigor which, as was said, was little in harmony with her bare neck and arms—a style then in vogue at court. She never judged persons by their reputations, but by their *esprit*; thus, it was possible for her to receive people of the most diverse tendencies. When the Marquise de La Ferté-Imbault, one of the few virtuous women of the time, and of the highest aristocracy, was invited to attend the salon of Mme. Necker and was told that the Maréchale de Luxembourg, Mme. du Deffand, Mme. de Boufflers, and Mme. Marchais were frequenters, she said: "These four women are so discredited by manners, and the first two are so dangerous, that for thirty years they have been the horror of society."

The two portraits by Marmontel and Galiani are interesting, as throwing light upon the doings of her salon. Marmontel wrote: "Mme. Necker is very virtuous and instructed, but emphatic and stiff. She does not know Mme. de Sévigné, whom she praises, and only esteems Buffon and Thomas. She calculates all things; she sought men of letters only as trumpets to blow in honor of her husband. He never said a word; that was not very recreating."

Galiani leaves a different impression: "There is not a Friday that I do not go to your house *en esprit*. I arrive, I find you now busy with your headdress, now busy with this duchess. I seat myself at your feet. Thomas quietly suffers, Morellet shows his anger aloud. Grimm and Suard laugh heartily about it, and my dear Comte de Greuze does not notice it. Marmontel finds the example worthy to be imitated, and you, madame, make two of your most beautiful virtues do battle, bashfulness and politeness, and in this suffering you find me a little monster more embarrassing than odious. Dinner is announced. They leave the table and in the café all speak at the same time. M. Necker thinks everything well, bows his head and goes away."

In summer her receptions were first held at the Château de Madrid, and, later on, in a château at Saint-Ouen; the guests were always called for and returned in carriages supplied by the hostess. It was in her salon, in 1770, that the plan originated to erect the statue of Voltaire, which is to-day the famous statue of the *Palais de l'Institute.*

When, during the stirring times before the Revolution, her salon took on a purely political nature, Mme. Necker played a very secondary rôle. In 1788 she and her husband were compelled to leave Paris; but being recalled by Louis XVI., Necker managed affairs for thirteen months, after which he retired with Mme. Necker to Coppet, where, in 1794, the latter died.

Mme. Necker never became a thorough Frenchwoman; she always lacked the grace and charm which are the necessary qualifications of a salon leader; intelligence was her most meritorious quality. Her dinners were apt to become tiresome and to drag. A very interesting story is told of her by the Marquis de Chastellux, which was reported by Mme. Genlis, one of her intimate friends:

"Dining at Mme. Necker's, the marquis was first to arrive, and so early that the hostess was not yet in the salon. In walking up and down the room, he noticed a small book under Mme. Necker's chair. He picked it up and opened it. It was a blank book, a few of the pages of which had been written upon by Mme. Necker. Certainly, he would not have read a letter, but, believing to find only a few spiritual thoughts, he read without any scruples. It contained the plan for the dinner of that day, to which he had been invited, and had been written by Mme. Necker on the previous evening. It told what she would say to the most prominent of the invited guests. She wrote: 'I shall speak to the Chevalier de Chastellux about public felicity and Agatha; to M. d'Angeviller, I shall speak of love; between Marmontel and Guibert I shall raise some literary discussion.' After reading the note, he hurriedly replaced the book under the chair. A moment later, a valet entered, saying that madame had left her notebook in the salon. The dinner was charming for M. de Chastellux, because he had the pleasure of hearing Mme. Necker say, word for word, what she had written in her notebook."

This woman was ever preoccupied with style, and, throughout her life, retained the solemn, studied, and academic air, as well as the simple, rural, innocent manner and spirit of her early surroundings. A mere bourgeoise, unaccustomed to elegance or to the manners of French social life, upon entering Parisian society she set her mind to observing, and immediately began to change her provincial ways and to make over her *esprit* for conversation, for circumstances, and for characters; she adjusted her provincial spirit to that of Paris, thus making of it an entirely new product. Later on, her salon became the first of the modern political salons, but it was far from reaching the prominence of that of Mme. Geoffrin, whose characteristics were social prudence and strict propriety, while those of Mme. Necker were virtue and goodness.

Mme. Necker was never in perfect sympathy with her visitors, the philosophers, the common basis of ideas and sentiments never existing between her and her friends as it did between Mme. Geoffrin and her frequenters; her tie was always artificial. "She represented the Swiss spirit in Parisian society; those serious and educated souls, virtuous and sentimental, somewhat sad and strictly moral, were rather tiresome to the Parisian world." Marmontel well describes her in another of his famous portraits:

"A stranger to the customs of Paris, Mme. Necker had none of the charms and accomplishments of the young French woman. In her manner and language she had neither the air nor the tone of a woman reared in the school of arts, formed at the school of high society. Without taste in her headdress, without ease in her bearing, without fascination in her politeness, her mind—as was her countenance—was too properly adjusted to show grace. But a charm more worthy of her was that of propriety, of candor, of goodness. A virtuous education and solitary studies had given to her all that culture can add to an excellent nature. In her, sentiment was perfect, but her thought was often confused and vague; instead of clearing her ideas, meditation disturbed them; in exaggerating them, she believed to enlarge them; in order to extend them, she wandered off into abstractions and hyperboles. She seemed to see certain objects only through a fog, which augmented their importance in her eyes; and then her expression became so inflated that the pomposity of it would have been laughable if one had not known her to be entirely ingenuous."

"In summing up the character of Mme. Necker, we find," says Sainte-Beuve, "first of all, a genuine individuality and a personality with defects which at first impression are shocking, but which only helped to render the woman and all her aspirations the more admirable. Entering a Parisian society with the firm decision of becoming a woman of *esprit* and of being in relation with the *beaux esprits*, she was able to preserve the moral conscience of her Protestant training, to protest against the false doctrines about her, to give herself up to duties in the midst of society, to found institutions for the sick and needy,— and to leave a memory without a stain."

While, among the famous salon leaders of the eighteenth century, Mme. Necker stands out preëminently for her strict moral integrity and fidelity to her marriage relations, Mme. d'Epinay is unique for the constancy of her affections for the men to whom she owes her celebrity, Rousseau and Grimm. Born in 1725, the record of her life runs like that of most French women. At the age of twenty she was married to her cousin, La Live, who later took the name of d'Epinay, from an estate his father, the wealthy M. de Bellegarde, had bought—a man who was really in love with her for a whole month after their marriage, but who, tiring of the pure affections of a loving wife, soon began to lavish his time and fortune upon a *danseuse*. The poor young wife was between two fires, the extravagance and wild dissipations of her husband and the rigid discipline and orthodoxy of her mother. Never was a woman treated so outrageously and insultingly as was this woman by a man who contrived in every manner to corrupt her morals by throwing her among his dissolute companions, Mme. d'Artz, the mistress of the Prince de Conti, and Mlle. d'Ette, an intriguing woman of the time; to the latter, Mme. d'Epinay confided her troubles, and, as the result of her counsels, fell into the hands of a M. de Francueil, handsome, clever, accomplished, but as morally depraved as was her husband.

When Mme. d'Epinay was finally convinced that her husband was untrue to her, she felt nothing but disdain and contempt for him, and decided to live a virtuous life; after holding for a short time to her resolution "that a woman may have the most profound and tender sentiment for a man and yet remain faithful to her duties," she lost herself under the influence of the professional seducer Francueil, and, completely carried away by that passion, she cries out, in her memoirs: *Francueil, Francueil, tu m'as perdue, et tu disais que tu m'aimais* [You have undone me—and you said you loved me]! Such was the lot, as was seen, of most women of those days, who had noble intentions, but a woman's weakness. The century did not demand faithfulness to the marital vows; but when a woman had once abandoned herself to love, it required that the attachment be to a man of honor and standing. Marriage was simply a preliminary step to freedom; after that ceremony came the natural election of the heart and mutual tenderness of the beings who could be mated only through the freedom which married life afforded. A superior illegitimate liaison was nothing unnatural—on the contrary, it was but a natural human selection; such was the nature of the affection of Mme. d'Epinay for this débauché Francueil.

As she enjoyed absolute liberty, her lover paid his respects to her at Epinay; there he inaugurated amusements and took his friends. It was he who suggested the erection of a theatre at which her friends' productions might be offered to the world of critics. Through his efforts, the great men who made her salon famous were gathered at "La Chevrette," where the actors and players soon drew the attention of literary Paris. After a year or two of attachment, Francueil became indifferent to Mme. d'Epinay and transferred his affections to an actress—the sister of M. d'Epinay's mistress. Thus runs the story of the life of the average married woman. If she remained virtuous, she usually became resigned to her fate and lived happily; if she undertook to imitate her husband's tactics, she fell from the good graces of one lover to those of another, ending her life in absolute wretchedness.

These two men—the lover and the husband—carried on with two sisters their licentious living and extravagances to such an extent that the injured wife demanded a separation of her fortune from that of her husband, in which project her father-in-law aided her and gave her thirteen thousand francs income. Mme. d'Epinay, in the midst of success, became acquainted with Mlle. Quinault, the daughter of the famous actor of the time, and herself a great actress. This woman invited Mme. d'Epinay to her so-called salon, which was, possibly, the most licentious and irreligious of the salons then in vogue, where she met Duclos, with whom she immediately formed a strong friendship.

After the death of M. de Bellegarde, her wealth was considerably increased, a piece of good fortune which enabled her to carry out all her plans. It was at this time, 1755, that she induced Rousseau to live in her cottage, "l'Hermitage;" and for about two years she enjoyed perfect happiness with him. By a peculiar freak of fate she fell in with Grimm, who was introduced to her by Rousseau and who had, for some time, been on the hunt for a "faithful mistress." This German by birth, but Frenchman in spirit, had championed her at a dinner, where she was the object of the severest reproach. She had burned the papers of her sister, Mme. de Jully, who had betrayed an honest husband. Stricken with smallpox, just before dying, she confessed all to Mme. d'Epinay. The latter owed Mme. de Jully fifty écus and the note was among the papers of Mme. de Jully. Mme. d'Epinay was accused of having burned the note to which it was asserted she had access; and Grimm undertook to plead her cause, an act which so elated madame that she turned all her affection upon her defender, whereupon Rousseau departed. Later on, the note having been found, Mme. d'Epinay was completely vindicated. Grimm then became her third lover.

This third marriage, so to speak, was one of reason; the first was one of mere emancipation; the second, one of passion and genuine love. In 1755, worn out physically, she took a trip to Switzerland, to be treated by the famous Dr. Tronchin; there she became so ill that Grimm was summoned. They remained together for about two years, and after her return to Paris she reopened her salon of "La Chevrette." Her reunions partook more of the nature of our house parties; the salon was an immense room, in which the members would pair off and divert themselves as they pleased; in that respect "La Chevrette" was unique. After her fortune, which at one time was quite large, became diminished, partly through her own extravagance and partly through that of her son, who was the very counterpart of his father, she was forced to rent "La Chevrette" and, later on, "La Briche," where she had opened her second salon.

The last years of her life she spent in Paris with Grimm. She had reached such a physical condition that her sufferings could be relieved only by the use of opium. Financial relief came to her in 1783, when the Academy awarded her the Montyon prize, then given for the first time, for her *Conversations d'Emilie*. She died in the same year, surrounded by her dearest friends— Grimm, M. and Mme. Belgunce, and Mme. d'Houdetot.

Mme. d'Epinay, in many respects, was a remarkable woman. Amid all her social duties, with all her physical and mental troubles, she found time to help others and to manage her own business affairs and those of her children, took an active interest in art, music, and literature, raised, with the utmost care, her granddaughter, produced one of the best works of the time for children, made tapestry, and wrote innumerable letters. Her fortune was lost through the reforms of Necker.

She was not a beautiful woman; but she was distinguished by a small, thin figure, an abundance of rich dark hair, which brought out in striking relief the peculiar whiteness of her skin, and large brown eyes. Her five lovers she called her five bears: Rousseau, Grimm, Desmoulin, Saint-Lambert, Gauffecourt. An epistle to Grimm begins thus;

"Moi, de cinq ours la souveraine,

Qui leur donne et present des lois,

Faut-il que je sois à la fois

Et votre esclave et votre reine,

O des tyrans le plus tyran?"

[I, sovereign over five bears,

Who give and prescribe laws for them—

Must I be your slave and queen at the same time,

O among tyrants, the greatest?]

As far as the care of the education of her children is concerned, with its sacrifice and real application to duty, she was sometimes called—and not unadvisedly—the type of the ideal mother. From 1757 on her ideas and thoughts ran to education. Her friends were all of the philosophical trend, and intellectual labor was their chief pleasure. After having passed through a career of excitement and love's caprices, she longed for a peaceful, quiet existence; at that point, however, her health gave way, and she entered upon a new territory at Geneva. There she conquered Voltaire, who was profuse with his compliments and kindnesses. Upon her return she became the recognized leader or champion of the philosophic and foreign group and the Encyclopædists, and was regarded as the central figure of the philosophical movement in general.

The ideas of the philosophers had been gaining ground, and were disseminated through all classes. The mere love of pleasure and luxury at first found under Louis XV. gave way to more serious reflections when society was confronted with those all-important questions which finally culminated in the Revolution. The salon of Mme. d'Epinay grew to be the most important and, intellectually, the most brilliant of the time. Rousseau, Diderot, Helvétius, Duclos, Suard, the Abbés Galiani, Raynal, the Florentine physician Gatti, Comte de Schomberg, Chevalier de Chastellux, Saint-Lambert, Marquis de Croixmare, the different ambassadors, counts and princes, were frequent visitors In this brilliant circle her letters from Voltaire, read aloud, were always eagerly awaited. Such dramas as Voltaire's *Tancred*, Diderot's *Le Père de Famille*, were given under her patronage and discussed in her salon; after the performance she entertained all the friends at supper.

Upon the departure of Abbé Galiani from Paris, Mme. d'Epinay and Diderot were intrusted with the revision and printing of his famous *Dialogues sur les Blés*; Grimm left to them the continuance of his *Correspondance Littéraire*. She was known for her wonderful analytical ability and her keen power of observation—faculties which won the esteem and respect of such men and caused her collaboration to be anxiously sought by them; however, she never attempted to rival them in their particular sphere. In her writings she displayed a reactionary tendency against the educational methods of the day, her chief work of real literary worth being mostly in the form of sound advice to a child. Being a reasonable, careful, and sensible woman,—in spite of the defects in her moral life,—she desired to show the possibilities of a moral revolution against the habits and customs of the time, of which she herself had been a most unfortunate victim. She was relieved of actual want by means of this work, which gained for her a pension from Catherine II. of Russia, who adopted her methods for her own children, and the award of the Montyon prize, which was given her in a competition with a large number of aspirants, the most famous of whom was Mme. de Genlis. It was her ability to gain and retain the respect of great men which won that honor for her.

The memoirs of Mme. d'Epinay leave one of the most accurate and faithful pictures of the polished society of the France of about 1750. "Her salon was the centre about which circled the greatest activity; it was filled with men who ordered events, thinkers whose minds were bent upon untangling the knotty problems of the age; it was her salon, more than any other, that quickened the philosophical movement of the day. Mme. d'Epinay made her reputation not so much through her *esprit*, intelligence, or beauty, possibly, as through the strength of her affection. Timid, irresolute, and highly impressionable, and amiable in disposition, she was constantly influenced by circumstances—a quality which led her on to the two principal occupations of her later life, education and philosophy. To-day, her name is recalled principally for its association with that of Rousseau, whose mistress and benefactress she was; it is to her that the world owes his famous *Nouvelle Héloïse*.

The last of the great literary and social leaders of the eighteenth century was Mme. de Genlis, a prodigy in every respect, an amateur performer upon nearly every instrument, an authority on intellectual matters as well, a fine story teller, a consummate artist, entertainer, and general charmer. Authoress, governess of Louis-Philippe, councillor of Bonaparte, her success as a social leader established her reputation and places her in the file of great women, although she was not a salon leader such as Mme. Geoffrin or Mme. du Deffand.

She was born in 1746, and at a very early age showed a remarkable talent for music, but her general education was much neglected. At the age of about seventeen she was married to a Comte de Genlis, who had fallen in love with her on seeing her portrait. As his relatives refused to welcome the young girl, she was placed in the convent of Origny, where she remained until 1764, after which her husband took her to his brother's estate, where they lived happily for a short time. When, in 1765, she became a mother, her husband's family became reconciled to his union, and, later on, took her to court.

Before her marriage, upon the departure of her father to San Domingo to retrieve his fortunes, her mother had found an asylum for her at the elegant home of the farmer-general M. de La Popelinière. This occurred at the time that Paris was theatre mad, and when great actors and actresses were the heroes and heroines of society. At this house the young girl became the central figure in the theatrical and musical entertainments. After passing through this schooling, she stood the test of the court without any difficulty, and completely won the favor of her husband's family, as well as that of the court ladies and the members of the other distinguished households where she was introduced. With an insatiable appetite for frolics, quite in keeping with the customs of the time, she plunged into social life with a vigor and an aptitude which soon attracted attention. She played all sorts of rôles at the most fashionable houses, "through her consummate acting and *bons mots* drawing tears of vexation from her less gifted sisters. She plays nine instruments, writes dramas, recasts others, organizes and drills amateurs, besides attending to a thousand and one other things."

Through the influence of her aunt, Mme. de Montesson, who was secretly married to the Duke of Orléans, Mme. de Genlis was appointed lady-in-waiting in the household of the Duchesse de Chartres, the duke's daughter-in-law, whose salon was celebrated in Paris. She soon won the confidence of the duchess, and became her confessor, secretary, guide, and oracle, but did not abandon in the least her pursuit of pleasure. She even took possession of the heart of the duke himself, and in 1782 was made "*gouverneur*" to his children, the Duc de Valois, later Louis-Philippe, the Duc de Montpensier, the Comte de Beaujolais, and Mlle. Adelaïde; for the education of her pupils she had the use of several châteaux. Many a piquant epigram and chanson were composed for the edification of the "*gouverneur.*" It is said that she acted as panderer for the princes, especially Louis-Philippe, of a "legitimate means of satisfying these ardent desires of which I am being devoured," by leading them to the nuns in the convents by means of a subterranean passage. The following passages from the journal of Louis-Philippe show the nature of his relations with her:

(December, 1790.) "I went to dine with my mother and grandfather. Although I am delighted to dine often with my mother, I am deeply sorry to give only three days out of the seven to my dear Bellechasse [that is, to Mme. de Genlis]."

(January, 1791.) "Last evening, returned to my friend [Mme. de Genlis]; remained there until after midnight; I was the first one to have the good fortune of wishing her a 'Happy New Year.' Nothing can make me happier; I don't know what will become of me when I am no longer with her."

(January, 1791.) "Yesterday, I was at the Tuileries. The queen spoke to my father, to my brother, and said nothing to me—neither did the king nor Monsieur, in fact, no one. I remained at my friend's until half-past twelve. No one in the world is so agreeable to me as is she." (February, 1791.) "I was at the assembly at Bellechasse, dined at the Palais-Royal, I was at the Jacobins, returned to Bellechasse, after supper went to my friend's. I remained with her alone; she treated me with an infinite kindness; I left, the happiest man in the world." Such language speaks for itself.

No sons of a nobleman ever received a finer, more typically modern education than did her pupils. She was, possibly, the first teacher to use the natural method system, teaching German, English, and Italian by conversation. The boys were compelled to act, in the park, the voyages of Vasco da Gama; in the dining room the great historical tableaux were presented; in the theatre, built especially for them, they acted all the dramas of the *Théâtre d'Education*. She taught them how to make portfolios, ribbons, wigs, pasteboard work, to gild, to turn, and to do carpentering. They visited museums and manufactories, during which expeditions they were taught to observe, criticise, and find defects. This was the first step taken in France in the eighteenth century toward a modern education. Although it was superficial, in consequence of its great breadth, yet this education inculcated manliness and courage.

In 1778 Mme. de Genlis published her moral teachings in *Adèle et Théodore*, a work which created quite a little talk at the time, but which eventually brought upon her the condemnation of the philosophers and Encyclopædists, because in it she opposed liberty of conscience. When, on the occasion of the first communion of the Duc de Valois, she wrote her *Religion Considered as the Only True Foundation of Happiness and of True Philosophy*, all the Palais-Royal place hunters, philosophers, and her political enemies, in a mass, opposed and ridiculed her. Rivarol declared that she had no sex, that heaven had refused the magic of talent to her productions, as it had refused the charm of innocence to her childhood.

One of the best portraits of her is in the memoirs of the Baroness d'Oberkirch (it was she who disturbed Mme. de Genlis and the Duc d'Orléans while they were walking in the gardens one night):

"I did not like her, in spite of her accomplishments and the charm of her conversation; she was too systematic. She is a woman who has laid aside the flowing robes of her sex for the costume of a pedagogue. Besides, nothing about her is natural; she is constantly in an attitude, as it were, thinking that her portrait—physical or moral—is being taken by someone. One of the great follies of this masculine woman is her harp, which she carries about with her; she speaks about it when she hasn't it—she plays on a crust of bread and practises with a thread. When she perceives that someone is looking at her, she rounds her arm, purses up her mouth, assumes a sentimental expression and air, and begins to move her fingers. Gracious! what a fine thing naturalness is!... I spent a delightful evening at the Comtesse de La Massais's; she had hired musicians whom she paid dear; but Mme. de Genlis sat in the centre of the assembly, commanded, talked, commented, sang, and would have put the entire concert in confusion, had not the Marquise de Livry very drolly picked a quarrel with her about her harp, which she had brought to her. Decidedly, this young D'Orléans has a singular governor. She holds too closely to her rôle, and never forgets her *jupons* [skirts] except when she ought most to remember them."

During her visit to England she was petted by everyone; but even in England there was a widespread prejudice against her—a feeling which the mere sight of her immediately dissipated. An English lady wrote about her:

"I saw her at first with a prejudice in her disfavor, from the cruel reports I had heard; but the moment I looked at her it was removed. There was a dignity with her sweetness and a frankness with her modesty, that convinced me, beyond all power of contrary report, of her real worth and innocence."

During the Revolution Mme. de Genlis travelled about Switzerland, Germany, and England. At Berlin, owing to her poverty, she supported herself by writing, making trinkets, and teaching, until she was recalled to France, under the Consulate. In Paris she produced some of her best works—although they were written to order. Napoleon gave her a pension of six thousand francs and handsome apartments at the Arsenal. To this liberal pension, the wife of his brother, Joseph Bonaparte, added three thousand francs.

From Mme. de Genlis, Napoleon received a letter fortnightly, in which epistle she communicated to him her opinions and observations upon politics and current events. Upon the return to power of the Orléans family, she was put off with a meagre pension. Like many other French women, she became more and more melancholy and misanthropic. She was unable to control her wrath against the philosophers and some of the contemporary writers, such as Lamartine, Mme. de Staël, Scott, and Byron. Her death, in 1830, was announced in these words: "Mme. de Genlis has ceased to write—which is to announce her death."

Throughout life she was so generous that as soon as she received her pensions, presents, or earnings from her work, the money was distributed among the poor. When she died, she left nothing but a few worn and homely dresses and articles of furniture. The diversity of her works and her conduct, the politics in which she was steeped, the satires, the perfidious accusations that have pursued her, have contributed to leave of her a rather doubtful portrait; however, those who have written bitterly against her have done so mostly from personal or political animosity. She was so many-sided—a reformer, teacher, pietist, politician, actress—that a true estimate of her character is difficult. A woman of all tastes and of various talents, she was a living encyclopædia and mistress of all arts of pleasing. She had studied medicine, and took special delight in the art of bleeding, which she practised upon the peasants, each one of whom she would present with thirty sous (thirty cents), after the bleeding—and she never lacked patients. Mme. de Genlis was an expert rider and huntress; also, she was graceful, with an elegant figure, great affability, and a talent for quickly and accurately reading character; and these gifts were stepping-stones to popularity.

She wrote incessantly, on all things, essaying every style, every subject. "She has discoursed for the education of princes and of lackeys; prepared maxims for the throne and precepts for the pantry; you might say she possessed the gift of universality. She was gifted with a singular confidence in her own abilities, infinite curiosity, untiring industry, and never-ending and inexhaustible energy. She wrote nearly as much as Voltaire, and barely excelled him in the amount of unreadable work, which, if printed, would fill over one hundred volumes."

"Let us remember," says Mr. Dobson, "her indefatigable industry and untiring energy, her kindness to her relatives and admirers, her courage and patience when in exile and poverty, her great talent, perseverance, and rare facility." In protesting vigorously against the universal neglect of physical development, against the absence of the gymnasium and the lack of practical knowledge in the education of her time, in advocating the study of modern languages as a means of culture and discipline, in applying to her pupils the principles of the modern experimental and observational education, Mme. de Genlis will retain a place as one of the great female educators—as a woman pedagogue, *par excellence*, of the eighteenth century.

A great number of minor salons existed, which were partly literary, partly social. From about 1750 to 1780 the amusements varied constantly, from all-day parties in the country to cafés served by the great women themselves, from playing proverbs to playing synonyms, from impromptu compositions to questionable stories, from laughter to tears, from Blind-man's-buff to Lotto. Some of the proverbs were quite ingenious and required elaborate preparations; for example, at one place Mme. de Lauzun dances with M. de Belgunce, in the simplest kind of a costume, which represented the proverb: *Bonne renommée vaut mieux que ceinture dorée* [A good name is rather to be chosen than great riches]. Mme. de Marigny danced with M. de Saint-Julien as a negro, passing her handkerchief over her face in the various figures of the dance, meaning *A laver la tête d'un More on perd sa lessive* [To wash a blackamoor white].

Among the social salons, the finest was the Temple of the Prince de Conti and his mistress, the Countess de Boufflers. It was a salon of pleasure, liberty, and unceremonious intimacy; his *thés à l'anglaise* were served by the great ladies themselves, attired in white aprons. The exclusive and élite of the social world made up his company. The most elegant assembly was that of the Maréchale de Luxembourg; it will be considered later on. The salon of Mme. de Beauvau rivalled that of the Maréchale de Luxembourg; she was mistress of elegance and propriety, an authority on and model of the usages of society.

A manner perhaps superior to that of any other woman, gave Mme. de Beauvau a particular *politesse* and constituted her one of the women who contributed most to the acceptance of Paris as the capital of Europe, by well- bred people of all countries. Her *politesse* was kind and without sarcasm, and, by her own naturalness, she communicated ease. She was not beautiful, but had a frank and open expression and a marvellous gift of conversation, which was her delight and in which she gloried. Her salon was conspicuous for its untarnished honor and for the example it set of a pure conjugal love.

The salon of Mme. de Grammont, at Versailles, was visited at all hours of the day and night by the highest officials, princes, lords, and ladies. It had activity, authority, the secret doors, veiled and redoubtable depths of a salon of the mistress of a king. Everybody went there for counsel, submitted plans, and confided projects to this lady who had willingly exiled herself from Paris.

The house of M. de La Popelinière, at Passy, was noted for its unique entertainment; there the celebrated Gossec and Gaïffre conducted the concerts, Deshayes, master of the ballet at the Comédie-Italienne, managed the amusements. It was a house like a theatre and with all the requisites of the latter; there artists and men of letters, virtuosos and *danseuses*, ate, slept, and lodged as in a hotel. With Mme. de Blot, mistress of the Duke of Orléans, as hostess, the Palais-Royal ranked next to the Temple of the Prince de Conti; it was open only to those who were presented; after that ceremony, all those who were thus introduced could, without invitation, dine there on all days of the Grand Opera. On the *petits jours* a select twenty gathered, who, when once invited, were so for all time. The "Salon de Pomone," of Mme. de Marchais, received its name from Mme. du Deffand on account of the exquisite fruits and magnificent flowers which the hostess cultivated and distributed among her friends.

"La Paroisse," of Mme. Doublet de Persan, was the salon of the sceptics and was under the constant surveillance of the police. All the members arrived at the same time and each took possession of the armchair reserved for him, above which hung his portrait. On a large stand were two registers, in which the rumors of the day were noted—in one the doubtful, in the other the accredited. On Saturday, a selection was made, which went to the *Grand Livre*, which became a journal entitled *Nouvelles à la Main*, kept by the *valet- de-chambre* of Mme. Doublet. This book furnished the substance of the six volumes of the *Mémoires Secrets*, which began to appear in 1770.

Besides these salons of the nobility, there were those of the financiers, a profession which had risen into prominence within the last half century, after the death of Louis XIV. According to the Goncourt brothers, the greatest of these salons was that of Mme. de Grimrod de La Reynière, who, by dint of shrewd manœuvring, by unheard-of extravagances, excessive opulence in the furnishings of her salon, and by the most gorgeous and rare fêtes and suppers, had succeeded in attracting to her establishment a number of the court and nobility.

The salon of M. de La Popelinière belonged to this class, although he was ranked, more or less, among the nobility. There were the weekly suppers of Mme. Suard, Mme. Saurin, the Abbé Raynal, and the luncheons of the Abbé Morellet on the first Sunday of the month; to the latter functions were invited all the celebrities of the other salons, as well as artists and musicians—it was there that the famous quarrel of the Gluck and Piccini parties originated. The Tuesday dinners of Helvétius became famous; it was at them that Franklin was one of the favorites; after the death of Helvétius, he attempted in vain to put an end to the widowhood of madame. No man at that time was more popular than Franklin or had as much public attention shown him.

There were a number of celebrated women whose reputations rest mainly on their wit and conversational abilities; they may be classed as society leaders, to distinguish them from salon leaders.

Chapter X

Social Classes

The belief generally prevails that devotion and constancy did not exist among French women of the eighteenth century; but, in spite of the very numerous instances of infidelity which dot the pages of the history of the French matrimonial relations of those days, many examples of rare devotion are found, even among the nobility. Love of the king and self-eliminating devotion to him were feelings to which women aspired; yet we have one countess, the Countess of Perigord, who, true to her wifehood, repels the advances of the king, preferring a voluntary exile to the dishonor of a life of royal favors and attentions. There is also the example of Mme. de Trémoille; having been stricken with smallpox, she was ministered to by her husband, who voluntarily shared her fate and died with her.

It would seem that the highest types of devotion are to be found in the families of the ministers and men of state, where the wife was intimately associated with the fortune and the success of her husband. The Marquis de Croisy and his wife were married forty years; M. and Mme. de Maurepas lived together for fifty years, without being separated one day. Instances are many in which reconciliations were effected after years of unfaithfulness; these seldom occurred, however, until the end of life was near. The normal type of married life among the higher classes still remained one of most ideal and beautiful devotion, in spite of the great number of exceptions.

It must be observed that in the middle class the young girl grew up with the mother and was given her most tender care; surrounded with wholesome influences, she saw little or nothing of the world, and, the constant companion of her mother, developed much like the average young girl of to-day. At the age of about eleven she was sent to a convent, where—after having spent some time in the *pension*, where instruction in religion was given her—she was instructed by the sisters for one year.

After her confirmation and her first communion, and the home visits to all the relatives, she was placed in a *maison religieuse*, where the sisters taught the daughters of the common people free of charge. The young girl was also taught dancing, music, and other accomplishments of a like nature, but there was nothing of the feverish atmosphere of the convent in which the daughters of the nobility were reared; these institutions for the middle classes were peaceful, silent, and calm, fostering a serenity and quietude. The days passed quickly, the Sundays being eagerly looked forward to because of the visits of the parents, who took their daughters for drives and walks and indulged them in other innocent diversions. Such a life had its after effects: the young girls grew up with a taste for system, discipline, piety, and for a rigid devotion, which often led them to an instinctive need of doctrine and sacrifice; consequently, in later life many turned to Jansenism.

However, the young girls of this class who were not thus educated, because their assistance was required at home, received an early training in social as well as in domestic affairs; they had a solid and practical, if uncouth, foundation, combined with a worldly and, often, a frivolous temperament. To them many privileges were opened: they were taken to the opera, to concerts and to balls, to the salons of painting, and it often happened that they developed a craving for the society to which only the nobly born demoiselle was admitted. When this craving went too far, it frequently led to seduction by some of the chevaliers who make seduction a profession.

The marriage customs in these circles differed little from those of to-day. The suitor asked permission to call and to continue his visits; then followed the period of present giving. The young girl was almost always absolute mistress of the decision; if the father presented a name, the daughter insisted upon seeing, receiving, and becoming intimately acquainted with the suitor, a custom quite different from that practised among the nobility. Instead of giving her rights as it did the girl of the nobility, marriage imposed duties upon the girl of the middle class; it closed the world instead of opening it to her; it ended her brilliant, gay, and easy life, instead of beginning it, as was the case in the higher classes. This she realized, therefore hesitated long before taking the final step which was to bind her until death.

With her, becoming a wife meant infinitely more than it did to the girl of the nobility; her husband had the management of her money, and his vices were visited upon her and her children—in short, he became her master in all things. These disadvantages she was taught to consider deeply before entering the marriage state.

This state of affairs developed distinctive physiognomies in the different classes of the middle-class society: thus, "the wives of the financiers are dignified, stern, severe; those of the merchants are seductive, active, gossiping, and alert; those of the artists are free, easy, and independent, with a strong taste for pleasure and gayety—and they give the tone." As we approach the end of the century, the *bourgeoisie* begins to assume the airs, habits, extravagances, and even the immoralities, of the higher classes.

Below the *bourgeoise* was the workingwoman, whose ideas were limited to those of a savage and who was a woman only in sex. Her ideas of morality, decency, conjugal happiness, children, education, were limited by quarrels, profanity, blows, fights. At that time brandy was the sole consolation for those women; it supplied their moral force and their moral resistance, making them forget cold, hunger, fatigue, evil, and giving them courage and patience; it was the fire that sustained, comforted, and incited them.

These women were not much above the level of animals, but from them, we find, often sprang the entertainers of the time, the queens of beauty and gallantry—Laguerre, D'Hervieux, Sophie Arnould. Having lost their virtue with maturity, these women had no sense of morality; in them, nothing preserved the sense of honor—their religion consisted of a few superstitious practices. The constituents of duty and the virtue of women they could only vaguely guess; marriage itself was presented to them under the most repugnant image of constant contention.

It was in such an atmosphere as this that the daughters of these women grew up. Their talents found opportunity for display at the public dances where some of them would in time attract especial attention. Some became opera singers, dancers, or actresses, and were very popular; others became influential, and, through the efforts of some lover, allured about them a circle of ambitious *débauchés* or aspirants for social favors. Through their adventures they made their way up in the world to high society.

From this element of prostitution was disentangled, to a large extent, the great gallantry of the eighteenth century. This was accomplished by adding an elegance to debauch, by clothing vice with a sort of grandeur, and by adorning scandal with a semblance of the glory and grace of the courtier of old. Possessing the fascination of all gifts, prodigalities, follies, with all the appetites and tendencies of the time, these women attracted the society of the period—the poets, the artists, even the scientists, the philosophers, and the nobility. Their reputation increased with the number and standing of their lovers. The genius of the eighteenth century circled about these street belles— they represented the fortune of pleasure.

As the church would not countenance the marriage of an actress, she was forced to renounce the theatre when she would marry, but once married a permit to return to the stage was easily obtained. Society was not so severe as the laws; it received actresses, sought out, and even adored them; it received the women of the stage as equals, and many of them were married by counts and dukes, given a title, and presented at court. The regular type of the prostitute was tolerated and even received by society; "a word of anger, malediction, or outrage, was seldom raised against these women: on the contrary, pity and the commiseration of charity and tenderness were felt for them and manifested." This was natural, for many of them—through notoriety —reached society and, as mistresses of the king, even the throne itself. "If such women as Mme. de Pompadour were esteemed, what principles remained in the name of which to judge without pity and to condemn the *débauchés* of the street," says Mme. de Choiseul, one of the purest of women.

This class usually created and established the styles. There is a striking contrast between the standards of beauty and fashions of the respective periods of Louis XIV. and Louis XV.: "The stately figure, rich costume, awe- inspiring peruke of the magnificent Louis XIV.—the satins, velvets, embroideries, perfumes, and powder of the indolent and handsome Louis XV., well illustrate the two epochs." The beauty of the Louis XIV. age was more serious, more imposing, imperial, classic; later in the eighteenth century, under Louis XV., she developed into a charming figure of *finesse, sveltesse et gracilité*, with an extremely delicate complexion, a small mouth and thin nose, as opposed to the strong, plump mouth and *nez léonin* (leonine nose). More animated, the face was all movement, the eyes talked; the *esprit* passed to the face. It was the type of Marivaux' comedies, with an *esprit mobile*, animated and colored by all the coquetries of grace.

Later in the century, the very opposite type prevailed; the aspiration then became to leave an emotion ungratified rather than to seduce; a languishing expression was cultivated; women sought to sweeten the physiognomy, to make it tender and mild. The style of beauty changed from the brunette with brown eyes—so much in vogue under Louis XV., to the blonde with blue eyes under Louis XVI. Even the red which formerly "dishonored France," became a favorite. To obtain the much admired pale complexion, women had themselves bled; their dress corresponded to their complexion, light materials and pure white being much affected.

In these three stages of the development of beauty, fashion changed to harmonize with the popular style in beauty. In general, styles were influenced by an important event of the day: thus, when Marie Leczinska, introduced the fad of quadrilles, there were invented ribbons called "quadrille of the queen"; and many other fads originated in the same way. French taste and fashions travelled over entire Europe; all Europe was *à la française*, yoked and laced in French styles, French in art, taste, industry. The domination of the French *Galerie des Modes* was due to the inventive minds of French women in relation to everything pertaining to headdress, to detailed and delicate arrangements of every phase of ornamentation.

Every country had, in Paris, its agents who eagerly waited for the appearance of the famous doll of the Rue Saint-Honoré; this figure was an exponent of the latest fashions and inventions, and, changing continually, was watched and copied by all Europe. Alterations in style frequently originated at the supper of a mistress, in the box of a dancer or in the atelier of a fine modiste; therefore, in that respect, that century differed little from the present one. Trade depended largely upon foreign patronage. Fortunes were made by the modistes, who were the great artists of the day and who set the fashion; but the hairdresser and shoemaker, also, were artists, as was seen, at least in name, and were as impertinent as prosperous.

An interesting illustration of the change of fashion is the following anecdote: In 1714, at a supper of the king, at Versailles, two English women wore low headdress, causing a scandal which came near costing them their dismissal. The king happened to mention that if French women were reasonable, they would not dress otherwise. The word was spread, and the next day, at the king's mass the ladies all wore their hair like the English women, regardless of the laughter of the women who, being absent the previous evening, had their hair dressed high. The compliment of the king as he was leaving mass, to the ladies with the low headdress, caused a complete change in the mode.

It now remains but to illustrate these various classes by types—by women who have become famous. The Duchesse de Boufflers, Maréchale de Luxembourg, was the woman who most completely typified the spirit and tone of the eighteenth-century *classique* in everything that belonged to the ancient régime which passed away with the society of 1789. She was the daughter of the Duc de Villeroy, and married the Duc de Boufflers in 1721; after the death of the latter in 1747, and after having been the mistress of M. de Luxembourg for several years, she married him in 1750. Her youth was like that of most women of the social world. A *savante* in intrigues at court, present at all suppers, bouts, and pleasure trips as lady-of-the-palace to the queen, intriguing constantly, holding her own by her sharp wit, in a society of *roués et élégants enervés* she soon became a leader. Mme. du Deffand left a striking portrait of her:

"Mme. la Duchesse de Boufflers is beautiful without having the air of suspecting it. Her physiognomy is keen and piquant, her expression reveals all the emotions of her soul—she does not have to say what she thinks, one guesses it. Her gestures are so natural and so perfectly in accord with what she says, that it is difficult not to be led to think and feel as she does. She dominates wherever she is, and she always makes the impression she desires to make. She makes use of her advantages almost like a god—she permits us to believe that we have a free will while she determines us. In general, she is more feared than loved. She has much *esprit* and gayety. She is constant in her engagements, faithful to her friends, truthful, discreet, generous. If she were more clairvoyant or if men were less ridiculous, they would find her perfect."

On one occasion M. de Tressan composed this famous couplet:

"Quand Boufflers parut à la cour,

On crut voir la mère d'Amour,

Chacun s'empressait à lui plaire,

Et chacun l'avait à son tour."

[When Boufflers appeared at court,

The mother of love was thought to be seen,

Everyone became so eager to please her,

And each one had her in his turn.]

One day Mme. de Boufflers mumbled this before M. de Tressan, saying to him: "Do you know the author? It is so beautiful that I would not only pardon her, but I believe I would embrace her." Whereupon he stammered: *Eh bien! c'est moi.* She quickly dealt him two vigorous slaps in the face. All feared her; no one equalled her in skill and shrewdness, or in knowing and handling men.

After her marriage to the Maréchal de Luxembourg, she decided, about 1750, to open a salon in Paris; it became one of the real forces of the eighteenth century, socially and politically. While her husband lived, she did not enjoy the freedom she desired; after his death in 1764 she was at liberty to do as she pleased, and she then began her career as a judge and counsellor in all social matters. She was regarded as the oracle of taste and urbanity, exercised a supervision over the tone and usage of society, was the censor of *la bonne compagnie* during the happy years of Louis XVI. This power in her was universally recognized. She tempered the Anglomania of the time, all excesses of familiarity and rudeness; she never uttered a bad expression, a coarse laugh or a *tutoiement* (thee and thou). The slightest affectation in tone or gesture was detected and judged by her. She preserved the good tone of society and permitted no contamination. She retarded the reign of clubs, retained the urbanity of French society, and preserved a proper and unique character in the *ancien salon français*, in the way of excellence of tone.

The Marquise de Rambouillet, Mme. de La Fayette, Mme. de Maintenon, Mme. de Caylus, and Mme. de Luxembourg are of the same type—the same world, with little variance and no decadence; in some respects, the last may be said to have approached nearest to perfection. "In her, the turn of critical and caustic severity was exempt from rigidity and was accompanied by every charm and pleasingness in her person. She often judged [a person] by [his] ability at repartee, which she tested by embarrassing questions across the table, judging [the person] by the reply. She herself was never at a loss for an answer: when shown two portraits—one of Molière and one of La Fontaine—and asked which was the greater, she answered: 'That one,' pointing to La Fontaine, 'is more perfect in a *genre* less perfect.'"

By the Goncourt brothers, her salon has been given its merited credit: "The most elegant salon was that of the Maréchale de Luxembourg, one of the most original women of the time. She showed an originality in her judgments, she was authority in usage, a genius in taste. About her were pleasure, interest, novelty, letters; here was formed the true elegance of the eighteenth century—a society that held sway over Europe until 1789. Here was formed the greatest institution of the time, the only one that survived till the Revolution, that preserved—in the discredit of all moral laws—the authority of one law, *la parfaite bonne compagnie*, whose aim was a social one—to distinguish itself from bad company, vulgar and provincial society, by the perfection of the means of pleasing, by the delicacy of friendship, by the art of considerations, complaisances, of *savoir vivre*, by all possible researches and refinements of *esprit*. It fixed everything—usages, etiquette, tone of conversation; it taught how to praise without bombast and insipidness, to reply to a compliment without disdaining or accepting it, to bring others to value without appearing to protect them; it prevented all slander. If it did not impart modesty, goodness, indulgence, nobleness of sentiment, it at least imposed the forms, exacting the appearances and showing the images of them. It was the guardian of urbanity and maintained all the laws that are derived from taste. It represented the religion of honor; it judged, and when it condemned a man he was socially-ruined."

A type of what may be called the social mistress of the nobility—the personification of good taste, elegance and propriety such as it should be—was the Comtesse de Boufflers, mistress of the Prince de Conti, intimate friend of Hume, Rousseau, and Gustave III., King of Sweden. The countess was one of the most influential and spirituelle members of French society, her special mission and delight being the introduction of foreign celebrities into French society. She piloted them, was their patroness, spoke almost all modern languages, and visited her friends in their respective countries. She was the most travelled and most hospitable of great French women, hence the woman best informed upon the world in general.

She was born in Paris in 1725, and in 1746 was married to the Comte de Boufflers-Rouvrel; soon after, becoming enamored of the Prince de Conti, she became his acknowledged mistress. To give an idea of the light in which the women of that time considered those who were mistresses of great men, the following episodes may be cited: One day, Mme. de Boufflers, momentarily forgetting her relations to the Prince de Conti, remarked that she scorned a woman who *avait un prince du sang* (was mistress of a prince of the blood). When reminded of her apparent inconsistency, she said: "I wish to give by my words to virtue what I take away from it by my actions...." On another occasion, she reproached the Maréchale de Mirepoix for going to see Mme. de Pompadour, and in the heat of argument said: "Why, she is nothing but the first *fille* (mistress) of the kingdom!" The maréchale replied: "Do not force me to count even unto three" (Mme. de Pompadour, Mlle. Marquise, Mme. de Boufflers). In those days, the position of mistress of an important man attracted little more attention than might a petty, trivial, light-hearted flirtation nowadays.

After the death of M. de Boufflers, in 1764, the all-absorbing question of society, and one of vital importance to madame, was, Will the prince marry her? If not, will she continue to be his mistress? In this critical period, Hume showed his friendship and true sympathy by giving Mme. de Boufflers most persuasive and practical advice in reference to morals—which she did not follow. Her relations with Rousseau showed her capable of the deepest and most profound friendship and sympathy. According to Sainte-Beuve, it was she who, by aid of her friends in England, procured asylum for him with Hume at Wootton. When Rousseau's rashness brought on the quarrel which set in commotion and agitated the intellectual circles of both continents, Mme. de Boufflers took his part and remained faithful to him, securing a place for him in the Château de Trie, which belonged to the Prince de Conti.

All who came in contact with her recognized the distinction, elevation of *esprit*, and sentiment of Mme. de Boufflers. With her are associated the greatest names of the time; being perfectly at home on all the political questions of the day, she was better able to converse upon these subjects than was any other woman of the time. When in 1762 she visited England, she was lionized everywhere. She was fêted at court and in the city, and all conversation was upon the one subject, that of her presence, which was one of the important events of London life. Everyone was anxious to see the famous woman, the first of rank to visit England in two hundred years. She even received some special attention from the eccentric Samuel Johnson, in this manner: "Horace Walpole had taken the countess to call on Johnson. After the conventional time of a formal call had expired, they left, and were halfway down stairs, when it dawned upon Johnson that it was his duty, as host, to pay the honors of his literary residence to a foreign lady of quality; to show himself gallant, he jumped down from the top of the stairway, and, all agitation, seized the hand of the countess and conducted her to her carriage."

No woman at court had more friends and fewer enemies than did Mme. de Boufflers, because "she united to the gifts of nature and the culture of *esprit* an amiable simplicity, charming graces, a goodness, kindness, and sensibility, which made her forget herself always and constantly seek to aid those about her." She made use of her influence over the prince in such ways as would, in a measure, recompense for her fault, and thus recommended herself by her good actions. She was the soul of his salon, "Le Temple." The love of these two people, through its intimacy and public display, through its constancy, happiness, and decency, dissipated all scandal. Always cheerful and pleased to amuse, knowing how to pay attention to all, always rewarding the bright remarks of others with a smile, which all sought as a mark of approbation, no one ever wished her any ill fortune.

The last days of the Prince de Conti were cheered by the presence of Mme. de Boufflers and the friends whom she gathered about him to help bear his illness. The letter to her from Hume, on his deathbed, is most pathetic, showing the influence of this woman and the nature of the impression she left upon her friends:

"Edinburgh, 20th of August, 1776.

"Although I am certainly within a few weeks, dear Madame, and perhaps within a few days, of my own death, I could not forbear being struck with the death of the Prince of Conti—so great a loss in every particular. My reflection carried me immediately to your situation in this melancholy incident. What a difference to you in your whole plan of life! Pray write me some particulars, but in such terms that you need not care, in case of my decease, into whose hands your letter may fall.... My distemper is a diarrhœa or disorder in my bowels, which has been gradually undermining me for these two years, but within these six months has been visibly hastening me to my end. I see death approach gradually, without any anxiety or regret. I salute you with great affection and regard, for the last time.

"DAVID HUME."

Hume died five days after this letter was written.

The last years of her life she spent with her daughter-in-law, at Auteuil, where she lived a happy life and received the best society of Paris. When she died or under what circumstances is not known. During the Revolution she lived in obscurity, busying herself with charitable work; she was one of the few women of the nobility to escape the guillotine, "This woman, who had kept the intellectual world alive with her *esprit* and goodness, of a sudden vanishes like a star from the horizon; she lives on, unnoticed by everyone, and, in that new society, no one misses her or regrets her death."

In order to fully appreciate the mistress of the eighteenth century, her power and influence, her rise to popularity and social standing, the general and accepted idea and nature of the sentiment called love must be explained; for it was to the peculiar development of that emotion that the mistress owed her fortune.

In the eighteenth century love became a theory, a cult; it developed a language of its own. In the preceding age love was declared, it spoke, it was a virtue of grandeur and generosity, of courage and delicacy, exacting all proofs of decency and gallantry, patient efforts, respect, vows, discretion, and reciprocal affection. The ideal was one of heroism, nobleness, and bravery. In the eighteenth century this ideal became mere desire; love became voluptuousness, which was to be found in art, music, styles, fashions—in everything. Woman herself was nothing more than the embodiment of voluptuousness; it made her what she was, directing and fashioning her. Every movement she made, every garment she wore, all the care she applied to her appearance—all breathed this *volupté*.

In paintings it was found in impure images, coquettish immodesties, in couples embraced in the midst of flowers, in scenes of tenderness: all these representations were hung in the rooms of young girls, above their beds. They grew up to know *volupté*, and, when old enough, they longed for it. It was useless for women to try to escape its power, and chastity naturally disappeared under these temptations. The young girl inherited the impure instincts of the mother, and, when matured, was ready and eager for all that could enchant and gratify the senses.

True domestic friendship and intimacy were rare, because the husband given to a young girl had passed through a long list of mistresses, and talked—from experience—gallant confidences which took away the veil of illusion. She was immediately taken into society, where she became familiar with the spicy proverbs and the salty prologues of the theatre, where supposedly decent women were present, in curtained boxes. At the suppers and dinners, by songs and plays, at the gatherings where held forth Duclos and others like him, in the midst of champagne, *ivresse d'esprit*, and eloquence, she was taught and saw the corruption of society and marriage, the disrespect to modesty; in such an atmosphere all trace of innocence was destroyed. She was taught that faithfulness to a husband belonged only to the people, that it was an evidence of stupidity. Manners, customs, and even religion were against the preservation of innocence and purity; and in this depravity the abbés were the leaders.

Such conditions were dangerous and disastrous not to young girls only, they affected the young men also; the latter, amidst this social demoralization, developed their evil tendencies, and, in a few generations, there was formed a Paris completely debauched. Love meant nothing more elevated than desire;

for man, the paramount idea was to have or possess; for woman, to capture. There was no longer any mystery, any secret; the lover left his carriage at the door of his love, as if to publish his good fortune; he regularly made his appearance at her house, at the hour of the toilette, at dinner and at all the fêtes; the public announcement of the liaison was made at the theatre when he sat in her box.

There came a period when so-called love fell so low that woman no longer questioned a man's birth, rank, or condition, and vice versa, as long as he or she was in demand; a successful man had nearly every woman of prominence at his feet. The men planned their attacks upon the women whom they desired, and the women connived, posed, and set most ingenious traps and devised most extraordinary means to captivate their hero. As the century wore on and the vices and appetites gradually consumed the healthy tissues, there sprang up a class of monsters, most accomplished *roués*, consummate leaders of theoretical and practical immorality, who were without conscience. To gain their ends, they manipulated every medium—valets, chambermaids, scandal, charity; their one object was to dishonor woman.

Women were no better; "a natural falseness, an acquired dissimulation, a profound observation, a lie without flinching, a penetrating eye, a domination of the senses—to these they owed their faculties and qualities so much feared at the time, and which made them professional and consummate politicians and ministers. Along with their gallantry, they possessed a calmness, a tone of liberty, a cynicism; these were their weapons and deadly ones they were to the man at whom they were aimed."

There were, in this century, superior women in whom was exhibited a high form of love, but who realized that perfect love was impossible in their age; yet they desired to be loved in an intense and legitimate manner. This phase of womanhood is well represented by Mlle. Aïssé and Mlle. de Lespinasse, both of whom felt an irresistible need of loving; they proclaimed their love and not only showed themselves to be capable of loving and of intense suffering, but proved themselves worthy of love which, in its highest form, they felt to be an unknown quantity at that time. Their love became a constant inspiration, a model of devotion, almost a transfiguration of passion. These women were products of the time; they had to be, to compensate for the general sterility and barrenness, to equalize the inequalities, and to pay the tribute of vice and debauch.

All the customs of the age were arrayed against pure womanhood and offered it nothing but temptation. Inasmuch as the husband belonged to court and to war more than to domestic felicity, he left his wife alone for long periods. The husbands themselves seemed actually to enjoy the infidelity of their wives and were often intimate friends of their wives' lovers; and it was no rare thing that when the wife found no pleasure in lovers, she did not concern herself about her husband's mistresses (unless they were intolerably disagreeable to her), often advising the mistress as to the best method of winning her husband.

It must be admitted that this separation in marriage, this reciprocity of liberty, this absolute tolerance, was not a phase of the eighteenth century marriage, but was the very character of it. In earlier times, in the sixteenth century, infidelity was counted as such and caused trouble in the household. If the husband abused his privileges, the wife was obliged to bear the insult in silence, being helpless to avenge it. If she imitated his actions, it was under the gravest dangers to her own life and that of her lover. The honor of the husband was closely attached to the virtue of the wife; thus, if he sought diversion elsewhere, and his wife fell victim to the fascinations of another, he was ridiculed. Marriage was but an external bond; in the eighteenth century, it was a bond only as long as husband and wife had affection for one another; when that no longer existed, they frankly told each other and sought that emotion elsewhere; they ceased to be lovers and became friends.

A very fertile source of so much unfaithfulness was the frequent marriage of a ruined nobleman to a girl of fortune, but without rank. Giving her his name was the only moral obligation; the marriage over and the dowry portion settled, he pursued his way, considering that he owed her no further duty. Very frequently, the husband, overcome by jealousy or humiliated by the low standard of his wife who injured or brought ridicule upon his name, would have her kidnapped and taken to a convent. This right was enjoyed by the husband in spite of the general liberty of woman. A letters-patent was obtained through proof of adultery, and the wife was imprisoned in some convent for the rest of her life, being deprived of her dowry which fell to her husband.

At one time, the great ambition of woman was to procure a legal separation— an ambition which seems to have developed into a fad, for at one period there were over three hundred applicants for legal separation, a state of affairs which so frightened Parliament that it passed rigid laws. A striking contrast to this was the custom connected with mourning. At the death of the husband, the wife wore mourning, her entire establishment, with every article of interior furnishing, was draped in the sombre hue; she no longer went out and her house was open only to relatives and those who came to pay visits of condolence. Unless she married again, she remained in mourning all her life; but it should not be understood that the veil concealed her coquetry or prevented her from enjoying her liberty and planning her future. Then, as to-day, there were many examples of fanaticism and folly; one widow would endeavor to commit suicide; another lived with the figure of her husband in wax; another conversed, for several hours of the day, with the shade of her husband; others consecrated themselves to the church.

This all-supreme sway of love and its attributes, left its impression and lasting effect upon the physiognomy of the mistress; in the early part of the century, the mistress was chosen from the respectable aristocracy and the nobility; gradually, however, the limits of selection were extended until they included the *bourgeoisie* and, finally, the offspring of the common *femme du peuple*. A woman from any profession, from any stratum of society, by her charm and intelligence, her original discoveries and inventions of debauch and licentiousness, could easily become the heroine of the day, the goddess of society, the goal and aspiration of the used-up *roués* of the aristocracy. Under Louis XIV., such popularity was an impossibility to a woman of that sort, but society under the Regency seemed to have awakened from the torpor and gloom of the later years of the monarchy to a reign of unrestrained gayety and vice.

The first woman to infect the social atmosphere of the nobility with a new form of extravagance and licentiousness was Adrienne Le Couvreur, who was the heroine of the day during the first years of the Regency. She was the daughter of a hatter, who had gone to Paris about 1702; while employed as a laundress, she often gave proof of the possession of remarkable dramatic genius by her performances at private theatricals. In 1717, through the influence of the great actor Baron, she made her appearance at the Comédie Française; the reappearance of that favorite with Adrienne Le Couvreur as companion, in the plays of Corneille, Racine, and Voltaire, reëstablished the popularity of the French theatre. Adrienne immediately became a favorite with the titled class, was frequently present at Mme. de Lambert's, gave the most sumptuous suppers herself, and was compelled to repulse lovers of the highest nobility.

Her principal lovers were Voltaire, whom she nursed through smallpox, spending many hours in reading to him, and Maurice of Saxony; she had children of whom the latter was the father, and it was she who, by selling her plate and jewelry, supplied him with forty thousand francs in order to enable him to equip his soldiers when he proposed to recover the principality of Courland. She was generous to prodigality; but when she died, the Church refused to grant consecrated ground for the reception of her remains, although it condescended to accept her munificent gift of a hundred thousand francs to charity. Her death was said to have been caused by her rival, the Duchesse de Bouillon, by means of poisoned pastilles administered by a young abbé. In the night, her body was carried by two street porters to the Rue de Bourgogne, where it was buried. Voltaire, in great indignation at such injustice, wrote his stinging poem *La Mort de Mademoiselle Le Couvreur*, which was the cause of his being again obliged to leave Paris.

The popularity of the Comédie Française declined after the deaths of Baron and Adrienne Le Couvreur, until the appearance of Mlle. Clairon, who was one of the greatest actresses of France. Born in Flanders in 1723, at a very early age she had wandered about the provinces, from theatre to theatre, with itinerant troupes, winning a great reputation at Rouen. In 1738 the leading actresses were Mlle. Quinault, who had retired to enjoy her immense fortune in private life, and Mlle. Dumesnil, the great *tragédienne*. When Mlle. Clairon received an offer to play alternately with the favorite, Mlle. Dumesnil, she selected as her opening part *Phèdre*, the *rôle de triomphe* of her rival.

The appearance of a débutante was an event, and its announcement brought out a large crowd; the presumption of a provincial artist in selecting a rôle in which to rival a great favorite had excited general ridicule, and an unusually large audience had assembled, expecting to witness an ignominious failure. Mlle. Clairon's stately figure, the dignity and grace of her carriage, "her finely chiselled features, her noble brow, her air of command, her clear, deep, impassioned voice," made an immediate impression upon the audience. She was unanimously acknowledged as superior to Mlle. Dumesnil, and the entire social and literary world hastened to do her homage.

Mlle. Clairon did as much for the theatre as did Adrienne Le Couvreur, especially in discarding, in her *Phèdre*, the plumes, spangles, the panier, the frippery, which had been the customary equipments of that rôle. She and Lecain, the prominent actor of the day, introduced the custom of wearing the proper costume of the characters represented. The grace and dignity of her stage presence caused her to be sought by the great ladies, who took lessons in her famous courtesy *grande révérence*, which was later supplanted by the courtesy of Mme. de Pompadour.

Mlle. Clairon became the recipient of great favors and honors, her most prominent slave being Marmontel, to whom she had given a room in her hôtel after Mme. Geoffrin had withdrawn from him the privilege of occupying an apartment in her spacious establishment. She contributed largely to the success of his plays, as well as to those of Voltaire, whom she visited at Ferney, performing in his private theatre. Her success was uninterrupted until she declined to play, in the *Siège de Calais*, with an actor who had been guilty of dishonesty; she was then thrown into prison, and refused to reappear. When about fifty years of age she became the mistress of the Margrave of Ansbach, at whose court she resided for eighteen years. In 1791 she returned to Paris, where, poor and forgotten, she died in 1803.

An actress or a singer who left a greater reputation through her wit, the promptness and malignity of her repartee, and her extravagance, than through her voice was Sophie Arnould, the pupil of Mlle. Clairon. She was the daughter of an innkeeper; her first success was won through her charming figure and her flexible voice. Some of the ladies attached to the court of Louis XV., having heard her sing at evening service during Passion week, had induced the royal chapel master to employ her in the choir. There, and by the warm eulogies of Marmontel during one of his toilette visits to Mme. de Pompadour, the attention of the *maîtresse-en-titre* was called to her beauty and vocal charm.

Her début was made with unusual success, but she afterward eloped with the Comte de Lauraguais, who had made a wager that he could win the beautiful artist. After her reappearance at Paris her career became a long series of dissipations and unprecedented extravagances. She was as witty as she was licentious, and many of her *bons mots* have been collected. It was she who characterized the great Necker and Choiseul, on being shown a box containing their portraits: "That is receipt and expenditure"—the credit and debit. She was one of the few prominent women who died in favor and in comfortable circumstances.

The lowest and most depraved of this licentious class of women was Mlle. La Guimard, the legitimate daughter of a factory inspector of cloth. In 1758 she entered the opera as a ballet girl, but very little is known of her during the first years of her career except in connection with her numerous lovers. In about 1768 she was living in most sumptuous style, her extravagances being paid for by two lovers, the Prince de Soubise, her *amant utile*, and the farmer- general, M. de La Borde, her *amant honoraire*.

At this period she gave three suppers weekly: one for all the great lords at court and of distinction; the second for authors, scholars, and artists; the third being a supper of *débauchées*, the most seductive and lascivious girls of the opera; at the last function, luxury and debauch were carried to unknown extremes. At her superb country home, "Pantin," she gave private performances, the magnificence of which was unprecedented and admission to which was an honor as eagerly sought as was that of attendance at Versailles.

There was another side to the nature of Mlle. La Guimard: during the terrible cold of the winter of 1768, she went about alone visiting the poor and needy, distributing food and clothing purchased with the six thousand livres given her by her lover, the Prince de Soubise, as a New Year's gift. Her charity became so general that people of all professions and classes went to her for assistance—actors and artists to borrow the money with which to pay their debts, officers with the same object in view. To one of the latter to whom she had just lent a hundred louis and who was about to sign a note, she said: "Sir, your word is sufficient. I imagine that an officer will have as much honor as *fille d'opéra*."

Her performances at "Pantin" and her luxurious mode of life required more money than the two lovers were able to supply; therefore, another was accepted in the person of the Bishop of Orléans, Monseigneur de Jarente, who supplied her with money and other necessaries. In 1771 she decided to build a hôtel with an elegant theatre which would comfortably seat five hundred people. The opening of this Temple de Terpsichore was the great event of the year (1772). All the nobility was there, even the princes of the blood, and the "delicious licenses of the presentation were fully enjoyed by those who were fortunate enough to obtain admission."

Her costumes were of such taste and became so renowned that Marie Antoinette consulted her in reference to her own wonderful inventions; the dresses became known as the *Robe à la La Guimard*. Inasmuch as the management of the Opéra supplied all gowns, the expense for this one artist was enormous, in 1779 amounting to thirty thousand livres for dresses alone. In 1785, being in financial straits, she sold her hôtel on the Rue Chaussée-d'Antin by lottery, two thousand five hundred tickets at one hundred and twenty livres each. None of the salons of Paris could compare with hers in the "costliness of the crystal and the plate of her table service, in the taste and elegance of her floral decorations—choice exotics obtained from a distance, regardless of expense."

After appearing at the Haymarket Opera House in London in 1789, Mlle. La Guimard decided to retire to private life, and married M. Despréaux, the ballet master, fifteen years her junior. During the Revolution the government ceased to pay pensions, and as she had saved very little of her wealth the two lived in the most straitened circumstances. Her fate was similar to that of the average woman of pleasure—forgotten, half-witted, stooping to any act of indecency to gain a few sous.

Such were the principal heroines of the stage, opera, and ballet; they were in harmony with the general state of that depraved society of which they were natural products; transitory lights that shone for but a short space of time, consumed by their own sensuous instinct, they were forgotten with death. The royal mistresses lived the same life and followed the same ideals, but exerted a greater and more lasting influence in the state.

Chapter XI

Royal Mistresses

In the study of the royal mistresses of the eighteenth century, we encounter two in particular,—Mme. de Pompadour and Mme. du Barry,—who, though totally different types of women, both reflect the gradual decline of ideals and morals in the first and last years of the reign of Louis XV. The former dominated the king by means of her intelligence, but the latter swayed the sovereign, already consumed by his sensual excesses, through her peculiarly seductive sensuality.

During the first years of the reign of Louis XV., one of the most influential women was Mme. de Prie, who brought about the marriage of the king to Marie Leczinska, the daughter of the King of Poland, by which manœuvre she made herself *Dame de Palais de la Reine*. The queen naturally took her and her husband into favor, regarding them as her and her father's benefactors and as entitled to her warmest gratitude. Mme. de Prie succeeded in winning the queen's affection and confidence; however, these were of little value, inasmuch as the queen's influence upon society and morals was not felt, for she led a life of seclusion, shut up in her oratory and constantly on her *prie-dieu*, and was an object of pity and ridicule.

Mme. de Prie and M. le Duc, having planned to deprive M. Fleury, the minister, of his power,—he had been the king's preceptor,—suddenly had the tables turned against them. Both were exiled, and a new coterie of ladies came into power; the Duchesse d'Alincourt replaced Mme. de Prie, and the king and M. Fleury themselves took up the affairs of state.

M. Fleury, now cardinal, perceiving that a mistress was inevitable, consented to the choice by the dissolute men and women of court of Mme. de Mailly,—or Mlle. de Nesle,—who was supposed to be a disinterested person. The king, who had no love for her, accepted her as he would have accepted anything put before him by the court. The queen was incapable of exerting any beneficial influence upon him; in fact, the more he became alienated from her, the more humble and timid did she appear when in his presence. The reign of Mlle. de Nesle had lasted less than a year, when the beautiful Mme. de La Tournelle, created Duchesse de Châteauroux, replaced her; the latter lived but a short time, being the second mistress of Louis XV. to die within a year. After her death the king raised the beautiful Mme. d'Etioles to the honor of *maîtresse-en-titre*; she, as Mme. de Pompadour, was, without doubt, the most prominent, possibly the most intelligent and intellectual, certainly the most powerful, of all French mistresses. It was the first time that a *bourgeoise* of the financier class had usurped the position of mistress—that honor having belonged exclusively to the nobility.

After the first infidelities of the king, Marie Leczinska's life became more and more austere and secluded; she remained indoors, far from the noise and activity of Versailles, leaving only for charitable purposes or for the theatre. Her mornings were entirely occupied in prayers and moral readings, after which followed a visit to the king, a little painting, the toilette, mass, and dinner. After dinner, she retired to her apartments and passed the time making tapestry, embroidering, and in charity work—no longer the recreation of leisure, but the duty of charity which the poor expected. Her taste for music, the guitar, the clavecin, all amusements in which she delighted before her marriage, were abandoned. Under such circumstances the mistress had full control of everything.

It was prophesied of Mlle. Jeanne Poisson, at the age of nine, that she would become the mistress of Louis XV. (Mme. Lebon, who made this pleasing prediction, was later rewarded with a pension of six hundred livres.) Mlle. Jeanne was the natural daughter of a butcher, but received a good education and, at the age of twenty, was married to Le Normand d'Etioles, farmer of taxes. It was shortly after this that she managed to attract the king's attention, at a hunting party in the forest of Senart. With the assistance of her friends, she was successful in winning the king, and, in April, 1754, at a supper which lasted far into the early morning, reposing in his arms, she virtually became the mistress of Louis XV. The actual accomplishment of this, however, depended upon the disposal of her husband, which was easily arranged by Louis, who ordered Le Normand d'Etioles from Paris, thus securing her from any harm from him. The brothers De Goncourt write thus of her talents:

"Marvellous aptitudes, a scholarly and rare education, had given to this young woman all the gifts and virtues that made of a woman what the eighteenth century called a virtuoso, an accomplished model of the seductions of her time. Jeliotte had taught her singing and the clavecin; Guibaudet, dancing; Crébillon had taught her declamation and the art of diction; the friends of Crébillon had formed her young mind to *finesse*, to delicacies, to lightness of sentiment, and to irony of the *esprit* of the time. All the talents of grace seemed to be united in her. No woman mounted a horse better; none captured applause more quickly than did she with her voice and instrument; none recalled in a better way the tone of Gaussin or the accent of Clairon; none could tell a story better. And there where others could vie with her in coquetry, she carried off the honors by her genius of toilette, by the graceful turn she gave to a mere rag, by the air she imparted to a mere nothing which ornamented her, by the characteristic signature which her taste gave to everything she wore."

To please and charm, Mme. d'Etioles had a complexion of the most striking whiteness, lips somewhat pale, and eyes of an indescribable color in which were blended and compounded the seduction of black eyes, the seduction of blue eyes. She had magnificent chestnut hair, ravishing teeth, and the most delicious smile which "hollowed her cheeks into two dimples which the engraving of *La Jardinière* shows; she had a medium-sized and round waist, perfect hands, a play of gestures lively and passionate throughout, and, above all, a physiognomy of a mobility, of a changeableness, of a marvellous animation, wherein the soul of the woman passed ceaselessly, and which, constantly in process of change, showed in turn an impassioned and imperious tenderness, a noble seriousness, or roguish graces."

In September, 1745, she was formally presented to the queen and court as the Marquise de Pompadour, and, in October, was installed at Fontainebleau in the apartments formerly occupied by Mme. de Châteauroux, who had just died. Her position was not an easy one, for all the superb jealousy and hateful scorn which the aristocracy cherished against the power and wealth of the *bourgeoisie* were turned against her; but the court scandal-mongers and intriguers found their match in Mme. de Pompadour, who showed herself so superior in every respect to the court ladies that the hostilities gradually ceased, but not until the public itself had expended all its efforts against this upstart.

Her first move was to surround herself with friends, the first of whom she wisely sought in the queen. Paying her every possible attention, she persuaded the king to show her more consideration. The Prince de Conti, the Paris brothers, and others of the great financiers of France were added to her circle. After this she began her rule as first minister, in place of the dead Fleury, by giving places and pensions to her favorites. The reign of economy and domestic morality came to an end with the accession of Mme. de Pompadour; in fact, it was soon generally considered that those upon whom she did not shower favors were her enemies. At this time the nobility of France was too corrupt to raise any serious objections to the dispensing of favors by the *maîtresse-en-titre*, whether she were of noble birth or not.

As mistress, her duties were many: to manipulate and manage Versailles, please and captivate the king, make allies, win over the highest officials and keep control of them, put her own friends in office, attach to her favor every man of prominence,—princes and ministers,—keep in touch with the court, appease, humor, and win the honor of the courtiers, "attach consciences, recompense capitulations, organize about the mistress an emulation of devotion and servility by means of prodigality of the favors of the king and the money of the state; but what was a more burdensome task,—she must occupy the king, aid and agitate him, fight off constantly, from day to day and hour to hour, ennui."

This terrible ennui, indifference, enervation, this lazy and splenetic humor of the king, she succeeded in distracting, in soothing, and amusing. She understood him perfectly—therein lie the great secret of the favor of Mme. de Pompadour and the great reason of her long domination which only death could end. She had the patience and genius to soothe the many ills of the monarch, possessing an intuitive understanding of his moral temperament, and a complete comprehension of his nervous sensibility; these gifts were a science with her and enabled her to keep alive his taste for and enjoyment of life. Mme. de Pompadour is said to have taken possession of the very existence of Louis XV.

"She appropriates and kills his time, robs him of the monotony of hours, draws him through a thousand pastimes in this eternity of ennui between morning and night, never abandoning him for a minute, not permitting him to fall back upon himself. She takes him away from work, disputes him to the ministers, hides him from the ambassadors. In his face must not be seen a cloud or the slightest trace of care of affairs; to Maurepas, in the act of reading some reports to the king, she says: 'Come now, M. de Maurepas, you turn the king yellow.... Adieu, M. de Maurepas'; and Maurepas gone, she takes the king, she smiles upon the lover, she cheers the man."

In 1747, two years after her installation, she interested the king in a theatre, and inaugurated the famous representations at the Théâtre des Petits Appartements; she herself was one of its best actresses, singers, and musicians. All the members of the nobility vied with one another in procuring admission to these performances, as auditors or actors. Her contemporaries say that she was without a rival in acting, for in that art she found opportunity to show her vivacity, her *esprit* of tone, and her malice of expression, the effect of which was heightened by her voice, graceful figure, and tasteful attire, which became the envy of every court lady.

Almost all rising young artists and men of letters were encouraged or pensioned by Mme. de Pompadour. Her salon would have become one of the most distinguished of the period, as she was, herself, the most remarkably talented and beautiful woman of her time, had not lack of moral principles and an intense love of power led her to seek the gratification of her ambitions in the much envied position of mistress of the king. To assist at her toilette became a favor more eagerly desired than presence at the *petit lever* of the king. The court became more brilliant, the middle class rose, the prestige of the nobility declined; the last became, in general, but a crowd of *cordons bleus*, eager to claim the favor of any of her protégés. Every noble house offered a daughter in marriage to her brother, whom she made *intendant* of public buildings, and who looked with much displeasure upon the actions of his sister.

Mme. de Pompadour made a thorough study of the politics of Europe in relation to the affairs of the nation—a proceeding in which she was aided by her extraordinary intelligence, acute perception of difficulties and conditions, domestic and foreign; by the exercise of these qualities, she put herself in touch with the politics of France, always consulting the best of minds and winning many friends among them. In 1749 she succeeded in ridding herself of her pronounced enemy, Maurepas, minister and confidential adviser of the king, and subsequently began her reign as absolute mistress and governor of France.

Her life then became one of constant labor, which gradually undermined her health. Appreciating the mental indolence of Louis, she would place before him a clear and succinct résumé of all important questions of state affairs, which she, better than any other, knew how to present without wearying him. Realizing that her power depended upon her influence over the king, and that she was surrounded by men and women who were simply waiting for a favorable opportunity to cause her downfall, she was constantly on the defensive. She considered it "the business of her life to make her yoke so easy and pleasant, and from habit so necessary to him, that an effort to shake it off would be an effort that would cause him real pain." Her happiest hours—for she did not love the king—were those spent with her brother, the Marquis de Marigny, in the midst of artists, musicians, and men of letters.

As for the queen, she was in the background, absolutely. "All the prerogatives of a princess of a sovereign house were, at this time, about 1750, conferred by the king upon Mme. de Pompadour, and all the pomp and parade then deemed indispensable to rank so exalted were fully assumed by her." At the opera, she had her *loge* with the king, her tribune at the chapel of Versailles where she heard mass, her servants were of the nobility, her carriage had the ducal arms, her etiquette was that of Mme. de Montespan, Her father was ennobled to De Marigny, her brother to be Marquis de Vandières. The marriage of her daughter to a son of the king and his former mistress was planned, then with a son of Richelieu, then with others of the nobility; fortunately, the girl died.

Mme. de Pompadour gradually amassed a royal fortune, buying the magnificent estate of Crécy for six hundred and fifty thousand livres; "La Celle," near Versailles, for twenty-six thousand livres; the Hôtel d'Evreaux, at Paris, for seventy-five thousand livres—and these were her minor expenses; her paintings, sculpture, china, pottery, etc., cost France over thirty-six million livres. Her imagination in art and inventions was wonderful; she retouched and decorated the château in which she was received by the king; she made "Choisy"—the king's property—her own, as it were, by all the embellishments she ordered and the expenditures which her lover lavished upon it at her request. All the luxuries of the life at "Choisy," all the refinements even to the smallest detail, had their origin in her inventions. It was she who planned the fairy château with its wonderful furniture, her own invention.

At that time, her whole life was spent in adding variety to the life of the king and in distracting the ennui which pursued him. In her retreats she affected the simplicity of country life; the gardens contained sheepfolds and were free from the pomp of the conventional French gardens; there were cradles of myrtle and jasmine, rosebushes, rustic hiding places, statues of Cupid, and fields of jonquils filled the air with the most intoxicating perfume. There she amused her sovereign by appearing in various characters and acting the parts —now a royal personage, now a gardener's maid.

However, in spite of all cunning study of the sensuous nature of the king, in spite of this perpetual enchantment of his senses, this favorite was obliged to fight for her power every minute of her existence. If hers were a conquest, it was a laborious one, held only through ceaseless activity; continual brainwork, all the countermoves and manœuvres of the courtesan, were required to keep Mme. de Pompadour seated in this position, which was surrounded by snares and dangers.

To possess the time of the king, occupy his enemies, soothe his fatigue, arouse his wearied body condemned to a milk diet, to preserve her beauty— all these were the least of her tasks. She must be ever watchful, see evil in every smile, danger in every success, divine secret plots, be on guard to resist the court, the royal family, the ministry. For her there was no moment of repose: even during the effusions of love she must act the spy upon the king, and, with presence of mind and calmness, must seek in the deceitful face of the man the secrets of the master.

Every morning witnessed the opening of a new comedy: a gay smile, a tranquil brow, a light song, must ever disguise the mind's preoccupation and all the machinations of her fertile brain. At one time the Comte d'Argenson, desiring to succeed Fleury as minister, almost arrived at supplanting Mme. de Pompadour by young Mme. de Choiseul, who, having charmed the king on one occasion, obtained from him a promise that he would make her his mistress—which would necessitate desertion of Mme. de Pompadour; but, by the natural charms of which age had not robbed her and by bringing all her past experience into play, Mme. de Pompadour once more scored a triumph and remained the actual minister to the king. All this nervous strain was gradually killing her, and, to overcome her physical weakness, her weary senses, her frigid disposition, she resorted to artificial stimulants to keep her blood at the boiling point and enable her to satisfy the phlegmatic king.

Undoubtedly the most disgraceful act of this all-powerful woman was the maintaining of a house of pleasure for the king, to which establishment she allured some of the most beautiful girls of the nobility, as well as of the *bourgeoisie*. These young women supposed that they were being supported by a wealthy nobleman; their children were given a pension of from three thousand to twelve thousand livres, and the mother received one hundred thousand francs and was sent to the provinces to marry; a father and mother were easily bought for the child. Thus was this clandestine trade carried on by those two—the king satisfying his utter depravity, and Mme. de Pompadour making herself all the more secure against a possible rival.

All this time her active brain was ever planning for higher honors and greater power. She aspired to becoming *dame de palais*, but as an excommunicated soul, a woman living in flagrant violation of the laws of morality and separated from her husband, she could not receive absolution from the Church, in spite of her intriguing to that effect. She did succeed, however, in influencing the king to make her lady of honor to the queen; therefore, in gorgeous robes, she was ever afterward present at all court functions.

She began to patronize the great men of the day, to make of them her debtors, pension them, lodge them in the Palais d'Etat, secure them from prison, and to place them in the Academy. Voltaire became her favorite, and she made of him an Academician, historiographer of France, ordinary gentleman of the chamber, with permission to sell his charge and to retain the title and privileges. For these favors he thanked her in the following poem:

"Ainsi donc vous réunissez

Tous les arts, tous les goûts, tous les talents de plaire;

Pompadour vous embellissez

La Cour, le Parnasse et Cythère,

Charme de tous les cœurs, trésor d'un seul mortel,

Qu'un sort si beau soit éternel!"

[Thus you unite all the arts, all the tastes, all the talents, of pleasing; Pompadour, you embellish the court, Parnassus, and Cythera. Charm of all hearts, treasure of one mortal, may a lot so beautiful be eternal!]

Voltaire dedicated his *Tancrède* to her; in fact, his influence and favor were so great that he was about to receive an invitation to the *petits soupers* of the king, when the nobility rose up in arms against him, and, as Louis XV. disliked him, the coveted honor was never attained. To Crébillon, who had given her elocution lessons in her early days and who was now in want, she gave a pension of a hundred louis and quarters at the Louvre. Buffon, Montesquieu, Marmontel, and many other men of note were taken under her protection.

It was Mme. de Pompadour who founded, supported, and encouraged a national china factory; the French owe Sèvres to her, for its artists were complimented and inspired by her inveterate zeal, her persistency, her courage, and were assisted by her money. She brought it into favor, established exhibits, sold and eulogized the ware herself, until it became a favorite. Also, through her management and zeal the Military School was founded.

The disasters of the Seven Years' War are all charged to Mme. de Pompadour. The motive which caused her to decide in favor of an alliance with Austria against Frederick the Great was a personal desire for revenge; the latter monarch had dubbed her "Cotillon IV," and had rather scorned her, refusing to have anything to do with a Mlle. de Poisson, "especially as she is arrogant and lacks the respect due to crowned heads." The flattering propositions of the Austrian ambassador, Kaunitz, who treated with her in person and won her over, did much to set her against Germany, and induced her to influence Louis XV. to accept her view of the situation—a scheme in which she was victorious over all the ministers; the result was the Austrian alliance. The letter of Kaunitz to her, in 1756, will illustrate her position:

"Everything done, Madame, between the two courts, is absolutely due to your zeal and wisdom. I feel it and cannot refuse myself the satisfaction of telling you and of thanking you for having been my guide up to the present time. I must not even keep you ignorant of the fact that their Imperial Majesties give you the full justice due you and have for you all the sentiments you can desire. What has been done must merit, it seems to me, the approbation of the impartial public and of posterity. But what remains to be done is too great and too worthy of you for you to give up the task of contributing and to leave imperfect a work which cannot fail to make you forever dear to your country. I am, therefore, persuaded that you will continue your attention to an object so important. In this case, I look upon success as certain and I already share, in advance, the glory and satisfaction which must come to you, no one being able to be more sincerely and respectfully attached to you than is your very humble and obedient servant, the Count de Kaunitz-Rietberg."

She received her first check when, Damiens having attempted to assassinate the king, the dauphin was regent for eleven days. She was confined to her room and heard nothing from the king, who was in the hands of the clergy. Among the friends who abandoned her was her protégé Machault, the guard of the seals, who conspired with D'Argenson to deprive her of her power and went so far as to order her departure. After the king's recovery, both D'Argenson and Machault were dismissed and Mme. de Pompadour became more powerful than before.

Her influence and usurpation of power bore heavily upon every department of state; she appointed all the ministers, made all nominations, managed the foreign policy and politics, directed the army and even arranged the plans of battle. Absolute mistress of the ministry, she satisfied all demands of the Austrian court, a move which brought her the most flattering letter from Kaunitz, in which he gives her the credit for all the transactions between the two courts.

Despite all her political duties and intrigues, she found time for art and literature. Not one minute of the day was lost in idleness, every moment being occupied with interviews with artists and men of letters, with the furnishers of her numerous châteaux, architects, designers, engineers, to whom she confided her plans for embellishing Paris. Being herself an accomplished artist, she was able to win the respect and attention of these men. Her correspondence was immense and of every nature, political and personal. She was an incessant reader, or rather student, of books on the most serious questions, which furnished her knowledge of terms of state, precedents of history, ancient and modern law; she was familiar with the contents of works on philosophy, the drama, singing, and music, and with novels of all nations; her library was large and well selected.

During the latter years of her life she was considered as the first minister of state or even as regent of the kingdom, rather than as mere mistress. Louis XV. looked to her for the enforcement of the laws and his own orders. She was forced to receive, at any time, foreign ambassadors and ministers; she had to meet in the Cabinet de Travail and give counsel to the generals who were her protégés; the clergy went to her and laid before her their plaints, and through her the financiers arranged their transactions with the state.

Notwithstanding all this influence and power, the record of her last years is a sorrowful one. More than ever queen, she was no longer loved by the king, who went to Passy to continue his liaison with a young girl, the daughter of a lawyer. When Louis XV. as much as recognized a son by this woman, Mme. de Pompadour became deeply concerned; but the king was too much a slave to her domination to replace her, so she retained favor and confidence; the following letter shows that she enjoyed little else:

"The more I advance in years, my dear brother, the more philosophical are my reflections. I am quite sure that you will think the same. Except the happiness of being with the king, who assuredly consoles me in everything, the rest is only a tissue of wickedness, of platitudes, of all the miseries to which poor human beings are liable. A fine matter for reflection (especially for anyone born as meditative as I)!..." Later on, she wrote: "Everywhere where there are human beings, my dear brother, you will find falseness and all the vices of which they are capable. To live alone would be too tiresome, thus we must endure them with their defects and appear not to see them."

She realized that the king kept her only out of charity and for fear of taking up any energetic resolution. Her greatest disappointment was the utter failure of her political plans and aspirations, which came to naught by the Treaty of Paris. There was absolutely no glory left for her, and chagrin gradually consumed her. Her health had been delicate from youth; consumption was fast making inroads and undermining her constitution, and the numerous miscarriages of her early years as mistress contributed to her physical ruin. For years she had kept herself up by artificial means, and had hidden her loss of flesh and fading beauty by all sorts of dress contrivances, rouges, and powders. She died in 1764, at the age of forty-two.

Writers differ as to the true nature of Mme. de Pompadour, some saying that she was bereft of all feeling, a callous, hard-hearted monster; others maintain that she was tender-hearted and sympathetic. However, the majority agree as to her possession of many of the essential qualifications of an able minister of state, as well as great aptitude for carrying on diplomatic negotiations.

She was the greatest patroness of art that France ever possessed, giving to it the best hours of her leisure; it was her pastime, her consolation, her extravagance, and her ruin. All eminent artists of the eighteenth century were her clients. Artists were nourished, so to speak, by her favors. It may truthfully be said that the eighteenth-century art is a Pompadour product, if not a creation. The whole century was a sort of great relic of the favorite. Fashions and modes were slaves to her caprice, every new creation being dependent upon her approbation for its survival—the carriage, the *cheminée*, sofa, bed, chair, fan, and even the *étui* and toothpick, were fashioned after her ideas. "She is the godmother and queen of the rococo." Such a eulogy, given by the De Goncourt brothers, is not shared by all critics. Guizot wrote: "As frivolous as she was deeply depraved and base-minded in her calculating easiness of virtue, she had more ambition than comported with her mental calibre or her force of character; she had taken it into her head to govern, by turns promoting and overthrowing the ministers, herself proffering advice to the king, sometimes to good purpose, but still more often with a levity as fatal as her obstinacy."

In *The Old Régime*, Lady Jackson has given an unprejudiced estimate of her: "She was the most accomplished and talented woman of her time; distinguished, above all others, for her enlightened patronage of science and of the arts, also for the encouragement she gave to the development of improvements in various manufactures which had stood still or were on the decline until favored by her; a fresh impulse was given to progress, and a perfection attained which has never been surpassed and, in fact, rarely equalled. *Les Gobelins*, the carpets of the Savonnerie, the *porcelaine de Sèvres*, were all, at her request, declared *Manufactures Royales*. Some of the finest specimens of the products of Sèvres, in ornamental groups of figures, were modelled and painted by Mme. de Pompadour, as presents to the queen.... The name of Pompadour is, indeed, intimately associated with a whole school of art of the Louis Quinze period—art so inimitable in its grace and elegance that it has stood the test of time and remains unsurpassed. Artists and poets and men of science vied with each other in admiration of her talents and taste. And it was not mere flattery, but simply the praise due to an enlightened patroness and a distinguished artist."

If we consider the morals of high society, we shall scarcely find one woman of rank who could cast a stone at Madame de Pompadour. While admitting her moral shortcomings, it must nevertheless be acknowledged that she showed an exceptional ability in maintaining, for twenty years, her influence over such a man as Louis XV. Such was the power of this woman, the daughter of a tradesman, mistress, king in all save title. She was, however, less powerful than her successor,—that successor who was less clever and less ambitious, who "never made the least scrupulous blush at the lowness of her origin and the irregularity of her life,"—Mme. du Barry.

Mme. du Barry was the natural daughter of Anne Béqus, who was supported by M. Dumonceau, a rich banker at Paris. The child was put into a convent, and, after passing through different phases of life, she was finally placed in a house of pleasure, where she captivated the Comte du Barry, at whose harem she became the favorite. The count, who had once before tried to supply the king with a mistress, now planned for his favorite. The king ordered the brother of Du Barry, Guillaume, to hasten to Paris to marry a lady of the king's choice. The girl's name had been changed officially and by the clergy, and a dowry had been given her. Thus was it possible for the king, after she had become the Comtesse du Barry, to take her as a mistress. Her husband was sent back to Toulouse, where he was stationed, while his wife was lodged at Versailles, within easy access of the king's own chamber.

After much intriguing and diplomacy on the part of her friends, especially Richelieu, she was to be presented at court. The scene is well described by the De Goncourt brothers, and affords a truthful picture of court manners and customs of the latter part of the reign of Louis XV.:

"The great day had arrived—Paris was rushing to Versailles. The presentation was to take place in the evening, after worship. The hour was approaching. Richelieu, filling his charge as first gentleman, was with the king, Choiseul was on the other side. Both were waiting, counting the moments and watching the king. The latter, ill at ease, restless, agitated, looked every minute at his watch. He paced up and down, uttered indistinct words, was vexed at the noise at the gates and the avenues, the reason of which he inquired of Choiseul. 'Sire, the people—informed that to-day Mme. du Barry is to have the honor of being presented to Your Majesty—have come from all parts to witness her *entrée*, not being able to witness the reception Your Majesty will give her.' The time has long since passed—Mme. du Barry does not appear. Choiseul (her enemy) and his friends radiate joy; Richelieu, in a corner of the room, feels assurance failing him. The king goes to the window, looks into the night—nothing. Finally, he decides, he opens his mouth to countermand the presentation. 'Sire, Mme. du Barry!' cries Richelieu, who had just recognized the carriage and the livery of the favorite; 'she will enter if you give the order.' Just then, Mme. du Barry enters behind the Comtesse de Béarn, bedecked with the hundred thousand francs' worth of diamonds the king had sent her, coifed in that superb headdress whose long scaffolding had almost made her miss the hour of presentation, dressed in one of those triumphant robes which the women of the eighteenth century called 'robes of combat,' armed in that toilette in which the eyes of a blind woman (Mme. du Deffand) see the destiny of Europe and the fate of ministers; and it is an apparition so beaming, so dazzling, that, in the first moments of surprise, the greatest enemies of the favorite cannot escape the charm of the woman, and renounce calumniating her beauty."

According to reports, her beauty must have been of the ideal type of the time. All the portraits and images that Mme. du Barry has left of herself, in marble, engraving, or on canvas, show a *mignonne* perfection of body and face. Her hair was long, silky, of an ashen blonde, and was dressed like the hair of a child; her brows and lashes were brown, her nose small and finely cut. "It was a complexion which the century compared to a roseleaf fallen into milk. It was a neck which was like the neck of an antique statue...." In her were victorious youth, life, and a sort of the divinity of a Hébé; about her hovered that charm of intoxication, which made Voltaire cry out before one of her portraits: *L'original était fait pour les dieux!* [The original was made for the gods!]

In her lofty position, Mme. du Barry sought to overcome the objections of the titled class, to quell jealousies and petty quarrels; she did not usurp any power and always endeavored not to trouble or embarrass anyone. After some time, she succeeded in winning the favor of some of the ladies, and, when her influence was fairly well established, she began to plan the overthrow of her enemy, De Choiseul, minister of Louis XV. She became the favorite of artists and musicians, and all Europe began to talk and write about this woman whom art had immortalized on canvas and who was then controlling the destinies of France. She succeeded, under the apprenticeship of her lover, the Duc d'Aiguillon, who was the outspoken enemy of De Choiseul, in accomplishing the fall of the minister and the fortune of her friend. This success required but a short time for its culmination, for in 1770 he was deprived of his office and was exiled to Chantilly.

Mme. du Barry was never an implacable enemy; she was too kind-hearted for that; thus, when her friend D'Aiguillon insisted on depriving De Choiseul of his fortune, she managed to procure for the latter a pension of sixty-thousand livres and one million écus in cash, in spite of the opposition of D'Aiguillon. After the fall of that minister all the princes of the blood were glad to pay her homage. She became almost as powerful as Mme. de Pompadour, but her influence was not directed in the same channels.

Her life was a mere senseless dream of *femme galante*, a luxurious revel, a constant whirl of pleasures, and extravagance in jewelry, silks, gems, etc. A service in silver was no longer rich enough—she had one in solid gold. To house all her gems of art, rare objects, furniture, she caused to be constructed a temple of art, "Luciennes," one of the most sumptuous, exquisite structures ever fitted out. The money for this was supplied by the *contrôleur général*, the Abbé Ferray, whose politics, science, duty, and aim in life consisted in never allowing Mme. du Barry to lack money. All discipline, morality, in fact everything, degenerated.

She had no rancor or desire for vengeance; she never humiliated those whom she could destroy; she always punished by silence, yet never won eternal silence by letters patent; generous to a fault, giving and permitting everything about her to be taken, she opened her purse to all who were kind to her and to all who happened in some way to please her. Keeping the heart of Louis XV. was no easy matter, as the case of Mme. de Pompadour clearly showed. The majority of his friends and her enemies endeavored to force a new mistress upon the king; surrounded on all sides by candidates for her coveted position, Mme. du Barry managed to hold her own. When the king was prostrated by smallpox, he sent her away on the last day.

The reign of Mme. du Barry was not one of tyranny, nor was it a domination in the strict sense of that word; for she was a nonentity politically, without ideas or plans. "Study the favor of Mme. du Barry: nothing that emanates from her belongs to her; she possesses neither an idea nor an enemy; she controls all the historical events of her time, without desiring them, without comprehending them.... She serves friendships and individuals, without knowing how to serve a cause or a system or a party, and she is protected by the providential course of things, without having to worry about an effort, intrigues, or gratitude."

Her power and influence cannot be compared with those of her predecessor, Mme. de Pompadour. Modes were followed, but never invented by her. "With her taste for the pleasures of a grisette, her patronage falls from the opera to the couplet, from paintings and statuaries to bronzes and sculptures in wood; her *clientèle* are no longer artists, philosophers, poets—they are the gods of lower domains, mimics, buffoons, dancers, comedians." She was the lowest and most common type of woman ever influential in France.

After the death of the king, she was ordered to leave Versailles and live with her aunt. Later on, she was permitted to reside within ten leagues of Paris; all her former friends and admirers then returned, and she continued to live the life of old, buying everything for which she had a fancy and living in the most sumptuous style, never worrying about the payment of her debts. After a few years she was entirely forgotten, living at Luciennes with but a few intimate friends and her lover, the Duc de Brissac.

At the outbreak of the Revolution, she was living at Luciennes in great luxury on the fortune left her by the duke. Probably she would have escaped the guillotine had she not been so possessed with the idea of retaining her wealth. Four trips to England were undertaken by her, and on her return she found her estates usurped by a man named Grieve, who, anxious to obtain possession of her riches, finally succeeded in procuring her arrest while her enemies were in power. From Sainte-Pélagie they took her to the Conciergerie, to the room which Marie Antoinette had occupied.

Accused of being the instrument of Pitt, of being an accomplice in the foreign war, of the insurrection in La Vendée, of the disorders in the south, the jury, out one hour, brought in a verdict of guilty, fixing the punishment at death within twenty-four hours, on the Place de la République. Upon hearing her sentence, she broke down completely and confessed everything she had hidden in the garden at Luciennes. On her way to the scaffold, she was a most pitiable sight to behold—the only prominent French woman, victim of the Revolution, to die a coward. The last words of this once famous and popular mistress were: "Life, life, leave me my life! I will give all my wealth to the nation. Another minute, hangman! *A moi! A moi!*" and the heavy iron cut short her pitiful screams, thus ending the life of the last royal mistress.

Chapter XII

Marie Antoinette and the Revolution

The condition of France at the end of the reign of Louis XV. was most deplorable—injustice, misery, bankruptcy, and instability everywhere. The action of the law could be overridden by the use of arbitrary warrants of arrest —*lettres de cachet*. The artisans of the towns were hampered by the system of taxation, but the peasant had the greatest cause for complaint; he was oppressed by the feudal dues and many taxes, which often amounted to sixty per cent of his earnings. The government was absolute, but rotten and tottering; the people, oppressively and unjustly governed, were just beginning to be conscious of their condition and to seek the cause of it, while the educated classes were saturated with revolutionary doctrines which not only destroyed their loyalty to the old institutions, but created constant aspirations toward new ones.

Thus, when Louis XVI., a mere boy, began to reign, the whole French administrative body was corrupt, self-seeking, and in the hands of lawyers, a class that dominated almost every phase of government. In general, inefficiency, idleness, and dishonesty had obtained a ruling place in the governing body; the few honest men who had a minor share in the administration either fell into a sort of disheartened acquiescence or lost their fortunes and reputations in hopeless revolt.

Under these conditions Louis XVI. began his reign; and although peace seemed to exist externally, the country was in revolution. France was as much under the modern "ring rule" as any country ever was—a condition of affairs largely due to the nature of the young king, whose predominant characteristics might be called a supreme awkwardness and an unpardonable lack of will power. He was a man who, during the first part of his reign, led a pure life; he possessed good and philanthropic intentions, but was hampered by a weak intellect and a stubbornness which bore little resemblance to real strength of will. Also, he entertained strong religious convictions, which were extremely detrimental to his policy and caused disagreements with his ministers— Turgot, on account of his philosophical principles, Necker, on account of his Protestantism.

His wife had those qualities which he lacked, decision and strength of character; unfortunately, she wielded no influence over him in the beginning, and when she did gain it, she used it in a fatal manner, because she was ignorant of the needs of France. Throughout her career of power, she evinced headstrong wilfulness in pursuing her own course. Thus, totally incapable of acting for himself, Louis XVI. was practically at the mercy of his aunts, wife, courtiers, and ministers, who fitted his policy to their own desires and notions; therefore, the vast stream of emoluments and honors was diverted by the ministers and courtiers into channels of their own selection. There were formed parties and combinations which were constantly intriguing for or against each other.

At the time of the accession of Louis XVI., when poverty was general over the kingdom, the household of the king consisted of nearly four thousand civilians, nine thousand military men, and relatives to the enormous number of two thousand, the supporting of which dependents cost France some forty- five million francs annually. Luckily there was no mistress to govern, as under Louis XV., but, in place of one mistress who was the dispenser of favors, there were numerous intriguing court women who were as corrupt and frivolous as the men. These split the court into factions. As the finances of the country sank to the lowest ebb, odium was naturally cast upon the whole court, without exception, by the people; hence, the wholesale slaughter of the nobility during the Revolution.

In this period, the most critical in the history of France, the queen, Marie Antoinette, as the central figure, the leader of society, the model and example to whom all looked for advice upon morals and fashions, played an important rôle. Although not of French birth, she deserves to be ranked among the women influential in France, since she became so thoroughly imbued with French traits and characteristics that she forgot her native tongue. French life and spirit moulded her in such fashion that even the French look upon her as a French woman.

Before judging this unfortunate princess who has been condemned by so many critics, we must take into consideration the demands that were made upon her. Parade was the primary requisite: she was obliged to keep up the splendor and attractiveness of the French monarchy; in this she excelled, for her manner was dignified, gracious, and "appropriately discriminating. It is said that she could bow to ten persons with one movement, giving, with her head and eyes, the recognition due to each one." It is said, also, that as she passed among the ladies of her court, she surpassed them all in the nobility of her countenance and the dignified grace of her carriage. All foreigners were enchanted with her, and to them she owes no small part of her posthumous popularity.

She was reproached by French women for being exclusively devoted to the society of a select, intimate circle. Moreover, her conduct brought slander upon her; as her companions she chose men and women of bad reputation, and was constantly surrounded by dissipated young noblemen whom she permitted to come into her presence in costumes which shocked conservative people; she encouraged gambling, frequented the worst gambling house of the time, that of the Princesse de Guéménée, and visited masked balls where the worst women of the capital jostled the great nobles of the court; her husband seldom accompanied her to these pleasure resorts.

During part of the reign of Marie Antoinette the country was waging an expensive war and was deeply in debt, but the queen did not set an example of economy by retrenching her expenses; although her personal allowance was much larger than that of the preceding queen, she was always in debt and lost heavily at gambling. Generally, she avoided interference with the government of the state, but as the wife of so incapable a king she was forced into an attempt at directing public matters. Whenever she did mingle in state affairs, it was generally fatal to her interests and popularity. She usually carried out her wishes, for the king shrank from disappointing his wife and dreaded domestic contentions.

He permitted her to go out as she did with the Comte d'Artois, her brother-in-law, to masked balls, races, rides in the Bois de Boulogne, and on expeditions to the salon of the Princesse de Guéménée, where she contracted the ills of a chronically empty purse and late hours. When attacked by measles, to relieve her ennui—which her ladies were not successful in doing—she procured the consent of the king to the presence of four gentlemen, who waited upon her, coming at seven in the morning and not departing until eleven at night; and these were some of the most depraved and debauched among the nobility—such as De Besenval, the Duc de Coigny, and the Duc de Guines.

While in power, she always sided with extravagance and the court, against economy and the nation. If we add to all these defects a vain and frivolous disposition, a nature fond of admiration, pleasure, and popularity, and lending a willing ear to all flattery, compliments, and counsels of her favorites, her Austrian birth, and as "little dignity as a Paris grisette in her escapades with the dissipated and arrogant Comte d'Artois," we have, in general, the causes of her wide unpopularity.

It will be seen that as long as she was frivolous and imprudent, she was flattered and admired; as soon as she became absolutely irreproachable, she was overwhelmed with harsh judgments and expressions of ill will. The first period was during the first years of the reign of Louis XVI., while he was still all-powerful and popular; the second phase of her character developed during the trying days of the king's first fall into disfavor and his ultimate imprisonment and death. From this account of her career, it will be seen that Marie Antoinette, as dauphiness and queen, was rather the victim of fate and the invidious intrigues of a depraved court than herself an instigator and promulgator of the extravagance and dissipation of which she was accused.

We must remember the atmosphere into which Marie Antoinette was thrust upon her arrival in France. One of the first to sup with her was that most licentious of all royal mistresses, Mme. du Barry, who asked for the privilege of dining with the new princess—a favor which the dissipated and weak king granted. Louis XV. was nothing more than a slave to vice and his mistresses. The king's daughters—Mmes. Adelaïde, Victoire, and Sophie—were pious but narrow-minded women, resolutely hostile to Mme. du Barry and intriguing against her. The Comtes de Provence and d'Artois were both pleasure-loving princes of doubtful character; their sisters—Mmes. Clotilde and Elisabeth—had no importance. The family was divided against itself, each member being jealous of the others. The dauphin, being of a retiring disposition and of a close and self-contained nature, did little to add to the happiness of the young princess. Thus, she was literally forced to depend upon her own resources for pleasure and amusement and was at the mercy of the court, which was never more divided than in about 1770—the time of her appearance.

At that time there were two parties—the Choiseul, or Austrian, party, and those who opposed the policy of Choiseul, especially in the expulsion of the Jesuits; the latter were called the party of the *dèvôts* and were led by Chancellor Maupeau and the Duc d'Aiguillon. This faction, with the mistress —Mme. du Barry—as the motive power, soon broke up the power of Choiseul. The young and innocent foreign princess, unschooled in intrigue and politics, could not escape both political parties; upon her entrance into the French court, she was immediately classed with one or the other of these rival factions and thus made enemies by whatever turn she took, and was caught in a network of intrigues from which extrication was almost impossible.

Here, in this whirl of social excesses, her habits were formed; hers being a lively, alert, active nature, fond of pleasure and somewhat inclined toward raillery, she soon became so absorbed in the many distractions of court life that little time was left her for indulgence in reflection of a serious nature. Her manner of life at this time in part explains her subsequent career of heedlessness, excessive extravagance, and gayety.

At first her aunts—Mmes. Adelaïde and Sophie—succeeded in partially estranging her from Louis XV., who had taken a strong fancy to his granddaughter; but this influence was soon overcome—then these aunts turned against her. Her popularity, however, increased. Innumerable instances might be cited to show her kindness to the poor, to her servants, to anyone in need—a quality which made her popular with the masses. In time almost everyone at court was apparently enslaved by her attractions and endeavored to please the dauphiness—this was about 1774, when she was at the height of her popularity.

However, there developed a striking contrast between the dauphiness and the queen; Burke called the former "the morning star, full of life and splendor and joy." In fact, she was a mere girl, childlike, passing a gay and innocent life over a road mined with ambushes and intrigues which were intended to bring ruin upon her and destined eventually to accomplish their purpose. By being always prompt in her charities, having inherited her mother's devotion to the poor, she won golden opinions on all sides; and the reputation thus gained was augmented by her animated, graceful manner and her youthful beauty.

Little accustomed to the magnificence that surrounded her, she soon wearied of it, craving simpler manners and the greater freedom of private intercourse. When, as queen, she indulged these desires, she brought upon herself the abuse and vilification of her enemies. While dauphiness, her actions could not cause the nation's reproach or arouse public resentment; as queen, however, her behavior was subject to the strictest rules of etiquette, and she was responsible for the morals and general tone of her court. This responsibility Marie Antoinette failed to realize until it was too late.

Upon the accession of Louis XVI., a clean sweep was made of the licentious and discredited agents of Mme. du Barry, and a new ministry was created. The former mistress, with her lover, the Duc d'Aiguillon, was banished, although Mme. Adelaïde succeeded in having Maurepas, uncle of the Duc d'Aiguillon, made minister. Marie Antoinette had little interest in the appointment after she failed to gain the honor for her favorite, De Choiseul, who had negotiated her marriage.

The queen then proceeded to carry out her long-cherished wishes for society dinners at which she could preside. Her every act, however, was governed by inflexible laws of etiquette, some of which she most impatiently suffered, but many of which she impatiently put aside. With this manner of entertaining begins her reign as queen of taste and fashion, for Louis XVI. left to his wife the responsibility of organizing all entertainments, and her aspiration was to make the court of France the most splendid in the world. From that time on, all her movements, her apparel, her manners, to the minutest detail, were imitated by the court ladies. This custom, of course, led to reckless extravagance among the nobility, for whenever Marie Antoinette appeared in a new gown, which was almost daily, the ladies of the nobility must perforce copy it.

Tidings of these extravagances of the queen and her court in time reached the empress-mother in Vienna. Marie Thérèse severely reproached her daughter, writing: "My daughter, my dear daughter, the first queen—is she to grow like this? The idea is insupportable to me." Yet, "to speak the exact truth," said her counsellor, Mercy, when writing to the empress-mother, "there is less to complain of in the evil which exists than in the lack of all the good which might exist." It is chronicled to her credit that all her expenditure was not upon herself alone, but that she was equally lavish when she attempted charity.

Her first political act, the removal of Turgot, was disastrous. She thought she was humoring public opinion, which was strongly against the minister on account of his many reforms, but her primary reason was rather one of personal vengeance. Turgot had been openly hostile to her friend and favorite, the Duc de Guines. She was then in the midst of her period of dissipation; "dazzled by the glory of the throne, intoxicated by public approval," she overstepped the bounds of royal propriety, neglecting etiquette and forgetting that she was secretly hated by the people because of her origin; her greatest error was in forgetting that she was Queen of France and no longer the mere dauphiness.

Under the escort of her brother-in-law, the Comte d'Artois, she was constantly occupied with pleasures and had time for little else. The king, retiring every night at eleven and rising at five, had all the doors locked; so the queen, who returned early in the morning, was compelled to enter by the back door and pass through the servants' apartments. Such behavior gave plentiful material to M. de Provence, the king's brother, who remained at home and composed, for the *Mercure de France*, all sorts of stories, from so- called trustworthy information, on the king, on society, and especially on the doings of the queen.

Marie Antoinette's fondness for the chase and the English racing fad, for gambling, billiards, and her *petits soupers* after the riding and racing, gave ample opportunity to the gossipmongers and enemies. In spite of the vigorous remonstrances of her mother, the empress, she persisted in her wild career of dissipation and extravagance, and drew upon herself more and more the disrespect of the people, especially in appearing at places frequented by the disreputable of both sexes, by entering into all noisy and vulgar amusements, by her disregard and disdain of all the conventionalities of the court. She increased her unpopularity by reviving the sport of sleighing; for this purpose she had gorgeous sleighs constructed at a time when the population of France was in misery. Such proceedings caused libels, epigrams, and satirical chansonnettes to flow thick and fast from her enemies. Her one idea was to seek congenial pleasures: she appeared to be wholly oblivious to the disapproval of public opinion.

The slanderous tongues of her husband's aunts, the "jealousies and bitter backbiting of her own intimate circle of friends," the infamous accusations brought against her by her sisters-in-law, the attacks of the Comte de Provence, and the indifference of the king himself, all helped to increase her unpopularity.

Among her personal friends was the Princesse de Lamballe, whose influence was preponderant for several years; she was not a conspicuously wise woman, but one of spotless character. Her ambitions, personal and for her relatives, often caused much trouble, for she became the mouthpiece of her allies and her clients, for whom she "solicited recommendations with as much pertinacity as if she had been the most inveterate place hunter on her own account." Her favors were too much in one direction to suit the queen, for, much attached to the memory of her husband, the princess naturally sympathized with the Orléans faction. As superintendent of the household of the queen, replacing the Comtesse de Noailles, she gave rise to much scandal. Her salary, through intrigues, had been raised to fifty thousand écus, while her privileges were enormous; for instance, no lady of the queen could execute an order given her without first obtaining the consent of the superintendent. The displeasure and vexation which this restriction caused among the court ladies may be imagined; complaints became so frequent that the queen tired of them, and her affection for her friend was thus cooled.

She sought other friends, among whom Mme. de Polignac was the favorite and almost supplanted the Princesse de Lamballe in the regard of the queen. To her she presented a large grant of money, the tabouret of a duchess, the post of governess to the children of France; and her friends received the appointments of ambassadors, and nominations to inferior offices. She was not by nature an intriguing woman, but was soon surrounded by a set of young men and women who made use of her favor and took advantage of her influence; the result was the formation of a regular Polignac set, almost all questionable persons, but an exclusive circle, permitting no division of favor, and undoing all who endeavored to rival them. This coterie of favorites may be said to have caused Marie Antoinette as much unpopularity and contributed as much to her ruin, and even to that of royalty, as did any other cause originating at court. Mme. de Lamballe was no match for her rival, so she retired, a move which increased the influence of Mme. de Polignac, to whose house the whole court flocked. The queen followed her wherever she went, made her husband duke, and permitted her to sit in her presence.

By spending so much of her time at the salons of Mme. de Polignac and the Princesse de Guéménée, the queen excited the displeasure and enmity of many of the court and the people; at those places, De Besenval, De Ligny, De Lauzun,—men of the most licentious habits and expert spendthrifts,—seemed to enjoy her intimate friendship, a state of affairs which caused many scandalous stories and helped to alienate some of the greatest houses of France. This injudicious display of preference for her own circle of friends also fostered a general distrust and dislike among the people. The first families of France preferred to absent themselves from her weekly balls at Versailles, since attendance would probably result in their being ignored by the queen, who permitted herself to be so engrossed by a bevy of favorites and her own amusements as scarcely to notice other guests.

Her eulogists find excuse for all this in her lightness of heart and gay spirits, as well as in the manner of her rearing, having been brought up in the court of Louis XV., where she saw shameless vice tolerated and even condoned. Although she preserved her virtue in the midst of all this dissipation, she became callous to the shortcomings of her friends and her own finer perceptions became blunted. Thus, in the most critical years of her reign, her nobler nature suffered deterioration, which resulted fatally.

Despite many warnings, she could not or would not do without those friends. She excused anything in those who could make themselves useful to her amusement: everyone who catered to her taste received her favor. M. Rocheterie, in his admirable work, *The Life of Marie Antoinette*, gives as the source of her great love of pleasure her very strongly affectionate disposition, —the need of showering upon someone the overflowing of an ardent nature, —together with the desire for activity so natural in a princess of nineteen. As a place in which to vent all these emotions, these ebullitions of affections and amusements, the king presented her with the château "Little Trianon," where she might enjoy herself as she liked, away from the intrigues of court.

Marie Antoinette has become better known as the queen of "Little Trianon" than as a queen of Versailles. At the former place she gave full license to her creative bent. Her palace, as well as her environments, she fashioned according to her own ideas, which were not French and only made her stand out the more conspicuously as a foreigner. From this sort of fairy creation arose the distinctively Marie Antoinette art and style; she caused artists to exhaust their fertile brains in devising the most curious and magnificent, the newest and most fanciful creations, quite regardless of cost—and this while her people were starving and crying for bread! The angry murmurings of the populace did not reach the ears of the gay queen, who, had she been conscious of them, might have allowed her bright eyes to become dim for a time, but would have soon forgotten the passing cloud.

There was constant festivity about the queen and her companions, but no etiquette; there was no household, only friends—the Polignacs, Mme. Elisabeth, Monsieur, the Comte d'Artois, and, occasionally, the king. To be sure, the amusements were innocent—open-air balls, rides, lawn fêtes, all made particularly attractive by the affability of the young queen, who showed each guest some particular attention; all departed enchanted with the place and its delights and, especially, with the graciousness of the royal hostess. There all artists and authors of France were encouraged and patronized—with the exception of Voltaire; the queen refused to patronize a man whose view upon morality had caused so much trouble.

Music and the drama received especial protection from her. The triumph of Gluck's *Iphigénie en Aulide*, in 1774, was the first victory of Marie Antoinette over the former mistress and the Piccini party. This was the second musical quarrel in France, the first having occurred in 1754, between the lovers of French and Italian music, with Mme. de Pompadour as protectress. After Gluck had monopolized the French opera for eight years, the Italian, Piccini, was brought from Italy in 1776. Quinault's *Roland* was arranged for him by Marmontel and was presented in 1778, unsuccessfully; Gluck presented his *Iphigénie en Aulide*, and no opera ever received such general approbation. "The scene was all uproar and confusion, demoniacal enthusiasm; women threw their gloves, fans, lace kerchiefs, at the actors; men stamped and yelled; the enthusiasm of the public reached actual frenzy. All did honor to the composer and to the queen."

Marie Antoinette, however, also gave Piccini her protection. Gluck, armed with German theories and supporting French music, maintained for dramatic interest, the subordination of music to poetry, the union or close relation of song and recitative; whereas, the Italian opera represented by Piccini had no dramatic unity, no great ensembles, nothing but short airs, detached, without connection—no substance, but mere ornamentation. Gluck proved, also, that tragedy could be introduced in opera, while Piccini maintained that opera could embrace only the fable—the marvellous and fairylike. This musical quarrel became a veritable national issue, every salon, the Academy, and all clubs being partisans of one or the other theory; it did much to mould the later French and German music, and much credit is due the queen for the support given and the intelligence displayed in so important an issue.

All singers, actors, writers, geniuses in all things, were sure of welcome and protection from Marie Antoinette; but she permitted her passion for the theatre to carry her to extremes unbecoming her position, for she consorted with comedians, played their parts, and associated with them as though they were her equals. Such conduct as this, and her exclusiveness in court circles, encouraged calumny. Versailles was deserted by the best families, and all the pomp and traditions of the French monarchs were abandoned. The king, in sanctioning these amusements at the "Little Trianon," lost the respect and esteem of the nobility, but the queen was held responsible for all evil,—for the deficit in the treasury, and the increase in taxes; to such an extent was she blamed, that the tide of public popularity turned and she was regarded with suspicion, envy, and even hatred.

In the spring of 1777 the queen's brother, the Emperor Joseph II. of Austria, arrived in Paris for a visit to his sister and the court of France. The relations between him and Marie Antoinette became quite intimate; the emperor, always disposed to be critical, did not hesitate to warn his sister of the dangers of her situation, pointing out to her her weakness in thus being led on by her love of pleasure, and the deplorable consequences which this weakness would infallibly entail in the future. The queen acknowledged the justness of the emperor's reasoning, and, though often deeply offended by his frankness and severity, she determined upon reform. This resolution was, to some extent, influenced by the hope of pregnancy; so, when her expectations in that direction proved to be without foundation, so keen was the disappointment thus occasioned, that, in order to forget it, she plunged into dissipation to such an extent that it soon developed into a veritable passion. Bitterly disappointed, vexed with a husband whose coldness constantly irritated her ardent nature, fretful and nervous, there naturally developed a morbid state of mind which explains the impetuosity with which she attempted to escape from herself.

In December, 1778, a daughter was born to the queen, and she welcomed her with these words: "Poor little one, you are not desired, but you will be none the less dear to me! A son would have belonged to the state—you will belong to me." After this event the queen gave herself up to thoughts and pursuits of a more serious nature. In 1779 the dauphin was born, and from that period Marie Antoinette considered herself no longer a foreigner.

After the death of Maurepas, minister and counsellor to the king, the queen became more influential in court matters. She relieved the indolent monarch of much responsibility, but only to hand it over to her favorites. The period from 1781 to 1785 was the most brilliant of the court of Louis XVI. and Marie Antoinette, one of dissipation and extravagance, the rich *bourgeoisie* vying with the nobility in their luxurious style of living and in lavish expenditure. "The finest silks that Lyons could weave, the most beautiful laces that Alençon could produce, the most gorgeous equipages, the most expensive furniture, inlaid and carved, the tapestry of Beauvais and the porcelain of Sèvres—all were in the greatest demand." Necker was replaced by incompetent ministers, the treasury was depleted, and the poor became more and more restless and threatening. Once more, and with increased vehemence, was heard the cry: *A bas l'Autrichienne!*

During the American war of the Revolution, Marie Antoinette was always favorable to the Colonial cause, protecting La Fayette and encouraging all volunteers of the nobility, who embarked for America in great numbers. She presented Washington with a full-length portrait of herself, loudly and publicly proclaiming her sympathy for things American. She assured Rochambeau of her good will, and procured for La Fayette a high command in the *corps d'armée* which was to be sent to America. When Necker and other ministers were negotiating for peace, from 1781 to 1785, she persisted in asserting that American independence should be acknowledged; and when it was declared, she rejoiced as at no political event in her own country.

Her political adventures were few; in fact, she disliked politics and desired to keep aloof from the intrigues of the ministers. She may have been instrumental in the downfall of Necker—at least, she secured the appointment, as minister of finance, of the worthless Calonne, who, it will be remembered, brought about the ruin of France in a short period. In time, however, the queen recognized his worthlessness and would have nothing to do with him, thus making in him another implacable enemy.

Events were fast diminishing the popularity of the queen. When, after the long-disputed question of presenting the *Marriage of Figaro*, she herself undertook to play in *The Barber of Seville* in her theatre at the Trianon, she overstepped the bounds of propriety. Then followed the affair of the diamond necklace, in which the worst, most cunning, and most notorious rogues abused the name of the queen. That was the great adventure of the eighteenth century. Boehmer, the court jeweler, had, in a number of years, procured a collection of stones for an incomparable necklace. This was intended for Mme. du Barry, but Boehmer offered it to the queen, who refused to purchase it, and he considered himself ruined. It may be well to add that the queen had previously purchased a pair of diamond earrings which had been ordered by Louis XV. for his mistress; for those ornaments she paid almost half her annual pin money, amounting to nine hundred thousand francs. The jeweler, therefore, had good reason to hope that she would relieve him of the necklace.

An adventuress, a Mme. de La Motte, acquainted at court and also with the Prince Louis de Rohan, who had incurred the displeasure of the queen, informed the cardinal that Marie Antoinette was willing to again extend to him her favor. She counterfeited notes, and even went so far as to appoint a meeting at midnight in the park at Versailles. The supposed queen who appeared was no other than an English girl, who dropped a rose with the words: "You know what that means." The cardinal was informed that the queen desired to buy the necklace, but that it was to be kept secret—it was to be purchased for her by a great noble, who was to remain unknown. All necessary papers were signed, and the necklace turned over to the Prince de Rohan, who, in turn, intrusted it to Mme. de La Motte to be given to the queen; but the agent was not long in having it taken apart, and soon her husband was selling diamonds in great quantities to English jewelers.

In time, as no payments were received and no favors were shown by the queen, an investigation followed. The result was a trial which lasted nine months; the cardinal was declared not guilty, the signature of the queen false, Mme. de La Motte was sentenced to be whipped, branded, and imprisoned for life, and her husband was condemned to the galleys. Nevertheless, much censure fell to the share of the queen. It was the beginning of the end of her reign as a favorite whose faults could be condoned. She was beginning to reap the fruits of her former dissipations. In about 1787, when she least deserved it, she became the butt of calumny, intrigues, and pamphlets.

During these years she was the most devoted of mothers; she personally looked after her four children, watched by their bedsides when they were ill, shutting herself up with them in the château so that they would not communicate their disease to the children who played in the park. In 1785 the king purchased Saint-Cloud and presented it to the queen, together with six millions in her own right, to enjoy and dispose of as she pleased. That act added the last straw to the burden of resentment of the overwrought public; from that time she was known as "Madame Deficit." Also she was accused of having sent her brother, Joseph II., one hundred million livres in three years. She was hissed at the opera. In 1788 there were many who refused to dance with the queen. In the preceding year a caricature was openly sold, showing Louis XVI. and his queen seated at a sumptuous table, while a starving crowd surrounded them; it bore the legend: "The king drinks, the queen eats, while the people cry!" Calonne, minister of finance, an intimate friend of the Polignacs, but in disfavor with the queen, also made common cause with the enemies, in songs and perfidious insinuations. Upon his fall, in 1787, the queen's position became even worse.

The last period of the life of the queen, La Rocheterie calls the militant period —it was one in which the joy of living was no more; trouble, sorrows upon sorrows, and anxieties replaced the former care-free, happy radiance of her youth. At the reunion of the States-General, while the country at large was full of confidence and the king was still a hero, the queen was the one dark spot; calumny had done its work—the whole country seemed to be saturated with an implacable hatred and prejudice against her whom they considered the source of all evil. Throughout the ceremonies attending the States- General, the queen was received with the same ominous silence; no one lifted his voice to cheer her, but the Duc d'Orléans was always applauded, to her humiliation.

Whatever may have been the faults and excesses of her youth, their period was over and in their place arose all the noble sentiments so long dormant. When the king was about to go to Paris as the prisoner of the infuriated mob, La Fayette asked the queen: "Madame, what is your personal intention?" "I know the fate which awaits me, but my duty is to die at the feet of the king and in the arms of my children," replied the queen. During the following days of anxiety she showed wonderful courage and graciousness, "winning much popularity by her serene dignity, the incomparable charm which pervaded her whole person, and her affability."

Upon the urgent request of the queen the Polignac set departed, and Mme. de Lamballe endeavored to do the honors for the queen, by receptions three times a week, given to make friends in the Assembly. At those functions all conditions of people assembled, and instead of the witty, brilliant conversations of the old salon there were politics, conspiracies, plots; instead of the gay and laughing faces of the old times there were the worn and anxious faces of weary, discouraged men and women. There was, indeed, a sad contrast between the gay, frivolous, haughty queen of the early days, and this captive queen—submissive, dignified, "majestic in her bearing, heroic, and reconciled to her awful fate."

Her period of imprisonment, the cruelty, neglect, inadequate food and garments, her torture and indescribable sufferings, the insults of the crowd and the newspapers, her heroic death, all belong to history. "The first crime of the Revolution was the death of the king, but the most frightful was the death of the queen." Napoleon said: "The queen's death was a crime worse than regicide." "A crime absolutely unjustifiable," adds La Rocheterie, "since it had no pretext whatever to offer as an excuse; a crime eminently impolitic, since it struck down a foreign princess, the most sacred of hostages; a crime beyond measure, since the victim was a woman who possessed honors without power."

Because Marie Antoinette played a romantic rôle in French history, it is quite natural to find conflicting and contradictory opinions among her biographers. The most conflicting may be summed up in these words: the queen's influence upon the Revolution was great—her extravagances, her haughty bearing, her scorn of the etiquette of royalty, her enemies, her prejudices, the arrests which she caused, etc. Then her pernicious influence upon the king, after the breaking out of the Revolution—she caused his hesitancy, which led to such disastrous results, and his plan of annihilating the States Assembly; the gathering of the foreign troops and his many contradictory and uncertain commands were all laid at her door, making of her an important and guilty party to the Revolution. Another estimate is more humane and, probably, is the result of cooler reflection, yet is not always accepted by Frenchmen or the world at large. It represents her as neither saint nor sinner, but as a pure, fascinating woman, always chaste, though somewhat rash and frivolous. Proud and energetic, if inconsiderate in her political actions and somewhat too impulsive in the selection of friends upon whom to bestow her favors, she is yet worthy of the title of queen by the very dignity of her bearing; always a true woman, seductive and tender of heart, she became a martyr "through the extremity of her trials and her triumphant death."

Although history makes Marie Antoinette a central figure during the reign of Louis XVI. and the period of the Revolution, yet her personal influence was practically limited to the domain of the social world of customs and manners; her political influence issued mainly from or was due to the concatenation of conditions and circumstances, the results of her friends' doings, while her social triumphs were products of her own activity. The two women—her intimate friends—who during this period were of greatest prominence, who owed their elevation and standing entirely to the queen, were women of whom little has survived. In her time, Mme. de Polignac was an influential woman, wielding tremendous power, contributing largely to the shaping and climaxing of France's fate; yet this influence was centred in reality in the Polignac set, which was composed of the most important, daring, and consummate intriguers that the court of France had ever seen. She escaped the guillotine, and by doing so escaped the attention of posterity.

Mme. de Lamballe, who wrote nothing, did nothing, effected nothing, is better known to the world at large, is more respected and honored, than is Mme. de Polignac or even the great salon leaders such as Mme. de Genlis or Mlle. de Lespinasse. She owes this prominence to her undying devotion to her queen, to her marvellous beauty, and to her tragic death on the guillotine. She was not even bright or witty, the essentials of greatness among French women —not one *bon mot* has survived her; but she may well be placed by the side of her queen for one sublime virtue, too rare in those days,—chastity. She was Princess of Sardinia; upon the request of the Duke of Penthièvre to Louis XV. to select a wife for his son, the Prince of Lamballe, she was chosen. A year after the marriage the prince died; and although the marriage had not been a happy one, because of the dissolute life of the prince, his wife forgave him, and "sorrowed for him as though he deserved it."

When in 1768 the queen died, two parties immediately formed, the object of both of them being to provide Louis XV. with a wife: one may be called the reform party, striving to keep the old king in the paths of decency; while the other was composed of the typical eighteenth century intriguers, endeavoring to revive the "grand old times." The candidate of the former was Mme. de Lamballe, that of the latter, the dissolute Duchesse du Barry. This state of affairs was made possible by the disagreement of the political and social schemes of the court and ministry. Soon after, in 1770, the king negotiated the marriage of Marie Antoinette and the dauphin, and from that time began the friendship of the future queen and the Princesse de Lamballe. Entering the unfamiliar circle of this highly debauched court, the young dauphiness sought a sympathetic friend, and found her in the princess. No figure in that society was more disinterested and unselfishly devoted. In all the queen's undertakings, fêtes, and other amusements, she was inseparable from the princess, who was indeed a rare exception to the majority of the women of that time.

The friendship of these two women was uninterrupted, save for a period extending from 1778 to 1785, when Mme. de Polignac and her set of intriguers succeeded in estranging them and usurping all the favors of the queen. When the outside world was accrediting to Marie Antoinette every popular misfortune, when she lost by death both the dauphin and the Princess Beatrice, when fate was against her, when the future promised nothing but evil, she found no stauncher friend, better consoler, more ardent admirer, than her old companion. Learning of the removal of the royal family to the Tuileries, she rejoined the queen. In 1791, with the escape of the royal fugitives, the princess left for England, to seek the protection of the English government for her royal friends.

Mr. Dobson says she was scarcely the *discrète et insinuante et touchante Lamballe*, with a marvellous sang-froid, hardly the astute diplomatist, that De Lescure makes her. "She was rather the quiet, imposing Lamballe of old, interested in her friends and what she could do for them, but never shrewd and diplomatic." In November she returned to France, to meet her queen and to suffer death for her sake,—and for this unswerving devotion she has a place in history. She stands out also as the one normal woman in the crowds of impetuous, shallow, petty, and, in many cases, pitifully debauched women of the time. Not majestic greatness, but a direct, unaffected sweetness and consistent goodness entitle her to rank among the great women of France.

Chapter XIII

Women of the Revolution and the Empire

Many women of the revolutionary period have no claim for mention other than a last glorious moment on the guillotine—"ennobled and endeared by the self-possession and dignity with which they faced death, their whole life seems to have been lived for that one moment." The society which had brought on and stirred up the Revolution was enervated and febrile. Paris was one large kennel of libellers and pamphleteers and intriguers. The salon frequenters were trained conversationalists and brilliant beauties who danced and drank, discoursed and intrigued. It was a superficial elegance, with virtue only assumed. The art of pleasing had been developed to perfection, but, instead of the actual accomplishments of the old régime, there was merely the outward appearance—luxury, dress, and magnificence; the bearing and language were of the ambitious common people. "The great women are those who, the day before, were taken from the cellar or garret of the salon."

During the Directorate, luxury and libertinism reigned almost as absolutely as during the monarchy. Barras was supreme. He had his mistress, or *maîtresse-en-titre*, in the beautiful Mme. Tallien, the queen of beauty of the salon of *la mode*. Ease and dissolute enjoyment were the aims of Barras, and in these his mistress was his equal. They gave the most sumptuous dinners, prepared by the famous chefs of the late aristocratic kitchens, while the people were starving or living on black bread. She impudently arrayed herself in the crown diamonds and appeared at the reception given to Napoleon.

The salons under the Empire are said to have preserved French politeness, courtesy, and the usages of *la bonne compagnie*, but intolerance and tyranny reigned there; the spirit of intrigue only was obeyed. From the beginning of the Revolution to the Empire, it may be said that the streets of Paris from one end to the other were a wild turmoil of people in fever heat—ready for any crime or cruelty, anxious for anything promising excitement. Where formerly the elegant lovers of the nobility were wont to promenade, the rabid populace held undisputed possession.

These were years, about 1780 to 1800, during which women shared the same fate with men; and, consigned to the same prisons, ever resigned and ready to die for principle, they knew how to die nobly. It was truly an age of the martyrdom of woman—an age in which she lived, through almost superhuman conditions, at the side of man. She was all-powerful, triumphant as never before; not, however, through her intellectual superiority as in the previous age, but through her courage. There was not one powerful woman standing out alone, but groups of them, hosts of them. It was during the

Directorate especially that woman controlled almost every phase of activity.

The woman who embodied all the heterogeneous vices of the past nobility and the rising plebs was Mme. Tallien, the goddess of vice and of the vulgar display of wealth. Her caprices were scrupulously followed, while about her jealousy and slanders were thick. Then immorality had no veil, but was low, brutish, and open to everyone. With the accession of Napoleon to absolute power, there was a fusion of the element just described with the remnant of the old régime. Josephine soon formed a select and congenial social circle, excluding Mme. Tallien and the Directorate adherents. Evidences of saddening memories of the past and a general gloom were visible everywhere in this circle. The disappointment of the nobility on returning from their exile was somewhat lessened by the very select bi-weekly reunions in the salon of Talleyrand, and by the brilliant suppers of the old régime, which were revived at the Hôtel d'Anjou.

The salon of Mme. de Staël was a political debating club rather than a purely social reunion. She being an ardent Republican, it was in her salon that the Royalist plot to bring back the Bourbons was overthrown. In a short time there were a number of brilliant salons, each one showing a nature as distinct as those of the eighteenth century. Thus, Joseph Bonaparte received the distinguished governmentals and the intriguing women of society at the Château de Mortfoulaine; at Lucien Bonaparte's hôtel youth and beauty assembled; at Mme. de Permon's salon there were music and conversation, tea, lemonade, and biscuits, twice a week. It remains but to characterize these different ages of French social and political evolution by the great women who, each one of her age, are the representative types.

The woman who, during the Revolution, not only added her name to the long list of martyrs, but who also made history and contributed to the very nature of those days of terror and uncertainty, was Mme. Roland, whom critics both extol and condemn—the fate of all historical characters. It would be difficult to estimate this remarkable person and her work without some details of her life.

When a mere girl she showed signs of a tempestuous future; she was seductive, but impulsive, with an inborn love for the common people—which is not always credited to her—and for democracy. These qualities were quickened during her experience at Versailles, for while there for a few days' visit she saw the pitiless social world in all its orgies, revelries of luxury, and wanton extravagances. There, also, she contracted that deep-seated hatred for the queen and royalty.

There was, indeed, a long list of suitors for the hand of the impulsive maiden; but owing to her views as to a husband and her restless, unsettled state of mind, she could not decide upon any one of them. To her mother, when urged to accept one, she said: "I should not like a husband to order me about, for he would teach me only to resist him; but neither do I wish to rule my husband. Either I am much mistaken, or those creatures, six feet high, with beard on their chins, seldom fail to make us feel that they are stronger; now, if the good man should suddenly bethink himself to remind me of his strength he would provoke me, and if he submitted to me he would make me feel ashamed of my power." For such a woman marriage was certainly a difficult problem. Finally, Roland de la Platières came within her circle; and although somewhat adverse to him at first, after a number of his visits she wrote: "I have been much charmed by the solidity of his judgment and his cultured and interesting conversation." Just such a man appealed to her nature and was in harmony with her views. After months of monotonous life in the convent to which she had retired, she at last consented to become the wife of Roland, not from expectations of any fortune, but purely from a sense of devoting herself to the happiness of an honorable man, to making his life sweeter.

Roland, scrupulously conscientious, painstaking, and observing, had won the position of inspector of manufactures, which took him away on foreign travels part of the time. He had acquired a thorough knowledge of manufacturing and the principles of political economy. The first years of their life were spent in each other's society exclusively, as he was insanely jealous of her; she rarely left his side, and they studied the same works, copied and revised his manuscripts, and corrected his proofs. In this she was indispensable to him. But her activity did not stop with literary work; she managed her husband's household, and for miles around her home the peasants soon learned to know her through her charitable deeds. She was the village doctor, often going for miles to attend the poor in distress. With her own hands she prepared dainty dishes with which to tempt her husband's appetite. Thus, her best years were spent upon things for which much less ability would have sufficed. She watched with breathless interest the installation of Necker and the dismissal of Turgot, the convocation of the notables, the struggles for financial recovery, and, finally, the calling of a States-General, which had not been in session since 1614. During the first stormy years, 1789-1790, she wrote burning missives to her friend Bosc, at Paris, which appeared anonymously in the *Patriote Français*, edited by Brissot, the future Girondist leader. Soon came the commission of Roland as the first citizen of the city of Lyons, which had a debt of forty million francs, to acquaint the National Assembly with its affairs.

When, in 1791, Mme. Roland arrived at Paris—for she accompanied her husband—she had already become an ardent Republican. She immediately threw herself into the whirlwind of popular enthusiasm. Her house became the centre of an advanced political group, which met there four times a week to discuss state questions. There Danton, Robespierre, Pétion, Condorcet, Buzot, and others were seen. She ably aided her husband in all his work as commissioner to the National Assembly. She was indefatigable in penning stirring letters and petitions to the Jacobin societies in the different departments. A staunch friend of Robespierre, she did much to protect him in his first efforts in public. On returning home, after her husband had completed his mission, she was no longer the same quiet, contented, submissive woman; she longed for activity in the midst of excitement.

With the meeting of the Legislative Assembly, in 1791, the group of men sent up from the Gironde immediately became the leaders, and when Mme. Roland returned to Paris she became the centre of this circle, exhorting and stimulating, advising and ordering. Through her friend Brissot, who was all-powerful in the Assembly, about February, 1792, as leader of the Girondists, who were looking for men not yet practically involved in politics, but qualified by experience for political life, her husband was made minister of the interior, and in March, 1792, he and his wife entered upon their duties. She was a keen reader of human nature, at first glance giving her husband a penetrating and generally truthful judgment of men. Being able to comprehend the temperaments of the ministers, she managed them with inimitable tact. Although all the Girondist ministers were supposed friends, she readily saw how difficult it would be for a small group of men with the same principles to act in concert. Seeing the political machine in motion at close range, she lost some of her enthusiasm for revolutionary leaders; above all, she recognized the need of a great leader. As wife of the minister, installed in the ministerial residence with no other woman present, she gave two dinners weekly to her husband's colleagues, to the members of the Assembly, and to political friends.

Her husband, the French Quaker of the Revolution, in all his simplicity of dress and honesty, was being constantly duped by the apparent good nature and sincerity of the king, against whom his wife was constantly warning him. It was she who, convinced of the king's duplicity and the need of a safeguard for the country, originated the plan of a federate camp of twenty thousand men to protect Paris when war had been declared against Austria. It was she who wrote a letter to the king in the name of the council, but sent in Roland's own name, imploring him not to arouse the mistrust of the nation by constantly betraying his suspicion of it, but to show his love by adopting measures for the welfare and safety of the country. The effect of this letter, which became historical, was the fall of the ministers. After their recall, her husband became more and more powerful. The political circulars which were published by his paper, *The Sentinel*, were composed by her. Then came the horrible massacres and executions by the hundreds, which inspired Mme. Roland with hatred for Danton, a feeling she communicated to the whole Girondist party. She desired above everything to see punished the perpetrators of the September massacres. In this plan the Girondists failed. Robespierre, Danton, and Marat were victorious, and Mme. Roland and her party fell.

When all parties and the whole populace vied with each other in welcoming back the victorious General Dumouriez, there seemed to be a possibility of a reconciliation between Danton and Mme. Roland, for when the general went to dine with her he presented her with a bouquet of magnificent oleanders.

This dinner, on October 14th, auguring good fortune to all, was the last success of Mme. Roland. She had been pushed to the very front of the Revolution. She coöperated in composing and promulgating the numerous writings of her husband by which public opinion was to be instructed. But she retained her implacable hatred for Danton, who, when her husband, ready to resign, was pressed to remain in office, cried out in the convention: "Why not invite Mme. Roland to the ministry, too! everyone knows that Roland is not alone in the office!" At this period her husband made the fatal mistake of appropriating a chest of important state papers and examining them himself instead of calling together a commission. As is known, the papers turned out to be fatal to Louis XVI. Libels and denunciations were pronounced against Roland, but his wife, called before the convention, not only succeeded in turning aside all accusations, but was voted the honors of the sitting.

At the time of the trial of the king, the power and influence of the Girondists were waning; then the Rolands became the butt of many violent and unreasonable outbursts. With the resignation of Roland on January 22, 1792, the day of the execution of the king, the fate of the Girondists was sealed. This time the minister was not asked to reconsider; in fact, his exposure of the pilfering then going on among the officials made him one of the most unpopular men in Paris. Upon their return to private life, Mme. Roland was accused of forming the plot to destroy the republic. When an armed force arrived one morning at half-past five o'clock to arrest her husband, she resisted them, herself going to the convention to expose the iniquity of such a proceeding. Failing in this, she returned to her husband, to find him safe with a friend. Being again arrested, she met the ordeal with her accustomed courage; and when the officers offered to pull down the blinds of the carriage, to shield her from the gaze of the unfriendly public, she said: "No, gentlemen! innocence, however oppressed, should not assume the attitude of guilt. I fear the eyes of no one, and do not wish to escape even those of my enemies." "You have much more character than many men," they replied; "you can calmly await justice." "Justice!" she cried; "if it existed, I should not be in your power! I would go to the scaffold as calmly as if sent by iniquitous men. I fear only guilt, and despise injustice and death!"

She has been deeply criticised for her letters written to her friend Buzot while she was in prison; yet it should be remembered that there was not the slightest chance of their meeting again, and, besides, the letters reveal the terrible struggle through which she had passed. While in prison, her beauty, grace, and fearlessness won and humanized nearly all who came under her spell. She was once unexpectedly set at liberty, but only to be sentenced to the lowest of prisons—Sainte-Pélagie. There, in the space of about one month, her memoirs, now among the French classics, were written. At the Conciergerie, where the lowest criminals and the filthiest paupers were crowded into cells with the highest of the nobility, and where the cowardly Mme. du Barry spent her last hours, Mme. Roland, by her quiet dignity and patient serenity, commanded silence and respect, and calmness and peace replaced angry and pitiful wrangling. The prisoners clung to her, crying and kissing her hand, while she spoke words of advice and consolation to the doomed women, who "looked upon her as a beneficent divinity." Her conduct under these circumstances alone is sufficient to keep alive her memory. In the last days, she clung to and upheld most passionately her principles of liberty and moderation, and in her conversation with Beugnot it was evident that she had been the real inspiration in the Girondist party for all that was best and most uplifting.

The charge against her when before the bar of judgment of Fouquier-Tinville, the terrible prosecutor, consisted in her relation to the Girondists who had been condemned to death as traitors to the republic. She met her death heroically, as became a woman who had lived bravely. At the very last moment of her life, she offered consolation to fellow victims. Her death was that of the greatest heroine of the Revolution, the climax of a life the one ambition of which had been to save her country and to shed her blood for it. As she rode through the city in her pure white raiment, serenely radiant in her own innocence, she was the embodiment of all that was highest and purest in the Revolution—one of the best and greatest women known to French history. She stands out as a representative of the French Republic.

There are a number of traits of Mme. Roland which should be considered before giving a final estimate of her character, of her rôle in French history, and of her right to be ranked among the most illustrious women of France. Critics in general seem to show her a marked hostility; such men as Caro assert that she had no modesty, that she lacked sentiment, delicacy, and reserve. M. Saint-Amand said that she reflected the vices and virtues of her age, summing up the passions and illusions, being intellectually and morally the disciple of Rousseau, but socially personifying the third estate, which in the beginning asked for nothing, but later demanded all. Politics made her cruel at times, although by nature she was good and sensible. He declared that with her acquaintance with Buzot began her career of love and ambition. In love, she believed herself a patriot, but all the various phases of her public career were simply the results of her emotions. Thus, for example, in order to see Buzot, she persuaded her husband to return to Paris to seek his fortune and make the realization of her dreams possible. She desired to play a rôle for which her origin had not destined her, which made her actions appear theatrical and affected. It is evident that she hated both the king and the queen, and at the council for the Girondist ministry demanded the death of the royal couple. And yet, Saint-Amand cites her as the most beautiful of that group of martyrs who lost their lives in the first heat of the Revolution—as the genius among them by her force, purity, and grace—the brilliant and austere muse in all the saintliness of martyrdom.

The two maxims which Mme. Roland followed throughout her career had much to do with her fall: security is the tomb of liberty; indulgence toward men in authority is the means of pushing them to despotism. These maxims as her motto or impulse, united with the spirit of push, energy, and at times rashness and impropriety, naturally led her to her ruin in those days of revolutionary ideas. She was a woman of powerful passion controlled by reason, and with frankness, devotion, courage, and fidelity as forces impelling her to activity. But there was one great defect which was at the bottom of her misfortunes,—a too great ambition, which often led her into perilous paths, even to the scaffold, which, in its turn, covered her errors.

She is said to have married M. Roland more as a theory than as a husband, for her ideas of marriage were such as to make pure, disinterested love impossible. Her husband was in many respects her intellectual superior, but she excelled him in versatility. Being her senior by twenty years, when he grew old and infirm he depended upon her for a great deal, all of which contributed to her restlessness and unhappiness. Then there developed in her that terrible struggle between loyalty to her husband and passion for Buzot, in which reason conquered. This devotion to duty was indeed rare in those days, when passion was supreme and pure love was almost unknown. Mr. Dobson says that this one trait by which she gave real expression of virtue is profoundly a product of her mental self. Her instinct would have led her to self-abandonment, so common in that day, but her "man by the head" self was stronger than her "woman by the heart" self. These two sides of her character, fostered by incessant reading, incited her fearful and unrelenting hatreds as well as her passion, "masculine enough to be mistrusted and feminine enough to be admired." These two qualities made her a power and an attraction. Her better side will continue to shine clearer as the horror of those days is revealed. Whatever may be the effects of her ambitious nature and of her unfortunate passion for Buzot, by the very virtue of her intellect and reasoning she will remain the one great woman of the Revolution who willingly and conscientiously sacrificed her life for her country.

A type perhaps more universally known in her relation to the Revolution than is Mme. Roland, though no better understood, was Charlotte Corday. Possessed of a most intense patriotism and an unusual emotional nature, she represented better than any other woman of her age the peculiar French trait —namely, the emotional perfectly combined with the mathematical. She was unique; her compatriots practised the art of studying themselves, in order to be attractive, and thus accomplished their ends, while her ambition was not to please merely, but to be of some real, practical value to her troubled country. She stands out, however, as the product of the end of the eighteenth century, a natural result of the reading of philosophy and political pamphlets. Quite naturally, she entertained such philosophical sentiments as this: "No one will lose in losing me, and the country may be better off for the sacrifice. Death comes only once, and let us use it to the good of the country or the greatest number of people." Thus, her philosophy led her to a complete detachment from her individual self, and fostered the idea of dying for her country.

Her decision to rid France of Marat was arrived at by degrees of silent brooding over the evils which beset her native land; at last she felt herself called to some great act which would necessitate the loss of her life. "The time brought forth desperation, intense warmth of feeling, concentrated upon some purpose or object;" the reasoning self seemed to be stifled by the intensity of the emotion. Yet, reason was to conquer in her. When the Girondists returned to Caen and described Robespierre and Marat in the darkest colors, she at once felt moved to put forth all her efforts to rid France of that evil blot—Marat. She was beautiful, strong, and graceful, presenting a most striking appearance. Loved by all, she felt love and devotion only for her country. Desperate and determined, she set out to fulfil her mission. She was a mere expression of the conservative element which acts only when driven by sheer necessity. Her reason impressed her with her duty and circumstances; the time acted upon her mind. "Easy, calm, resigned, she looked upon the angry masses of people who cursed her," confident that she had done her country a service, and proud that she had been the fortunate one to render it. This was her glory, and for this she will be remembered in history.

Possibly the rarest phenomenon in the history of the illustrious women of France is Mme. Récamier, who, by force of her beauty and social fascination, and without intellectual gifts or even wit, won for herself the position of queen of French society, which she held for nearly half a century. The very name of Récamier has come to evoke a vision of beauty, a beauty so well known to every lover of art who has visited the Luxembourg and gazed upon the figure "so flexible and elegant, with head well poised, brilliant complexion, little rosy mouth with pearly teeth, black curling hair, soft expressive eyes, and a bearing indicative of indolence and pride, yet with a face beaming with good nature and sympathy." Her beauty has been considered perfect, but a recent writer has proved this to be an error. M.J. Turquan, in a new volume on Mme. Récamier, is everything but sympathetic to the woman at whom criticism has rarely been pointed. "Quite a contrast to her extraordinary beauty of face," he declares, "were her hands, with big fingers square at the end and having flat nails. The same may be said of her feet, which were not only big, but were without the slightest trace of *finesse* in their lines." But though Turquan has raised numerous points in her disfavor, they are not at all likely to detract from her unrivalled reputation for beauty.

Critics have made of her a sort of enigmatic figure, supernatural and having only the form of the human. Thus, in Lamartine we find the following description: "The young girl was, they say, a *sous-entendu* of nature: she could be a wife, she could not be a mother. These are the two mysteries we must respect, but which we must know to have been the secret of the entire life of Mme. Récamier—a mournful and eternal enigma which will never have its words divined,… All her looks produced an intoxication, but brought hope to no heart. The divine statue had not descended from its pedestal for anyone, as though such a performance would have been too divine for a mortal." Her beauty was so marked, so singular, that wherever she appeared
—at the ball, the theatre—it caused a sensation; all turned to look at her and admire in subdued astonishment. Her form was said to be marvellously elegant and supple, her neck of an exquisite perfection, her mouth "deliciously small and pink, her teeth veritable pearls set in coral, her arms splendidly moulded, her eyes full of sweetness and admiration, her nose most attractive in its regularity, her physiognomy candid and spiritual, her air indolent and haughty, and her attitude reserved. Before this ensemble, you remained in ecstasy." All this beauty was particularly well set off by an exquisite white dress adorned with pearls—a style she affected the year around.

But her beauty alone could hardly have contributed to the marvellous success of Mme. Récamier, as some critics assert. Guizot, for instance, suspects her nature to have been less superficial than other writers might lead one to suppose. He said: "This passionate admiration, this constant affection, this insatiable taste for society and conversation, won her a wide friendship. All who approached and knew her—foreigners and Frenchmen, princes and the middle classes, saints and worldlings, philosophers and artists, adversaries as well as partisans—all she inspired with the ideas and causes she espoused." Her qualities outside of her beauty were tact, generosity, and elevation of soul, combined with an amiable grace which was unlimited, however superficial it may have been. Knowing how to maintain, in her salon, harmony and even cordial relations between men of the most varied temperaments and political ideas, it was possible for her to remain all her life an intelligent and warm-hearted bond between the élite minds and their diverse sentiments, which she tactfully tempered. Though ever faithful to one cause, she admitted men and women of all parties to her salon. She was moderate and just in the midst of the most arduous struggles, tolerant toward her adversaries, generous toward the conquered, sympathetic to all, and remarkably successful in conciliating all political, literary, and philosophical opinions as well as the passions which she aroused in her worshippers. To these qualities, as much as to her beauty, were due the harmony of her life, the unity of her character—which were never troubled by the turmoils of politics or the emotions of love. She was not wife, mother, or lover; "she never belonged to anyone in soul or sense." Always mistress of her imagination as well as of her heart, she permitted herself to be charmed but never carried away—receiving from all, but giving nothing in return. Her life was brilliant, but there was lurking in the background the demon of sadness and lassitude and the terrible disease of the eighteenth century,—ennui.

Two splendid portraits of Mme. Récamier are left to us: one by her passionate but unsuccessful lover, Benjamin Constant, picturing her as the personification of attractiveness; the other by M. Lenormant, showing that she desired constant admiration: "She lacked the affections which bring veritable happiness and the true dignity of woman. Her barren heart, desirous of tenderness and devotion, sought recompense for this need of living, in the homage of passionate admiration, the language of which pleases the ears." Mme. Récamier, while still a child, seemed to realize the power of her beauty, and even before her marriage in 1793 she would often say, when demanded in marriage: "Mon Dieu! how beautiful I must be already!" A mere girl when married, being only sixteen years of age, she felt no love for her husband, who was her senior by twenty-five years. Soon after the terrible times of "the Reign of Terror" she found herself one of the most beautiful women in Paris, and her husband one of the wealthiest of bankers. The three rival women of the times were Mme. Récamier, Mme. Tallien, and Josephine. The terrible days of the guillotine were succeeded by an uninterrupted reign of pleasure, "when a fever of amusement possessed everyone, and the desire for distraction of all kinds seemed to have been pushed to its limits." M. Turquan states that in the reign of dissolute extravagance, immorality, and gorgeous splendor, Mme. Récamier formed a striking contrast by her simplicity. Her first triumph was at the church Saint-Roche, the most fashionable of Paris, where she was selected to raise a purse for charity. On one occasion the collection amounted to twenty thousand francs, all due to the beauty of the woman passing the plate. She was soon invited by her friend Barras to all the balls and fêtes under the Directorate.

In 1798 M. Récamier bought the house formerly tenanted by Necker, and later established himself in a château at Clichy, where he received his friends, among whom was Lucien Bonaparte, who attempted the ruin of the beautiful hostess, but without success. Napoleon himself attempted in vain to win her to his court as maid of honor and as an ornament, her refusal incurring his anger, especially as she was the height of fashion and courted by all the great men of the age. Through her preference for the Royalists—persisting in her line of conduct in spite of her friend Fouché—she finally incurred the enmity of the emperor. Even the Princess Caroline endeavored to obtain Mme. Récamier's friendship for Napoleon, "but, although the princess gave her *loge* twice to the favorite, and upon each occasion the emperor went to the theatre expressly to gaze upon her, she remained firm in her refusal, which was one of the causes of the downfall of her banker husband, whom Napoleon might have saved had his wife been the emperor's friend." Napoleon certainly resented her refusal, for when requested to save Récamier's bank he replied: "I am not in love with Mme. Récamier!" Thus, because his wife preferred the aristocracy to the favors of Napoleon, the banker lost his fortune.

She, however, bore her misfortunes with great reserve, immediately selling her jewels and her hôtel; after which they both retired to small apartments, where they were even more honored and had greater social prestige than ever. She at once made her salon the centre of hostility against the emperor, who, according to Turquan, did not banish her, but her friend Mme. de Staël, with whom she passed over into Switzerland. Here began her romance with Prince August of Prussia, who became so enamored of her that he asked her hand in marriage. Encouraged by Mme. de Staël, she even went so far as to ask her husband for a divorce, that she might wed the royal aspirant. Her husband generously consented to this, but at the same time set forth to her the peculiar position which she would occupy, an argument that opened her eyes to her ingratitude, and she refused the prince.

Upon the fall of Napoleon, Mme. Récamier returned to Paris and, her husband's fortune being restored, gathered about her all the great nobles of the ancient régime. But fortune was unkind to her husband for the second time, and she withdrew to the Abbaye-au-Bois, where she occupied a small apartment on the third floor. Here her distinguished friends followed her— such as Chateaubriand and the Duc de Montmorency. Between her and the famous author of *Le Génie du Christianisme* there sprang up a friendship which lasted thirty years. During this time it is said that he visited her at a certain hour each day, the people in the neighborhood setting their clocks by his appearance. When he was absent on missions, he wrote her of every act of his life. Both, weary of the dissipations of society and its flatteries, sought a pure and lofty friendship, spiritual and affectionate, with no improper intimacy. There was mutual admiration and mutual respect. Even Chateaubriand's wife, who was an invalid and with whom he spent every evening, encouraged his friendship with Mme. Récamier. When, through the fall of Charles X., Chateaubriand lost his power, the friendship did not cease.

M. Turquan insists that he did not really care seriously for Mme. Récamier, that his visits were the outgrowth of mere habit. But it is to be seen that throughout his book Turquan has little sympathy for his subject, whom he pictures as a beautiful, heartless, intriguing woman with immense hands, flat, square fingers, and large feet.

The influence possessed by Mme. Récamier was most remarkable; for with the new statesmen, Thiers, Guizot, Mignet, De Tocqueville, Sainte-Beuve, as well as the nobles and princes, she was on most cordial terms, and was received in any salon which she chose to visit. Her unbounded sympathy, tact, and common sense made her friendship and counsel much in demand by great men. One trait, however, her exclusiveness, caused much discomfort in her life, such as bringing upon her the ill will of Napoleon.

In her later years her physical beauty gradually developed into a moral beauty. She was never a passionate woman, but rather passively affectionate; purely unselfish, her one desire always was to make people love her and to be happy. Her friendship with Chateaubriand in the later days was possibly the most ideal and noble in the history of French women. He never failed to make his appearance in the afternoon at the *abbaye*, driven in a carriage to her threshold, where he was placed in an armchair and wheeled to a corner by her fireplace. On one of those visits, he asked her to marry him—he being seventy-nine, she seventy-one—and bear his illustrious name. "Why should we marry at our age?" Mme. Récamier replied. "There is no impropriety in my taking care of you. If solitude is painful to you, I am ready to live in the same house with you. The world will do justice to the purity of our friendship. Years and blindness give me this right. Let us change nothing in so perfect an affection." Her charm never deserted her, and she continued to the very last to receive the greatest men and women of the day. Still the reigning beauty and the queen of French society, she died at the age of seventy-two, of cholera.

There is a wide difference between Mme. Récamier and Josephine, the two women of the Napoleonic era who exerted so powerful an influence upon the social and political fortunes of France. At the time of Napoleon's first success, the former was only twenty-one, with Madonna-like charms and attractiveness; the latter, thirty-five, but with exquisite taste in dress and skill in beautifying. Possessed of unstudied natural grace and elegance, and always attired in perfect harmony with her beauty of face and form, she could easily stand a comparison with the other beauties of the day, all of whom studied her air and manner and marked the aristocratic ease and poise of her real *noblesse* of the old régime.

"Josephine had a faded and brown complexion, which she remedied with rouge and powder; her small mouth concealed her bad teeth; her elegant figure and graceful movements, refined expression, gentle voice and dignity, all dexterously expressed with an air of coquetry, made her delightful." The happiest part of the life of Napoleon and Josephine was during their stay in Italy, when he was absolutely faithful to her. As soon as Napoleon left for Egypt, Talleyrand secured the erasure of many noble names from the list of the proscribed exiles and soon gathered about him a large number of Royalists, who immediately began to pay court to Josephine. Napoleon had enjoined her to keep her salon according to the means he provided and to entertain all influential people. To this she was equal; and all men of elevated rank, the most distinguished artists, men of letters, orators, and musicians, found her salon an enjoyable retreat. No greater galaxy of talent and genius ever assembled under the old régime than was found there,—David, Lebrun, Lesueur, Grétry, Cherubini, Méhul, J. Chénier, Hoffman, Ducis, Désaugiers, Legouvé, and others.

But her life was not without its difficulties. She was always annoyed by the Bonaparte family, who were jealous of her influence over Bonaparte. Exceedingly extravagant, in fact a spendthrift, she was always in need of money. Her virtues, however, easily offset these defects. Josephine never offended anyone, never argued politics; she made friends in all classes, thus conciliating Republicans and aristocrats; therefore, her greatest influence was as a mediator between two classes of society, by which she, more than any other woman, unconsciously contributed to the forming of a new social France. Napoleon was wise enough to recognize such diplomacy, and encouraged her to intrigue like an experienced diplomat. She was the most efficient aid and means to his future plans, and M. Saint-Amand says that without her he would possibly never have become emperor. When he returned from Egypt and found her away,—she had gone to meet him, but missed him,
—his suspicions were aroused as to her fidelity, as she had been accused of many misdeeds. When the reconciliation finally took place, after a day of sobbing and pleading, she put to work all her tact and knowledge of Parisian society to help her husband to the *coup d'état*.

She was always of great service to Napoleon in his relations with the men of whom he wished to make use; fascinating them and drawing them over to him, she charmed such persons as Barras, Gohier, Fouché, Moreau, Talleyrand, Sièyes, and others. By her skill she kept hidden Napoleon's plans until all was ripe for them. She was in the secret of the 18th Brumaire; "nothing was concealed from her. In every conference at which she was present, her discretion, gentleness, grace, and the ready ingenuity of her delicate and cool intelligence were of great service." During the Directorate she allayed jealousies and appeased the differences between Republicans and Royalists. As wife of the First Consul, she conciliated the *émigrés*. At that time she was probably the most important figure in France. The *émigrés* would call at her salon in the morning so as to avoid meeting her husband, with whom they refused to associate. Her task was not easy, but she knew so well how to say a kind word to all, and her tact was so great that when she became empress the duties and requirements of that office were natural to her. She won the Republicans by her friendship with Fouché, the representative of the revolutionary element—the aristocracy, by her dignity and refinement. Her whole appearance had a peculiar charm.

In 1803 the conditions began to be reversed. In 1796 Josephine had worried Napoleon on account of her inconstancy; she was then young and beautiful, while he was penniless and ailing. In 1803 he was thirty-four and she forty—he in his prime, wealthy and popular, she faded and powerless, no longer able to give cause for suspicion. However, nothing could make Napoleon reject her, because she was useful to him. "Her kindness was a weapon against her enemies, a charm for her friends, and the source of her power over her husband." "I gained battles, Josephine gained me hearts," are the well-known words of Napoleon. As empress she had every wish gratified, but she realized that a woman of her age could not continue indefinitely her fascination over a man as capricious as Napoleon. In the brilliant court of Fontainebleau she held the highest place, and no one could suspect the anxieties that tormented her, so cool and happy did she appear.

Josephine did many things that later on gradually helped reconcile Napoleon to a divorce: her pride, her aristocratic tendencies, extravagance and lavishness; her objection to the marriage of Hortense to General Duroc on the grounds of humble birth; her religious tendencies; her difficulty in keeping secrets, which led to highly tragic scenes between her and Bonaparte; the encouragement she gave to the jealousies and hatred of her brothers and sisters-in-law, who maliciously slandered her at every opportunity; and finally, her barrenness.

Her career after her divorce was honorable, and to-day Josephine is still held in the highest esteem in France and in the world at large. Her greatness is not in having been the wife of a great emperor, but in knowing how to adapt herself to the conditions in France into which she was suddenly thrust. As a conciliator and a mediator between two almost hopelessly irreconcilable classes of society, she deserves a prominent place among great French women.

Chapter XIV

Women of the Nineteenth Century

Among the unusually large number of prominent French women which the nineteenth century produced, possibly not more than a half-dozen names will survive,—Mme. de Staël, George Sand, Rosa Bonheur, Sarah Bernhardt, Mme. Lebrun, and Rachel. This circumstance is, possibly, largely due to the character of the century: its activity, its varied accomplishments, its wide progress along so many lines, its social development, its absolute freedom and tolerance—all of which tended to open a field for women more extensive than in any preceding century.

The salon, in its old-time glory, became a thing of the past; and the passing of this institution lessened, to a large extent, the possibility of great influence on the part of women. In short, the mode of life became, in the nineteenth century, unfavorable to the absolute power exercised by woman in former times. She was now on a level with man, enjoying more privileges and being looked upon more as the equal and possible rival of man. It became necessary for woman to make and establish her own position, whereas, under the old régime, her power and position were established by custom, which regarded her vocation as entirely distinct from that of man. The result was a host of prominent and active women, but few really great ones. Undoubtedly by far the most important and influential was Madame de Staël, but her influence and work are so intimately associated with her life that any account of her which aims at giving a true estimate of her significance must necessarily involve much biography.

Her mother, the Mme. Necker of salon fame, endeavored to bring up her daughter as the *chef d'œuvre* of natural art,—pious, modest in her conversation, dignified in her behavior, without pride or frivolity, but with wide knowledge. In this ambition she partly succeeded. At the age of eleven the young girl was present at receptions, where she listened to discussions by such men as Grimm, Buffon, Suard, and others. Her parents took her to the theatre, and she would subsequently compose short stories on what she had heard and seen. Rousseau became her ideal, but she enjoyed all literature, showing an insatiable desire for knowledge. From her early youth to her death, her conversation was ever the result of her own impulse; consequently, it was uncontrolled and lacked the seriousness imparted by deep reflection.

Interested in all things except Nature, which seemed mournful to her, while solitude horrified her, society was her delight. At the age of twenty she wrote: "A woman must have nothing to herself and must find all power in that which she loves." Her masculine ideal was a man of society, of success, a hero of the

Academy, a superior genius, animated more by the desire to please than to be useful. During these early years she wrote a great deal, her work being mostly in the form of sentimental utterances, but very little has survived her.

When she reached marriageable age, many ambitions of her parents were frustrated by her independent will. Pitt, Mirabeau, Bonaparte, were considered, but destiny had in store for her a Swedish ambassador, Staël- Holstein, a man of good family, but with little money and plenty of debts, who had been looking out for a comfortable dowry. In 1786, at the time when Marie Antoinette was at the height of her popularity, this girl of twenty years was married to a man seventeen years her senior, who had no affection for her and whom she could not love.

At Paris she immediately opened a salon, which soon eclipsed, both in beauty and wit, that of her mother; there her eloquence, enthusiasm, and conversational gifts captivated all, but her imprudent language, the recklessness of her conduct, her scorn of all etiquette, her outspoken preferences, frightened away women and stunned men. Her sympathy for her friends, Talleyrand, Narbonne, De Montmorency, together with the approaching Revolution, drew her into politics. When her father was called by the nation to the control of its finances, his daughter shared his glories.

Her salon was the centre of the élite and of all literary and political discussions; but as the majority of its frequenters were partisans of the English constitution and expressed their views openly and freely, her enemies became numerous. When Narbonne was made minister of war, a great triumph for her and her party, the eloquence of his reports was attributed to her, and when he fell into disgrace she rescued him. However, the atmosphere of Paris was too unfriendly, so she left in 1792 for her home at Coppet, which became an asylum for all the proscribed. When she visited England, she began a thorough study of its mode of life, its customs, and its parliamentary institutions. Upon her return to Coppet she wrote *Réflexions sur le Procès de la Reine*, to excite the commiseration of the judges. After the death of her mother in 1794, she devoted her energies to the education of her two boys.

After the violence of her love for Benjamin Constant, who drew her back to politics, was somewhat cooled, she became an ardent Republican, writing her treatise *Réflexions sur la Paix adressées a M. Pitt et aux Anglais*, which facilitated her return in 1795 to Paris, where she found her husband reinstalled as ambassador. Her hôtel in the Rue de Bac was reopened, and she proceeded to form a salon from the débris of society floating about in Paris. It was an assembly of queer characters—elements of the old and new régime, but not at all reconciled, converts of the Jacobin party returning for the first time into society, surrounded by the women of the old régime, using all imaginable efforts and flattery to obtain the *rentrée* of a brother, a son, or a lover; it was composed of the most moderate Revolutionists, of former Constitutionalists, of exiles of the Monarchy, whom she endeavored to bring over to the Republican cause.

Through the influence of Mme. de Staël, the decree of banishment was repealed by the convention, thus opening Paris to Talleyrand. In 1795 appeared her *Réflexions sur la Paix Intérieure*; the aim of that work being to organize the French Republic on the plan of the United States; it strongly opposed the restoration of the Monarchy. The Comité du Salut Publique accused her of double play, of favoring intrigues, and, seeing the plots of the Royalists, she adopted a new plan in her salon; politics being too dangerous, she decided to devote herself more to literature. In her book *Les Passions* she endeavored to crush her calumniators; she wrote: "Condemned to celebrity, without being able to be known I find need of making myself known by my writings."

It was not safe for her to return to Paris until 1797, when her friend Talleyrand was made minister of foreign affairs. Her efforts to charm Napoleon led only to estrangement, although he appointed her friend Benjamin Constant to the tribunate; but when he publicly announced the advent of the tyrant Napoleon, she was accused of inciting her friends against the government, and was again banished to Coppet, where she wrote the celebrated work *De la Littérature Considérée sous ses Rapports avec les Institutions Sociales*, a singular mixture of satirical allusions to Napoleon's government and cabals against his power; in that work she announced, also, her belief in the regeneration of French literature by the influence of foreign literature, and endeavored to show the relations which exist between political institutions and literature. Thus, she was the first to bring the message of a general cosmopolitan relationship of literatures and literary ideas.

In 1802 she returned to Paris and began to show, on every possible occasion, a morbid hatred for Napoleon. When her father published his work *Dernières Vues de Politique et de Finance*, expressing a desire to write against the tyranny of one, after having fought so long that of the multitude, the emperor immediately accused Mme. de Staël of instilling these ideas into her father. Her salon and forty of her friends were put into the interdict.

After the death of her husband in 1802, she was free to marry Benjamin Constant; and after refusing him, she wrote her novel *Delphine* to give vent to her feelings. The two famous lines found in almost every work on Mme. de Staël may be quoted here, as they well express her ideas on marriage: "A man must know how to brave an opinion, and a woman must submit to it." This qualification Benjamin Constant lacked, and at that time she was unable to give the submission.

Her travels in Germany, Russia, and Italy were one great succession of triumphs; by her brilliancy, her wonderful gift of conversation, and her quickness of comprehension, she everywhere baffled and astounded those with whom she conversed. Schiller declared that when she left he felt as though he were just convalescing after a long spell of illness. One day she abruptly asked the staid old philosopher Fichte: "M. Fichte, can you give me, in a short time, an *aperçu* of your system of philosophy, and tell me what you mean by your ego? I find it very obscure." He began by translating his thoughts into French, very deliberately. After talking for some ten minutes, in the midst of a deep argument she interrupted him, crying out: "Enough, M. Fichte, quite enough! I understand you perfectly; I have seen your system in illustration—it is an adventure of Baron Münchhausen." The philosopher assumed a tragic attitude, and a spell of silence fell upon the audience.

The result of her visit to Italy was her novel *Corinne*, in which the problems of the destiny of women of genius—the relative joys of love and glory—are discussed. This work remained for a whole generation the standard of love and ideals, and at the same time revealed Italy to the French, After a second visit to Germany, she began to labor seriously on her work on that country, in 1810 going *incognito* to Paris to have it printed. Ten thousand copies, ready for sale, were destroyed before reaching the public. This work opened the German world to the French; it applied, to a great nation, the doctrine of progress, defending the independence and originality of nations, while endeavoring to show that the future lay in the reciprocal respect of the rights of people, declaring that nations are not at all the arbitrary work of men or the fatal work of circumstances, and that the submission of one people to another is contrary to nature. She wished to make "poor and noble Germany" conscious of its intellectual riches, and to prove that Europe could obtain peace only through the liberation of that country. The censors accused her of lack of patriotism in provoking the Germans to independence, and of questionable taste in praising their literature; consequently, the book was denounced, all the copies obtainable were destroyed, and a vigorous search for the manuscript was undertaken. After this episode, her friends were not permitted to visit her at Coppet.

In 1811 she was secretly married to a young Italian officer, Albert de Rocca, a handsome man of twenty-three—she was then forty-five. In him she realized the conditions which she described in *Delphine*, namely, a man who braved an opinion and prejudices; and she was ready to submit herself to him, Coppet became the centre for endless pleasures and fêtes; Mme. de Staël began to write comedies and to forget Paris entirely. This blissful happiness was suddenly checked by the emperor, who determined to show his displeasure and also to give evidence of his power by banishing Schlegel and exiling Mme. Récamier and De Montmorency, who continued to visit Mme. de Staël. Fear for the safety of her husband and children influenced her to leave for Russia, where the czar ordered all Russians to honor her as the enemy of Napoleon. Indeed, she was everywhere received like a visiting queen.

In the autumn of 1816 she returned to Paris, and spent a number of months very happily in her old style—in the society of the salon. Though devoured by insomnia, enervated by the use of opium, and besieged by fear of death, she accepted all invitations, and kept open house herself, receiving in the morning, at dinner, and in the evening; and though at night she paced the floor for hours or tossed about on her bed until morning, she was yet fresh for all the pleasures of the next day. But this mode of existence was undermining her health.

She endured this constant strain until one evening in February, 1817, when, at a ball at the Duke of Decazes's, in the midst of her pleasure, she was stricken with paralysis. At the Rue des Mathurins, she had all her friends come and dine with her. Chateaubriand, who was one of the party, entered her room upon one occasion and found her suffering intensely, but able to raise herself and say: "Bonjour, my dear Francis! I am suffering, but that does not hinder me from loving you." She lingered until July, when there ended a life which not only influenced but even modified politics and the institutions of nations, which exercised, by writings, an incalculable influence upon French literature, opening paths which previously had not been trod.

The most important of her works is *De l'Allemagne*, in writing which her only desire was to make Germany known to the French, to explain it by comparison with France and to make her people admire it, and to open new paths to poetry. According to her, Germany possessed no classic prose, because the Germans attributed less importance to style than did the French. German poetry, however, had a distinct charm, being all sentiment and poetry of the soul, touching and penetrating; whereas French poetry was all *esprit*, eloquence, reason, raillery.

In her treatise on the drama, she was the first in French literature to use the term "romantic" and to define it; but she had not invented the word, Wieland having used it to designate the country in which the ancient Roman literature flourished. Her definition was: "The classic word is sometimes taken as a synonym of perfection. I use it in another acceptance by considering classic poetry that of the ancients and romantic poetry that which holds in some way to the chivalresque traditions. The literature of the ancients is a transplanted literature with us; but romantic or chivalresque literature is indigenous. An imitation of works coming from a political, social, and religious midst different from ours means a literature which is no longer in relation with us, which has never been popular, and which will become less so every day. On the contrary, the romantic literature is the only one which is susceptible of being perfected, because it bears its roots from our soil and is, consequently, the only one which can be revived and increased. It expresses our religion and recalls our history." This opinion alone was enough to create a revolt among her contemporaries. Almost all other interpretations of *Faust* were based on her conception.

At the time of its publication, her book was considered to have been written in a political spirit, but her motive was far from that; it was the action of a generous heart, a book as true and loyal to the French as was ever a book written by a Frenchman. In her work *Considérations sur la Révolution Française* she expressed the most advanced ideas on politics and government. The Revolution freed France and made it prosper; "every absolute monarch enslaves his country, and freedom reigns not in politics nor in the arts and sciences. Local and provincial liberties have formed nations, but royalty has deformed the nation by turning it to profit." Mme. de Staël found nothing to admire in Louis XIV., and to Richelieu she attributed the destruction of the originality of the French character, of its loyalty, candor, and independence. In that work she advocated education, which she considered a duty of the government to the people. "Schools must be established for the education of the poor, universities for the study of all languages, literatures, and sciences;" these ideas took root after her death.

Mme. de Staël was a finished writer; because of its force, openness, and seriousness, her style might be termed a masculine one; she wrote to persuade and, as a rule, succeeded. Her grave defect seemed to be in her inspirations, which were always superior to her ideas, and in her sentiments, which she invariably turned to passions.

Few French writers have exercised such a great influence in so many directions, and it became specially marked after her death; while living, the gossip against her salon prevented her opinions from being accepted or taking root. Her political influence was great at her time and lasted some twenty years. Directly influenced by her were Narbonne, De Montmorency, Benjamin Constant, and the Duc Victor de Broglie, her son-in-law. By her and her father, the Globe, the orators of the Academy and the tribune, and the politicians of the day, were inspired. The greatest was Guizot, who interpreted and preached in the spirit of Mme. de Staël. In history her influence was equally felt, especially in Guizot's *Essays on the History of France*, and in his *History of Civilization*, wherein civilization was considered as the constant progress in justice, in society, and in the state. To her Guizot owed his idea of *Amour dans le Mariage*. *The Historical Essays on England*, by Rémusat, an ardent admirer of hers, was largely influenced by her *Considérations*, while Tocqueville's *Ancien Régime* contains many of her ideas.

Literature owes even more to her works, which encouraged the study of foreign literatures; almost all translations were due to her works. Michelet, Quinet, Nodier, Victor Hugo, so much influenced by German literature, owe their knowledge of it mainly to her. Too much credit may be given her when it is stated that all Mignons, Marguerites, Mephistopheles, etc., proceeded indirectly from her work, as well as nearly all descriptions of travels. Lamartine undoubtedly used her *De l'Allemagne* and her *Des Passions* freely. The heroine of *Jocelyn* is called but a daughter of *Delphine*, and the same author's terrible invective against Napoleon was inspired by her.

Mme. de Staël had an indestructible faith in human reason, liberty, and justice; she believed in human perfection and in the hope of progress. "From Rousseau, she received that passionate tenderness, that confidence in the inherent goodness of man. Believing in an intimate communion of man with God, her religion was spirit and sentiment which had no need of pomp or symbols, of an intermediary between God and man." She was not so much a great writer as she was a great thinker, or rather a discoverer of new thoughts. By instituting a new criticism and by opening new literatures to the French, she succeeded in emancipating art from fixed rules and in facilitating the sudden growth of romanticism in France.

In her life, her great desire was to spread happiness and to obtain it, to love and to be loved in return. In politics it was always the sentiment of justice which appealed to her, in literature it was the ideal. Sincerity was manifested in everything she said and did. Pity for the misery of her fellow beings, the sentiment of the dignity of man and his right to independence, of his future grandeur founded on his moral elevation, the cult of justice, and the love of liberty—such were the prevailing thoughts of her life and works.

Mme. de Staël's chief influence will always remain in the domain of literature; she was the first French writer to introduce and exercise a European or cosmopolitan influence by uniting the literatures of the north and the south and clearly defining the distinction between them. By the expression of her idea that French literature had decayed on account of the exclusive social spirit, and that its only means of regeneration lay in the study and absorption of new models, she cut French taste loose from traditions and freed literature from superannuated conventionalities. Also, by her idea that a common civilization must be fostered, a union of the eastern and western ideals, and that literature must be the common expression thereof, whose object must be the amelioration of humanity, morally and religiously, she gave to the world at large ideas which are only now being fully appreciated and nearing realization. In her novels she vigorously protested against the lot of woman in modern society, against her obligation to submit everything to opinion, against the innumerable obstacles in the way of her development—thus heralding George Sand and the general movement toward woman's emancipation. France has never had a more forceful, energetic, influential, cosmopolitan, and at the same time moral, writer than Mme. de Staël.

The events in the life of George Sand had comparatively little influence upon her works, which were mainly the expression of her nature. As a young girl, she was strongly influenced by her mother, an amiable but rather frivolous woman, and by her grandmother, a serious, cold, ceremonious old lady. Calm and well balanced, and possessing an ardent imagination, she followed her own inclinations when, as a girl of sixteen, she was married to a man for whom she had no love. After living an indifferent sort of life with her husband for ten years, they separated; and she, with her children, went to Paris to find work.

After a number of unsuccessful efforts of a literary nature, she wrote *Indiana*, which immediately made her success. Her articles were sought by the journals, and from about 1830 her life was that of the average artist and writer of the time. Her relations with Chopin and Alfred de Musset are too well known to require repetition. After 1850 she retired to her home, the Château de Nohant, where she enjoyed the companionship of her son, her daughter-in- law, and her grandchildren; she died there in 1876.

To appreciate her works, it is more important to study her nature than her career. This has been admirably done by the Comte d'Haussonville. George Sand is said to have possessed a dual nature, which seemed to contradict itself, but which explains her works—a dreamy and meditative, and a lively, frolicsome nature; the first might throw light upon her religious crisis, the second, upon her social side. The combination of these two phases caused the numerous conflicts of opinions and doctrines, extending her knowledge and inciting her curiosity; the not infrequent result was an intellectual and moral bewilderment and the deepest melancholy, from which she with great difficulty freed herself. Because of these peculiarities she was constantly agitated, her strongly reflective nature keeping her awake to all important questions of the day.

Her intellectual development may be traced in her works, which, from 1830 to 1840, were personal, lyrical, spontaneous—a direct flow from inspiration, issuing from a common source of emotions and personal sorrows, being the expressions of her habitual reflections, of her moral agitations, of her real and imaginary sufferings. These first works were a protest against the tyranny of marriage, and expressed her conception of a woman in love—a love profound and naïve, exalted and sincere, passionate and chaste: such is pictured in *Indiana*. In *Valentine* she portrays the impious and unfortunate marriage that the sacrilegious conventions of the world have imposed, and the results issuing therefrom. In all of these early works are seen an inventiveness, a lively *allure*, an exquisite style, a freshness and brilliancy, *finesse* and grace; but they show an undisciplined talent, giving vent to feelings that her unbounded enthusiasm would not allow to be checked—there is emotion, but no system.

In her second period, from about 1840 to 1848, her reflection and emotion combined produced a system and theories. The higher problems took stronger hold on her as she matured; philosophy and religious science in their deeper phases excited her emotive faculties, which threw out a mere echo of what she had heard and studied. Her inspiration thus came from without, throwing out those endless declamatory outbursts which we meet in *Consuelo* and in *Comtesse de Rudolstadt*. These theory-novels were soon followed by novels dealing with social problems, now and then relieved by delightful idyllics such as *La Mare au Diable* and *François le Champi*. This third tendency M. d'Haussonville considers the least successful.

After 1850 there appeared from her pen a series of historical novels, especially fine in the portrayal of characters, variety of situations, movement, and intrigues; these are free from all social theories; in these, reverting to her first tendencies, she is at her best in elegance and clearness, in analysis of characters. Thus does the work of George Sand change from a personal lyricism, in which the emotions, held in check during a solitary and dreamy youth, burst forth in brilliant and passionate fiction, to a theoretical, systematic novel, finally reverting to the first efforts, but tempered by experience and age.

M. d'Haussonville says that in the strict sense of the word George Sand had no doctrines, but possessed a powerful imagination that manifested itself at various periods of her life. Whatever the principles might have been at first, they were made concrete under a sentiment with her, for her heart was her first inspiration, her teacher in all things. The ideas are thus analyzed through her sentiments under a threefold inspiration,—love, passion for humanity, sentiment for Nature.

According to other novels, love is the unique affair of life; without love we do not really live, before love enters life we do not live, and after we cease to love there is no object in life. This love comes directly from God, of whom George Sand had ideas peculiar to herself. The majority of her characters have a sort of mystic, exalted love, looking upon it as a sacred right, making of themselves great priests rather than genuine human lovers. This love, issuing from God, is sacred; therefore, the yielding to it is a pious act; he who resists commits sacrilege, while he who blames others for it is impious; for love legitimizes itself by itself. Such a theory naturally led her to a sensual ideality, and her heroes rose to the highest phase of fatalism and voluptuousness; this impelled her to protest against the social laws. Jacques says:

"I do not doubt at all that marriage will be abolished if humankind makes any progress toward justice and reason; a bond more human and none the less sacred will replace this one and will take care of the children which may issue from a man and woman, without ever interfering with the liberty of either. But men are too coarse and women are too cowardly to ask for a law more noble than the iron law which binds them—beings without conscience—and virtue must be burdened with heavy chains."

Yet, in none of her books did George Sand ever submit any theories as to how such children would be cared for; apparently, such a difficulty never troubled her, since almost all of the children of her books die of some disease, while to one—Jacques—she gives the advice to take his own life, so that his wife may be free to love elsewhere.

Her social theories are marked by an exaltation of sentiment, a weakness, an incoherency in conception, caused by her ardent love for theories and ideas, but which, in her passionate sentiment and her loyal enthusiasm, she always confounds and confuses. From early youth she manifested an immense goodness, a profound tenderness, and a deep compassion for human misery. She rarely became angry, even though she suffered cruelly. Her own law of life and her message to the world was—be good. The only strong element within her, she said, was the need of loving, which manifested itself under the form of tenderness and emotion, devotion and religious ecstasy; and when this faith was shaken, doubt and social disturbances overwhelmed her.

Throughout life her consolation was Nature. "It was half of her genius and the surest of her inspirations." No other French novelist has been able to "express in words the lights and shades, harmonies and contrasts, the magic of sounds, the symphonies of color, the depth and distances of the woods, the infinite movement of the sea and the sky—the interior soul of Nature, that vibrates in everything and everybody." With Lamartine and Michelet, she has best reflected and expressed the dreams and hopes and loves of the first half of the nineteenth century.

George Sand saw Nature, lived in her, sympathized with her, and loved her as did few other French writers; therefore, she showed more memory than pure imagination in her work, for she always found Nature more beautiful in actuality than she could picture her mentally, while other great writers, like Lamartine, saw her less beautiful in reality than in their imagination; hence, they were disappointed in Nature, while for George Sand she was the truest friend. The world will always be interested in her descriptions of Nature, because with Nature she always associated something of human life—a thought or a sentiment; her landscapes belonged to her characters—there is always a soul living in them, for, to George Sand, man and Nature were inseparable.

Thus, every novel of this authoress consists of a situation and a landscape, the poetic union of which nothing can mar. "Man associated with Nature and Nature with man is a great law of art; no painter has practised it with instinct more delicate or sure." Because Nature, in her early youth, was her inspiration, guide, even her God, she returned to her later in life. M. Jules Lemaître wrote that her works will remain eternally beautiful, because they teach us how to love Nature as divine and good, and to find in that love peace and solace. There are many parts of her work which show as detailed, accurate, and realistic descriptions as those by Balzac. She constantly employed two elements—the fanciful and the realistic.

George Sand never studied or knew how to compose a work, how to preserve the unity of the subject or the unity in tone in characters; hence, there was nothing calculated or premeditated—everything was spontaneous. No preparation of plan did she ever think of—a mode of procedure which naturally resulted in a negligent style and caused the composition to drag. Her inspiration seemed to go so far, then she resorted to her imagination, to the chimerical, forcing events and characters. "There are many defects in the style
—such as the sentimental part, the romanesque in the violent expression of sentiments or invention of situations, the exaggerated improbabilities of events, the excessive declamation; but how many compensating qualities are there to offset these defects!"

Her method of writing was very simple. It was the love of writing that impelled her, almost without premeditation, to put into words her dreams, meditations, and chimeras under concrete and living forms. Yet, by the largeness of her sympathy and the ardor of her passions, by the abundant inventions of stories, and by the harmonious word-flow, she deserves to be ranked among the greatest writers of France. Her career, taken as a whole, is one of prodigious fecundity—a literary life that has "enchanted by its fictions or troubled by its dreams" four or five generations. Never diminishing in quality or inspiration, there are surprises in every new work.

No doubt George Sand has, for a generation or more, been somewhat forgotten, but what great writer has not shared the same fate? When the materialistic age has passed away, many famous writers of the past will be resurrected, and with them George Sand; for her novels, although written to please and entertain, discuss questions of religion, philosophy, morality, problems of the heart, conscience, and education,—and this is done in such a dramatic way that one feels all to be true. More than that, her characters are all capable of carrying out, to the end, a common moral and general theme with eloquence seldom found in novels.

An interesting comparison might be made between Mme. de Staël and George Sand, the two greatest women writers of France. Both wrote from their experience of life, and fought passionately against the prejudices and restrictions of social conventions; both were ideal natures and were severely tried in the school of life, profiting by their experiences; both possessed highly sensitive natures, and suffered much; both were keenly enthusiastic and sympathetic, with pardonable weaknesses; both lived through tragic wars; both evinced a dislike for the commonplace and strove for greater freedom, but for different publics, after unhappy marriages, both rose up as accusers against the prevalent system of marrying young girls. But Mme. de Staël was a virtuoso in conversation, a salon queen, and her happiness was to be found in society alone; while George Sand found her happiness in communion with Nature. This explains the two natures, their sufferings, their joys, their writings.

The greatest punishment ever inflicted upon Mme. de Staël was her exile, for it deprived her of her social life, a fact of which the emperor was well aware. Her entire literary effort was directed to describing her social life and the relation of society to life. "She belongs to the moralists and to the writers who wrote of society and man—social psychologists." Not poetic or artistic by nature, but with an exceptional power of observation, she shows on every side the influence of a pedagogical, literary, and social training; she was the product of an artificial culture.

George Sand, on the contrary, was a product of Nature, reared in free intercourse and unrestrained relation with her genius and Nature. A powerful passion and a mighty fantasy made of her a poetess and an artist. These two qualities were manifested in her intense and deep feeling for the beauty of Nature, in her power of invention, in a harmonious equilibrium between idealism and realism. Her fantasy overbalanced her reason, impeding its development and thus relegating it to a secondary rôle. "She is possibly the only French writer who possessed no *esprit* (in the sense that it is used in French society)—that playful, epigrammatic, querulous wit of conversation."

She never enjoyed communion with others for any length of time, or the companionship of anyone for a long period; the companions of which she never tired were the fields and woods, birds and dogs; therefore, she enjoyed those people most who were nearer her ideals, the peasants and workmen, and these she best describes. Thus, her whole creation is one of instinct rather than of reason, as it was with Mme. de Staël. George Sand was a genius, a master-product of Nature, while Mme. de Staël was a talent, a consummate work of the art of modern culture; she reflects, while George Sand creates from impulse; the latter was a true poetess, communing with Nature, while the banker's daughter was an observing thinker, communicating with society—but both were great writers.

Intimately associated with George Sand is Rosa Bonheur, in all of whose canvases we find the same aim, the same spirit, the same message, that are found in so many of the novels of George Sand. They were two women who have contributed, through different branches, masterworks that will be enjoyed and appreciated at all times. "It would be difficult not to speak of *La Mare au Diable* and the *Meunier d'Angibault* when recalling the fields where Rosa Bonheur speeds the plow or places the oxen lowering their patient heads under the yoke."

In the evening, at home, while other members of the family were at work, one member read aloud to the rest; and George Sand was a favorite author with the Bonheur group of artists. It was while reading *La Mare au Diable* that Rosa conceived the idea of the work which by some critics is pronounced her masterpiece, *Plowing in Nivernais*. The artist's deep sympathy was aroused by her love of Nature, which no contemporary novelist expressed or appreciated as did George Sand. In all her works, and throughout the long life of the artist, there is absolutely nothing unhealthy or immoral to be found. The novelist had theories which were inspired by her passion, and these became unhealthy at times; she belongs first of all to France, while Rosa Bonheur belongs first of all to the world, her message reaching the young and old of every clime and every people. The novelist is to be associated with the artist by virtue of her exquisite, simple, and wholesome peasant stories.

The entire Bonheur family were artists, and all were moral and genuinely sympathetic. As a young girl, Rosa manifested an intense love for Nature, sunshine, and the woods; always independent in manners, she used to caricature her teachers; and while walking out into the country, she would draw, with charcoal or in sand, any objects that met her eye. Her father was not long in detecting her talent. She was wedded to her art from the very beginning, showing no taste for or interest in any other subject. As soon as her father gave permission to follow art as a profession, she devoted all her energy to advancing herself in what she felt to be her life's work. For four years the young girl could be seen every day at the Louvre, copying the great masters and receiving principally from them her ideas of coloring and harmony, while from her father she learned her technique. After she had mastered these two principles, she decided to specialize in pastoral nature.

From that time her whole life was given up to the study of Nature and animals. Not able to study those near by, she procured a fine Beauvais sheep, which served as her model for two years. From the very first her work showed accuracy, purity, and an intuitive perception of Nature, and these qualities soon placed her among the foremost artists of the time. Her struggle for reputation and glory was not a long and arduous one, for after 1845 her fame was established—she was then but twenty-three years old; and after 1849, having exhibited some thirty pictures, her reputation had become European.

In order to be able to study her models with greater ease and freedom from the annoyance and coarse incivilities of the workmen at the slaughter houses, farmyards, and markets that she was in the habit of visiting, she adopted the garb of man.

Her honors in life were many, though always unsought. The Empress Eugénie, while regent during the absence of Napoleon III., went in person to her château and put around her neck the ribbon of the decoration of the Grand Cross of the Legion of Honor, then for the first time bestowed upon woman for merit other than bravery and charity. The Emperor Maximilian of Mexico conferred upon her the decoration of San Carlos; the King of Belgium created her a chevalier of his order, the first honor won by a woman; the King of Spain made her a Commander of the Royal Order of Isabella the Catholic; and President Carnot created her an Officer of the Legion of Honor.

With qualities such as she possessed, Rosa Bonheur could not fail to attain immortality. Her success was due in no small degree to the scientific instruction which she received when a mere child; having been taught, from the very first, how to paint directly from a model, she supplemented this training by a period of four years of copying great masters. In the latter period she studied Paul Potter's work rather slavishly, but was individual enough to combine only the best in him with the best in herself; this gave her an originality such as possibly no other animal painter ever possessed—-not even Landseer, who is said to be "stronger in telling the story than in the manner of telling it."

Rosa Bonheur was too independent and original to follow any particular school or master, for her only inspiration and guide were her models, always living near by and upon intimate terms with her. Thus, in all her paintings, we instinctively feel that she painted from conviction, from her own observation, nothing being added for mere artistic effect. To some extent her pictures impress one as a perfect French poem in which there is no superfluous word, in which no word could be changed without destroying the effect of the whole; thus, in her paintings there is not a superfluous brush stroke; everything is necessary to the telling of the story; but she excels the perfect poem, for, in French literature, it seldom has a message distinct from its technique, while her pictures breathe the very essence of sympathy, love, and life. We feel that she thoroughly knew her subjects as a connoisseur; but her animals do not impress one as the production of an artist who knew them as do horse traders and cattle dealers, who know their stock from the purely physical standpoint; the animals of this artist are from the brush of one who was familiar with their habits, who loved them, had lived with and studied them—who knew and appreciated their higher qualities. Rosa Bonheur most harmoniously united two essential elements in art—a scientific as well as sympathetic conception of her subject. Possibly this is the reason that her pictures appeal to animal lovers throughout the world.

As was stated, she was independent, hence kept aloof from the corruptions of contemporary French art and its technique lovers, always pursuing an even tenor in her art and never permitting one of her pictures to leave her studio in a crude or unfinished state. In all her long career she kept her original sketches, never parting with one, in spite of the most tempting offers; and this explains the fact that the work of her later years exhibits the freshness and other qualities of that of her youth. Thus, her art has gained by her experience, even though her best work was done between about 1848 and 1860, and is especially marked by its excellence in composition, the anatomy, the breadth of touch, the harmony of coloring, and the action, although it is said to lack the spontaneity, the originality, and the highly imaginative quality which are at their best in *The Horse Fair*; the same qualities seem to have been possessed by many of her contemporaries, such as Troyon.

Notwithstanding these apparent defects, Rosa Bonheur stands for something higher in art than do most of her contemporaries. She was not influenced by the skilled and often corrupt technicians; she perfected her technique by study of the old masters and learned her art from Nature; wisely keeping free from the ornamental, gorgeous, and highly imaginative and exaggerated historical Romantic school, in French art she stands out almost alone with Millet. Whatever may be said of the more virile and masculine art of other great animal painters, Rosa Bonheur, by her truthfulness, her science, her close association and intimate communion with her animal world, by the glad and healthy vigor which her paintings breathe, has taught the world the great lesson that there are intelligence, will, love, and even soul, in animals.

Her art and life inspired respect and admiration; we have nothing to regret, nothing to conceal; we desire to love her for her animals, and we must esteem her for her grand devotion to her art and family, for her purity and charity, for her kindness to and love for those in the lower walks of life, for her goodness and honesty. An illustration of the last quality may be taken from her dealings with art collectors. After having offered her *Horse Fair*, which she desired should remain in France, to her own town for twelve thousand francs, she sold it for forty thousand francs to Mr. Gambert, but with the condition which she thus expressed: "I am grateful for your giving me such a noble price, but I do not like to feel that I have taken advantage of your liberality. Let us see how we can combine matters. You will not be able to have an engraving made from so large a canvas; suppose I paint you a small one of the same subject, of which I will make you a present." Naturally, the gift was accepted, and the smaller canvas now hangs in the National Gallery of London.

In all her dealings she showed this kindness and uprightness, sympathy and honesty. Although numberless orders were constantly coming to her, she never let them hurry her in her work. She was, possibly, the highest and noblest type—certainly among great French women—of that strong and solid virtue which constitutes the backbone and the very essence of French national strength. The reputation of Rosa Bonheur has never been blemished by the least touch of petty jealousy, hatred, envy, vanity, or pride—and, among all great French women, she is one of the few of whom this may be said. She won for herself and her noble art the genuine and lasting sympathy of the world at large.

The only woman artist in France deserving a place beside Rosa Bonheur belongs properly under the reign of Louis XVI., although she lived almost to the middle of the nineteenth century. At the age of twenty, Mme. Lebrun was already famous as the leading portrait painter; this was during the most popular period of Marie Antoinette—1775 to 1785. In 1775, but a young girl, admitted to all the sessions of the Academy as recognition of her portraits of La Bruyère and Cardinal Fleury, she made her life unhappy and gave her art a serious blow by consenting to marry the then great art critic and collector of art, Lebrun. His passion for gambling and women ruined her fortune and almost ended her career as an artist. Her own conduct was not irreproachable.

Mme. Lebrun will be remembered principally as the great painter of Marie Antoinette, who posed for her more than twenty times. The most prominent people of Europe eagerly sought her work, while socially she was welcomed everywhere. Her famous suppers and entertainments in her modestly furnished hôtel, at which Garat sang, Grétry played the piano, and Viotti and Prince Henry of Prussia assisted, were the events of the day. Her reputation as a painter of the great ladies and gentlemen of nobility, and her entertainments, naturally associated her with the nobility; hence, she shared their unpopularity at the outbreak of the Revolution and left France.

It is doubtful whether any artist—certainly no French artist—ever received more attention and honors, or was made a member of so many art academies, than Mme. Lebrun. It would be difficult to make any comparison between her and Rosa Bonheur, their respective spheres of art being so different. Only the future will speak as to the relative positions of each in French art.

In the domain of the dramatic art of the nineteenth century, two women have made their names well known throughout Europe and America,—Rachel, and Sarah Bernhardt, both tragédiennes and both daughters of Israel. While Rachel was, without question, the greatest tragédienne that France ever produced, excelling Bernhardt in deep tragic force, she yet lacked many qualities which our contemporary possesses in a high degree. She had constantly to contend with a cruel fate and a wicked, grasping nature, which brought her to an early grave. The wretched slave of her greedy and rapacious father and managers, who cared for her only in so far as she enriched them by her genius and popularity, hers was a miserable existence, which detracted from her acting, checked her development, and finally undermined her health.

After her critical period of apprenticeship was successfully passed and she was free to govern herself, she rose to be queen of the French stage—a position which she held for eighteen years, during which she was worshipped and petted by the whole world. As a social leader, she was received and made much of by the great ladies of the Faubourg Saint-Germain. Her taste in dress was exquisite in its simplicity, being in perfect harmony with the reserved, retiring, and amiable actress herself.

Possibly no actress, singer, or other public woman ever received such homage and general recognition. With all her great qualities as an actress, vigor, grandeur, wild, savage energy, superb articulation, irreproachable diction, and a marvellous sense of situations, she lacked the one quality which we miss in Sarah Bernhardt also—a true tenderness and compassion. As a tragédienne she can be compared to Talma only. Her greed for money soon ended her brilliant career; unlike her sister in art, she amassed a fortune, leaving over one million five hundred thousand francs.

Compared with Bernhardt, Rachel is said to have been the greater in pure tragedy, but she did not possess as many arts of fascination. There are many points of similarity between the two actresses: Rachel was at times artificial, wanting in tenderness and depth, while at times she was superhuman in her passion and emotion, and often put more into her rôle than was intended; and the acting of Sarah Bernhardt has the same characteristics. Rachel, however, was much more subject to moods and fits of inspiration than is Bernhardt— especially was she incapable of acting at her best on evenings of her first appearance in a new rôle. Her critical power was very weak in comparison with her intellectual power, the reverse being true of her modern rival. Rachel's greatest inspiration was *Phèdre*, and in this rôle Bernhardt "is weak, unequal. We see all the viciousness in *Phèdre* and none of her grandeur. She breaks herself to pieces against the huge difficulties of the conception and does not succeed in moving us…. Rachel was the mouthpiece of the gods; no longer a free agent, she poured forth every epithet of adoration that Aphrodite could suggest, clambering up higher and higher in the intensity of her emotions, whilst her audience hung breathless, riveted on every word, and dared to burst forth in thunders of applause only after she had vanished from their sight."

Both of these artists were children of the lower class, and struggled with a fate which required grit, tenacity, and determination to win success. The artist of to-day is no social leader—"never the companion of man, but his slave or his despot." It is entirely her physical charms and the outward or artificial requisites of her art that make her what she is. According to Mr. Lynch, her tragedy "is but one of disorder, fury, and folly—passions not deep, but unbridled and hysterical in their intensest display. Her *forte* lies in the ornate and elaborate exhibition of rôles," for which she creates the most capricious and fantastic garbs. She is a great manager,—omitting the financial part,— quite a writer, somewhat of a painter and sculptor, throwing her money away, except to her creditors, adored by some and execrated by others. Her care of her physical self and her utter disregard for money have undoubtedly contributed to her long and brilliant career; rest and idleness are her most cruel punishments. All nervous energy, never happy, restless, she is a true *fin de siècle* product.

Among the large number of women who wielded influence in the nineteenth century, either through their salons or through their works, Mme. Guizot was one of the most important as the author of treatises on education and as a moralist. As an intimate friend of Suard, she was placed, as a contributor, on the *Publiciste*, and for ten years wrote articles on morality, society, and literature which showed a varied talent, much depth, and justness. Fond of polemics, she never failed to attack men like La Harpe, De Bonald, etc., thus making herself felt as an influence to be reckoned with in matters literary and moral.

As Mme. Guizot, she naturally had a powerful influence upon her husband, shaping his thoughts and theories, for she immediately espoused his principles and interests. In 1821, at the age of forty-eight, she began her literary work again, after a period of rest, writing novels in which the maternal love and the ardent and pious sentiments of a woman married late in life are reflected. In her theories of education she showed a highly practical spirit. Sainte-Beuve said that, next to Mme. de Staël, "she was the woman endowed with the most sagacity and intelligence; the sentiment that she inspires is that of respect and esteem—and these terms can only do her justice."

Mme. de Duras, in her salon, represented the Restoration, "by a composite of aristocracy and affability, of brilliant wit and seriousness, semi-liberal and somewhat progressive." Her credit lies in the fact that, by her keen wit, she kept in harmony a heterogeneous mixture of social life. She wrote a number of novels, which are, for the most part, "a mere delicate and discreet expression of her interior life."

Mme. Ackermann, German in her entire makeup, was, among French female writers, one of the deepest thinkers of the nineteenth century. A true mystic, she was, from early youth, filled with ardent, dreamy vagaries, to which she gave expression in verse—poems which reflect a pessimism which is rather the expression of her life's experiences, and of twenty-four years of solitude after two years of happy wedded state, than an actual depression and a discouraging philosophy of life. Her poetry shows a vigor, depth, precision of form, and strength of expression seldom found in poetry of French women.

One of the most conspicuous figures in the latter half of the nineteenth century is Mme. Adam,—Juliette Lamber,—an unusual woman in every respect. In 1879 she founded the *Nouvelle Revue*, on the plan of the *Revue des Deux Mondes*, for which she wrote political and literary articles which showed much talent. In politics she is a Republican and something of a socialist, a somewhat sensational—but modestly sensational—figure. She has been called "a necessary continuator of George Sand." Her salon was the great centre for all Republicans and one of the most brilliant and important of this century. In literature her name is connected with the movement called neo-Hellenism, the aim of which seems to have been to inspire a love and sympathy for the art, religion, and literature of ancient and modern Greece. In her works she shows a deep insight into Greek life and art. Her name will always be connected with the Republican movement in France; as a salon leader, *femme de lettres*, journalist, and female politician, no woman is better known in France in the nineteenth century.

A woman who might be called the rival of Mme. Adam, but whose activity occurred much earlier in the century, was Mme. Emile de Girardin,— Delphine Gay,—who ruled, at least for a short time, the social and literary world of Paris at her hôtel in the Rue Chaillot. Her very early precocity, combined with her rare beauty, made her famous. In 1836, after having written a number of poems which showed a weak sentimentality and a quite mannered emotion, she founded the *Courrier Français*, for which she wrote articles on the questions of the day—effusions which were written upon the spur of the moment and were very unreliable. Her dramas were hardly successful, although they were played by the great Rachel. Her present claim to fame is based upon the brilliancy of her salon.

The future will possibly remember Mme. Alphonse Daudet more as the wife of the great Daudet than as a writer, although, according to M. Jules Lemaître, she possessed the gift of *écriture artiste* to a remarkable degree. According to him, sureness and exactness and a striking truth of impressions are her characteristics as a writer. She exercised a most wholesome power over Alphonse Daudet, taking him away from bad influences, giving him a home, dignity, and happiness, and saving him from brutality and pessimism; she was his guardian and censor; she preserved his grace and noble sentiments. The nature of her relations to him should ensure the preservation of her name to posterity.

We are accustomed to give Gyp—Sybille Gabrielle Marie Antoinette de Riquetti de Mirabeau, Comtesse de Martel de Janville—little credit for seriousness or morality, associating her with the average brilliant, flippant novelists, who write because they possess the knack of writing in a brilliant style. Her object is to show that man, in a civilized state in society, is vain, coarse, and ridiculous. She paints Parisian society to demonstrate that the apparently fortunate ones of the world are not to be envied, that they are miserable in their so-called joys and ridiculous in their pleasures and their elegance. She has described the most *risqué* situations and the most delightful women, but she gives us to understand that the latter are not to be loved. The vanity of the social world might be called her text.

Mme. Blanc—Thérèse de Solms—is known to us to-day as the first woman to reveal English and American authors and habits to her contemporaries. By advocating American customs she has done much to ameliorate the condition of French girls, by giving them a freer intercourse with young men and permitting them to see more of the world before entering upon married life.

Mme. Gréville, who died recently, deserves a place among the prominent women writers of France. No *femme de lettres* ever received more honors, prizes, and decorations than she; a number of her writings were crowned by the Academy. A member of the Société des Gens de Lettres, with all her literary work she was a domestic woman, keeping aloof from all feminist movements. Her husband, Professor Durand, to show his esteem and admiration for her, adopted her name—a wise act, for it may preserve his name with that of his talented wife.

Many other names might be cited, but, as the list of prominent women is practically without end, owing to the indefiniteness of the term "prominent," we shall close with these names, which have become familiar in both continents.